SINEATER

SINEATER

ELIZABETH MASSIE

Carroll & Graf Publishers, Inc.
New York

First Carroll & Graf edition June 1994

Carroll & Graf Publishers, Inc.
260 Fifth Avenue
New York, NY 10001

Library of Congress Cataloging-in-Publication Data

Massie, Elizabeth,
    Sineater / Elizabeth Massie. — 1st Carroll & Graf ed.
       p.   cm.
    ISBN 0-7867-0061-0 : $21.00 ($28.50 Can.)
    1. Mountain life—Virginia—Fiction.   2. Young men—Virginia—
Fiction.   I. Title.
PS3563.A79973S56   1994
813'.54—dc20   94-4659
                                                              CIP

Manufactured in the United States of America

To Barbara, my best friend, soul sister, and true sister.
Thanks for being there.
Thanks for being.
Thanks.

ACKNOWLEDGMENTS

To those who were soul-buds during the creation and gestation of this American edition: my husband Roger, daughter Erin, and son Brian I give a hearty thanks and much love. To the rest of my extensive family: Barb, Charlie, Jenni, Becky, Charles, Joe, Butch, Mom, and Al—I say, "Wouldn't it have been nice if MeDot were here for this?" To my friends around and about—Brian, Von, Jeff, Wayne, Gary, Mark, Dave, Kurt, Amy, Andrew, Joan, Lisa, and Stan, I ask, "When the hell we gettin' that commune? I'll bring Plinko." To Don Curtis, thanks for the support during the SMS years. Great appreciation goes to Peter for traveling these miles with me, and to Kent for taking the baton at the end of the line.

SINEATER

PROLOGUE

The young boy stands by his mother's bed, watching her scream. Beside the boy is his younger sister, a tiny blond-haired five-year-old. The little girl's pale hair is plastered to her cheeks with tears and sweat. Her eyes are tightly closed. They wince with each scream. It is mid-June, and the room is hot and wet like a soaked wool blanket.

At the foot of the bed, sitting on a kerosene can, is the teenaged midwife. Her name is Jewel Benshoff. Jewel's eyes are nearly closed, too. The boy knows she does not want to be in this room; she does not want to be birthing the child who is soon to come. The boy's own fear terrifies him. But the midwife's fear excites him.

Curry Barker, the seven-year-old boy, the oldest of the two children, does not close his eyes. It is his duty to watch his mother. She said a new baby was the family's business, and it was not a private thing. Curry can see his mother's private things, though. They are splayed out between her spread legs, hairy and gaping and red. He makes himself look at them, and at the blood and wetness running out onto the mattress.

Curry's mother screams into the dishrag clamped in her teeth. She bucks her shoulders. Her fingers slash the air. Mottled, leaf-stained sunlight from the cabin window patterns her face. The rest of the room is dark, the walls of black wood and pitch. The mother's feet flex in the darkness, then draw up and push out violently. She takes

1

a breath, a moment of silence, allowing faint goat bleats to be heard from outside. Then she screams again. The sound is loud and long, a throaty wail that rattles the bed frame.

Birthing is a family matter. Curry is there. His sister, Petrie, is there.

But, of course, the father is not there.

"Feel it coming!" cries the mother around the rag.

Curry clamps his teeth down. His eyes want to shut but he makes them stay open, and they sting. He watches the place between his mother's legs for it to come. The blood reminds him of the blood of the chickens he kills for the family meals; of the fresh, stinking blood of the deer his mother is teaching him to hunt. The white of the mattress makes him think of the white muscle of the stripped oak branches his mother is training him to form into simple baskets. Jewel's bloodied, grasping fingers make him think of the hands of the damned in the lake of fire of the Bible, reaching out for pity and salvation.

Curry's father's hands would be eternally damned if Curry were not alive. Curry's father, Avery, is the sineater. Curry knows he was born to keep Avery from God's holy and terrible burning lake when he dies.

Petrie squeaks, a muffled scream. Curry gives her a stern look, and then looks back at his mother.

"Push," says Jewel.

Curry's mother growls with the pain. "I feel . . ." she begins, and then cries out with the contraction.

Jewel frees the heels, and her trembling hands reach between the thick, vein-marbled legs. A slick black mass appears at the opening. The mother's feet rise slightly, the toes spread and clutching, then fall back to the mattress.

Petrie utters a loud gasp of fear. Curry takes her firmly by the arm.

"You hush now," he whispers.

"Mama's dying!"

"I'll slap you you don't hush," says Curry. "She ain't gonna die. And if she do, Avery will send her to heaven."

Petrie wails louder then, and Curry drives his palm against her cheek. Petrie chokes, shudders, and falls silent, wiping the red spot on her face.

"You got to push now," the midwife says. The mother strains and grunts.

"Coming!" screams the mother on the bed. Jewel shudders visibly. Curry feels blood rush the veins of his hands, and cold rush the skin over his skull. If Mama died having this baby, Avery would have to come and send her to heaven. Curry and Petrie would have to put food on her chest. They would have to turn away to the wall while the sineater came in, ravenous with hunger, slobbering and seething with the heat of sin. He would eat up the food. Curry wonders if sineater's drool is poisonous.

Jewel's hands cup about the baby's head.

"Now!" the mother barks into the rag. She bends at the waist, her face rising toward the midwife like a phantom in the shadowed room. Wet baby shoulders jump out. A rank, rich smell of blood and fluids hits Curry in the face. He gasps.

The mother twists herself back and forth, as if trying to shake the baby free. "Now!" she screams again, and the dishrag is spit into the air. She grunts hoarsely and slams her fists into the bulge of her belly.

The baby shoots out, red, gummy face squashed and silent. The midwife quickly folds it within a white scrap of flannel, then snips and ties the cord. The baby squeaks once, weakly. Jewel puts it onto the bed between the mother's legs and leans over to press the mother's stomach to help the afterbirth along. She begins to hum a Jesus song. Curry has heard his mother sing this song. She sings it when she is afraid. She sings it late at night when there is no wake and she knows Avery will come home to eat supper alone in the kitchen after everyone has gone to bed.

"Mama?" says Petrie. Her hands are clasped together as if she were trying to pray.

"It's all done now, Petrie," says the mother. She seems to sink into the mattress, her voice faint and small. She sighs and slowly licks her lips. It seems as if she is trying to lick away the spots of sunlight. "So what we got then?" she asks the midwife.

Jewel says, "Boy."

There is a long silence. Curry tries to see the baby, but it is covered in the cloth. "A boy." The mother's words are soft now, the abating pain edged with wonder. "His name is Joel."

"Joel," says Petrie.

"Curry," says the mother. "Is Avery outside?"

Curry's mouth goes dry. He has to work his jaw in order to speak. "I think he's near the mailbox, Mama." Curry's father is the sineater; he knows when to be where he needs to be. About an hour ago, Curry had gone out to the porch with Petrie to bring in an armload of towels from the bench. Down in the deep shadows, something had moved. Something huge, thick, and dark.

The sineater.

"Call to him, then. Tell him it's a boy."

Curry's heart tries to turn inside out. It scrapes against his ribs, and he digs his fingers against his chest through the thin cotton of his T-shirt. He doesn't want to call out to the sineater. He didn't know he was going to have to say something to the sineater. It is too dangerous.

"Curry, what's matter with you? I say, go now."

"Mama, I don't want to," Curry says. The family has little to do with the sineater. Curry, Petrie, and Lelia are to be asleep on nights when the sineater comes to eat his meal. The family is to be hiding in bedrooms, clinging to the blanket of night's oblivion when Avery Barker has no wake to attend, and takes his midnight supper in the cabin's small kitchen. Curry doesn't want to call out to the sineater.

Petrie rubs her fist under her running nose.

The mother coughs. "Give me the baby," she says to Jewel. "Give Joel to me." And to Curry, "You hear me, boy?"

Curry watches as his mother puts the baby under her chin and strokes its ugly wrinkled face. The baby has dark hair like his mother. It is still for a moment, then it flails its legs suddenly, loosening itself from the white flannel. It startles itself and begins to cry.

Petrie reaches out and touches the thin baby arm.

Curry's teeth fight each other, making scraping noises in his ear. Then he says, "Yes, Mama."

Jewel draws herself up on the kerosene can and tucks her face down as if the sineater is going to come into the room with her. Curry grits his teeth, then goes out of the bedroom and down the short hall to the kitchen. Petrie's baby kitten, found with its dead mother several weeks ago down by West Path when Curry went to look for mayapples, lies in its wooden box near the stove.

Curry puts his hand on the door to pull it open. He does not want to call to the sineater. What if your voice carries your soul?

Mama would not ask him if it were dangerous. Mama knows what to do.

What if your soul comes out when you scream? What if it comes out and the sineater sucks it up?

Mama would not make him do something dangerous. He thinks for a second that Jewel Benshoff should have to call to Avery. Her soul didn't matter as much as Curry's, because he would have to be sineater when Avery died. Jewel is only a midwife.

Curry pulls the door open. He steps one step out onto the porch. He digs his fingers into his hurting chest, where his heart waits to see what he will do. He puts his other hand to his mouth. The fingers cup. He calls, ''It's a boy!''

The words fly down the stone walkway toward the trees and the mailbox and what hides in the seething summer shadows. He feels a hot wind whip back up the walkway, like a stinking, devil's belch.

And before Curry can feel or hear more, he slams the door and throws himself against the safety of the sturdy wood, panting.

PART ONE

JOEL AND LELIA

1

"You trust me, don't you boy?"

'*Jesus,*' the boy thinks. 'She's crazy. I knew it.' He moves his head a little, and hears ringing in his skull. He thinks he is drugged, but his mind is too numb to decide.

"Don't you, Burke?"

Faces shift behind the woman's voice. A nameless Brother, a nameless Sister.

"Burke, if you don't trust me, this will be in vain. I want to care for you. Your mama and daddy entrusted me to this. I promised I would do what was necessary. We're of the same flesh . . ."

Burke tries to clear his throat. The sound burrs in his ears, a worthless distraction.

". . . and the same spirit."

Burke looks over the woman's shoulders at the Sister and Brother. Then he tries to focus again on his Aunt Missy. He does not understand her. He knows little of God except for what he has been told since he moved here. His own mama and daddy never spoke of God, so Burke does not know if they believed or not. Burke senses that there is indeed a peculiar love for him here. And yet, it bounces off him, reflected like a dull light from the mirror shard that is his heart. He had no love at his other home, and cannot fathom if what Aunt Missy offers now is good or bad.

"Listen to me, boy. Remember. Have you forgotten all I've told you?"

Burke shakes his head.

"What then? Tell me."

Burke blinks and tries his mouth. His tongue is fat and dead. He cannot make words come out.

"It's the evil come home to us here in Beacon Cove, Burke. Those what live here are trampling on our holy traditions. They chew them up and spit them into the mouth of Satan. Now Satan's mouth is waiting to have us."

Burke's gaze moves from Aunt Missy to the wrapped bundle she holds to her like a dead newborn. He knows what is in the bundle. He tries to lick his lips, but whatever is in his veins will not let him.

"You got to see it, Burke. You got to know what is out there, and what you must be vigilant against so you're safe."

Burke nods faintly. There is rampant sin, Missy has told him. It is settling and growing thick like sludge on a boiling pot. Many will suffer the sin. Many will be crushed under its weight. But those of the light will be spared.

Those with the sign of the Light. The mark of God.

No, Burke has not forgotten what he's been told. And now, Aunt Missy's hand is outstretched, offering to hold him above the sin around him. She is crazy for what she is about to do, she has scared him, and she loves him. Burke cannot make his hand move to hers.

"Burke," says Aunt Missy.

Burke cannot answer.

"Repeat me, boy."

The Brother and Sister drop to their knees. They fold their hands.

"Lord God of creation!" Missy says to the air above Burke's head.

"Lord God of creation," say the Brother and Sister. Burke says, "Of creation."

"Sin has found our neighbors and friends. Sin has crept in and made them unclean."

The Sister and Brother repeat. Burke says, "Unclean."

"And now the sin of them what die," Missy says.

"Die," Burke manages.

"Is consumed in deadly excess by the sineater."

"Sineater," says Burke.

"Protect us from the sin come back to harm us. Protect us from the sineater."

Burke tries to focus on his aunt. The rim of his vision swims. "Sineater," he says.

"Give me your arm," says Missy. The Brother and Sister stand up, two solemn and silent specters. "Burke, it's time."

Satan's mouth will open wider and wider, Aunt Missy has said. Burke knows that without the mark of God, he will fall into that maw. But he is also afraid of the mark of God because he knows it will hurt.

"You are all I have now that Patsy is lost. Trust me."

At his other home, hate meant pain. Here, love is going to mean pain, too.

"Here, Burke."

Burke wonders if there is a difference between love and hate. The only difference he can see is salvation.

"Burke."

Burke looks at his arm, and then raises it clumsily toward Missy. The arm is covered with freckles and red-gold hairs. The faces of the Sister and Brother move closer. Their hands reach out for Burke's arms, and hold them firmly down against the wood of the table. Aunt Missy pushes the sleeve of his T-shirt up to his armpit, and twists the inner flesh of his arm to face her. As she moves, the short sleeve of her own cotton shirt pulls up, revealing that which Burke is about to receive. Burke thinks about pain, and wonders what he is supposed to think about while it is happening.

"Think about the safety of God," Missy answers for him. She unrolls a small knife from the bundle. It looks like the knife he used two days ago when he brought in three trout from the Beacon River on his fifth day in Ellison. But this knife, he thinks, is not the same. It is a special knife.

"Think of God," and Aunt Missy presses the point to the smooth flesh of Burke's inner arm. "Think of the sineater and his evil. He is filled with more sin than can be held. He will rise up like the devil and chew us up. Think of . . ."

And the point slices down and under the skin and Burke arcs backward, sucking air in surprise and exquisite pain. He bolts straight again, but the Sister and Brother are strong. Aunt Missy's fingers tighten about his thin arm, and the knife begins to slice up and down, carving, severing, working out the pattern.

"Jesus!" Burke cries.

"Yes!"

Burke's eyes roll futilely; his feet dig against the floor beneath him.

"Yes!" repeats Aunt Missy. "Think of Jesus!"

Burke pants, swallowing air, gnashing teeth. He cannot think of God or love. He can only think of what he had at his other home, of BETRAYAL, and of HATE, and of PAIN. He can only watch the knife dancing through his living skin, gouting out blood and making the pattern of God. There is lava in his arm. He closes his eyes and howls through the anguish and sweat. If this is love, his tortured body screams, then God be damned! If this is good, he wants evil!

And then Aunt Missy says, "It's done, boy. Look at this beautiful sign."

Burke's eyes cannot open right away, but he feels her withdraw the knife and place something heavy and cold on the fire of the wound. Then her hand touches his face. "Look, Burke. It is a good thing." Burke opens his eyes. Missy is watching him. The Sister and Brother had stepped back. Missy lifts the wet washrag from his arm. There is a raw, bleeding star where smooth flesh had been. "He is the Light," Missy says. "Say it, boy."

'God be damned. You be damned, Aunt Missy,' Burke thinks.

"Say it, Burke."

"He is the light," Burke whispers. He stares at the crude star. He is nauseous.

Aunt Missy slathers her hands in a thinned tar solution and she rubs it into the cut. "In the morning," she says. "I'll take turpentine to this. It'll clean off but what is in the pattern." She turns Burke's arm all around, looking it over. "Fine job here."

Burke tastes blood and Aunt Missy's spiced cabbage in the back of his throat, trying to come out.

Missy takes the bundle and knife across the room and puts them on the mantel. She rubs her hands with a towel. "We're growing stronger," she says finally. "The sins of this generation will not have dominion over the saved. The consort of the devil will not destroy us.''

The Brother and Sister nod, watching Burke.

Burke feels the coppery strangle of vomit shoot into his mouth. He gags, but swallows it down. He will not let her see him weak. His shoulders shudder, his stomach contracts, and he feels his body fold over with another heave. He grits his teeth. He swallows it down.

Missy shows the Brother and Sister to the door. The three go outside to the stoop. Moths and mosquitoes hurry into the kitchen on the wake of the closing screen door. Burke stands uneasily from the table. He head reels. When his stomach cramps this time, he lets it out onto the floor. He clutches himself weakly, wondering why Aunt Missy wouldn't come now and put him to bed. Couldn't love at least do that for pain? But as the nausea recedes, he is glad she didn't. She has reminded him that love is a fake. In the real world, strength is the only truth that matters. If Missy knew his mind now, she would throw him to the demons without a second thought, screaming ''Blasphemer!'' to his back.

Missy comes back into the kitchen, alone. She takes a cup from the cupboard counter and hands it to Burke. ''Drink this. It'll make things easier.''

The pain screams through Burke's arm, forcing him to drink. It soothes his burning throat, but as the liquid moves into his stomach, it blossoms into an unnatural warmth. More drugs. He doesn't care.

Missy then takes his hand, and leads him gently out back to the dark yard. ''I need your help,'' she says as she opens the door to one of the sheds.

The job for which Missy needs him is made much easier by the drugs.

2

Earlie Grant's eyes and her right shoulder ache. She crooks the glasses from her nose and drops her red felt tip marking pen beside them. She rubs her shoulder and sits back in the plastic chair.

She is in the teachers' lounge, the only room in the school where, after hours, she can have some privacy. In the halls are Joshua Munsen and his band of merry no-works with their obnoxious radios and their stinking cigarettes. Sometimes, too, stray children with nothing else to do but hang around after the buses have left hide and try to scare whomever happens along. All of the other teachers bowed out early, chasing the tails of the school buses and watching for their chance to get around and in front of them so they don't have to stop every tenth mile for the students to amble off. But Earlie prefers to stay on this first day of school, as she will each school day, and grade her papers and record her marks. She brings a bag supper of some sort; occasionally a sandwich and a piece of fruit or cold, cut vegetables, but more often a can of soup to heat up in the lounge's microwave. It is partly dedication that keeps her there, partly the fact that since her husband Larry passed on nearly two years ago this November, she prefers not to have to rattle about in the empty house more than she has to. School is home now.

At four o'clock, Earlie finishes her grading, and puts the final touches on the plans for the rest of the week. She opens her can of bean with bacon and watches it through the clear microwave window until she sees it boil, then takes it out and pours it into one of the bowls by the sink. The soup was to have been her lunch, but, of course, on the first day of school there is no time for any good teacher to eat. She must be on duty in the lunchroom, walking between the tables and watching for signs of littering and fighting and trading of food. Not all the teachers feel this way, but she knows that as one of the oldest teachers at Ellison Elementary, she is watched by the younger ones, and she must serve as an example.

As Earlie sits to eat, one of the janitors comes in to buy a Coke from the machine. He is one of the older assistants, with all manner of tattoos on his arms. Earlie had heard that he had been in Vietnam, and had something to do with demolition, and that he had a small tattoo of a skull for each enemy his explosives had killed. He grunts at Earlie, some sort of crude acknowledgment. She says nothing, because the greasy, tattooed man has on a set of headphones and there is some sort of loud music playing through them. Then, as the janitor unscrews the cap to the drink and leans against the machine, he pulls the phones down around his neck and says, "Here kind of late, it being the first day of school and all. You give the kids a lot of work?" He tips his head, indicating the stack of papers beside Earlie's large green plan book.

Earlie swallows beans. She looks at the man, and can hardly keep from frowning at him. This is the same worthless pay-check collector who had not touched the floor of her classroom the entire summer, and who had laughed when Earlie had come back in early August to make bulletin boards and found a nest of mice in her construction paper storage shelf. Earlie had had a fit, running down the hall to the office, her hands cold as a winter's day and her heart making painful cuts in her chest. She couldn't remember specifically, but she thought she had cried there at the office counter. Her heart had gone into painful palpitations, and for the next twenty-four hours she had to survive by downing ten Advils, way over the bottle-recommended limits, and by moving slowly and eating little. Mr. Fort, the principal, had spoken with Joshua Munsen, and the mess had been cleared, but even when the heart pain was gone, Earlie had nightmares for nearly a week. She could tolerate most of God's creatures. She'd had them all, from hamsters to gerbils to ring-necked snakes as pets in her classroom. But rats and mice were vermin in the greatest sense.

Diseased, manic, with instinct that would as soon drive them to taste human flesh as any other morsel of food.

The assistant janitors had giggled mercilessly, undaunted by Joshua Munsen's admonitions. Earlie knew they now referred to her as the Rat Lady behind her back, and although she was hard pressed to care what they thought of her, she could not bear the thought of the children hearing one of their careless side remarks.

"Yes," Earlie says, in answer to the janitor's question regarding the papers. "It's never too early to get down to business."

"Kind of tough on the little guys, ain't it?" The janitor sniffs, twisting his nose sideways with the peculiar agility of a contortionist. "My little niece goes here. She ain't in your grade yet, though. You gotta let up if them kids is gonna like you."

It is all Earlie can do to keep from standing, pointing her finger, and giving him one of her well-honed speeches on respect. But her shoulder hurts, and she stays seated. She says, "If I let up, they would not learn. If they do not learn, they cannot reach their full potential." She looks at the hippie for a moment, wondering if he can make that connection. He obviously cannot. He merely contorts his nose and takes a long drink of Coke. Then he sniffs and lets out a long burp.

"Well," he says then. "Guess I best get out to finish cleaning up the little kids' shit." He puts his headphones up on his ears again and goes to the door. Then he looks back and says, "You didn't give 'em so much work, we wouldn't have so much mess. You know how many papers you grade that get tossed in the trash can or we find out against the fence by the bus stop?"

Earlie takes a bite of her bean-with-bacon soup and can't taste it. She acts as though she is reading a VEA flyer although she can't see it without her glasses. When the janitor leaves, she angrily flushes the soup down the sink, crams her glasses back onto her face, and takes her materials out to her car. She slams the door shut, starts the engine, and pulls out onto Route 536.

She turns on the radio as she drives northeast toward town. The station is one she enjoys, one that plays show tunes and forties hits. Most of the static-ridden stations she can pick up in the Ellison vicinity are of the gospel kind, and although Earlie is a religious woman, she is a Methodist, and does not go for the holy-rolling rigmarole that many of her students' families hold to. The song on the air now is "Bali Hai" from *South Pacific*, and Earlie mouths the words that she knows. She takes a doughnut from the bag on the seat beside her. Her doughnuts are always homemade, always cinnamon and sugar coated, and are always her breakfast on the way to school. This one is a leftover, as is the other one in the bag, because first day duties had Earlie moving faster than usual this morning. Now with papers done and her school routine smoothly moving into gear, her appetite is peeked. She bites into the doughnut and hums "Bali Hai" around a clot of pastry.

When Earlie passes Hodge's Hardware, she slows her car, watching as several children race across the road in front of her toward the West Path bridge. Then she stops at the grocery store next door, pulling way off onto the narrow gravel drive between the grocery store and the Exxon so there will be no chance for any mad-driving maniac to hit her car on the side of the road. She goes in for a can of tomato juice to put into the vegetable soup she'd made last night. While there, she decides to add two Hostess cherry pies, thinking it was the first day of school and a little extra treat can't hurt that much. The grocery store owner, Pete Johnson, rings the amount up wrong the first go around, and Earlie has to wait with her cherry pies in hand until he can get the cash register to go right. He punches the keys, snorts, and growls. Earlie stands with a pie on each hip, losing her patience for the second time today.

"Got it," Pete says, then grins, as if speaking to the teacher constituted an apology. Earlie is not appeased. Pete takes her money and gives her the change.

Outside, Earlie squints through the sunstreaks on her glasses and wonders for a moment if she should eat a pie in the car. She decides against it, knowing if she can't manage a little self-control herself, how can she ask it of the students? She goes around to the gravel driveway and puts the small paper bag onto the back floor of the car.

Then she stops short as she notes a folded piece of notebook paper stuck beneath the windshield wiper.

"Mother of pearl!" she swears.

She goes around front and pulls the paper out. Was this here before she left school? Certainly not, her eyes are bad but not that bad. Earlie smooths the paper across the hood of the car and squints at the print. Before her mind even acknowledges what is written there, the tenured teacher sees several misspelled words.

It reads, "You teach the one who should'nt be taut. You deal with the unholly. The blessed act of consuming will save."

Earlie frowns, and her feet go suddenly cold. She reads the note again, wondering if she should be able to recognize the handwriting.

"You teach the one who should'nt be taut . . ."

Who shouldn't be taught?

"The unholy . . ."

Unholy?

Earlie's mouth is tight with confusion and fear. She glances up and about, wondering who would be watching. Who had put this note on her car?

"The blessed act of consuming will save."

Earlie presses dry lips together. '*Foolishness*,' she thinks. That was all this was, someone's silly personal joke, meaning nothing but to the one who wrote it out and possibly the nasty little friend, hanging back and goading the jokester on.

Earlie balls up the note with one quick motion of both hands. Then she gets into her car and takes the key chain out of the zippered compartment of her purse. She starts the car, and before putting it into reverse, she reaches into the bag for the remaining doughnut.

Her hand jerks out immediately. There was something warm and soft inside the bag.

Earlie hesitates, her eyes widening behind the scratched glasses. She slowly picks up the bag by the edge, and dumps the contents.

A dead rat falls out, its feet curled up and tail slack. One set of toes appears to twitch, scratching meekly in the heat of the automobile. The thing is newly dead; blood soaks into the worn cloth seat upholstery, and the blood on the gray fur is dark and thick and shimmering. The rat's head is gone.

Earlie shrieks and throws herself back against the car door. Her purse is knocked free by her flailing arm, tossing wallet and lipstick and pennies and loose M&Ms in a wide arc.

"My God!" Earlie cries.

The rat is silent.

But there is another note, smaller than the first. It's lying beside the rat body, having fallen from the bag where the cinnamon sugar doughnut should have been.

There is a single word on the note. ''Consume.''

Earlie grapples for the door handle and climbs free of the car. She finds a stick beside the driveway and then hurries around to the other side of the car. Slowly then, she opens the door, and without looking directly at the rat, she rakes it off the seat. The rat bounces on the sill and onto the toe of Earlie's shoe. She screams and dances, hurling the rat into oblivion in the driveway-side weeds.

Earlie grapples the hood of the car with her fingers, and presses her face into them. The eyeglasses are knocked askew. Convulsions cramp her stomach. Her heart flips, threatening to turn inside out, and she gasps with the short burst of pain. For the first time in her twenty-two-year career, Earlie wishes there was a cigarette-smoking, tattooed hippie janitor around so he could find the rat and burn it and look about for the criminal who did such a thing to an elderly schoolteacher.

But they are all back at school, drinking the teachers' Cokes and spinning brooms around in dust circles until quitting time.

3

The Beacon River is low, traveling the center of its rocky bed like a lost stream. White and silvered stones, round and smooth as balls, lay heaped and exposed and naked on each side of the trickling water. Tiny, trapped puddles are filled with half-grown tadpoles, budding limbs whirling, eyes bulging and stupid, a stranded delicacy for the snapping turtles which forage the vicinity of the river. Branches that had grown thick coatings of moss while underwater now lay drydocked, dusty, and brittle, the moss reduced to gray fringes of crust. Day leaves spin about the rocks in a hot, late-August breeze.

Joel jumps from the end of the bridge and slides, pebbles showering, down to the rocky river bed. Under one arm is a blue spiral notebook and a spelling book with a Keep Virginia Green book jacket. He uses his free hand to flap for balance as he steps gingerly along the round stone tops. Behind him on the bridge, which is part of the West Path that branches from Route 536 by the Beacon Baptist Church, several other elementary-school children chase each other and hit each other on the backs with gravel and bits of chipped concrete. A girl with straight hair and bug eyes, one of Joel's sixth-grade classmates, leans over the bridge railing and from her safe distance, calls, "Joel, Joel, beanpole, his daddy eats sin from out your soul!" But the other children are oblivious to the boy on the river bed. When Joel stops and peeks around, the brown-haired girl flips back a loose strand from her face and runs on with the others.

20

Joel continues along the river bottom, skipping pebbles and flipping smaller stones over with his toe to look for treasures. He is a small boy, not unusually short for eleven, but willowy and loose-jointed. His hair is wavy and black, cut with precision for the first day of school. He sweats in the shade of the blowing oak trees. His nose runs with a summer cold. His T-shirt, a faded red hand-me-down from Curry, sucks his skin like a damp and hungry leech. The new jeans are a gift from Andy and Andy's mother, but they are too big, and Joel has gathered them about his waist with Curry's old hand-tooled belt.

The boulder Joel seeks is on the second river bend past the West Path Bridge. It is large, three times as tall as Joel and as broad as the Exxon tow truck is long. It stands a good ten yards back from the trickling remnant of the river, a granite giant over the round, naked stones. Its back is wedged into the sheer slope of the forest. Roots and brambles from the hillside curl around the sides of the boulder like spiny lovers' arms.

Joel thinks very little as he works his way to the boulder. The day at school was for the most part uneventful, as is usually the case. A few taunts, but very few. One third-grader Joel does not know shouted something in the lunchroom that made very little sense to Joel, something like "the demon of below has come to earth in servant's flesh." Joel, of course, ignored the child. Joel doesn't think the little boy knew what he was saying, either. He was talking like some grownup, his mama probably, at one of those nighttime Christian meetings. Joel conjures up a little flutaphone tune he heard the fourth graders working on in the music room that afternoon, and it fills the empty spaces of his brain with a lilting rhythm; a sweet and soulful chant that sounds like summer's end.

He reaches the base of the boulder and pauses, looking down at his feet. A dead crayfish is wedged between two white stones, and Joel picks it up. He turns it over in his hand, wondering about crayfish spirits. And then he pinches it between his fingers. The hull shatters in a spray of copper scales. Joel watches the scales fall to the stones, and then wipes his hands on his jeans.

Dropping his books, Joel runs his hands on the side of the boulder, setting his fingers into the niches, and begins to climb. His toes and fingers find the holds without the aid of vision; his sights are set on the swaying, hypnotic tangle of branches above the slices of ivory sky beyond them. The tips of his shoes work tiny showers of dirt from the holds. A deep, dry scent of lichens swirls about his face. The decaying surface is as slippery as moisture beneath Joel's fingertips, but he scales the stone side deftly. When he reaches the top, he throws his legs over and straddles the saddle-shaped indentation on the side, facing back up the river.

He sits for a long time. After the distant squealing of the schoolchildren fades into the thick woods behind him, the river bottom is quiet. Through the heavy material of the new jeans, Joel feels the unrelenting cool of rock. He bounces the heels of his rubber-soled shoes on the boulder. A sulfur butterfly hangs on a spear of sunlight and then drops to Joel's knee. Joel stares as it probes the dark denim, turning itself around like a dowser seeking water. Joel grabs for the butterfly, but it flits from his knee and sails down toward the river.

In Joel's pocket is a lace-bordered handkerchief that his mother insisted he carry to school. He pulls it out and swipes at his nose. The handkerchief is white, embroidered in the corner with Lelia Barker's initials. During lunch, Joel had tugged it out, to the snickers of Rennie and Ed. Ed had dangled a limp wrist and Ed had said, behind the flat of his palm but loud enough for Joel, "Bad genes breed fags." If Andy had been there, he and Joel would have gone into their two-man idiot routing, rolling foreheads on the tabletop and making pig snort sounds and giddily stuffing the handkerchief into each other's pockets like it had cooties or boogers. Ed and Rennie would have then crossed their eyes and stuck their tongues out at the space cadets across the table, and then searched for something elsewhere that was more worth their while. But Andy hadn't been there. Andy was gone, moved all the way to Arlington. And so Joel had sat at his table, alone with Ed and Rennie and Mary Skipp. When Rennie and Ed had giggled at the lacy handkerchief, Joel had merely balled it up and crammed it back into his jeans pocket. After lunch, he had nearly left it purposefully on his tray to be dumped with the garbage, but even though there was a certain sense of satisfaction in imagining the lacy white among the slop, he could not do it. It was his mother's. It was one of her favorites. She had made the lace and the initials before Joel was even born. Back before she had three children and no time for fancy work.

Back before she was married, Joel guessed. Back before Avery was the sineater.

Beside Joel, on the flat crest of the boulder, are scores of childish hieroglyphics. They are shallow, sketched into the stone by penknife point. The coded messages have no direction, but link into each other at strange angles, each independent messages dating back over the past two years. Joel runs the handkerchief under his nose and sniffs. He touches the jumbled graffiti.

The first message he touches is Andy's, carved near the end of fourth grade in the basic code he and Joel invented by reversing the alphabet. Andy's message, like most of the others, is misspelled. "SR QVLO," it says. "HI JEOL." Another message, one of Joel's from fifth grade, was a secret he shared only with Andy. "R OLEV QFORV." "I LOVE JULIE." In the boulder top are important dates, newly learned curse words, answers to riddles. Joel allows his hand to brush the tops of the messages, brailling with his palm the scratches that link with each other, that link him with Andy.

"Arlington," Andy had said as he and Joel had sat atop the rock in mid-July just five weeks earlier. "Near D.C. Sounds like a dumb place to me. Daddy said we'll get a really big parsonage with three floors." Andy had squinted across the river to where something was rustling the brush. After a moment, a woodchuck emerged and waddled to the river's edge. "What do you think?"

Joel shrugged. He wasn't exactly sure where Arlington was. North. He'd seen it on a map in school, but it was summer and school things lost substance and form in the comfortable catatonia that was vacation.

"Daddy said it's God's will that we move," said Andy.

Joel grunted.

"He said God'll send somebody else to the church here."

"Don't matter to me, anyhow," said Joel. "We don't go to church." He patted the pocket of his worn shorts, a pair of balding corduroys his mother had cut off above his knees to give them another year's wear. In his pocket was his penknife. He took it out and pulled open the blade. He began etching in the stone.

"I think us moving stinks," said Andy. "What do you think?"

"I don't know."

"Who you gonna play with when I leave?"

"I don't know," Joel scratched, forming a "W."

"Maybe if God sends new preachers to places, he sends new friends, too. What do you think?"

"Maybe," said Joel. His knife picked at the stone.

"Nobody will play with you but me," said Andy. "God better get off His tail and send you a new friend, huh?" Andy chuckled.

Joel sniffed. What Andy had said was true, and had been said with no malice. It was just a fact. But it sounded strange coming from Andy. It was like splitting your pants while goofing around with your best friend, but instead of just ignoring it like best friends do when something embarrassing happens, the friend points and grins and says, "You just split your pants."

"Mom wants to get you something," said Andy.

"Why?"

"For us going away. What do you want?"

"Nothing," said Joel. A large piece of oak bark was in the way of his knife and he flicked it away. Then he looked at Andy. "Yeah, I do want something."

Andy's face lightened. "What's that?"

"I want to come visit you one more time."

Andy swallowed and his mouth puffed up.

"I want to come play like I did last spring."

Andy's brows bunched in anger and he turned away from Joel, crossing his arms.

"Can I come to visit?" Joel pressed, leaning toward Andy.

Andy pulled away even farther and looked across the river again.

"Ask your daddy if I can come over to play before you leave. Ask him if he thinks Missy Campbell would think it's okay."

"Why don't you ask yours?" said Andy under his breath. "Ask your daddy if *I* can come play at *your* house."

Joel sat back. He stared at Andy. Then he managed, "You turd."

"You, too," said Andy.

Joel took a heavy, shuddering breath. He worked at his penknife, rapidly opening the blade and snapping it shut. His nose ran and he let it go. Finally, he said, "Hey."

Andy didn't say anything.

"Hey, Andy, I'm sorry."

"Sure."

"Really."

Andy's shoulders lifted and fell. Joel coughed and put his penknife down. He wiped his nose with the side of his hand. He looked at Andy, whose face was turned too far to see if he was still mad. Joel reached over and poked Andy under the ribs. Andy jerked away. Joel dug harder, and made a hooting sound into Andy's ear. Andy squirmed, and then laughed. He looked back at Joel and grinned.

The boys tossed rock chips and talked at length about Alfred Coon's wreck out on 321 and Greggie Dublin, whose mother wouldn't get his cleft lip fixed because all doctors were quacks and because she didn't have time. They mused briefly on the June disappearance of twelve-year-old Patsy Campbell, concluding as they had before, that she'd tempted the limits of the Beacon River the night it had stormed and had been swept away and buried somewhere downstream.

When the afternoon sky had cooled with a coming shower, Andy had gone home so his dad could take him shopping in Staunton. Joel had stayed alone on the rock until dark and finished his message to Andy.

"WLMG TL ZMWB." "DON'T GO ANDY."

Andy had never read it because Joel didn't see Andy for two weeks after that, and when he finally did, it was really awful because it wasn't at the boulder, it was at Joel's cabin. Andy and his mother, Mrs. Mason, had driven their Buick as far up West Path as possible without tearing out the guts of the car, then had parked along the side of the path and taken the twisting, strangled trail leading to the Barker cabin. Andy and his mother did not make it to the cabin; Lelia Barker had stopped them down by the mail bucket. But civil words were exchanged, and from the sagging front porch of his home, Joel could see Mrs. Mason hand Lelia a brown paper bag. Mrs. Mason had nodded and smiled. Joel's mother had wiped her neck and tucked the bag uncomfortably beneath her arm. Andy had spun the toe of his shoe in the dust of the path and bit at his fingernails. Mrs. Mason had gestured toward the cabin. Lelia shook her head. Mrs. Mason's smile never faltered, and she extended her hand to Lelia. Lelia did not take it; she had pushed the air urgently with upturned palms, then turned away toward the cabin. Joel opened the screen door, and for a moment was going to call out to Andy. But

Lelia's face locked on his as she came up the crumbling walkway, and her eyes, tightened with age and embarrassment, said, "Let it be, boy." And so Joel held the door for his mother and watched as his friend vanished beneath the pines.

Joel had not seen Andy again. The gift in the brown Penny's bag was a new pair of jeans. Lelia took up an inch of hem, but could not quite manage the waistband for fear of ruining them. She found an old belt Curry used to wear and punched three new holes into the leather with the tip of her filleting knife.

A granddaddy longlegs feels its way along the back of Joel's hand, and Joel, unaware until it entangles itself in the long dark hairs on the base of his wrist, flinches. The granddaddy longlegs rolls to the rock. Joel pounds it with his fist, then turns the side of his hand over and looks at the smashed body. He wipes his hand off along one of the messages.

Joel's mother had grabbed his elbow on the porch after Andy and his mother were gone, twisting it just enough to make him stand straight, and speaking in a low, harsh whisper.

"What did you have to do with the reverend's missus and her boy coming up here?"

Joel had looked away to where Petrie was folding laundry at a wooden bench at the end of the porch. Petrie's face was slack, drained with her chore, but Joel could see faint streaks of forbidden makeup.

"Nothing," said Joel.

"Joel."

Joel looked at his mother.

"Joel, I know that the reverend's boy is your friend. What's his name, then?"

"Andy."

"Andy." One side of Lelia's dark lip twitched. She nodded with her eyes. "I know you is friends with him. I can't have nothing against a boy having friends."

Joel rolled his eyes.

"Joel!"

Joel looked at his toes, and danced them within his shoes.

"Joel, what you done is dangerous. Having your friend come here with his mama is foolishness. You want harm to come to those of the Lord's family? To them that spread the gospel?''

"Avery ain't here," Joel said slowly. "It's just us, Mama."

Lelia's eyes flew open wide. "Joel!" And then she caught herself, pulling her lips inward momentarily, swallowing heavily. "Petrie," she said. "Get them clothes into the house."

"Ain't finished," said Petrie.

"Leave what ain't done and get the rest put away."

Petrie swore something unintelligible under her breath and the bench scraped the porch floor with an angry whine. Petrie brushed past Joel and Lelia and slammed through the front door. Joel looked back up at his mother. Her narrow eyes made him feel like a tick in a pair of tweezers. Her voice was hardened into granite.

"Where is this from, Joel? Have I done wrong in letting you go into public and get schooling? Have you lost your sense of who you are? God forgive me if this is true." Lelia's large dark hand moved to her face; the fingertips feathered her cheekbone, dabbing at the sheen of sweat. The hand dropped. "We are the least of all, Joel. We got our place, our duty. I chose mine, though a few in the Cove would say I chose wrong. Curry has no choice; he is the oldest. Petrie had no choice, she is a girl. And you have more freedom because of your place in the family, but you have no choice in being a Barker. We was assigned of God, Joel." Lelia's neck moved forward a fraction. To Joel it seemed as if someone had flipped to the magnifying side of a mirror. Her visage filled the entirety of his sight. "Assigned of God. Our early desires can't hinder us."

Behind Joel, somewhere in one of the two huge pines that stood to the sides of the rock path, an owl whistled.

"Never again, Joel. Don't never invite nobody to come here. It's a sin."

"I didn't invite them," said Joel. "They came by theirselves."

"It's a sin, boy."

"But I didn't ask them to come."

"It's wrong."

"But they brought me a present."

Lelia tugged the bag from under her arm. She held it out to Joel. It shook in the hot air like an enormous, dried bean pod. "You think whatever's in this bag's worth a soul?"

Joel couldn't answer.

"It's a sin," she repeated. She crumpled the thin bag and shoved it beneath her arm again. "You knew that. And there's got to be punishment."

Joel squeezed his toes together until he could feel a throbbing pulse at the ball of his feet. He knew punishment. It was never a whipping. His mother didn't believe in raising her hand in anger, although Joel had tried to imagine her doing so, and he knew her blow would be as hard as her eyes.

Lelia turned briskly and went to the front door. She grasped the rusting latch and threw her hip against the weathered wood. The door swung open. Petrie's gray cat skittered out. Lelia looked back at Joel. "Get your blanket," she said. "Time alone to think about your sin will purge your heart."

Joel spent the next twenty-four hours alone, locked in the toolshed.

And now, with Andy gone, he sits on the rock, alone.

Joel looks down at the river. If water could care, then he thinks this water would be his friend. It has let him play, let him fish, let him bathe, let him dream, all without kicking up a fuss or turning tide on him. It has risen and fallen, it has flooded and dried, but it has done nothing because of Joel and has done nothing for Joel but accept the boy and tolerate his presence. Joel thinks that's what friends do. Accept and tolerate.

Andy had accepted him. Joel had felt tolerated.

But now . . .

The third grader at school had stared, pointed his little third-grade finger at Joel and had shouted, "The demon of below has come to earth in servant's flesh." Several of Joel's classmates had turned to Joel then, lunch trays in hand, and watched to see what Joel would do. Joel had not understood the boy, but several of the other students had nodded silently as if they did.

Now, in his aloneless on the boulder, the statement begins to bother Joel.

"The demon of below." That had to be Satan. Joel knows the Bible; his family does not attend church, but they study the Lord's word every day. But Joel does not know what "servant's flesh" means. And why did the boy say this to Joel?

Suddenly, Joel believes that school is indeed going to be very different. And not just because of Andy's absence. As the coldness of the boulder spreads upward toward his shoulders, he thinks what the third grader was saying was something others wanted to say. Even though it made no sense, and Andy would have laughed it off.

Joel finds several small twigs on the boulder and weaves a tiny raft to toss to the river below.

It is when Joel hears Wayne's four-wheeler crossing West Path Bridge, its hole-riddled muffler firing off a round of irregular blasts that echo up the river bed on its mail delivery route, that Joel knows it is late, it is nearing suppertime, and he must get the animals fed if he hopes to receive supper himself. He tosses his tiny raft to the water. He cannot see where it lands, or if it takes sail. Then he runs his finger across the last message to Andy, and slides to the bottom of the boulder and claws up his books. His feet cut pebbly divots along the river side as he hurries back toward the road. The bridge comes into view; it is empty, the four-wheeler long gone. Joel slips several times, going down palm first into the rocks. He reaches the bank beside the bridge and scrabbles up the side. From somewhere south, down toward the town limits of Ellison, he hears a mother calling her child to dinner. Imagining Lelia is on the stone path by the mail bucket doing the same, he spurs his legs to take the upward sloping West Path, swiping his nose along the shoulder of his dusty shirt.

4

Wayne Nelson slams the rusted door of the Vias' mailbox closed as the Barker boy comes panting up the West Path. Wayne shifts on the seat of his Honda and watches. He knows the boy has been taught to have nothing to do with adults other than school personnel, but that kind of crap has always nagged at Wayne. That kind of crap belongs to his mother and stepfather, and to the religious biddy, Missy Campbell.

On impulse, Wayne says, "Howdy."

The boy glances over, but continues to walk up the rutted path, one arm wrapped about books, the other swinging hard like a piston.

Wayne sniffs and plants both feet firmly on the West Path dirt, keeping his butt on the Honda's seat. "You take your mail now," he says, "then I don't have to come all the way up to your house."

The boy crosses in front of Wayne and the Honda, and he slows but does not stop. It is obvious he feels strange being addressed. Wayne does not want to scare the boy, but he wants to talk to him. He wants to loosen the kid up a bit, so he can ask him some questions he's been wanting to ask about Pasty Campbell.

The boy looks hard at the road, and at his moving feet, as though he's afraid they might start running on him.

"Checking the mail is your job, ain't it?" asks Wayne.

The boy moves on up the road, his back to Wayne, still looking down at his feet. But it seems as though he is walking even more slowly.

"You late getting home?"

The boy stops. He keeps staring up the road. He says nothing.

"Well, then, don't let me hold you up. I do have your mail, though. Why don't you come get it? Ain't much, some advertisements and credit card stuff is all, but your mama might want to look at it all the same."

The boy sighs, and shrugs, then slowly turns around. Wayne is surprised that there is no sign of concern or worry on the boy's face, just a great irritation. Maybe there is hope here after all. A little fire of independence.

"Here go," says Wayne, and he takes a step off the four-wheeler toward the boy. The boy moves down to Wayne and grabs for the mail in the mailman's hand. But before the boy can pull it free, Wayne tightens his grip.

"I don't bite," Wayne says.

The boy frowns and tugs on the mail.

"I really don't."

The boy jerks the mail out of Wayne's grasp, then turns and trots off up the path.

Wayne sits down on the Honda's seat. He rubs his face, clears his throat, and spits on the dry road. Someday soon, he is going to have a talk with the Barker boy. He doesn't know how much good it would do; certainly the Barker kid had nothing at all to do with Missy Campbell's daughter. That would be as likely as a black bear and a goat choosing each other as playmates. As likely as a snowfall on a hot August evening. But Wayne has talked to a great many people in both the town of Ellison and in Beacon Cove, and the pisser is, nobody seems to know anything, and worse, they don't seem to care. A twelve-year-old girl disappears just eight weeks ago, and the community seems to have forgotten. Or they have chosen to remain piously tight-lipped and silently prayerful. Or somebody knows something and won't let it out.

Wayne swings his leg over and straddles his four-wheeler, then leans on the handlebars. Somewhere up the path to the Vias' cabin, several of the children scream at each other. A pet dog bounds out of the brush past the mailbox and Wayne races several yards down the road, then noses after the scent of some animal that had crossed the path. A child calls out for the dog but it goes on across the road and into the trees, undeterred.

Some of the people of the cove have told Wayne to let it go. Even Wayne's mother has said that it must have been God's will to take Patsy to whatever destiny she has met. Without telling her that was bullshit, Wayne told her that was bullshit. Nobody ignores the absence of a child, for pity's sake. Even Christians should turn over every pebble to find that which is missing. But Mrs. Stone merely directed her son to read his Bible and see that all good things come to those who love the Lord. Wayne wanted to say that even the Good Shepherd looked high and low for the missing lamb, but he knew it would go nowhere. His mother could quote more scriptures than Wayne had ever heard of, and probably make up a few in the bargain. And so, Wayne has formed himself into the one-man search and rescue team. He has decided to use his interest and knowledge of police and detective procedures, inspired and keened by a faithful following of *Hill Street Blues*, *Miami Vice*, and *Crime Story* reruns, to find out what has become of the daughter of the cove's religious leader.

He is going to talk to the Barker boy soon. If anyone would know about the goings-on in the higher and darker parts of these mountains, it would be the son of Avery Barker.

Wayne gives the Honda's handlebar a twist, and the machine bites the road, spraying dirt and rock. Wayne leans in, bearing down for the next stretch of the relentless, uphill climb of the West Path.

5

The Barkers' four-room cabin is on the back ridge of Beacon Cove, straddling the ground near the top of the south side of Slayman's Ridge, almost three miles from the town limits of Ellison. The cabin faces southwest in a weedy, four-acre clearing, surrounded by a rail fence which holds back the thick forest of oak, pine, locust, and poplar. Queen Anne's lace and honeysuckle, both living and dead, twine the knotty rails of the fence, a weaving left untouched for decades. The front gate is built of flat board left over from the barn. It is hinged with a chain and lead block. Nailed to the gate post is a galvanized pail from Hodge's Hardware. A piece of tin is attached to the top with two squeaky springs, put in place to keep rain off the mail. A stone walkway leads from the gate to the cabin; to either side of the walk are two immense loblolly pines, left when the lot was cleared by Lelia Barker's great-grandfather. One end of a braided clothes cord is tied to a lower branch of the pine on the right. The other end of the cord is nailed to the cabin's screened porch. Bits of tin are tied to the branches over the end of the cord so birds won't perch and leave messes on the clean clothes. The front of the cabin sits in the eternal shadows of the trees. Chicory stubs, trimmed by the grazing of Joel's goats, have shattered most of the stones of the walkway to jagged chunks and powdered chips.

There is a toolshed to the far right of the cabin, beside it a hooded well, and behind it a small animal barn. Weeds give way to raw dirt around the barn, and a sagging chicken-wire enclosure does not keep the goats confined. Hens, roosters, and chicks scavenge the dust around the rock foundation of the barn, hopping in and out through the holes in the wire fencing, yet keeping near the barn in hopes of feed.

At the far end of the back acre is the compost pile, an elephantine mass of weed trimmings from Lelia's vegetable garden, discarded and splintered splits from Curry's handmade basket business, goat droppings, compressed garbage, and ash. When younger, Joel had played in the compost pile, bidding for king of the mountain with his goats, until he got a long and vile case of the flu at age seven. Lelia Barker swore the illness was due to the germs which lived in the ash and garbage and goat manure. Too sick to argue, Joel agreed to let the compost pile alone. Now, only the goats take turns climbing the pile and butting each other off.

Between the pile and the cabin are Lelia's large vegetable garden and the privy. Tiny cedars grow among the tall clots of grasses against the privy's rear and sides. Orb spiders' webs tie the grass to the wood siding with fragile lines. A dusty path is carved through the weeds along the garden to the roofed back stoop of the cabin. Cut wood is stacked to age in a pine box nearly half the length of the cabin. At one corner stands the remnants of a doghouse Curry had built before Joel was born. Lelia still tells tales of Curry and his dog. The dog had been a stray, and Lelia had been set against it, knowing dogs did nothing but chew up things and eat chickens. But this dog had been faithful and mannered, and Lelia and Curry had been equally attached to it. But someone down the road found out that the dog belonged to the Barkers and had shot it for fun, then left dog biscuits on its chest. A joke for the sineater's son's dog. Beside the doghouse in a tin trough float Curry's white oak splits. The backyard is blindingly sunny on late-summer evenings; the squash and beets and lettuce in the garden are shaded with bushy pine-branch implants. A sturdy barbed-wire fence keeps the goats out of the vegetables.

In the barn, Joel sits on the lid of the grain barrel, flinging hands full of cracked corn and seed from the milk jug scoop. The hens twirl madly, ramming into each other, into the chicks beneath them. Joel's goats have been tied inside the pen. Their angular heads jut through the boards. Rectangle pupils are fixed, unblinking, on the milk-jug scoop. There are two windows in the barn, a tiny one above the pen and a larger one by the doorway. A square of sunlight from the larger window hits the wall just above Joel's head. Sunlight from the doorway streaks the floor beside the barrel, washing the scattered hay with tainted gold.

"Brock, brock, brock," says Joel. He swings his foot. The peeps of the chicks are drowned in the throaty chortling of the hens. Joel braces the jug between his knees for a moment so he can touch the painful briar scratch on his left arm. Whenever he is late after school, he is careless on his shortcut. Sometimes a banged knee, sometimes a twisted ankle. But the shortcut, which makes a crow's path from the otherwise twisting West Path, reduces his traveling time to and from school from an hour to only thirty-five minutes. School buses do not take West Path, or the South Branch that leads left just over the West Path Bridge. They cater only to the children who live along Route 536 and the offshoots that are to the east. So far, the county school administration has not seen fit to notice this discrepancy, and the parents, as children, had walked to school and therefore find no fault. Joel's scratch is not bleeding anymore, and Joel carefully pats the sticky trace of browned red. Blood is funny, he thinks. Cells and water, they told him in health class. But Mama says your spirit is in your heart, in your blood. And it can be a clean spirit, washed in Jesus' own blood, or a spirit full of dirt and foul thoughts.

A shadow cuts through the sunlight on the floor. Joel looks up. Petrie stands in the doorway, arms splayed out, hands braced on each side of the frame.

"How long you been out here?" she asks.

Joel shrugs. He throws a handful of grain in the direction of the goats' heads and the heads flinch and draw back, twisting, through the pen boards.

"Mama don't know you's home from school yet."

"So she didn't look," says Joel. He waggles his tongue and bugs his eyes.

One of Petrie's hands loosens from the doorsill and she leans against one side. Her foot draws up, flat on the wood, her knee poking out in front. She looks out at the yard, then back in at Joel. Her hair is long, curly, and straw-colored. It hangs loosely down her arms. Her eyebrows are sunbleached. Her eyes are a dark, shadowed blue. Looking at Petrie is like looking at a miniature reflection of Curry. She is no more feminine than Curry. Her sharp nose is his; her narrow face and full mouth are Curry's.

"You best get in for supper."

Joel says, "Brock, brock, brock."

"Get in to supper."

"You can't boss me."

"Mama'll be mad."

"What time is it?"

"Don't know. After six."

"Why ain't you in?"

"Ate already." Petrie's foot comes down. A puff of hay dust floats upward. "Ate already, done chores, and got stuff to do now. You're finished with the chickens. They can't eat all what you got on the floor as it is."

Joel looks down at the grain on the floor. The hens have buried much of the seeds in the dirt. Some have grain in their feathers and they peck at the floor and each other.

"They'll eat theirselves to death."

"Nuh-uh," says Joel.

"Yeah, they will. Chickens is dumb like turkeys. They'll eat till they bust, they don't have sense to stop."

"What do you know?" Joel throws a handful of seed at Petrie. She bats at them with her hand.

"Get to supper. Now," says Petrie.

Joel's head tips. "Why you so fired to get me into supper? Don't want me in trouble? Don't want me to starve to death?"

Petrie's cheeks puff threateningly. Her brows become a single white line across her forehead. She takes a step into the barn, fists clenching. The goats' heads have reappeared through the pen rails, and they watch Petrie.

"Get to supper, Joel!"

Joel drops the milk-jug scoop onto a hay bale behind the barrel. "I know why you want me out of the barn," he says.

Petrie licks her lip. "What are you saying, little boy?"

Joel opens his mouth, but then shuts it again. He says, "Nothing."

"What are you talking about?" demands Petrie.

"Nothing, Petrie," he says. He really doesn't want to get into this conversation. He wouldn't know where it would lead, or how to get out of it if he found himself in too deep. He slips from the barrel and steps over the hens. As he passes Petrie, he squishes his nose. Petrie smells funny, like the school secretary, Mrs. Fort. Weird perfume, or some kind of soap Mama doesn't use.

"Chickens ain't dumb," he says as he steps into the barnyard. "No dumber than some people I know." Without looking back, he climbs the latched gate and crosses the yard to the cabin. He knows that as soon as he is on the back stoop, Petrie will find whatever it is she keeps hidden in the barn and then go out to find her fat boyfriend in the woods. Petrie thinks nobody knows about her hiding things in the barn. She thinks nobody knows about her boyfriend from town. Joel knows she hides things because she hates the hens and goats and yet she always finds reasons to go into the barn. He knows about the boyfriend because one evening in May Joel had followed her to the old crumbling chimney of Great-Aunt Ellen's cabin site a quarter-mile north of their own cabin, and saw a fat boy with a white rolled-sleeve shirt and blue ball cap. Joel remembered the boy as Ozzy's help down at the Exxon. Joel had watched from behind a dead sycamore until Petrie and her boyfriend had stopped tickling and started kissing. Seeing Petrie disappear as the white shirt folded around her, seeing Petrie's mouth grinding against the sweaty face beneath the blue cap, had driven a sickening knot of disgust into Joel's chest, and he had run away. Joel does not want to know more about the boyfriend. He cannot even imagine how Petrie met the boy, and does not want to know that, either.

On the stoop, Petrie's cat stitches a frantic pattern about Joel's legs. Joel kicks the cat free. The cat stumbles off the stoop, then jumps back to wind its body along Joel's calves. Its fur is short and matted with hitchhiker and chicken dung. Joel cannot understand the belief that cats clean themselves. He has never seen Petrie's cat do anything but chew ticks. Joel thinks the cat has a dog's soul. When Joel opens the back door, the cat races in ahead of him.

"Joel?" It is Lelia's voice, coming from the kitchen. Joel squints his eyes. He is in the pantry, and although he could make his way into the hall and to the kitchen with his eyes closed, he waits until his vision focuses before moving.

"It's me, Mama," Joel says. He stands still. The pantry smells heavily of Clorox and onions and dust. A jar of pickled crabapples has cracked; the odor is at once dull and sour. Joel breathes deeply, and as the smells fill his head, his tongue curls and waters.

"Joel, get in here to supper!"

Joel blinks. There are ceiling-high shelves to either side of him, lined precariously with Mason jars and cartons. A plastic bin of cleaning rags sits beside the door. A stack of rusted buckets forms an irregular, lopsided column as high as Joel's shoulder. When he turns his head, he can see fragments of himself reflected in the shelved jars, like the damaged vision of some enormous insect. Joel looks away from the jars and goes into the hall.

Directly across from the pantry is Joel and Curry's tiny, windowless bedroom. To the left is the closed door to Lelia's room. Joel turns right and enters the large kitchen. Lelia, kneeling in front of the wood cookstove, is wrangling a half-burned log into a better position with an ash-coated poker. Curry is seated at his place at the table, one foot propped up on the seat of Joel's chair. Curry weaves thin white oak splits, lacing them and drawing them up tightly, forming the bottom of a large hamper.

Lelia looks over her shoulder. Her face is blotched with heat. "Joel, your supper been ready a half hour. Where you been?"

Joel goes to the table. He stares at Curry's leg. "Feeding goats and hens. Went straight to chores after school. Guess you didn't see me get home." Joel crosses his arms. Curry's foot twitches, but Curry does not take notice of Joel.

"School been out long time," says Lelia. She stands and lifts the lids from a boiling pot. Steam roars upward, enveloping her face and hair. When she turns back to Joel, there are pearls of water on her nose. "You ain't been chorin' since school. What you been up to?"

"Nothin'," says Joel. Curry's eye narrows as he studies his twining. Joel makes google eyes at Curry's leg.

"Nothin'?"

"Nothin'. Just piddling with goats is all."

Lelia scoops a ladle full of beans and onions from the pot and pours it into a brown bowl. She brings it to the table and puts it in front of Joel's chair. She nudges the opened jar of pickle relish in the direction of the bowl. "You think I think you's out with them goats three hours?"

"Yes, Mama, I was." Joel crosses his arms. The heel of Curry's foot twists slightly on the seat of the chair. It makes a coughing sound. Joel clears his throat loudly. Curry's blue eyes cut from the weaving. In spite of himself, Joel flinches.

Curry's gaze travels slowly from Joel's face to his knees and back up again. Joel cannot remember a time when Curry ever spoke without first taking complete appraisal of the person to whom he would speak. At seventeen, Curry is almost a foot taller than his mother. He has the beginnings of an orange-colored beard. His hair is light and cut close to his head. Joel thinks that touching the top of Curry's head would be like stepping barefoot on one of the thistle weeds in the side yard.

"What's wrong with you?" Curry asks Joel. Curry's voice is husky and low. Joel has often wondered if Curry really talks like that or if he just works at it.

"Gotta eat," says Joel.

"Move to Petrie's seat. I've work to do."

"This is my chair," says Joel.

"Got work to do," says Curry.

"This is *my* chair."

"Got *work* to do."

"Mama." Joel turns toward Lelia.

"Move to Petrie's seat, Joel. Curry's work to do."

Joel looks at Lelia. She is by the stove again, a dishrag over her large, bare arm, sweat pinning the bodice of her plaid cotton dress to her breast. She scoots an aluminum coffeepot onto a front eye of the stove and then swivels the pot handle around to the back.

"Mama," says Joel. He hears Curry's foot make a satisfied squeak on the seat of the chair. "Mama," Joel repeats.

"Move, Joel," says Lelia. She wipes her face with the dishrag and moves the pot of beans to a back burner.

Joel's throat tightens. He grabs the bowl of beans and shoves it across the tabletop to Petrie's place. He steps around the table and kicks Petrie's chair back with his heel. Curry smiles and pushes the relish jar toward Joel. Joel drops onto Petrie's chair and stabs his spoon into the center of the beans and onions.

"Ain't fair," he mutters.

Joel hears Lelia clinking around pans and bowls and utensils. He knows she is trying to think of something pleasant to say. She does not like confrontation where Curry is concerned.

"Good day at school?" she asks finally, and Joel rolls his eyes.

" 'S okay," he says.

"What's Mrs. Grant like?"

" 'S okay. Old."

"Lots of kids in your class?"

"Same as usual."

"Same ones as last year?"

"Yeah," Joel says, and thinks, except for Andy. He spins the spoon in the beans, making a tiny, muddy whirlpool.

"You really feeding goats all this time?"

"Yeah. What'd you think I was doing?"

Lelia does not answer. She bumps the pots around some more, and when Curry groans lightly at a mistake, there is a second of silence, followed by more banging. Joel watches Curry work the oak splits. Curry makes baskets, hampers, and an occasional chair that Benton Hodge sells to tourists down at the Hardware. The people of Ellison and Beacon Cove know who makes the baskets and chairs, but Benton only tells the tourists that they are handmade by the natives. The people of Ellison don't buy Curry's handiwork; Curry makes money from city people who come to the mountains to see the fall leaves or who pass through in the spring on their way to the Sugar Maple Festival in Monterey or who just pleasure ride on weekends. Curry, as well as Petrie, has never been to school. Petrie because she is the only daughter, and Curry because he is the firstborn Barker. Lelia showed him what she knew about weaving and woodwork when Curry was ten, and Curry took it from there. Curry can't read, but he can write his name and figure out how much he needs from the baskets in order to help Lelia pay for kerosene and meat. Joel has a secret thrill when he reads the mail aloud to Mama, Petrie, and Curry. But Curry never seems to be concerned. It is almost as though reading is beneath him. He listens with most of his attention clamped to the woodwork. Joel isn't crazy about Curry's bulky hampers, but he likes the way Curry makes sturdy, straight-back chairs from pine wood and shaved splits.

"Trying to stir some flies in with that?" Lelia is right behind Joel, and he jumps.

"No," he says.

"Then eat. You got homework. You got more chores before the sun is gone."

"Yes, Mama."

"And here, 'fore I forget. Some mail come for you this afternoon."

Joel turns in his seat. Lelia is holding a small white envelope. He cannot see the return address because Lelia's thumb is over it. Joel holds out his hand, and is surprised to see his fingers shaking. Lelia presses the envelope into his hand.

"From Andy," Lelia says, then turns away to the stove.

Joel puts the envelope on the table and smooths it down. He takes a bite of onions and beans and keeps his eye on the letter.

"Ah," says Curry. He holds up the smoothly crafted hamper base.

"Nice, Curry," says Lelia.

Curry stands and puts loose splits into a burlap bag at his feet. He cups his hand and scoops tiny shavings onto the kitchen floor. He snaps his sharp pocket knife closed and slips it and his clamp into his pocket. He walks around beside Joel and taps the table with a stiff index finger.

"Best eat up, brother," he says.

Joel ignores Curry. He puts a spoonful of beans into his mouth, but he cannot taste it now because of Andy's letter. He has not heard from Andy since the end of July, when the Masons moved away. Joel rubs the side of his hand across the crooked pencil print.

Curry clamors in the dish cabinet, but Lelia stops him.

"He ain't coming," she says. "Got a note in the bucket today from Mannie Vicks along with the food cans I ordered. Carter's throat cancer took her last night. Wake's this evening."

"Ahh," says Curry, and the sound is much different from the sound he made for the hamper base. Curry closes the cabinet door, and crosses the floor to leave by the porch door.

Neither Joel nor Lelia speak for a moment. An unexpected stream of cool air rolls in through the porch door that Curry has left open. Air that is not of late summer, but hints at the autumn soon to come. Little pinpricks of skin stand up on the back of Joel's arms. Somewhere beneath Petrie's sofa on the back wall of the kitchen, the cat has found a rattley ball of paper, and is bouncing it along in the shadows. Lelia scuffs her foot on the rough wooden floor, making a sound close to that of sniffing.

Then she says, "Eat, Joel," and Joel shovels a spoonful of beans and onions through his teeth. He strums the envelope with his finger-tips, scooting the letter closer to his bowl.

6

After supper, Joel helps Lelia with the dishes and sweeps Curry's shavings from the floor. Lelia suggests that Joel bring in the wood, which is Curry's chore, and Joel does it because whenever Avery is gone for a whole night, Curry goes away, too. Joel isn't sure where Curry goes, just as he isn't sure where Avery spends his days, but Joel knows wherever Curry goes, it is to fast and pray. It has only been since the last few wakes that Joel has realized why Lelia waits until after Curry dines to tell him that Avery has a wake to attend. Lelia thinks Curry is sickly, but she only tells Joel that. She thinks the Lord's servant should strengthen himself before his life's service is begun.

After sundown, Joel takes his lantern into his bedroom and sits on his cot. Curry's cot is a hairbreadth away from Joel's, and Joel puts his feet up on the tubular framework. He twists his feet along the steel, making goat-dust streaks on the metal. He then tosses his spelling book on the bed and pulls Andy's wrinkled letter from the pocket of his jeans. It is still unopened.

Joel listens through his closed door. There is no sound except for Lelia talking to the cat. Petrie hasn't gotten home yet. Curry is still out, and will be until morning, probably. Joel turns back to the envelope, and slowly tears away one small end. He taps the envelope, and a folded piece of school paper falls free. He looks at his spelling book and wonders if he should do his homework first and save the

43

good stuff until later, but the draw of the folded paper is too strong. He unfolds the letter.

"Dear Joel,

Hope this gets to you. Daddy says you don't have a real adress but that every body knows where you Barkers live since they don't want to run up on you all by accident."

Joel pauses and looks at the envelope. It reads, "Joel Barker, West Path, Ellison, VA 29202."

"We live in a dumb house with alot of wall paper. Flowers and stuff. Mom thinks it is nice but I say KLLK LM RG, if you know what I mean." Joel grins; continues reading. "It is really hot up here. Alot of dust and alot of cars and people. I don't like it too good. I don't have enough money to run away. If I did where would I go but Ellison and I didn't have too many friends there excep for you and I couldn't stay with you. Do you know up here nobody does stuff like in Ellison? No wakes or stuff like that. No meetings excep on Sunday and sometimes on Wednesday when there is a dinner and movie in the soshal hall. A soshal hall is like a big room hooked to the rest of the church and they got a stage and a kitchen.

I wish I could run away. Daddy says he likes it here but I don't think he is real happy. He won't let me talk about Ellison. Says we need to think of the future. I say all the boys here that are my age play socker and I don't even know how. At one supper last Sunday I herd one of the boys call me a country dummtrie. He was ugly like Ed and plays socker on the church youth teem."

The kitchen door thumps and Joel freezes. He looks at the tiny alarm clock that Curry has on a crate between his cot and the wall. It is still early, not yet nine. The door thumps again, and Lelia clears her throat. Joel figures she just tossed the cat, and he lets his shoulders relax again.

"I wonder what school's gonna be like. I bet all the kids dress like those church kids. I bet all the kids will think I'm a country dummtrie.

Gotta go. Write, okay?

Your frend,

Andy."

Joel grapples for his spelling book and tips it upside down. Several sheets of paper fall out and he flips them open to see if any of them are blank. One is covered with doodles drawn in math class. One is the beginnings of the spelling homework assignment. The third is blank. In the mug on the crate by the alarm clock, Joel finds a pencil with a point.

He flattens the notebook paper on the top of the book and chews the eraser. Then he writes,

"Dear Andy,

Got your letter today. Today was the first day of school. Got old Mrs. Grant. Julie ain't in my class this year. They got too sixth grades this year. Our class is pretty little. Only about ten girls and seven boys, I think. We don't have stations. Just desks in rows. Remember the old white eye dog that used to hang around school. Joe said somebody shot it over the summer. I bet it was Joe."

Joel picks up the pencil. He looks at what he has written. It sounds dumb. But he doesn't know what he is supposed to say. He has only written letters in English class when he had to pretend he had gone away to summer camp or to Europe.

"My goats are okay. None of them had no babies since you moved. The spotted one is prenent. Mama says we keep getting more goats we'll have to start eating them since they eat so much and don't give milk worth worrying about. I'd let them run away in the woods first. Nothing out there can hurt them but bears and Avery. Ha ha ha. Hope Mama don't see this letter.

"Oh yeah, Carter Vicks died today. Throat rotted out finally.

"Oh yeah, thanks for the jeans. I wore them today. They fit but for the waste. It was hot and all."

Joel lifts the pencil again and taps his cheek. He lowers the pencil.

"Got spelling to do. I hate school since I can't sit behind you or at a station with you. We got the baby room, you know, with that stinky rug. Well, by. Write me again."

Joel looks to see how Andy has signed his letter. He doesn't want to put "love" if Andy hasn't. Andy hasn't. Joel signs, "Your friend, Joel."

He reads the letter, then reads it over again. He puts it into his jeans pocket until he can sneak an envelope from the box in the kitchen, then props up with his pillow and lantern and finishes his spelling homework. Somewhere between Part C Synonyms and Part D Antonyms, he hears Petrie thumping through the kitchen door, then wake up Lelia who has fallen asleep on Petrie's sofa. There is a brief, indiscernible conversation, and then Joel hears Lelia shuffle past his bedroom door toward her own. Petrie hums something low as she gets ready for bed.

When the homework is done, Joel slips the book onto the floor. He strips from his jeans and shirt, and lies on top of the covers in his underwear. He fingers the door open a crack, and tilts his head to catch the fresh air. His eyes close. Although Avery will be gone all night, his mind begins to draw down into sleep immediately, through training. Joel moves his fingers across his bare arms, his chest, touching the skin and bringing chill bumps through the wash of sweat. He wonders briefly what Carter's skin feels like tonight. He pokes at the sloped angle of his flared rib, a condition his mother told him was nothing but a little unimportant variation on the Lord's blueprint, but what the school nurse had said was a result of poor nutrition. He tries to think again of how nice it might be to have a window in the bedroom, of how Mama could probably talk Curry into cutting one in the wall if they can get a bit of glass, but he cannot focus on the thought. He rocks with the room, moves with the night and the heat, uncertain if the cat yeowling on the porch is real or a dream, and not caring.

7

Burke stands just inside the Vicks' cabin door, his back against the rough framework, allowing enough room for mourners to enter and leave, and enough room for him to bolt if need be. The wooden door itself, blackened and splinter-ridden and much like Aunt Missy's cabin door, is flung wide and braced back with a cinder block. Burke watches intently as a smooth-bodied spider works to build a web from door latch to cinder block. It scrambles up the wood and dives down to the block, time and time again, trailing its unseen silk. Burke knows the web won't last longer than the wake, when Mannie moves the block and shuts the door to spend a last night with his dead wife, but it is enough to keep Burke distracted while the visitors pay their respects.

He does not want to look into the room. The crying is enough; the wailing and laughlike, hitching sounds of grief from the men and women. The shuffling bootsteps and whispers from the children, heard in the clips of silence as the adults inhale. The heat of the small front parlor is worse. Candles and lanterns ring the walls, placed at sporadic heights on the floor, on shelves, on overturned buckets, on seats of unoccupied chairs. The living bodies pressed all around give off their own steam, adding to that of the humid summer air outside. But it is the smell which is the worst. Not a smell of dead flesh as Burke had feared there would be, but a smell of death welcomed, of death embraced. There are flowers, certainly, but the blooms compete with heavy spices and homemade perfumes, which, as Missy has explained, have been worked into Carter's skin in the tradition of the Old Testament. The rancid sweat of the living tinges the perfume on the dead, creating a nauseating assault on Burke's nostrils. And there is the scent of foods, meats and buttered vegetables and dessert, wafting in pockets of air and making Burke take breaths through his mouth and focus even more intently on the diving spider. The food, he knows, is not for the gathered mourners. Their feast is outside on simple tables, covered with stained tablecloths and awaiting the end of the ceremony. The food which is in the parlor is for one who has not come yet. One who is not yet invited.

Missy weeps with the visitors. She moves about through the crowd and holds hands and pats shoulders and embraces the bereaved. Burke hears a man, Mannie Vicks, he is certain, speak softly with Missy, his voice breaking with sobs. Missy quotes Bible verses to the man, and he thanks her.

Missy and Burke came to the wake with the members of Missy's Brotherhood. There are eight who wear the secret engraved star, including Missy and Burke. Missy told Burke that her heart was blessed, because just a month earlier, there had been a total of five Brothers and Sisters. However, she said also that her heart was troubled, because although she still retained the position of religious leader of Beacon Cove, many of the people had been sliding away from the truth and were continuing to slide. She could not sleep soundly until the mote of sin was washed from her neighbors and they were all part of the holy gathering.

Soon, Missy quiets the mourners with her voice. "My friends, my family," she says, and the sobbing softens. The visitors turn from their conversations and look at her. Burke looks, too, happy that there are so many in the small room that the body is still hidden on the cot near the back wall. When first he entered the cabin, he had glimpsed prone legs beneath an ironed cotton skirt, and his heart had lurched. He had turned then and found the industrious spider at work. "My friends," Missy continues. A baby cries out, and is shushed by its mother. "Our sister Carter Vicks is on the threshold now of eternity with the Lord Jesus. Her faith will see her clearly to the other side. We are grieved at her leaving. We are happy for her tribulation what is gone like a moulting skin. She leaves a world what is filling so with sin that only the holy can hold out and be pure of heart.''

"Amen," says an old man. "Amen," repeats a little child of five or six.

"Carter lived the good life. She deserves to be cleansed and sent to paradise to sit at the right hand of God."

The man Burke believes to be Mannie Vicks chokes, and pushes a knotty, coarse hand to his mouth. His eyes are wild and white. Burke remembers a funeral in West Virginia, when his mother's sister died. At the funeral home, nobody cried outright. They just walked around with puffy faces and glazed eyes. Burke's father said most of them had taken pills to calm them down, because it wasn't right to make a scene in front of anybody. Burke wonders why this man wasn't given pills for his dead wife.

Missy closes her eyes and turns her face up. The others close their eyes as well. Burke pretends his eyes are closed, and he watches.

"Lord have mercy on the soul of our sister, Carter. Bless her and take her to live with Thee in the promise of eternal life. Let those of us what is left behind live such that we may join her and our other departed when Thou sees fit to take us onto Y'Self.'' And then Missy's voice slides into a song, one Burke does not know, but everyone else in the parlor knows. It is a whining, swaying song, and as Missy sings, her head flops from side to side. Her long, graying black hair, unadorned and gathered in a green rubber band, sways like a horse tail brushing at flies. Again, Burke wonders at his aunt's age. She is his father's older sister, but how old, he cannot know. She is small and thin, and sometimes, from the back, she looks like a young girl. But her face is old. Her thoughts are as ancient as the Old Testament.

The hymn ends. Two women move through the crowd to the side of the room where the food is waiting on a steel platter. The shifting of bodies makes part of the corpse visible, and as Burke sees the white arms, crossed like bones across the sunken chest, he looks back at the spider.

"Stop," says Missy.

Burke looks back at her. He has no idea of the ceremonies of these strange people, nor does he want to be part. His arm still aches with the week-old scar. And yet the way Missy spoke, he feels there is a breech here, and he wants to see.

The women who have picked up the tray of food stare at Missy, confused.

Mannie Vicks says, "What is it?"

"There was a vision," Missy says. "And the Lord commands that I share it with you."

"Vision?" says Mannie. His face says that he doesn't understand. The faces of the other mourners reflect his lack of understanding.

"We are at a crossroads," says Missy. "The time to be watchful is here. The Lord has shown me the evil that has manifested itself among us. It is love that causes me to speak to you tonight, Mannie."

Burke notices that the Brothers and Sisters, scattered throughout the other mountain people, nod in solemn agreement. Mannie shakes his head. "Missy, we got work to do here. We must send Carter to her holy place."

"Mannie, tonight must be the night of new beginnings. We must seek a new tradition. We cannot do as we have always done. The blister has grown to a head. The face on that head is the devil."

"What?" Minnie's head shakes more vehemently. There is saliva on his lower lip, and it flies as his head shakes. "What are you saying?"

"It is the time for faith . . ."

"Carter's dead! She can't lie and wait forever!"

"You trust me, don't you, Mannie?"

Mannie looks around at his family. They all stare at Missy. Mannie looks back at Missy and begins to cry.

"What are you saying, Missy?" asks an older woman. "We don't understand your vision."

"He is not to be let in tonight," says Missy.

"He . . . ?" begins the older woman.

"He cannot come tonight. He cannot be allowed in this room."

"We never look at his face!" says Mannie. "We know how to protect ourselves."

"Listen, Mannie . . ." says Missy. She steps toward the man, but he jerks backward, stumbling into another man.

"Carter is a good woman! She must be sent to the Lord!"

"We must find another way."

"There is no other way!" Mannie is screaming now. His arms fly
about, hitting those around him. But they do not move out of his
way. They clutch their breasts and hold their children tightly. "You
want her soul damned!"

"Heed me, Mannie!" Missy shouts. "Do not let him enter!"

"Go away!" Mannie screams. "Leave my house, Missy Campbell! Carter will go to God a pure soul!" He turns toward the women
with the food. "Quickly," he says to them. "Put out the food."

One woman tugs the tray, but the other stares at Missy Campbell
in awe.

Missy says, "Heed me."

The uncertain woman lets go of the tray of food, and it nearly
falls. The other woman catches it up and holds it close.

"What are you doing, Missy?" cries Mannie. "There should be
peace for the dead!"

"Do not put the food out. Do not let him enter."

"Leave my house!"

Missy's face is hard and controlled, and yet she says, "It is love
that bids me warn you, Mannie. This is the season of Satan. You
will see."

"Please leave!" His voice is a sob.

Missy turns and brushes past Burke, out the door. The Brothers
and Sisters follow quickly. The woman who let go of the tray follows
as well. Burke gazes in bewilderment at the mourners, and sees the
lone woman hasten the tray of food to the cot on which the dead
Carter Vicks lies. Burke again catches a glimpse of the body, this
time brushed silver hair arranged about tiny shoulders like a scarf.
The woman begins to place small plates of food on the dead woman's
chest. The mourners turn their faces to the walls and step away from
the center of the room. The candles flicker with their movement.

Burke hurries out the cabin door, following his aunt into the night,
fearful of what he has seen, and filled with a greater dread for that
which he has not seen. And as he runs, he hears something near him
in the night, something heavy and dark, moving past him toward the
cabin where the mourners cower like children before an insane
parent.

8

Joel Barker's classroom is halfway down the hall from the office, across the hall from the big kids' bathrooms, and on the corner of the perpendicular hall heading to the cafeteria and the playroom. The classroom is one of the smallest in the school; it originally was a kindergarten class. There are cubbies along the inner wall of the room, and a gold carpet on the floor. Near the blackboard, there is a large pee stain on the floor. Mrs. Grant has tried to make the room look like sixth grade; there is a World Event map on the bulletin board in the back, a Star Speller chart, and no birthday train or helper list. But the room is still the baby class to the rest of Ellison Elementary students, and the thrill is in teasing the babies of Mrs. Grant's class.

The desks are in rows, all facing the blackboard. Mrs. Grant's massive teacher desk is at the front of the room, but in the back is her favorite stool. She sits there much of the time so nobody will know when she is looking at them. Sometimes she goes to the board and draws science pictures or writes sentences for English. But mostly she rides shotgun on her stool, giving curt directions from the back of the classroom. Everybody is afraid to cheat. Mrs. Grant's face always looks heavy, like it's hard to carry around.

In August, when school had just begun, Mrs. Grant had put tissue paper butterflies across the cork strip over the blackboard. Last month, in September, construction paper leaves had gone up. But it is now October, and lopsided, sherbet-colored pumpkins parade over the board top. Mrs. Grant doesn't like Halloween, and so when she tore down the "Welcome Back to School" bulletin board, she took a mental leap into November and put up cornucopias and Pilgrims. On the first day of October, she also rearranged her seating chart, moving boys to one side of the room and girls to the other. Greggie Dublin was shifted into Joel's desk, and Joel was moved back a slot. Rennie said Mrs. Grant put Greggie closer to the front so she wouldn't have to hear those weird slurping sounds all day. From his new space, Joel can look out into the hall when the door is open and see much of what is coming or going.

"Try again, Ed," says Mrs. Grant. She is seated on her stool, pinching off bites of a raised doughnut from the teachers' lounge and putting them into her mouth. "You've forgotten something. What is it?"

Ed stamps his foot and then grins at the class over his shoulder. He shrugs.

"You've divided thirteen into the first two numbers, and sub-tracted, but what have you forgotten to do?"

Ed scratches a crusty patch on his cheek and flips the chalk and catches it. He looks at the blackboard and shrugs again.

Rennie mumbles something and Ed whirls about. He points the chalk threateningly in Rennie's direction.

"Tell him to shut his mouth, Mrs. Grant. He said something about my mother."

"Did not, moron," says Rennie. Rennie and Ed are best friends. This ploy has wasted a good number of minutes out of a good number of boring class periods.

"Did, too," says Ed. "Want me to smack them words back out your mouth?"

Mrs. Grant sighs and swallows some doughnut. "Rennie, I don't want to hear any more. We've got work to do here."

Rennie sticks out his tongue, then grins. Ed grins back and flips the chalk. "I just don't get it, Mrs. Grant. Better have me sit down and let somebody show me how to do it."

Mrs. Grant't throat rumbles, softly, impatiently. "Mary," she says. "Go show Ed what he's forgotten."

Mary Skipp, a tall girl of eleven with short blond hair and three pierced holes in each earlobe, pops up from her desk and trots to the chalkboard. She takes the chalk from Ed, and with a flourish, begins to correct the division problem. Ed stands back and makes tiny but elaborate faces at Mary.

Joel looks from the blackboard to the completed math work on his desk to the wall calendar which is marked off up to October 18. Then he looks outside the open classroom door. If this had been last year, he would have been watching Mary Skipp, because last year he liked her for a little while. He got a signed valentine from her, and liked her for three whole weeks. But then he found out that the valentine was only a joke played by Rennie, so Mary no longer held that secret charm. She was just another kid who had nothing nice to do with Joel.

Joel scratches his thumb and watches out the door. He hears foot-steps in the hallway. After a moment, the head janitor, Mr. Munsen, passes with his wobble-wheeled garbage bag. Mr. Munsen has a lower jaw that looks as if someone crushed it like an aluminum drink can. The kids say he got it in a fight one night when he was drunk. Lelia told Joel that when Joshua Munsen was younger, a mule kicked him in the face, and he didn't get medical attention until it was too late and some of his jawbone had to be taken out.

Last week, there was a rumor that Mr. Munsen had come to school early, while it was still dark, and caught someone nailing a baby to a tree on the edge of school property. Only it wasn't a baby, it turned out to be a bloody doll. Ed said he heard Mr. Munsen and Mr. Fort, the principal, talking in the office. Mr. Munsen said he didn't know who had done it, but it was one of the sickest thing he'd ever seen. He said there was a note stuck on the doll that said, "Sacrifice or be damned." Ed said Mr. Fort had seemed concerned, but asked Mr. Munsen to keep quiet so as not to scare anyone. Joel thinks the head janitor looks pale almost as wobbly as his cart today. He knows the kids will laugh about the doll scare and taunt Mr. Munsen for at least another week for being so gullible.

Joel wonders who would nail a bloody doll to a school tree.

Behind Joel, Mrs. Grant calls Rennie to take his place at the chalk-board. Mary giggles. In the hall, a tall, red-haired boy stops at the door to the bathroom and stares in at Joel. Joel does not know this boy, except that he is a new seventh grader this year.

This boy has been giving Joel the hairy eyeball for almost a month, and Joel figures a beating is on the way, for whatever reason the red-haired boy has conjured up in his mind. The boy's eyes are white spots in a freckled and peeling face. His lips are thin, and they stretch across his face from high cheekbone to high cheekbone. The top of his hair sticks up from his forehead; the back is long and hangs in strings to the collar of his shirt. He tilts his head, mouthing something, and waves his middle finger in Joel's direction and grins. Then he pushes through the bathroom door.

Mrs. Grant calls for the math papers and there is an instant, unanimous rustling throughout the classroom. Brent Weirs jabs Joel in the shoulder with several papers. Joel takes them, adds his own to the pile, and drops them over Greggie's shoulder. Greggie doesn't have his math work, and he drums the papers nervously and sucks noisily on his forked lip as Mary collects the work across the front of the room.

The class has social studies and spelling, and then Mrs. Grant lines the students up for lunch. On their way, Ed and Rennie pull at Mary's hair and she clings to Portia Marshall and the two laugh and bump into the hall walls like moths against a lamp globe.

Joel walks at the back of the line. Mrs. Grant walks beside the line, a dutiful drill sergeant. She parades her experience like a spirit squad rifle. The other teachers watch her with mixed awe and resentment. These other teachers are just out of college, and have come to Ellison thrilled to have a teaching position. After a year or two, however, they pack their apple-printed tote bags and clear out. The area is too isolated, they say. Joel wishes that Miss Burnette had stayed in the sixth grade. All the kids who had been in her class last year said she was the best teacher they'd ever had. The boys had crushes on her; the girls tried to wear their hair in high twists like Miss Burnette. But Miss Burnette found a boyfriend in Roanoke somehow, and she left at the end of the year. Her replacement is Mr. Glass from Harrisonburg, who has a tic in his right eye and always wears the same tweed jacket.

The cafeteria is long and wide, with rows of vinyl-topped folding tables. The large bulletin board across the back of the large room, decorated for October Nutrition Month, has happy, bouncing construction-paper fruits proclaiming the importance of nutrition. The seventh-grade boys had gotten a kick out of the bouncing banana that says, "Eat me!" On the side of the cafeteria is the kitchen. At the other side is a pile of construction materials that will become a school stage. Miss Hewitt had organized the new expenditures last January. Miss Hewitt's minor was drama, and after a spring of creative movement workshops and dramatics inservices of which Miss Hewitt was the driving force, preparing the teachers to better use the stage, she found a part-time job in New York by way of her sister, and packed her apple tote in June.

Because the workmen have been busy this morning with their two-by-fours and plywood, and because it is warm, the students are allowed to eat outside on the playground. It is not yet Indian summer, there has been no freeze yet, but the air has the coppery scent of cooked autumn leaves. Student monitors watch for littering. Some students eat and swing, other older girls hold up the brick corner near the Bible trailer. Joel sits in the crooked base of an oak at the field edge of the playground. He sets his tray between his legs and chews his tuna boat. Leaf flakes drop into his applesauce and he spoons them out onto the grass. Last year, the week before Halloween, he and Andy had found some half-rotted string on the playground and had strung a bunch of dead, waxy oak leaves together and worn them as beards back into the classroom. The other kids made faces and comments, but as usual, let it drop quickly. None of them really wanted to mess with Joel, or with Joel's friend. Joel and Andy had had some unhampered and goofy times.

A shadow spills across Joel's tray and he looks up. The red-haired boy has his foot on a high root and his arms are crossed. One eye is squished shut. *Well,* thinks Joel. *The beating has arrived.*

The boy takes something from his pocket. "Want to see something?"

"No," says Joel, swallowing a soft lump of applesauce.

"Oh, you want to see this," says the boy. "It's a coon dick." A tiny, leathery bit of tissue on a length of blue yarn is swung in Joel's face. It bats Joel's nose and Joel swipes at it. It makes a wide arc and hits his face again. Joel sits back against the tree trunk and frowns. The red-haired boy twirls the string in his fingers. He looks as though he wants to laugh but no sound comes out through his open mouth. His eyes seem strained at the corners, nervousness pinched into red-rimmed daring. Joel looks from the boy to the coon dick and back again.

Finally, the boy's mouth closes and he grunts, once. He winds up the yarn and tucks the trophy into his pants pocket.

"Scare ya?" he asks. His voice is high and abrupt.

"No," says Joel. "Why'd I be scared?"

"Coon dicks is for cursing."

"Ha."

"Yes, sir. Make a curse on one and then dry it and the curse gets sealed up inside. Then you can use it over and over again."

There is a tiny bit of apple-seed hull on Joel's tonsil, and he tries to cough it free. "Who said?"

"Everybody knows."

"I don't know. Nobody I know knows."

"That's 'cause this is a dip-shit place. I'm from West Virginia." The boy burps and wipes his hand across his face. His hands and arms are as freckled and blotched as his face.

"So?"

"So West Virginia's the only place worth living in in this world. Virginia's nothing but moron assholes."

Joel clears his throat. The apple-seed hull comes up and he spits it out. "Why you here, then?"

The red-haired boy frowns, his eyes flash, and for a moment, Joel thinks fists will fly. But the boy merely grunts again, gives Joel the middle finger, then picks between his teeth with a pinky nail. He drops his hand and says, "Staying with my aunt. She needed someone to come stay with her."

"Who's your aunt?"

"My Aunt Missy."

"Missy who?"

"Missy Campbell. My mom and dad sent me to stay with her in June. She'd be all alone now that her daughter's gone if it weren't for me."

"Your aunt's Missy Campbell?"

The red-haired boy nods.

Joel feels a coldness in his shoulders. He knows Missy believes that neither he nor Curry nor Petrie should even have been born.

"I have been watching you," says the boy. "You know I been

watching, don't you? And you don't look like such a big deal to me. Look dumb like everybody else at this school. This is the dumbest-ass school with the dumbest-ass kids and teachers I ever seen.''

Joel shrugs at the boy. He wonders if the boy might know what happened to Patsy. He wonders if he might get the courage to ask. "We ain't dumb," says Joel.

"See there?" says the boy. "Dumb folks don't even know they's dumb." He laughs. He pulls the yarn from his pocket again. "Know what this dick's cursed against?"

"No."

"Cursed against sineaters."

The muscles of Joel's neck tighten. He cups the toe of his shoe in his palm and looks away from the boy, out toward the Bible trailer, pretending to study the girls who gather there.

"Keeps the sineater germs away," the boy presses.

Joel snorts silently.

"Aunt Missy told me 'bout your family. Said leave you alone. Leave you the high hell alone."

Joel looks back. The boy begins to spin the yarn lazily. Joel hates being trapped here. He says, "Why you got a hammer in your back pocket?"

The red-haired boy glances at his hip and hastily pulls his T-shirt back down over the protruding hammer head. "Never know what you'll need till you need it," he says.

"Weird," Joel says. He can hear the monitors beginning to call the children in from lunch.

"Your Aunt Missy warn you, why you standing here, then?" asks Joel.

"Got my sineater coon dick. Cursed to keep the germs away."

Joel picks up his tray and stands. The boy spins the coon dick around, faster and faster, like a June bug on a string. His eyes whirl like pinwheels, keeping up.

Joel crosses the playground for the open cafeteria door and the reluctant crowd filing into the darkness.

9

Benton Hodge's hunting dogs are bloodhounds, seventh generation from Benton's daddy's first bitch, Rosetta, and Benton doesn't trust them at home with his family. He keeps them at the Hardware while he is at work. Benton's wife, Philicia, and his four children had forgotten to feed the three dogs over one of Benton's fishing weekends and Benton had returned Sunday evening to find the dogs several pounds lighter and frantic. Now the hardware store boasts a smaller pen next to the side window and a trio of hyperactive, whining dogs spinning after each other and chasing bugs in the dust during store hours.

Many afternoons, Joel stops by Benton's store to play with the dogs. Before Andy moved away, he would take what money he and Joel could scrounge together and buy a handful of cheap, imitation chocolate drops to feed the hounds. Joel would wait by the pen, teasing the dogs until Andy came back with the candy. Then the boys would make the dogs jump for the treats. The fat hound named Creeper could jump so high that his hind toes would nearly push him over the top of the fence. Andy almost lost an index finger to Creeper once, and he lied to his father about the deep gash, saying he'd slipped on a sharp river rock so he wouldn't have to go to the doctor and get a tetanus shot. But he got the shot anyway, and the finger was stitched and bandaged, and when it healed, the scar was dark and scalloped, like some little old Ellison lady had tried to make the fingertip into a fancy melon dish.

Elizabeth Massie

From the side of the hound pen, Joel can see the edge of the Hardware's front porch. The porch is unscreened, the boards weathered and as gritty as sandpaper. The platform is narrow, and when men sit on the porch bench they can rest their heels off the front edge. Above the porch, in the interior of the roof, straws and grass form sparrow nests. Tiny mud dauber castles cling to the base of the roof and to the gutter that is strapped to the wall at the corner of the back of the porch. Joel thinks the hard dirt nests look like fairy pipes. Off the side of the porch, in the dirt, is a barrel that Benton has made into a trash container so the men who hang around the store would help keep the place clean. Joel has never seen the men use it except to try to spit in it from the bench on the porch.

Across the street from the Hardware is the tourist store. It is called Ellen's Antiques. It is run by Ellen and Rod Quarles. It is a building set sideways on the road, with the narrow end facing the street and the length of it stretching back toward the river. Ellen Quarles, who moved to Ellison when she married Rod, having lived most of her life in the Tidewater city of Williamsburg, said once that in colonial days, it was a law that houses sat longways on the road and businesses sat sideways. And so she and her husband constructed their store in colonial style. Benton Hodge once said that that was one slice of information he could have skipped over and never been the worse for ignorance. The antique store has a single twelve-pane window beside the door, and the display in the window shifts from week to week. Sometimes handmade teddy bears have noses smashed on the glass, looking balefully out at the road. Sometimes grapevine wreaths are clustered at various heights, dangling on velvet ribbons. Sometimes Rod puts little shelves of his wooden trucks and trains in the window. There is always a sign in the window that reads, "Sale, 20% Off Entire Stock." Ellen and Rod don't make much money, but Ellen says she has found peace away from the hubbub. Benton says that Ellen is walking hubbub and she can't get away from herself no matter how far away she moves.

Next to the antique store are two acres of weeds, then the unpaved West Path that branches from Route 536. Across the West Path from the weeds, sternly planted in its asphalt yard, is the Beacon Baptist Church. Built by Ellison's spiritual fathers in 1837, it is a building of gray stone and plain, steeple-shaped windows. Ivy splashes toward the spire in a thick green wave, concealing the proud scars of Ellison history. Beneath the ivy are three large cannon ball holes, holes made by Union forces in an attempt to roust out Confederate soldiers hiding in the church. The holes do not go all the way through the wall, and serve as testimony to the good faith of the congregation of 1864. The entire community had fled to the church at rumors of the approaching forces, full warned by couriers and traveling businessmen of the barbaric savagery of Northern militia, of the inhumane treatment of witting and unwitting Rebs alike. Three hundred and fourteen parishioners cleared their homes of food and blankets and Bibles, crammed the stone church, bolted the door, and prayed. Alfred Hodge had hid with his family; a good number of the Quarles clan had survived the ordeal along with the Reverend Eli Campbell and Moses Prichard, Lelia's great-grandfather. The Barkers hadn't moved into the area until after Reconstruction. The Union detachment had word that a band of deserted, fanatical Confederates were striking blows on small farms and communities in neighboring Kanawah, hiding in Ellison and Beacon Cove, attempting to create their own tiny nation within the failing Confederacy. In fact, Ellison had never seen this tribe of soldiers. They believed the rumor had been a Southern confusion tactic, and as they sat and shuffled silently within the damp, unventilated walls of the Beacon church, some of the elders declared that if Virginia was to treat her own that way, subjecting innocent citizens to an inane attack in attempt to postpone the inevitable, then they should link Ellison to the western mountaineers and secede from the South. What did they care for saving the institution of slavery? No one in Ellison had reason to own a slave, save having the money to buy one. What did they care for state's rights? They were not large farmers or plantation owners. Most had little concern for any law which was in existence, because their law was that of the God of the Bible.

The dreaded Union invaders consisted of four horses, one wagon and cannon, twenty-six infantrymen, and a weary lieutenant. They scavenged about the town, tore the insides out of the general store, and stole what supplies the wagon could hold. When it was realized that the people were in the church, a few rounds were fired at the shuttered windows. The cannon was then lowered from the wagon and loaded, and three cannon balls burrowed into the stone walls and then dropped out onto the grass. The cannoneer was cursed for aiming at the wall, and four more balls went for the door, tearing it out easily. Behind the door, they encountered a heavy mountain of piled pews and tables. These were downed with much effort with swords and rifle butts and sweating, bellowing men. The community was found under blankets around the altar, walls, and hiding up the steeple shaft. Eli Campbell had stood alone, unarmed and unshielded, facing the troops.

Eli and the lieutenant spoke briefly. Men of the town peered from the blankets and steeple-tower door. Children and women held motionless. Eli told the lieutenant that the men of Ellison had never had any ties to an army or regional cause. The lieutenant accused Eli of harboring enemies of the United States. Eli pointed a finger and called the lieutenant a soldier of Satan seeking out the godly in a holy place. The lieutenant, obviously a man of religious background, dropped his hand, in surprise, to his side. A slow-witted soldier took the motion as a sign to shoot, and he fired at Reverend Campbell, catching him in the shoulder. Eli stumbled back against the altar. Several men jumped to his aid, lifting him and turning him to face the army. "God knows His own!" Eli had shouted, a shrill condemnation recorded in all the stories ever told Ellison children about their heritage. "And God's own have dominion over all others!"

The lieutenant had stared at Eli, the two men issuing silent, visual challenges that seemed to the Ellison citizens to be ruthless and well matched. But the lieutenant had shuddered then, and blinked, and turned quickly to usher his stunned men from the church. Eli quietly began turning the smashed pews back over, setting destroyed ones by the door opening, straightening the usable ones back into place in the center of the sanctuary. Several weeks later, Ellison was informed that the detachment had sought the crazed rebels in the Penloe and Monterey areas to the north, and having failed to unearth the phantoms, drifted northeast where in May they were reunited with their units for the battle at The Wilderness.

When organized religion found its way to Ellison, and Baptists infiltrated the walls of the stone church without even a cannon ball, a number of families withdrew membership. Most, however, curious, stayed and gradually modified the services and rituals to Southern Baptist standards. The Campbells never returned to the church. They worshipped in their cabin, constantly warning neighbors of the evils of mediocrity in love for the Lord. Eli's vehement curse on the lieutenant was repeated for the backsliding community. "God knows His own!" Patrick Campbell, Eli's son, and his wife, Morina, would declare to shoppers at the general store. "We, as God's own, will and shall have dominion, in love and in holiness!" Morina and Patrick's children would crow on Sunday evenings as they passed the open windows of the Ellison Baptist church as congregational suppers were held. Eli's followers made house calls on Baptist families, urging them to return to the straight and narrow, and come, worship with the Campbells for true sanctified union. Eventually, Baptist members began to straddle the fence, attending the Ellison church on Sundays as their ministers insisted, and participating in old traditional rituals with the Campbells. At the chagrin of the ordained Baptist ministers, snake handlings were held, ceremonial poisons were drunk in back cabins on Wednesday-night witnessings. Elaborate wakes were held for deceased loved ones and friends, and the sineater, in terrifyingly reverent solitude provided by the averted faces of the families, the turned backs of the grieving, would consume the sin of the dead by eating food laid out on the corpse's chest.

In 1946, when Orville Campbell discovered a major still on a site near Pine Clearing a mile off West Path, he rallied the faithful, setting not only the still on fire, but igniting the bootlegger's cabin as well. Joe McDonald, the owner of the still and cabin, screamed and tore his hair, not, as was told, because of his great loss, but because the sight of Orville's face alight and drenched with the heat of the flames, gave Joe sudden realization of the eternal damnation he had in store for him come his day of reckoning. On that night also, Floyd Ramsey, Bobby Stone, and Donald Barker, drunk on the Spirit, went into the inferno that was the cabin to prove their faith and were burned to ashes. Floyd and Bobby, young single men, were mourned by their mothers; Donald Barker, a widower father with a two-year-old son, was less so grieved. Faithful yes, but irresponsible. The orphan Avery was taken in by Sister Sally, an elderly spinster who lived just south of Pine Clearing. The sineater, John Reid, ate food strewn in the cabin's charred remains to redeem the souls of the three dead men as the mourners hid their faces in the dense green of the woods which rimmed the clearing.

Baptist ministers throughout the years hammered the pulpit with pious fists, condemning the fanatical temptations, dangers, and deaths in the McDonald incident. Congregational members continued to hop from pew to late-night services at the cabins of the faithful. Until Andy Mason was transferred to Ellison with his father in 1983, discordance between the established church and the community in the Cove was an increasingly uncomfortable tradition. Reverend Mason, on the other hand, believed interference with the rites of Beacon Cove was unnecessary. "Let them have their ways," he declared to the stunned congregation. "God understands our deeds and our acts of dedication." When word of this open-minded preacher reached the ears of Missy Campbell and her followers, she declared that at last, God had heard her prayers and the flock would be torn no more.

Across from the Beacon Baptist Church is the Exxon filling station and garage. The building is the discarded hull of the old Ellison grocery, which closed in 1964. The exterior walls are of a strange, peach-colored tile in which are set rippling, beveled-edged windows. The corners of the building are rounded. There is a tin-roofed porch to the station, where customers can pump out of the rain. Inside, customers pay cash and stock up on Valvoline, nail clippers, and sunglasses.

Behind the station, on a downhill slope, is the three-door garage. There is not a steady flow of business at the garage, so the head mechanic Ozzy Stumps and his high school assistants spend the majority of their time tearing down and rebuilding old motorcycles. A tall fence topped with barbed wire encircles the garage lot. Ozzy and the boys are always test riding the cycles in and out of the gate, spinning wheelies and sliding in the gravel. Joel has never seen the garage closed. Petrie's boyfriend has his own small red Kawasaki, and it is forever in a stage of dismantle, its parts strewn along the garage wall, the body propped up on two-by-fours.

Between the Exxon and Hodge's Hardware is the new Ellison grocery store. The Hardware and grocery compete on sales of ice cream, roll candy, Cokes, and PecoPies, but the grocery holds the monopoly on meats and dairy products. The building is new red brick. Ellison's brick mason, Harold Raymond, had designed the building, using arch patterns over the windows and glazed headers every six bricks. Pete Johnson, who oohed and ahhed as the building progressed, had threatened to refuse payment to Harold when the bill came in. He said he'd never ordered a priss-pot building and to hell with it, Harold could just shave about four thousand off the price and Pete would reconsider. Harold said Pete didn't know shit from bricks and that was the going price even without the headers and the arches. After a months-long argument that almost wound up in the county court, Harold came down a bit and Pete went up slightly. Pete has a constant battle scar to flourish—because of the higher priced building, he could only afford a gravel parking lot behind the store instead of paved. When Linda Allen's little girl fell off her bike in the gravel and Linda wanted damages, Pete told her to go see Harold.

Except for Willie's Auto Mart a quarter of a mile north, and the Ellison Antique Shoppe two tenths of a mile to the south with the Ellison Elementary School beside it, there is nothing more to the town save the scattered residential dwellings. Even the Baptist parsonage is on Route 3909, a half mile east of Willie's.

Joel scoops a pile of dried leaves together and sits down beside the hound pen. Creeper jumps against the fence and howls. Joel spreads empty hands, showing them to the dog. The dogs haven't seen him since summer, but they seem to remember the candy.

"Sorry," says Joel.

Creeper whines and digs his nails into the chain links. Joel shakes his head. Creeper barks and leaps again, long ears trailing. Joel crosses his legs and rests his elbows on his knees.

After a few minutes, Creeper calms down. He sticks his nose through a link and tries to reach Joel with his tongue. "Hey, Creeper," says Joel. Creeper pushes his nose further, twisting it back and forth like he wants to cut it off. Joel sticks his index finger out and touches the tip of the dog's nose. The hound jerks his nose back through the link and barks again. Joel wishes Andy were here, or that he wasn't a Barker and he had some money.

"Oh, but no sir!" comes a loud female voice from the half-opened window above the hound pen, and Joel looks up sharply. He can see nothing but dusty screen and a bottle of Lysol sitting on the sill. "I can't take the man and nobody else here in his right mind would sit for it, either!"

"Now, Mrs. Campbell." It is Benton's voice, steady and emotionless.

"I love the church, Benton." Missy Campbell always sounds like she is either praying for you or damning you to eternal hell. Benton, it seems, is being wished into that lake of fire. "And if you was a church-going man you wouldn't stay still for it one minute. That church, built for the glory of our Lord and Savior, has the claws of the Demon deep in its flanks."

Joel doesn't hear the next bit of conversation; Benton is mad and his bagging the groceries is loud and definite. Creeper scratches his cheek along the wire. Joel rubs the short, dirty dog hair with his fingertips and Creeper does not jump back this time.

Then Missy Campbell says, "Benton, Benton, is love what causes me to speak with you today. This world is rolling downhill toward hell, with the weights round our necks. Them weights is the lyin' preachers that tell us not to be concerned, not to fret ourselves. Our town, or cove, is being pulled down into that pit."

Benton says something Joel cannot hear, and Missy says, "I'm throwin' pearls afore swine here, Benton. My family and me ain't to be on that train of damnation. If you heed me not, then the fire's comin' for you and you made that bed y'self!" Joel thinks of Missy Campbell's family, how there is nothing to it now except for that red-haired boy. Joel straightens and glances around, wondering if the boy has met his aunt at the store after school. All he sees is the side of Fitch Spencer's leg sticking off the front of the Hardware's porch and Sam Fielding, a third grader, going out of the grocery next door. Joel looks back at the window.

"That's seven forty-eight," says Benton.

"God's judgment will fall on these modern times," says Missy. "Looked like things was going to change, to go the Lord's way, when Reverend Mason come here. But the Lord seen fit to take him away, it seems, to bring on our heads trials and tests of our faith. Now Reverend Bowman, and saying the word 'reverend' afore his name is like chewing dandelion stems, the taste is so bitter, that man spits on what has been righteous and holy in our service to God. He tells the people what them other lyin' Baptist preachers been saying all along. Confusing the body of Jesus with rules and regulations made up by the flesh and mind, not by the spirit!"

"Thank you for your business, Mrs. Campbell," says Benton. "Good afternoon."

"Signs are comin', Benton," says Missy. "And after signs, the evil incarnate. Watch for it, Benton. The truth will set you free."

"Good afternoon."

There is stomping about inside the window, and Joel looks back toward the porch to watch Mrs. Campbell come out. Creeper whines and Joel whispers "Hush." After a moment, Fitch moves his leg and Missy steps off the side of the porch. Behind her, freckled arms wrapped around a bulging bag, is the red-haired boy. Joel swallows, hoping the boy doesn't look around, but the boy does, and when he sees Joel, his eyes widen in surprise and amusement. He tips his head down, indicating the blue yarn dangling from his pants pocket. Then he crosses his eyes and trots after his aunt Missy.

Joel turns back to Creeper. The other two dogs are splayed out in the dirt as though passively waiting to be butchered. Creeper is settled on his haunches, watching Joel. Joel thinks of how while Reverend Mason was around, Missy Campbell's hell-firing had virtually stopped, and now that the Masons are gone, it is all stoked up again. Mrs. Campbell and Patsy had even returned to the church when the Masons lived in Ellison, holding week-night ceremonies and then appearing on Sundays just as meek as the rest of the congregation. The community had mixed feelings about Reverend Mason's leniency toward the layman rituals, the frenzied spiritual trance meetings, the occasional snake handling, the wakes and the sineating. Half of the congregation was relieved to have Reverend Mason replaced by Bowman, another in the long line of outspoken, rigid Baptist ministers. The other half of the congregation saw it as the backsliders again at the reins. According to the scraps of information Joel gathered from the gossiping men on the Hardware porch as he passed to and from school alone, Missy again refused to set foot inside the Beacon Church. The disappearance of Patsy had not so much touched off visible sorrow in the woman as it had increased her religious vehemence. Joel has never spoken to Missy Campbell. He knows she has nothing but detest for the family of the sineater. But the woman's looks keep Joel satisfied that if she is the spokeswoman and judge for the Lord, then it is just as well to keep out of the Lord's way.

"Best be getting off my porch," laughs Benton. He is on the front porch now, out of sight, talking to Fitch.

"What's that now?" asks Fitch.

" 'Bout ready to go up in a ball of fire, this old store is. Praise the Lord." Benton chuckles.

Fitch lets out a heavy breath. Then he says, "Best not take vain." His leg begins to pump up and down on the porch floor.

"Oh, Fitch, let it go. That woman's always had loose bolts and nuts in her punkin. Worse off now that Patsy's gone and she's alone."

"Ain't alone. Got that boy with her."

"Maybe so, but he ain't no Patsy," says Benton. "Patsy loved her mama. Patsy believed all that sin-hoopla her mama believed. You remember how she was always quoting Missy, swearing we were gonna be damned and would all go to hell in a handbasket for listening to those modern-thinking preachers? Funny she disappeared. She wasn't one to try anything without Missy's permission. But now this boy, this nephew of hers. I don't know. He nods along with Missy but could you see that mischief in his eyes?"

Fitch coughs and spits into his tobacco can with a sharp pinging noise. He says, "Humph," and then he and Benton share silence.

Joel watches in the direction where Mrs. Campbell and the boy have gone. He wants to follow the boy and watch from a distance, but he hesitates at the thought of crossing beside Fitch and Benton. Neither man would make comment, of course. Both of them tolerate Barkers as well as any person in Ellison, but Joel doesn't want Benton to know that he's been messing with the dogs. A Barker in town might be one thing to Benton, but playing with his prized dogs might be another matter altogether. And so Joel scurries down around the back of the grocery store, digging up bits of soil and rock from the parking lot and coming up through the untrimmed brush of the store's north side.

Missy Campbell and the boy are already well onto West Path, nearing the bridge. The boy lags behind the woman, boredom reflected in the quick side-to-side motion of his head and the way he uses his feet as dirt plows. Joel slips across the road and holds still beside a woody, gnarled lilac bush. A car passes behind him on Route 536, strains of Randy Travis whining and fading on a pocket of fall air. A motorcycle at the Exxon coughs, screams, and cuts off. Joel watches Missy Campbell's steady retreat. He does not want to be seen by her; he knows she believes Barkers should not be seen *or* heard. And yet the boy, although unnerving in his own sense, is extremely curious to Joel. The boy is the first child to talk to him directly since Andy left. And yet this boy is so very different from Andy. Joel wonders if he ever back-talks his aunt. He wonders if the boy goes into those spells that he'd heard Patsy used to go into, shouting hallelujah and flailing on the floor at the late-night meetings.

The red-haired boy finds something on the path, a stick it seems, and he snatches it up, then does an underhanded flip, sending it up behind his back and into the shimmering air. It arcs and lands at his feet. As he stoops to pick it up again, his eyes turn back toward the road. He sees Joel by the lilac bush. Joel crouches slightly, trying to pull out of sight, but not certain that he wants to.

The boy smiles, then calls ahead to Mrs. Campbell. "Aunt Missy! I just remembered that I forgot something at school. My books. I got to go back or I'll be in deep trouble over my head on Monday."

Missy looks back. Joel pulls deeper into the bush. Missy's shoulders appear to droop slightly; her mouth pulls down. A breeze takes loose gray hairs and dances them out like fine, feathery thistledown. "If you must, then go," she says. "But I need you at home as soon as you get your books." Missy's voice sounds strange to Joel. He doesn't think he's ever heard her sound so rageless. She sounds almost like Joel's own mother when she is tired and not willing to debate an issue.

Joel does not breathe, thinking Missy might see him. She does not, and she turns back toward the bridge. The red-haired boy strides boldly in Joel's direction, glancing occasionally over his shoulder to make sure his aunt is gone on. As he gets close, he shoves his hands deep into his pockets and his coon-dick smile crosses his face.

"Hey, Barker, eaten any good sin lately?"

Joel frowns and swallows hard, but he cannot take his eyes off the boy. The boys knows it, and he saunters up until he is a mere three feet in front of Joel.

"What you doing out here? Get lost on the way home?"

Joel's eyes flick to the string dangling from the boy's pocket, then back to the boy's face. "Your auntie's looking back here," Joel says.

The boy looks around quickly, eyes widening. When he sees Missy trudging on, a tiny figure now on the other side of the bridge, moving into a veil of trees, he turns again to Joel. His eyes have a different look in them now; a look flecked with a humored appreciation.

"Think you got me, huh? Well, I might be staying with Aunt Missy, but like I told you, I'm a West Virginia boy. She don't bother me none."

"No?"

"No," says the boy. He puts his hands on his hips and gives Joel his second perusal for the day. "You ain't too tall when you're standing up, now are you? I figure to be a sineater you got to be a big one, least, say, six feet or so. How you gonna hold all that sin when you grow up if you're just a little shrimpy-shit?"

"Ain't a shrimpy-shit. What's that, West Virginia hick talk?" Joel is surprised at the ease of his defense. But it seems to be pulled out of him by this boy like a sponge pulls water out of a basin. It's like if he didn't talk to the boy in this way, the boy would give up and go on home with his Aunt Missy. Like being quiet with Andy was right a lot of the time, taking up for yourself was the right thing to do now, with this boy.

"Your whole family short?"

"Your whole family stupid?"

The boy's eyes narrow. His nose twitches barely, and he exhales slowly. He repeats, "Your whole family short?"

Joel sucks his upper lips into his mouth. It tastes like the dust around Creeper's pen. He eases it back out again. "No, we ain't all short."

"Your mama tall?"

"Not really. Maybe."

"Don't you know?"

"No, she ain't really. But my brother is."

"Big brother?"

"Yeah."

"Little brother tall?"

"Ain't got a little brother. Just a big brother and big sister."

"How about your daddy? He tall?"

Joel blinks. The shock of the question causes his thoughts to tremble slightly, shifting the heavy, sealant walls of his mind behind which his imaginings, avoided and forgotten, lie stored. Through the faint new fissure corners, edges, fragments ooze; shadows hint at the shape of a man, traces form a dark periphery. Joel's head jerks back as his inner mind gazes, trying to see what he has not been allowed to see, what he knows he must never see. A void fills the shape, a void that holds all of the vileness and evil that has ever been Beacon Cove. A void not empty, but full in its blackness. Joel hears echoes of bootsteps on the porch late at night. He feels the floor quaking under the footfalls in the kitchen. He hears his mother's soft breathing in her room as she hides her face to the mattress. He sees the trees shimmering back into position after parting for this man-shape in the blue light of a new morning. A cold fear clutches Joel's heart. He knows if he peers any longer, his own brain will betray him and condemn him to damnation: he will see Avery's face.

"Yes," says Joel, wrenching his mind's eye from the sight through the fissure. "He is tall."

"I'll bet he is. Tall as the damn day is long."

Joel looks away from the boy. He wishes he hadn't attracted his attention. This boy is abrasive; an offense to everything that is stable in Ellison and the Cove. Joel's mother has a term for the feeling this boy stirs. Vexation. The boy is a vexation to the spirit. Joel has been taught to avoid people and situations that are vexations to the spirit. Until now, Joel didn't truly know what that meant. Now he does. He steps from the lilac bush and quickens his step on the path, heading home.

There is no sound from behind Joel, no sound from the red-haired boy. Joel's steps take a rhythm; a distraction from the vexation the boy aroused. No one had the right to speak to him about his father. No one should dare.

"Hey," calls the red-haired boy. Joel steps onto the surface of the bridge. Below, the Beacon River has regained much of its proper majesty. Its sides have spread, making it twice the size it was in August. September rains have cleaned the sludge from its banks. The center of the river hurries along at a rapid clip, trailing on its skin a sundry collection of mountain debris, leaves, twigs, clots of buoyant, loamy humus. Joel likes the river best when it is like this. It seems to have a purpose on its mind: to clean up the mountain. To take the refuse onto itself and carry it away. Joel walks over the bridge, reaching out once to knock a cluster of walnut leaves from the railing into the water.

"Hey!" The voice is quite near now. Joel, feeling the rise of anger, looks back.

The red-haired boy is grinning, but the grin harbors a surprising hint of concern. "Where are you going?"

"Home."

"Where's home?"

"Why?"

"Just so I'll know where not to go. Or if I *do* decide to go there sometime, I'll be sure to bring my coon dick along with me." The boy pats his pocket.

Joel looks hard at the boy. Why would a nephew of Missy Campbell be so anxious to talk with him? It made no sense. "What's your name?"

"Mr. West Virginia Man."

Joel scowls; makes to turn away.

"No," says the boy. "It's Burke Campbell. Burke is my middle name. It's really David Burke Campbell. D. Burke Campbell. David B. Campbell. D. B. Campbell. At your service." He grins, a thin, lopsided motion.

Joel crosses his arms.

"You got a whole name?" asks Burke.

"Just Joel. Mama said people don't need middle names."

"Well, shit, I do. 'Cause then if I didn't have one I wouldn't be me. I wouldn't be Burke. Just David Campbell. That's somebody different. You see?"

"No."

Burke looks to his right, down at the river. Traces of varied expressions work on his face; it is worrisome to Joel, as this boy is unpredictable. Joel cannot fathom what he will say or ask next.

Burke looks back at Joel. "Got any friends?"

'*Great*,' thinks Joel. '*Another one.*' Still, he knows he should have figured this question, and have been ready for it.

"Yeah," says Joel. Andy is still his friend. Even if he is a hundred and fifty miles away.

"I didn't figure you for a liar," says Burke. "You ain't got no friends."

Joel shrugs. "Prove it."

"*You* prove it," says Burke. "Find one person in this whole town that'll say they's your friend. Aunt Missy says no one is friends with Barkers. It's Barkers' place not to have friends, and they know it. It's Barkers' duty to God to keep out of the way of everybody else. Missy says Barkers are glad not to have friends because that's the way it's got to be. That's the only way God'll keep from striking you all down 'cause you ain't supposed to be here in the first place. You glad for not having friends? You thank God every night for not having friends, Joel?" Burke is smiling. His tongue appears briefly at the front of his mouth, as though it can't wait to lick the lips in thrill of the knowledge that has been shared, and in anticipation of Joel's shocked reply.

"I have friends," Joel says very slowly. "My friend lives in Washington, D.C., and I bet you don't even know where that is."

Burke tips his head back, and looks down his nose at Joel. He takes time to feel out Joel's reaction. "You's a liar."

"I bet you don't even know where that is," repeats Joel.

"I ain't from Virginia, you musta forgot. I know a hell of a lot. A hell of a lot more than any damn sineater kid that hasn't got no friends."

"I gotta go," says Joel.

"Aunt Missy says it's wrong that you is alive. Wrong that a sineater has kids. She says that ain't the way it's supposed to be done. Sineaters is supposed to live alone."

"Shut up, Burke."

"Says your daddy gettin' married and havin' kids is wrong. Says it's a sign of the evil growin' in the Cove. Evil growin', Joel."

"Go get your school stuff. I gotta go," says Joel.

"You believe that stuff I told her? I ain't gettin' no school stuff. God, you're dumber than I thought."

"Good-bye, Burke." Joel strides off, crossing the bridge.

"Hey! Wait!" calls Burke. "I mean, hell, it's a Friday, ain't it? Where you got to rush off to?"

"Chores," says Joel, not stopping.

Burke laughs, and the laughter lacks the animosity it held earlier. "Chores, huh? What kind of chores does a Barker do?"

"I feed goats," calls Joel. He is off the bridge; his feet pick up stride for the uphill climb to the left. "I feed chickens. I clean the barn."

Burke is hurrying after him. "I got chores, too," he says. "Aunt Missy wants me to be a good-working holy boy. I say piss on it all. I never did chores back home. I ain't doing them here. Life's for a good time."

Joel stops and looks back. "Yeah, and you tell her that?"

Burke stops, too, several yards behind Joel. "I told you, I'm from West Virginia. I'm smart. I'll play her game, at least to where she thinks I'm getting along. But, Joel Barker, I'm my own man. I do what I want."

"That why you're talking to me? Because she told you not to?"

Burke's neck straightens, lengthening a bit. He squints at Joel, pondering this. "Probably," he says.

"Probably," echoes Joel. He looks down at the river. He thinks about the boulder, and how he hasn't visited it since August, though he has thought about Andy every day. He has had one other letter from Andy since the first one, a threat that Andy was going to leave a note on his pillow one night and run away from the city boys and come back to Ellison. Joel had thought for a few days that Andy would turn up at his front gate, and then the two of them would run away together to California. But it has been over a month since the letter, and Joel wonders how many of the city boys are now Andy's friends.

"Gotta go," says Joel softly. He leaves Burke and heads up the West Path.

"Watch our for the boogeyman!" calls Burke. Then he adds, "But Barkers don't have to worry about that, do they? The boogeyman's their daddy!"

10

Saturday morning at six-thirty, Benton Hodge arrives at his store to open up. As is true on every Saturday morning, there are pieces of Curry's work on the porch, this time three large egg baskets waiting to be priced and placed in the storefront with the other creations. Benton rubs his palms against both front pants pockets, feeling for the keys. He digs them from the deep right pocket, flicks through the massive collection, and produces the broad, flat key that fits the store's lock. As he turns the key and the door rattles open, he looks over at the new bits of workmanship Curry has delivered. They are fine-looking baskets with tall, curved sides and broad handles of bone white oak splits.

The air is chilly; the store is still in the shadow of the morning, the sun not yet over the trees to the rear of the store. There is a new clutter of dead leaves on the porch, and Benton picks a broom from inside the door and urges the leaves off with a series of brusque strokes. The leaves spin lightly in the air and settle on the roadside. Benton nods to himself and puts the broom back inside. He pulls the key from the door and follows the broom into the store.

Benton moves around the perimeter of the room, pulling up all the shades. Dusty, silver light fills the room. He unlocks the cash register and gets himself a pint carton of milk from the cooler. Philicia has long since quit trying to fix Benton breakfast; he'd rather spend his time at the store to keep an eye on the town.

Leaning back against the counter, Benton looks out his front window toward the street, letting the creamy milk swill in his mouth like a rich wine. He scratches his head just above his ear with one finger and lets the finger stay in the hair for a moment, musing on the time when all his hair was as thick, and the top didn't look like a meadow of dried, chopped corn stalks with most of the shucks blown away in the wind somewhere. He sighs, enjoying the silence of the early hour. If he had his way, he'd move into the store, set himself a cot right up in the back room, maybe remodel the bathroom to add a shower. It's not that he hates his wife, he just doesn't enjoy her company a whole hell of a lot. What they have in common are children, and that sums it up. But he loves being the center of town. He feels like its unofficial mayor, the man people seek out for advice, the one people bitch to when they've got reason to bitch. If Ellison wasn't unincorporated, he thinks he would run for mayor at that. He wouldn't care if it paid or not.

When the milk carton is nearly empty, he tosses it into the large yellow waste can by the front door. He goes out onto the porch to retrieve Curry's baskets and bring them in to the front corner of the store, where another basket and a caned chair await purchase by some exotic foreigner. Curry's work is something Benton has always admired. They don't sell like his cases of Coors do, but when that certain sightseer happens through the community, honed and ripe for quaint treasures, Curry's handiwork are stowed happily into the backs of recreational vehicles, or bundled into U-Hauls, or put on hold in Benton's back room until a suitable method of shipment can be arranged. Benton makes a small bit on storage fees, plus fifteen percent of the price of the chairs and baskets, which go for comfortably high sums. Benton has been urged by Fitch to charge more on commission, but Benton was never a man much concerned with money. As long as he has his store, and his dogs, he is content with the most of his lot.

Benton stops the front door with a rock kept against the wall for that purpose, then lifts the first two baskets and works them around into the store. He waltzes them between the front window and the center-aisle shelves. He places them carefully on the floor next to the handmade chair. Lovely things, he muses, fascinated once again by the Barker boy's ability to make beauty from such plain things.

He goes out for the last basket, pausing on the porch to wave briefly to Rod Quarles, who is opening up his antique shop across the road. And then, he wraps his fingers about the perfect handle of the basket.

Even as he lifts it, his fingers are screaming, the palm of his hand is full of fire, and there is a sudden rush of stickiness across his lifeline. Benton's fingers open, dropping the basket to the porch floor. There is blood on the basket handle; blood dripping from several gashes in the meat of Benton's hand.

Benton clenches his fist, shocked, and stares for a moment as blood oozes through the tightened knuckles. "Jesus Christ!" he swears, then opens his fist to look. Calloused lips of wounds gape at him, and continue to drool red. Benton closes his hand again. "Christ!" he whispers. He looks to the road, thinking ridiculously that maybe someone was watching and would come to his aid.

"It's not that bad, Benton," he tells himself, thinking *but it sure hurts that bad.* "'S only cuts." He looks at his balled-up fist. It burns exquisitely. He looks at the basket, at the slick pinkish-red on the white oak.

Keeping his hand clenched, he pulls his reading glasses from his shirt pocket with his good hand, jabs them onto his face, and stoops to see. He gingerly touches the top of the handle, and pushes the basket on its side to look at the handle's underside.

There are razor blades worked into the lacing of the handle. Sharp steel teeth, single-edged silver, all in a row, stuck between vine and split. Glued, perhaps, or just shoved into the grain of wood, but Benton can't really tell because of the smears of blood. Benton's fingers open once more, slowly. The cuts gape; bleed. A stupid prank. A painful, stupid, cruel prank. And played on him by whom? What little tough-ass kid, farting along the road before sunup, took the notion to doctor up an egg basket on the Hardware's porch? Even as Benton's mind tries to parade the local punks along the road in single file, in an attempt to pick one out on which to fit the crime, he knows it cannot be any one of them.

The town closes at dark, he thinks.

He rubs his throbbing fist along his hip.

Ellison rolls up with the night. The townspeople don't go out in the dark alone. The people of the Cove don't go out in the dark alone. In groups, sometimes. In pairs, rarely. But alone, no. Benton is the last man heading home in the evenings, the first one out in the mornings. It is nothing new. Tradition demands that the citizens remain inside after dark. They are afraid of what they might see if they peered too long into a midnight shadow; what might come upon them if they lingered in the blackness of a moonless wood.

But still, he thinks, there must be a few who are not afraid of the dark. Curry Barker delivers his baskets and chairs at the late hours so as not to offend anyone. The Baptist minister, Reverend Bowman, certainly puts no stock in the admonitions of the old beliefs. And certainly, on a dare, boys might come out together, frightened, but urging each other on to prove their lack of fear.

And then Benton stands straight, hearing in his brain the voice of Missy Campbell, rising in condemnation and certainty. ''The sinner shall feel the blade of the Lord, come to cut down the sin in His path and beneath His feet.''

''No,'' he says, closing his hand, the word more of an appeal than an exclamation. ''It's a kid, a boozed-up punk late-nighting it with his friends that did it. Some stupid kid angry 'cause his girl wouldn't give out and he can't take it out on her, so he takes it out on somebody else.'' Benton goes into the store, to the back room, where he washes his hand and bandages it. Then, taking the basket by the sides, he removes the blades and puts the basket on display with the others in the growing light of the store's front window. ''She ain't that crazy,'' he mutters, and with a damp sponge, dabs off the fading blood.

11

Miss Rexrode, the seventh-grade teacher at Ellison Elementary, is new, and in Burke's opinion, a looker. She is twenty-two, a new graduate of James Madison University in Harrisonburg. Burke figures she has some sort of personal Vista score to settle with herself, and so she has chosen Ellison in which to serve. Burke remembers Vista volunteers in West Virginia, because before moving to Tickton, Burke and his parents had lived in a town much like Ellison where there was little running water and a lot of disease and worms and scabies and mites, and the volunteers would take the dirty children to the doctor or teach the dirty mothers how to cook. Burke was very little, but the faces of those people will always remain as a vivid memory, pained smiles and polished teeth and a brand-new hairbrush with which he was instructed to never share with anyone or he might get lice.

Burke doubts that Miss Rexrode will serve more than a year, what with the standing teacher record he's heard about here, but by then he will be gone on to the high school, or maybe will have run away back to West Virginia, so it won't matter. If Burke has to be in school, he might as well have a decent pair of legs, a sexy head of blond hair, and never-ending boobs to watch in the meanwhile. Miss Rexrode has no discipline with her students, which suits Burke fine and makes for some interesting exchanges with the tougher kids. But usually the day drags on like a dog with sore feet and Burke finds himself on the edge of sleep most of the time.

On Monday, Miss Rexrode shows an hour-long film on whales. Because there is only one section of seventh grade, and because Miss Rexrode considers the film too good to keep only to themselves, she invites the two classes of sixth graders to join them in the cafeteria for the showing. Burke cranes around as the sixth-grade students are paraded in by their teachers, watching for the Barker boy. Most of the sixth graders are shrimps, with an occasional giant or porker in the bunch. Burke tips forward and back, trying to see around the jerk Jeff Kestner beside him. Finally, the Barker boy rounds the cafeteria door, and is ushered into a front-row seat by his nasty-looking teacher. Once seated, he is no longer visible, so Burke slides down in his seat, resting the heels of his thin, rubber-soled shoes on the tiled floor and closing his eyes to rest out the film. After a moment, Jeff jabs him in the ribs with a sharp elbow, and Burke's eyes fly open and he whips around, giving Jeff a deserved knuckle to the forearm.

"Keep your fucking hands off me."

"Miss Rexrode doesn't want anybody sleeping through the movie. I'll tell on you if you do. You always think you can get away with stuff that nobody else gets away with." Jeff is a little twerp with greasy brown hair and a nose as big as a school bus.

The twerp's nerve is constantly amazing Burke, and he says, "I'll ream out your asshole with a two-by-four if you do, so your mama will have to put you in diapers."

Jeff flinches slightly, then straightens in an attempt to hold his composure. His huge nose twitches. "Well," he says. "I hope we have a quiz on this when it's over."

"It'd give you a hard-on, wouldn't it, Jeff?" Burke rolls his eyes, then resumes his nap position.

The cafeteria lights go out. Burke listens to the din of the students begin to die, with the underlying hushes and finger snappings of the teachers. The projector begins to roll, jumping at first, the music slurring and sputtering. Someone punches the loop reset, and the music and words of the movie's narrator clear. Burke hears Jeff sniffing beside him, an impatient noise that makes Burke smile.

Burke breathes deeply through his mouth, feeling relaxation course through his ribs, his lungs. It would've been kind of fun to have sat near the Barker kid through the movie; to maybe have him near enough to pass a note to or kick his chair or poke him in the neck with a pencil tip. It is no fun doing little aggravating things to most of the other kids because they are afraid of him already. They look at him as the wild man from West Virginia. But the Barker kid seems to hold his own pretty well.

In the darkness, Burke's eyes feel like they are settling deeper into the sockets, happy to be without need for a while. Burke's shoulders loosen and droop, the smile on his face giving way to the easy fall of gravity.

He is tired.

It is not just boredom that calls him to rest, but weariness. Weariness brought on by Aunt Missy and her persistent following of Brothers and Sisters. Aunt Missy and her late-night Sunday worship services. Burke bears the sign of the Light; therefore his presence is a command performance. Even the other Sisters and Brothers call him Brother when in a torrid and holy frenzy. Most of the time, however, they do not notice him at all.

Last night was a particularly long service of witness, and to Burke, a particularly disturbing one. The Brothers and Sisters came to the Campbell cabin in the dying afternoon light, shedding wraps in the kitchen, gathering about the heavy wooden table in the center of the room. The Hertzes, the Stones, the Culbreths, the Marshalls. Those who, since Reverend Mason's replacement at the church, seek spiritual strength solely through the person of Missy Campbell. Those who share her initiation into the Brotherhood of the Light, those who shun the evil rantings of the clerical madmen and work for the kingdom in the private locked-door rituals of the Ellison mountains.

Joanie Marshall had a demon last night. Joanie, a young newlywed, and more newly pregnant, was ill. She was nauseous without relief; she had passed blood several times. Chills came with the night, and fever with the morning. Not typical pregnancy sickness, she knew. And so she spoke with Missy, and Missy arranged a gathering to be done to release the demon.

Joanie's husband, Rody, had come with Joanie, and he listened with a distraught, fidgeting silence from the shadows of the corner of the kitchen. He had a wad of tobacco in the side of his mouth, a chunk from his own harvest that he had laid up in his barn at the end of the summer. He had brought extra, and offered it to the men at the gathering. A few obliged Rody, including Burke. Burke pinched a clot of the green-brown stuff and worked it into his mouth, wishing in less than a minute that he hadn't done so. He had never chewed tobacco. It was a foul, creeping taste that made him want to retch. When the Brothers weren't watching, he hooked it from his cheek and pretended to chew as he held the slimy chunk in his sweating palm. Rody had a corn can; he spit frequently, clearing his throat with a frightened, apologetic quietness after each hawk. The other chewers spit directly onto the floor, taking no notice of the wet splashes on their pants legs.

Missy listened to Joanie as she retold her afflictions. Missy then stood from her backless chair and raised her eyes and hands to the ceiling in mute audience with the Lord. Rody ceased his spitting during those long moments.

"The day of reckoning is at hand," Missy said after the silence. She brought her head down, her eyes following a second later. She pivoted then, studying slowly every person in the small kitchen. "I do not know when this world will come to its end," she went on. Burke stopped chewing the stale air in his mouth. "The Bible says no one knows save the Lord when the last day comes. But, dearest ones, the signs are upon us. The days are short for those in our home, in our Cove, and our town of Ellison. Our community has debts to pay, and the devil has chosen his tax collector."

"Glory, yeah," muttered some of the Brotherhood.

Joanie looked around at Rody; he looked at her, aware obviously that his wife wanted him to come to her, but rooted to the spot by the words of the woman in the center of the room.

"Our debt will come down on our heads a thousandfold." Missy's gaze traveled across Burke's face, and Burke felt the cords on his neck stiffen into cold blades. Yet he did not look away from her. He would play her game in spite of the coals of fear she dredged from his soul. "Ellison has a festering sore. The sore of indifference, doubt, self-righteousness. And what shall happen when this sore splits open? My dearest, it already has."

A Brother, several Sisters, moaned in awe and terror. Someone said, "Help us, Jesus."

"It has happened. The sore that has been brought us by the sins of the children and the fathers and the grandfathers has opened in our time. It could not be held back." Missy closed her eyes. The gray brows above her wrinkled eyelids trembled. Something wet, tears or sweat, gathered on her lower lashes and dropped to the floor with the puddles of tobacco swill. The flesh beneath her neck flexed with her heavy breathing, bobbing like a crude and calloused wattle of a thin turkey. "Beware the devil's collector."

Burke thought, '*Who is she talking about? She is crazy.*'

Joanie again looked at Rody, but in that instant Missy spun on her, and took both of Joanie's arms in a strong grip. "Sister Joanie, get onto the table." Joanie's eyes widened, and she licked her lips feebly. But before she could protest, if indeed she was going to consider it, the gathering of Sisters and Brothers converged and moved forward, a wall of knowing and demanding faces. Burke was moved with them, and saw in Joanie's eyes what he knew had been in his own the night he had been given the star. He looked away from Joanie's face, finding the corner of the table and rooting his focus to it.

Joanie climbed onto the table and lay back. Reverent faces moved around the perimeter of the tabletop. Rody was among them coughing silently, apparently having swallowed a mouthful of tobacco juice. Missy took Joanie's hand in her own and patted it.

"Fire with fire, Sister," said Missy. "We shall rid you of the evil this very evening. Shall you do what must be done?"

Joanie mumbled something, and Missy repeated, "Shall you, Sister?"

Audibly, Joanie whispered, "Yes."

"Fire with fire," Missy said. "The Light driving out darkness. On your knees, my family, and pray for the release of this infant and its mother." The Brothers and Sister obeyed. Burke went down, looking away from the button toward Missy. Behind her, Rody was clutching his corn can as if it were an urn of myrrh. It shook with the undisguised shaking of his hands. Burke blinked; looked down at his own hands. He felt Missy moving away from the gathering, and after a moment she was back, mixing something in her wooden bowl. In the poor light and in the pretense of prayer, Burke could not tell what it was she was using.

When the mixing was done, Missy called for the Brotherhood to rise. And then she fed the mixture to Joanie.

For the half hour that followed, the Brothers and Sisters prayed and spoke in tongues and praised the Lord as Joanie was held to the table, writhing and twisting violently, heaving great spurts of stinking vomit onto herself and onto the arms of those that held her, crying and doubling up as if she was a woman giving birth to the devil.

There is a sharp whispering in Burke's ear, and he shakes it off as he would a bee, then settles his mind to the darkness again, seeing Joanie rise finally, to the grateful cries of the thankful gathering, watching Joanie's fouled and weary lips meet the wrinkled cheek of Missy in a kiss of respect and relief. But the darkness is short-lived; the bee returns and it has the obnoxious voice of Jeff Kestner.

"The movie's over, Burke. Get *up!*"

Burke sits straight, and grabs the collar of Joel's cotton shirt. "I'll get you up, you little shit. And you'll meet me in front of the hardware store after school. We got a bit of discussing to do, and it ain't about no damned whale movie."

"What?" Jeff manages, his eyes stretching wide.

"We gonna talk manners, you and me. You understand, little boy?"

Jeff nods in sudden desperation. Burke lets go. He knows Jeff won't come within a mile of the Hardware this afternoon, but the nod is good enough for Burke.

The sixth-grade classes are swarming on the exit, with Mrs. Grant and Miss Sanders riding shotgun. The Barker boy, Burke notices, walks with his face to the floor when he is at school. This will have to change. Nobody with the power of the Barkers should ever give in to the wimps of the world. Burke might not have a meeting with Jeff Kestner after school, but he sure as hell is going to arrange something with the young and strange Mr. Joel Barker.

12

He tells her that his chores are done, and his homework as well, and Lelia fumes about the kitchen for a while, not wanting him to go but not having a substantial reason not to let him go. Besides, as Joel knew it would be, the possibility of having fresh meat is a sweet deal to his mother.

"Curry started hunting when he was a year younger'en me," Joel says, and Lelia knows it to be true. "Curry ain't got nothing good to eat in almost two weeks. He's been on them old hampers too much. I'm tired of corn and cabbage and that old dried-up ham. Ain't you?" Lelia is, although she won't give in to outwardly acknowledging it. She compromises with a shrug. "I know how to use Curry's gun." Joel continues. "I shot a mess of cans offa that back board on the fence. You even clapped for me when I got five in a row, remember?" Lelia remembers. Joel had been reluctant to take up the gun, and Lelia had assumed that Joel felt a kinship between the deer Curry would bring home and the goats Joel cared for in the barn. But Joel had had a steady hand, as steady as Curry's had ever been. But he had never wanted to shoot for food. Curry seemed more suited for it; he was more like the wilderness man. Joel more like the shepherd.

And so Joel's request surprises Lelia, but the appeal of rabbit or squirrel takes the edge off the wonderment, and after some pacing around between the table and the stove, she tells him it will be all right.

"But make sure the lantern is full, Joel. Be home before midnight." She pauses, and Joel knows what she wants to say but is uncertain how to mention it. It is almost as though realizing the danger is one thing, but saying it aloud makes it more certain. Saying it makes it her fault if something goes wrong because she was aware ahead of time. And so after a pause during which she moved pots on the stove and kicked at the cat with a couple of unaimed swings of her foot, she says, "Stay on the paths, the ones you know. You understand me, Joel?"

"Sure, but Curry don't have to be home by midnight, he . . ."

"Curry's older than you."

"But I might not get anything before later."

"Curry's older. He knows more about the woods. I shouldn't even be saying yes. You stay on them paths, Joel. Lots of animals cross them paths at night. Keep to 'em and you'll be all right."

Joel nods, realizing it is all the blessing he'll get from his mother for this venture. In truth, Joel is anxious, his stomach fighting the bread and the strips of old ham as it settles into his stomach. But he has to go. It is not an option.

He clambers from the supper table when his plate is clean, and clears his dishes away as Curry comes into the room from the porch. Curry considers Joel briefly, and his gaze is difficult to interpret, but Joel does not stay long enough to let his mind worry about it.

Petrie is outside, loosening the soil around the pole beans. She gives her sisterly frown when she sees him, and he returns a wide, face-stretching grin that hurts his face. She raises on one knee to watch him as he pads around the garden in the cold light of the setting sun and goes toward the outhouse. She waits until he has gone inside and crammed the wooden stick through the steel ring clasp to call to him.

"What you so happy about?"

Joel pretends he doesn't hear, and he sits on the fanny-polished wood, looking down at the shit through the hole. The smile on his face has dropped, and there is a thought, a black spot hiding in his mind, that wants to come through, but he will not let it.

"What you smiling about, Joel Barker?" Petrie calls again.

Joel looks at the closed door. He knows she'll pester him until he gives her an answer, so he shouts, "Mama gave me ten dollars to spend at the Hardware after school tomorrow."

Joel can feel the earth shift beneath his feet as Petrie's surprise and then rage blossom. He hears her swear something, and then her heavy breath comes like a fast storm toward the privy door.

"What are you talking about?" She is right outside now.

Joel looks down at his toes. They clap together in appreciation of the frustration he has caused his sister. Normally he would feel the appreciation that his toes feel, but the black thought pushes again from the back of his mind. He pushes back.

"Ten dollars," he says. " 'Cause I got a B on my social studies test."

Petrie whoops, then grunts. He can imagine the red in her eyes. "She never gave you no ten dollars! She ain't got it to give! You didn't even get a B on your test, and you can't even go into the Hardware to spend it. God'll get you for lying to me, Joel. He'll have your tongue rot up and fall out your mouth!"

"Ain't lying," says Joel. "She says since I get to go to school I should do good. Says I should get rewards when I do good. Told me not to tell anybody, 'specially not you or Curry, since you don't go to school. But you and your big mouth had to bug me about it, so I told you. It's your fault now if you're mad."

There is a pause full of trembling, thick with fury. Then Petrie says, "She never gave me no ten dollars! I do the stupid garden, I wash your stinking underpants! It ain't my fault I don't go to school! It ain't fair! I'm gonna tell her so!"

Joel snickers, although the fluttering anxiety in his gut won't allow the snicker to become a full-fledged laugh. '*Hey, Joel*,' it says. '*Listen*.' But Joel won't listen. "I'm joking, Petrie," Joel says through the door. "Can't take a little joke?"

There is another whooshing of air, but this time is sounds like it is going in instead of out. "What did you say?"

"I'm joking. And you said chickens is dumb. No go on, I gotta crap."

"You turd! You think you can do just about anything you want just because you get to go all over town? You wait! Your time is comin', and it won't be pretty!"

"You mean it'll look like you?"

"You just wait, Joel Barker! You just wait!"

Joel wonders what he is supposed to wait for, but he doesn't have the time to wait and find out. He hears Petrie storm off, and he slumps on the seat. He thinks about Burke, and how Burke might already be at the clearing, waiting to show Joel what he called some " 'mazing things." It is not the " 'mazing things" Joel must go for, however. He must go because at the end of the quick invitation, dumped on him after school when Burke cornered him in the side parking lot, Burke added the challenge, "You better come, here me? Come show me what a Barker boy's made out of. Show me I ain't the only one in this damned place what's got balls instead of cream puffs."

Joel leaves the outhouse for the shed to retrieve the large lantern. It is a Hillary, only a couple of years old, traded to Curry for a small stool. Joel had wondered how Curry got the lantern, how Benton would ask Curry if he wanted a lantern in trade instead of money, but it didn't really matter. The lantern was super, much better than the old one. Curry takes the new one out when he delivers baskets and hampers to the store, or when he goes hunting. It is the lantern that Curry feels safe with, because the light is a beacon, and is strong, and is recognized by . . .

'By who, Joel?' the dark thought giggles. *'You know who!'*

Joel presses the thought out.

. . . by the Beacon Cove people who might be out together on a trip to Missy Campbell's cabin for a night service. They know who Curry is, but don't want to be around him.

'That's not who recognizes the light, Joel . . .'

Inside the shed, Joel lifts the lantern from the nail and shakes the base to see if there is any kerosene in it. It is nearly full. Joel goes outside. Petrie watches him cross the yard, her eyes, body, and hoe all turning in unison like a dirty, furious music-box dancer. Joel climbs over the back fence and trots through the weeds beyond.

"And where do you think you're heading?" screeches Petrie, but Joel is already vanished, leaving the faint shuddering of chicory stems in his wake.

Thirty yards into the woods, Joel stops to gather his bearings. He lights the lantern in the shadows of the trees, then pivots on his foot, looking about. He is supposed to meet Burke at eight o'clock at Pine

Clearing. It is not far from the the Barkers' home, sitting just due south, but the terrain between the two is vicious. There are paths spiraling through the trees, leading off from where Joel stands, trails flattened by Curry's search for suitable oak saplings. These lead south, west, and north. Joel has been to the clearing before, exploring the woods alone or with Andy. But he has never gone at night. And he hasn't truly been on the clearing. Nobody uses the clearing because it is a place of sacrifice and respect. Men gave their lives many years ago to the glory of God and in open, defiant faith.

Joel is going to be defiant tonight. He is going to do what he is not supposed to do, all on a stupid dare.

The black thought whispers, *'That's right, Joel. Think about it.'*

"I ain't going to think about it," Joel says aloud. "Ain't nothing to think about. Ain't no problem at all. You hear me, Burke Campbell?"

'You hear me, Joel Barker? Nobody in the woods at night. Nothing to worry about. Nobody out here except . . .'

"Fuck it," Joel says, and then feels a chill on his neck at the words. He looks back through the trees toward his house, in case his mother or Petrie has heard him. He does not curse; no one in his family uses dirty language. He feels like Burke is playing with his mind, making him do things he would never do.

Like curse.

Like go into the woods alone at night.

"Hang tough," Andy had said in his letter. With or without a clear meaning, it still sounds like good advice.

Joel takes one of Curry's paths leading south, knowing that in a few minutes it will break off to the east and wind down toward West Path. Joel will be left to carve his own way through the shin-clawing, face-mauling undergrowth of the mountain.

Small things skitter away form the path ahead of Joel. He waits once to let a long black snake scoot from one side of the path to the other. The snake is so long that for a moment, there is no head or tail. Then the tail comes into sight, and twitches across into the underbrush. Joel goes on, wiping occasional spiderwebs from his face, cringing once when not only the web but the spider falls to his cheek. Joel smacks himself, and the brown, leggy creature makes a dive for the ground, gossamer dragline trailing.

And then there is the sharp turn east, leading downward, and Joel gazes ahead into the brambled wall, the lantern coming to thump and then rest on his calf.

Chigga, chigga, CHIGGA, CHIGGA, chigga, chigga.

A short shot ahead, he tells himself. You've done this before. Less than a half mile. Maybe only a third. You know this place. Nothing here at night that ain't here in the daytime.

'Except . . .'

"No," says Joel, dodging the thought.

'Except . . .'

Joel lunges ahead into the wiry mesh of weeds, a bramble wrapping itself around his leg. Joel tugs it free. He tops the bank, and swings the lantern, looking behind him.

'Except for Avery, Joel . . .'

"Fuck!" cries Joel. He swipes the lantern in the dark; wide circles striking out at the black thought. Chills caress his arms as did the webs. Phantom spiders tickle his neck, up his pants legs, down the back of his shirt. He thinks it is sweat on his neck and legs, but he can't be sure and he can't put down the lantern to check because a lantern on the ground doesn't shed as much light as a lantern held up and it was his mother, Lelia Barker, who had reminded Curry, "He knows a lantern and will stay away from it. But it's the coming on him by surprise that is the harm." The coming on him . . .

The seeing of his face . . .

The fissure of imagination, the gap weakened by Burke on the West Path Bridge after school not long ago, shifts painfully, but Joel will not look into it. He looks at the sky, making himself see the sapphire-marbled swirls of cloud and air, he looks at the moths who display suicidal excitement at having found the lantern globe. He looks at the paper-crisp layers of leaves at his feet. He does not know if the fissure has closed back; he will not look to see if it has.

"Burke!" he calls. If Burke hears him, he will call back. It isn't far, the crickets cannot be louder than a human voice. The spider sweat plays along on the gooseskin on his back. "Burke!"

Burke does not answer.

Joel's mouth hitches up, an involuntary scream posing, waiting. He thinks of his mother's words. "He knows a lantern and will stay away from it." But in the thickness of this forested mountain, light is swallowed by ravenous plant life.

"Burke!"

A moth hits Joel in the face. He licks his lips with a dry tongue. He should count, he should think of Andy, he should picture the boulder drawing in his mind. He should move ahead. He should find Burke. Joel looks into the darkness to his right and sees the stark, straight tree trunks. The trees are the crack in his imagination; they sway, bowing from each other, threatening to reveal what God has ordained to be banned from human sight. Opening the night.

'*Look around, Joel*,' says the dark thought.

Joel whips his head back around, facing forward.

"In the Blue Ridge Mountains of Virginia," he begins a childhood song, speaking as though he were chanting. He begins walking up the steep slope. "On the trail of the Lonesome Pine; stood a nice . . ."

He switches the lantern to the other hand and digs his feet into the thick humus. He leans forward for traction. He works his head beneath low branches, his feet over tall roots.

". . . old cow, with eyes so kind, but how do you 'spect a cow to read a railroad sign?" He parts a clump of brush that has grown tall and angry in its search for sunlight. He continues up, the jigsaw patches of blackberry sky visible just above his sights, filled with the frantic, silent beat of bats' wings.

CHIGGA, CHIGGA, CHIGGA.

"She stood in the middle of the track, and the train came and hit her in . . ."

Movement to Joel's left, and he freezes. His eyes are the only part of him that turn toward the sound.

". . . the back . . ." he whispers unintentionally.

The sentinel trees do not move. Joel watches. And then there is a shudder, a slow, quiet rattling of leaves. A huge, wet-eyed opossum comes out of the brush, stares at the glowing lantern, hisses, winks, and waddles away.

Joel watches it go. He looks ahead again. A bitter-tasting liquid fills his mouth, and he forces it back down. He scratches his forehead slowly.

His mother had said, "You see your father and you see the sin of the world."

Missy Campbell had said, "You see the sineater, and your mind will boil with the evil he carries from all the souls he has cleaned for heaven. Your soul will explode from the foulness that shines from his eyes."

"Now her head's in the valley of Virginia," Joel says, forcing his feet on. "And her tail's on the lonesome spine."

The land goes up another few yards, and then levels off. Joel struggles onward, knowing it can't be that much farther, please God it can't be too much farther in these Allegheny Mountains of Virginia on the trail of the lonesome sixth-grader. Not far, not far. The swaying lantern gives him a moment of motion sickness, but the distraction of nausea is a relief. Not far, God, not far. His legs move more quickly. Crickets protest.

Chigga, CHIGGA, CHIGGA, CHIGGA, CHIGGA.

And then he sees a small fire, and he sees also that he has stepped clear of the woods and into a broad expanse of tall, dry grass. The fire is to the far side, and Joel raises his lantern and waves it. Someone stands up beside the fire, and calls out, "I hope the fuck you brought some marshmallows." Joel calls back, checking his voice for the trembling of adrenaline withdrawal, "Fuck, no. Didn't you?"

13

"You think bugs got souls?" asks Joel. He watches Burke intently. Burke has a long stick that he has whittled, and he is stirring in the hottest core of the campfire. He dared Joel to touch the tip of the stick to his tongue, but Joel wouldn't unless Burke did it first. Burke said he would later, when it was just hot enough. He is now working on making it hot enough.

"I don't know," Burke answers. "Who cares?"

The boys sit near each other by the fire, but at a respectful distance. According to Burke's watch, it was ten-twelve the last time Joel asked. Beside Burke is a lumpy burlap bag; the nose of the bag, tied with a string, sticks out from beneath the denim jacket he'd shed when he began to play with the fire. Several feet behind him is a hammer he'd had in his back pocket. Joel can't figure the red-haired boy's fascination with hammers. Burke's hair is pumpkin-bright in the light of the fire.

"Bugs would care," Joel says.

"You know what they got in West Virginia?" Burke asks. He stirs the stick. Ashes fly. "Bug zappers. Electric lights people put on poles so bugs can electrocute theirselves."

Joel has heard of bug zappers. Andy told him once that Benton was thinking about ordering a shipload, but decided against it because most people in Beacon Cove don't have electricity.

"We had one where I used to live. All night long in the summer-

93

time I could hear them damn bugs frying theirselves to death. Pop! Pop! When a big one would get caught it would buzz and sputter and if you looked out it would be smoking like a pork chop.''

"Think there was souls in that smoke?"

"I don't know. Maybe. Little bug souls all full of sin. But no sineaters for bugs, you know. Gotta go straight to hell with no chance of getting off.'' Burke's eyebrows arch, and he looks beyond the fire as if his thoughts are switching gears. When he speaks to Joel again, he looks at the dark-haired boy directly.

"Your mama care you come out here?"

"She don't mind. I told her I was hunting."

"Oh, yeah? So what you using, rocks?"

Joel glances down at the darkened lantern beside him. He has brought nothing but the lantern. The rifle is still at home in the kitchen. "Oh, no," he says.

"Hunt much?" laughs Burke.

"Don't have to," says Joel. "My brother does that. I don't really want to, anyway. Just thought I'd tell Mama that so she'd let me come. What'd you tell your Aunt Missy?"

"I don't have to tell her nothing. She don't own me."

"You told her something."

"No, I didn't."

Joel is doubtful, but says nothing. He watches as Burke stretches his feet closer to the fire and groans. He pokes the stick harder, three heavy jabs. Then Burke asks, "You believe in souls, Joel Barker?"

"Of course, who don't?"

"No," says Burke. "I mean, really believe in them. I mean, you say you do 'cause of your family. Hell, you say you do 'cause of this whole damn place. But deep down inside, do you really believe in souls?"

"Of course."

"Well, I don't know if I do. It don't make much sense. You're dead, you're dead. I think people made up souls so they could tell other people what to do."

"The Bible tells about souls."

"People wrote the Bible."

"No, they didn't," says Joel. "God did."

Burke laughs. "You think God picked him up a pencil, no, a quill pen, one day and got him some of that paperaya stuff they used to make paper out of and said, 'I'm gonna write me a book and tell people what to do.' You really think he did that, Joel Barker?''

"Well, not exactly."

"Not exactly. That's right. Even if there is a God he wouldn't be wasting time on writing stuff down for people to read. He'd be zappin' them for misbehaving, just like that old electric bug zapper we had in West Virginia.''

"You don't even believe in God?"

"I didn't say that, exactly. But that ain't the point. People tell each other that they got souls, see. Then they tell them that their souls will live forever on account of what they do or what they don't do when they're on the earth. Like if you are good, your soul will live forever all happy and peaceful. If you are bad, your soul will burn forever in hell. And if you tell people stuff long enough, they believe it. And then they don't have no power over theirselves anymore. The people what preached to them have the power. And they can say or do whatever they want, and everybody believes that it's right.''

"Shut up," says Joel.

"Come on," says Burke. "You ain't stupid. Who's got the power in this place? Who tells people what to do and they do it?''

"Teachers."

"Well, yeah, but they got a different power. We're talking souls here.''

"The preacher."

"Yep, he's one. But he's only got power over some of the people, 'cause some of the people go to church meetings. Who else?''

"My mom."

"Yep, that's another. Keep going."

"Your aunt."

Burke nods. "Now you're getting to it, Joel. My Aunt Missy's got so much power over people it makes me sick. They do what she says, you know?''

"But her power comes from God."

"Oh, yeah? Who says?"

"She knows about what God wants. Her family has always been a preaching family. Everybody knows that. But you being from West

Virginia wouldn't know that. Maybe God'll let you off the hook since you're from a stupid place that doesn't even believe in the Lord.''

Burke laughs again. He seems happy with Joel's reprimand. He pulls the stick out of the fire and offers it to Joel. ''Sure you don't want to try this?'' Joel shakes his head. ''Okay,'' says Burke. ''Watch this.'' He sticks his tongue out. His eyes widen with his mouth and cross as the stick comes close to his mouth. And then, with a quick motion, the stick point touches his tongue tip and then bounces off again. Burke holds the stick up and grins. ''No big deal,'' he says. ''Now you.''

''Ain't hot enough,'' says Joel. ''You wet it down with your tongue. Give it to me.''

Burke hands the stick to Joel. Joel scoots close to the campfire and works the stick point into the glowing ash.

''Tell me about sineating,'' says Burke.

'Of course,' thinks Joel. The main purpose of the night meeting. Joel sits straight. His face flushes hot, but is matched by the heat of the fire. He frowns at Burke. ''Don't you know when to shut up? Don't you know there is stuff you just don't talk about?''

''Who said we can't talk? The preachers? The teachers? Your mom? My Aunt Missy?''

''It ain't right, Burke.''

''I have my own power. I can talk about what I want to talk about.''

Joel groans; he looks over his shoulder to the dark mass that is the woods from where he came. He should leave now. That would be best. Talking about bug souls is one thing. Even listening to Burke say he doesn't believe in God is another. But this is not right. He should leave. If he were ready, he would.

But the dark of the forest seems to growl silently at him. Joel is not ready to leave, because the forest seems anxious to have him come in. Joel looks again at Burke, trapped with his vexing company and the subject that has the older boy so enthralled.

Burke goes on. ''Aunt Missy says that when a person dies, something's got to get rid of all the sin, so the dead person can go to heaven. Can't get into heaven with sin riding your coattail, right? So at a wake, after all the cryin' and prayin' and kissin' the dead person, the family puts food on the dead person's chest. Sound right?''

Joel nods.

"They put all sorts of tasty stuff like chicken and beef and vegetables and even some kind of dessert. All steamin' and smellin' good. A meal good enough for anybody, but especially for somebody what ain't ate anything all day. Yeah?"

"Yeah," says Joel.

"So after all this food is laid out, the family and all those who came to the wake turn round to the wall, and they close their eyes real tight. Tight so they can't see nothing for the next ten minutes or so. And when nobody's looking, the sineater comes out of the woods. He ain't had no food in a day, and he's hungry like a dog. He comes into the house and eats up all that food, right off the dead person's chest. Man, can you think about it? Food off an old dead person's stinking chest."

Joel presses the stick into the fire hard enough to break off the tip.

"So the sineater eats all that food, and what he is really doing is eating the sin from the dead person. Eating it so the dead person is pure again. And the sineater is all full of the sin of that person. So the sineater walks all around, hiding in the woods, full of dead people's sin."

Joel takes the stick from the fire. He looks at Burke with a sober expression of challenge. Then he lowers the stick to his tongue. He holds it there, and it sizzles.

Burke is impressed. "Feel good?"

Joel takes the stick away. His tongue hurts on the tip, burned like it was when he was five and Petrie got mad at him for knocking over one of Mama's bean pots on the stove, spilling beans, and Petrie made him lick the mess off the eye of the stove. But he grins at Burke. "Don't feel nothing."

"So," continues Burke, Joel's efforts at changing the subject foiled. "A sineater is like a garbage man. Cleans up after everybody. And then when the sineater dies, somebody got to eat the sin offa him, and that somebody becomes the new sineater, right?"

Joel nods, and hurls the stick into the distant weeds to his right.

"Thought so," says Burke. "Missy ain't lied to me about any of that, then, has she?"

Joel knows Burke wants him to say no, so he says nothing.

"But Missy says things are different now. She says that in the past, sineaters were sineaters and that was that. Hid in the woods and kept to theirselves till a wake. Now, though, Missy says things is changed. Says there is so much evil, it's like that crap that floats in the river in the fall. She says that people are backsliding and that's one of the worst sins of all. People going to listen to false preachers. Changing rituals to suit theirselves. Not many of them coming to witness meetings at her house, just a few of the faithful. Women dressing in men's clothes, kids getting taught about their bodies at school. The sineater getting married and having a family.''

"What time is it?'' asks Joel.

"Just wait a minute. Missy says things got to change. Know why? 'Cause where is all that extra sin going when the sinners die? Into the sineater, that's where. And he's got more now than he can handle. More than can keep him in his place, staying in the woods and out of people's way. He might have been dangerous to look at before, but now he's changed. He's become the devil. He's gonna do things. Bad things. Missy says the growing danger drove Patsy away from Ellison and the Cove. Says she ran away because she couldn't take the sin no more. She was too pure to handle it. What do you think about that?''

Joel shrugs.

"Know what I think?'' Burke says. "I think Patsy's dead. I think she got ate up by a bear. Maybe a wolf. I think she's dead as a old rusty nail.''

Joel sniffs. Burke has probably heard the story. Patsy's bones, rusting along the Beacon River.

"You know what else, Joel? I think all Missy says is crap in a barnyard. But it all comes down to the power I was talking about. You know who has the most power in Beacon Cove?''

"I ask you what time it was, Burke. Ain't your watch working no more?''

"Shit, man, it's ten forty-five, make you happy?''

"Yeah.''

"It's your daddy.''

Joel frowns. There is a catch in his lungs. "What?''

"Your daddy got more power in the whole place than anybody else does. Than anybody else ever did.''

Joel pulls his knees up abruptly. He looks over his shoulder at the forest. He should have left here long ago. He should not be listening to this. Burke is crazy. He is a nonbeliever. A vexation. Joel's heart races. He looks back at the older boy. Burke is licking his lips like a hungry man who has just found a feast. And that feast is . . .

"Power," says Burke. "It's what makes this old world go round and round. I want to know about your daddy, Joel. Tell me what you know."

"I don't know nothing."

"Bullshit. You're his kid."

"I don't want to talk about him."

"Does he live at your house? Come on, Joel. I want to know."

"No."

"No, what?"

"No, he doesn't live at our house," says Joel. His heart hitches. He cannot imagine why he is letting Burke do this to him.

"What do you mean? Where does he stay, then?"

'Don't tell him', Joel thinks, but again his mouth opens, and he gives Burke what he wants. "He stays in the woods mostly. He comes to our house very late at night when there ain't no wake. Mama leaves him supper."

"So he eats there late at night. What about you and your family?"

"We're in bed by then. We have to be asleep by then."

"What if you ain't asleep?"

"It ain't a matter of if we are or not. We have to be, and we are."

"He sleep there after he eats?"

"I . . ." Joel pauses. He does not want to answer, and honestly doesn't know the answer to that one. "I don't know."

"Your mama sleep with the sineater? She musta since you was born, Joel Barker, but does she still sleep with him? Does she look at the sineater?"

'God, this is wrong!' Joel's mind bolts, trying to avoid the topic. *'What are you doing, Joel? This ain't right, it's dangerous!'* And yet, something inside makes him want to go on. It feels . . .

"No, she don't, Burke."

. . . good, it feels scary, but good.

Burke nods like a teacher who has been given the correct answer. "I guess she wouldn't at that. Nobody can look at your daddy."

"No, of course not." Scary but good. Almost like a relief in Joel's brain. Almost like . . .

"You ever see your daddy on accident Joel?" asks Burke.

. . . like a sick blister getting popped, letting out all of the stinking bad stuff. "No. I know what would happen if I did."

"And what would happen?"

"I'd go insane. It would be seeing all the evil he has eaten. It would kill me, and I would go to hell and burn in eternal damnation."

Burke looks at the night sky. "See what I mean, Joel? Power."

Joel says nothing.

"And when your daddy dies, you gonna eat his sin? You gonna be the sineater?"

"No, Curry will."

"Curry's your big brother."

"Yeah."

"Missy gets her way, he won't have to be. She don't want no more sineater. She wants to get another way from the Lord to save the souls of the dead. Says people gonna be sorry if they don't heed her soon before it all gets unleashed."

Joel takes a deep breath of sooty air. The two boys sit in silence as the fire crackles and sputters, as strobing yellow streaks caress their arms and legs and faces. Burke is deep in thought. Joel struggles on the gangplank of which he was walked to the edge. He is safe on the platform; but there is an appeal in the deep depths of the dark water. Burke is in the water, calling for Joel to join him. Joel rubs the welt of a mosquito bite on his neck. Where is Andy? Why is he gone? He would know what to do.

And then Burke says, "Remember I said I had something neat to show you?" He grins, the shadows of his face making his mouth seem to cut from ear to ear. It is a frightening smile. He pulls himself up, like he's happy with himself, and he flips his jacket from the top of the burlap bag.

"Ever see something die, Joel?"

Joel looks quickly at the string tying the bag, and at faint movement within the fabric. "What do you mean?"

"No speaka da English, ma man? Do you want to see something

die? Want to see something el croako? Want to see a soul give up the ghost?''

"What's in there?"

"Nothing of importance, so don't worry a single hair." Burke tugs the string; it pulls loose. He upends the bag and gives it a shake. A small cat falls out onto the sooty ground beside Burke. It staggers and falls to its side, ears back, neck stretched out. Joel can see that its jaws are shut with heavy tape, the strip wound around its snout several times. It is skinny, with wild, rolling eyes. It seems dizzy and cannot stand erect. Joel then sees the tape holding the front and hind legs together.

"One of Missy's," explains Burke. "God, you wouldn't believe how many cats that woman has. 'A few mousers,' she calls them. She doesn't know that a 'few mousers' turns into thirty with no trouble at all. She got more cats than we got rats to chase. She's got names for some of them. But there ain't no name for this one."

Joel makes himself look at the cat's eyes. He thinks of Curry hunting. What do deer eyes look like when they know they are going to die? He has seen dead animals. Dead eyes are merely that, soft, dead marbles that know nothing. He can look at dead eyes. But looking at dying eyes is much harder.

"This one has four others what look just like it. Little ratty cats, all of the same litter. Think they have souls?"

"I don't know."

"Well, we can find out. What do you say? I got my pocket knife with me. We can toss for who does it."

"No."

"No, what? No, let's decide some other way? No, don't kill the cat?"

"No, don't kill the cat."

"We got two votes here. And since I brought the cat and the knife, I get both votes." Burke's shoulders drop a little; his smile falters. "Come on, Joel. This will be really neat. It'll be a way to see something we never get to see."

Jesus,' thinks Joel. '*This will be like looking behind those trees in the woods. It will be seeing what we ain't supposed to see. It'll be like looking at his face . . .*'

"It'll be good. It'll make us like blood brothers. Here, Joel, watch.'' And Burke tips the cat's muzzled nose toward the sky, and he inserts the blade of the knife. The cat jumps; blood pours. Joel jerks his head away, but then Burke speaks, his voice pinched and strange. ''Oh, man, oh, look at its eyes.'' Joel looks. He cannot see the cat's eyes in the shadow of Burke's body, but he can see Burke's eyes. They are wide and full of a shock that sends spears into Joel's gut. Burke's grin is gone. His face hovers above that of the cat's. The cat's taped legs flap back and forth like chains without swings attached, Burke drops the knife, and then the cat. His hands fly upward, fingers bent, a movement of horror and disgust.

''Oh, shit,'' Burke says. He scoots back from the cat, sending up puffs of dirt and ash. The cat writhes in the dirt, and then stops.

''It's dead now,'' says Joel.

Burke nods. One set of stiffened fingers moves to his hair and rakes it back from his forehead. The other set, swathed with oily cat's blood, hangs suspended in the air.

Joel feels himself falling from the gangplank into the water. ''Tell me,'' he says. ''What did its eyes look like?''

Burke moves his lips, and in the shadow of his body, it looks as if they form the word ''pain.'' But he does not repeat it audibly. He reaches for the burlap bag and drops it over the cat.

He looks at Joel, still holding out his bloody hand. ''Bring any water with you or just that damn lantern?''

''No.'' Joel looks at the lumpy burlap. Something hurts in his chest, and he puts one fist against it, feeling.

''Shit, no, you wouldn't, would you? Retard. No gun, no water.'' Burke tilts his head down to his fingers and spits on them. He spits until Joel thinks he could have no more spit in his head at all. Then he wipes the fingers in the grass. ''Why don't you just get the hell out of here?''

Joel pushes his fist into the pain of his chest. Under the pressure, the knot seems to spread outward and upward, making his ribs hurt as well, and then his throat. Joel tries to swallow, but it is too hard.

''Just get the hell out of here if you don't like what I just did,'' says Burke. He then spits on his hand again and wipes it off in the grass, even harder than before. ''If I'd brought marshmallows I could've put 'em on the cat and eaten its sin away.'' Burke looks at Joel, his eyes narrow, waiting for an answer to all of this.

Joel wishes he had watched the cat die, and is angry that Burke killed the cat. Pain flowers into his head, nose, and eyes. "How could you do that?" he asks. He recognizes the pain now; it is the pressure of angry, impotent tears. He pulls the lantern to him and jabs the pump. It lights with a whoosh. He clambers to his feet, afraid for Burke to see that the sineater's son is confused and has no power over something as simple as his own feelings.

"Shit, Joel, it was just a cat," Burke says. His teeth show yellow in the firelight.

"It wasn't ready to die. It wasn't time for it to die."

"It was just one of Aunt Missy's old cats. I wouldn't kill one of mine, or even one of yours."

Joel turns from the campfire and walks toward the forest. The black trees wait for him.

"Joel, wait!"

Joel stops and doesn't look back. "You ain't God, Burke. You can't kill stuff for the fun of it."

"I just wanted to let you see its eyes. To see if there was a soul. No big deal. I was doing it for you!"

"Don't do me no favors, Burke." Joel moves again. Across the clearing the blackness is hushed and hungry. Joel can feel wet through the seat of his jeans, and the rising of several new mosquito bites on his neck. He thinks it must be near eleven. He has got to get home.

"Hey, Joel . . ."

And he will vow never to talk to Burke again. A vexation to the soul. Making Joel feel things he shouldn't feel. Why had he cared if he could hang tough in front of Burke or not? Andy wouldn't care. Andy would understand what kind of person Burke was. Joel feels the first tear cut down his face. The rest will come without a doubt.

"Joel!" Burke calls. Joel walks on, the lantern light spotting his footsteps. "Hey, Joel!" Joel can hear scrambling behind him. It gets closer. Then a hand lands on his shoulder. Joel stops but does not look back. Burke comes around to face him. Joel is surprised that Burke doesn't mention the tears. "You didn't help me put out the fire. You want Smokey Bear on our case? Jesus Christ. You can't go until the fire's out."

"Put it out yourself. You started it."

"I need help."

"Bull you do."

"Help me," says Burke.

"I'm going home," says Joel. He moves again toward the tar-black edge of the clearing.

"Well, just wait a damn minute!" Burke runs across the grass. Joel looks back. Burke lifts his jacket from the ground, shakes it off, and begins quick side kicks, scuffing up showers of dust and dirt and aiming it into the fire. The flame flickers and spits, coughing and belching glowing ash in the air in angry death throes. And then the fire is completely out. Burke rolls the burlap bag and stuffs it beneath his arm. The cat is left, unseen but not forgotten, in the weeds. Burke returns, jogging, to Joel.

"Let's go," he says.

"Go where? You got to go south. You lost or what?"

"I know where Aunt Missy's cabin is," Burke replies.

"So?"

"So I thought I'd walk you back to your place. Now am I a West Virginia gentleman or what?"

"No. Take your own lantern and walk yourself home." Joel steps into the trees; into the woods.

"Wait one fucking minute, Joel, Jesus-God!" Burke is on Joel's elbow again, stooping beneath a gnarled branch, kicking at an unforgiving clump of chirring, cricket-filled chokeweed. The chirring stops. "You forgot your rifle, right, Mr. Smartass? So I'm due one, too, don't you think?"

"Get lost."

"So I came here when it was still light." Burke wriggles through brush, getting up into Joel's face. Joel crosses his arms and glares. "So I forgot a lantern," continues the red-haired boy. "Gonna sue me?"

"Ain't no surprise," Joel answers. "You're from West Virginia." He stomps ahead, stepping high, bending and dipping with the stern contour of the mountain. He hears Burke behind him, following. Joel picks up his pace, his mind distracted from the frights that linger beyond the lantern-paled trees. He hates Burke; and is glad that Burke is following.

Burke keeps his steps steady with Joel's, staying several yards behind. He mumbles as he goes, complaining about Joel's lack of humor, about the ridiculous fact that people could actually live in places as prehistoric as Ellison and not lose their sanity.

And then Joel stops and faces the older boy. "You coming home with me?"

"Well . . ." begins Burke.

"Then I want you to say something and mean it."

"What the hell are you . . ."

"Shut up, Burke. I want you to say something, and mean it."

"Say what?"

"I want you to say that it was wrong to kill the cat. I want you to say it made you feel bad to kill the cat. And I want you to say you won't do something like that no more. You won't kills things no more."

"What if I have to go hunting, how about that, Joel Barker?"

"You know what I mean."

Burke's shoulders jump. His lip wrinkles.

"Say it, Burke. Or I'm gonna run off and leave you without a lantern. I don't think no West Virginia boy knows his way in these hick mountains too good on just his sense of smell."

Burke looks at the ground, then at the trees, then at Joel. His eyes are crinkled and strange, the shadows of the night and the light of the lantern painting wrinkles around his lids that remind Joel of his mother's sorrow lines. "Okay," he says.

"Okay, what?" says Joel.

"Okay, I was wrong to kill that stinking cat. I won't kill anything else."

Joel switches the lantern from one hand to the other. "I don't think you really mean it."

"Fuck it, Joel. I mean it, all right? Christ!"

"I don't think so."

Burke swallows. He blinks. "Goddam it, Joel! I mean it!"

Joel holds the lantern up closer to Burke's face. Burke's eyes are wet and strained. As he watches, a tiny streak falls down Burke's sooty cheek. Joel's surprise almost causes him to point it out, but Burke had ignored Joel's tears, and so it is even.

"Well, okay, then," says Joel. "But keep close. It ain't exactly like walking on no Grand Central Highway."

They look at each other for another second, and it becomes uncomfortable, so Joel turns and they proceed through the trees. As the twigs and leaves snap beneath his shoes, and he hears the heavy breathing and the mumbled jokes of Burke from behind, Joel thinks briefly of power, and wonders if the sineater's son might not really have just a bit of it, and if he might be on the threshold of having a second friend in his whole life.

"Shit on it," says Burke as a thin branch smacks his face.

Joel smiles for the first time this evening, in spite of the unseen things beyond the light. And his arms, reaching out, lantern dangling, spreading stray brush and pushing it back, are like the arms of a swimmer in deep and dark water, steadied for a long and uncertain trip ahead.

14

"You barely made it," says Curry.

Joel pushes the kitchen door closed. He strains to see the old clock on the shelf over the potato bin, but it is dark. No lights are lit; only the stove sheds its pale light from the open cast-iron door, the yellow-white lying in a puddle that crosses half of the floor and ends at the foot of the table.

Curry shifts in the chair where he sits, and turns one newly polished boot about on his fist. It throws faint white light from the oily black. Curry puts it down on the table beside the tin of cream.

"I ain't late," says Joel. He is certain that he isn't. The trip back was quicker than the one going out. He steps over to the clock. It reads 11:42. "I'm early."

"Hmmmm," says Curry.

"Where is Petrie?" asks Joel. Usually Petrie is in bed by now, sacked out on her sofa, and Curry is usually on his cot in the small bedroom.

"I told her to sleep on my bed," says Curry. He picks up a glistening black rag and moves it back and forth across the toe of the polished boot. He watches it with the concentration he uses with his chairs and baskets. "She didn't want to, but I insisted. I wanted to wait up for you."

"Why?"

"I wanted to ask you what business you had in the woods tonight?"

"It's none of your business."

"Oh, but it is."

"I'm sure Mama told you."

"Where were you, Joel?"

"Hunting," says Joel. "You haven't done much these past weeks. Thought I could help the family since you weren't."

"Hunting? You never cared much for hunting, Joel."

"So I changed my mind. So I'm getting older."

"The woods at night are not for little-boy business. You don't realize that the woods can be very bad for little boys. You are his son, and yet you have so very little understanding. He won't be responsible for your carelessness."

"I was hunting. I had a lantern."

"So he saw your light? He heard your rifle?"

"Yes."

"Really." Curry stands, straightens his jeans, and moves to the dark wall behind the sofa, where Petrie's cat is curled into a furry pillow. Curry withdraws the rifle from the wall and holds it out in Joel's direction.

"I'm going to bed," says Joel. His throat has gone dry.

"What business did you have? Business worth the danger of the forest at night?"

"Your other boot needs polishing." Joel walks to the hall doorway. His heart is thundering at Curry's find, but he will not let it show.

"And the lantern, Joel? Where is it?"

Joel stops but does not turn back. Burke has the lantern. Joel gave it to him in the Barkers' side yard. Burke was going home by the long stretch of the West Path. He had promised to return the lantern in the morning at school. "In the shed, where it belongs."

"From the pantry, I saw a light come into the backyard. When you came into the kitchen, I could see a light moving down the front walk. What light was that, then, Joel?"

Joel looks back at Curry. His older brother is still holding the rifle, and is standing in the center of the kitchen. His tall frame is outlined in the glow of the oven's fire.

"It musta been your imagination," says Joel. "It musta been your damn imagination.'' It feels good to curse at Curry, good and daring. ''Shut up and polish your other shitty boot.''

Curry strides forward quickly, his face coming into Joel's sight, looming large and angry. Joel's heart lurches; he has always argued with Curry, although never over something of much matter. And Lelia has never allowed Joel to win such an argument, nor has she allowed any to bloom fully. But this time, Curry has several reasons, sound reasons, to correct his younger brother. Curry's righteousness is rooted in truth, and Joel is suddenly and acutely afraid of it. He grips the doorframe with his fingers.

Curry presses his face to Joel's. When he speaks, his voice is controlled as it has always been, but is full of rage. ''And do you find foul words like those in the woods at night? Dirty words?''

''No,'' says Joel softly.

''Do you want to repeat those words to Mama? Do you want her to know of the lie you told her tonight so you could do little-boy business?''

''No.''

''Do you want to tell her that the lantern is gone?''

''The lantern is in the shed,'' Joel says. His chest constricts against the repeated lie, but he cannot tell Curry the truth.

Curry's eyes narrow, and after a moment he stands straight. He looks at the ceiling, at Joel, at the rifle in his hand. He closes his eyes and looks for a dreadful moment that he might cry. Then he turns and strides back to the kitchen table and sits down.

Joel holds on to the doorframe. He wants to go to bed, to have this night over, but feels as if he needs to be dismissed. He wonders if Curry will tell Lelia. He could never forgive Curry if he does, but he knows Curry would only be doing what is right. Cursing is wrong. Lying is wrong. Hanging around with Burke is wrong. Wanting to see something's dying eyes is wrong. But the wrongs feel good, and it is the contradiction that is a dizziness spinning madly in his brain.

''You are my brother,'' says Curry finally. He is looking into the fire, his hands lying loosely on the tabletop, one on each side of a black boot. ''I don't want anything bad to happen to you.''

''I know,'' says Joel, and he is surprised that he said it. He blinks.

''You get hurt and it will tear me apart.'' Curry looks at Joel. ''It would kill me inside.''

Joel scratches a mosquito bite.

"Promise me you won't never go into the woods like that again, Joel. I can hunt. I know about Avery's movements. I can sense him like nobody else. Because I'm the firstborn, you see? Because one day I will take on his job. But you are not like him. You don't have the senses I was born with. Promise me, Joel." Curry's eyes study Joel. They seem to smoke with the residue of the stove. And even though the words are those of concern, Curry's tone is a demand.

"Yeah," says Joel. "I promise."

"Go to bed, then. It is later than you think, and we must both be asleep very soon. There was no wake today."

Joel loosens his fingers from the door. He backs into the hallway, then swings into his tiny room, easing the door shut. Leaning the side of his face on the surface of the door, he listens to the sounds of Curry in the kitchen. Above the beating of his own heart and the raspy breathing of Petrie on Curry's cot, he hears the scraping of the kitchen chair, the clearing of Curry's throat, the clump of boots on the tabletop. Joel thinks of power, and how big brothers have it over little brothers.

Joel straightens out on his cot, his arms thrown over his head, hugging his pillow. He is very glad he is not Curry. He knows what Curry will become when Avery dies. Joel wonders if Curry, in the late hours of the night, ever wishes he were not Curry, either.

15

Wayne Nelson delivers mail to the folks along West Path and the South Branch. He is not the regular mailman. The regular mailman is Tommy Taylor, who drives Route 536 through Ellison but will not take his car into the steep paths of the mountain that rise above the Beacon River. Wayne enjoys his treks on his Honda, up the graveled trail of the South Branch and the dirt track of West Path. He is paid a little by Tommy, but it is not money that sends him up the mountain.

Wayne is a sturdy man, twenty-six, with blond hair already streaked with gray. His good looks have frustrated the affections of several single women of Ellison, but Wayne is a confirmed bachelor, living in a three-room apartment over a garage on the low side of South Branch, the nearest building off the West Path Bridge that crosses the Beacon River. He is an only child; his mother, Candace Stone, and stepfather, Preston, live another mile and a half up the trail from Wayne's garage in a small cabin next to the home of Rody and Joanie Marshall. The Stones had kicked up a storm when Wayne had turned down the chance to marry Joanie, and had moved in with the local fix-it man, Charlie Draper. Charlie had been Wayne's boss, and he ran a good business repairing tractors and doing plowing and clearing jobs. Two years after Wayne left home, Charlie died of pneumonia. Wayne bought the business from Charlie's brother Jeff, who lived in Charlottesville and didn't give a shit about the meager inheritance.

Instead of being pleased that their son was securing his future, Candace and Preston were infuriated with Wayne's uppitiness. Wayne, they said, was now too good for his family, which had been on state aid since Wayne was five and Preston, an older man with a nervous condition, had married Wayne's mother. Wayne was never sure what they wanted him to do, perhaps sit on the porch with his stepdad and polish the rifles, or whittle those worthless canes which Candace was forever at work on. The canes that were stored in an ever-growing deadwood forest in the smokehouse. The canes Candace paraded about the mountain one at a time as if they, not the sinner Wayne, were her children.

Wayne fell from religious grace at the age of nineteen. Charlie Draper, who had lived in many places while in the Navy, had had lively, challenging discussions with his young apprentice. Wayne began to doubt the world as his parents saw it. Charlie told him of the Mediterranean, and of France, and of war and beautiful women left behind. Charlie talked of cities of millions of people, and of crimes and punishment and justice. Justice was not of God, Charlie would say. Justice was of people and of what those people decided was wrong and what was right. Charlie used to say it was a damn shame that there was never really a Superman, because the world needed a Superman a hell of a lot more than it needed a Missy Campbell. Charlie said truth, justice, and the American way was what the world needed now, in spite of what the Dionne Warwick song said. They're the only things that there was just too little of.

With his thoughts changed, and feeling pretty good about it, Wayne left home and moved in with Charlie. He became as good at repairs as Charlie ever was. He saved his money, not in a bank, but in the bottom drawer of his dresser. For a while, Wayne took occasional second jobs with Fitch Spenser, who at the time ran his own small excavation business. Wayne sent the extra money to his mother, but found out later that she was only squirreling it away for any grandchildren who might happen along in the future. So Wayne dropped the excavating work, telling Fitch the explosives were giving him migraines, furious that his mother was still attempting to control his life with her little rituals.

But Wayne has bigger plans than life in Beacon Cove. He is going to leave Ellison soon. Sell the small business he purchased and move to North Carolina and become a state policeman.

On the last Tuesday of October, Wayne stops by Benton's hardware store to pick up the mail. Benton accepts the delivery from Tommy twice a week, on Tuesdays and Fridays, and it is on those days that the Cove people can expect to hear Wayne on the run up the mountain. Benton is on the front porch this afternoon, side by side with Fitch, watching the misting rain fall onto the road. Wayne wears a dark-green poncho, and as he steps on the Hardware porch, he bends down and shakes like a wet dog.

"Whoa, boy," says Benton, pulling back his beer can. "Don't water this down no more. It's bad enough as it is."

"Why don't you make a longer stop up at Beecher's, see if John has any spare jugs?" adds Fitch. "I ain't seen that man in weeks. Don't he know how important his juice is to my well-being?"

Wayne smiles. "Yeah, bo'," he says. "Can't nobody brew it like old John. But he's crazy as an old fart. One day he likes you, one day he thinks you out to rob him blind or bring down the law in his lap. I try to tell him it's his business, 'cause justice don't have nothing to do with what a man wants to drink. But when he's in a mood, he won't listen. His mailbox is about as close as I want to get to his house without an invitation."

"Oh, just piss on that, Wayne," says Fitch. "John knows you good. Just go on up there, tell him Benton and me is dying of thirstation, that our lives is on his head if he don't come clean with one last jug."

"I bet you got some 'splosives left over since you retired, Fitch," says Benton. "Go blow us some jugs out of his storage shed. We'll stay down here and catch 'em."

Wayne wipes stray rain drops from his nose. "Forget it," he says. "John'll bring his stuff out when he's good and ready. And you know it's his best stuff that takes this long to brew. We got to be patient."

"Patient," scoffs Benton with a smile.

Wayne says, "And until then, I need a beer. My throat's sore."

"Fitch, get Mr. Deputy Mailman a drink while I get the mail," says Benton. He clambers from his seat. "I'd let you go in, but you're one wet, sorry mess and I just mopped. If you was a customer, it'd be different." He goes into the store, followed by Fitch.

Wayne waits outside, looking at the rain. A car hisses by, then another. Then Benton is back on the porch again.

"Got you two heavy bags today," he says. "Christmas time is just around the corner and the catalogs are coming in. Been through them all and I don't see nothing worth spending money on. If you ask me, you could save yourself some trouble by just ditching all them things and acting like they never came in the first place."

"Through rain and heat and all that shit," says Wayne. He takes the bags.

"Yeah, I hear you," says Benton. "And you flip over on that Honda from all those damn tons of junk mail and kill yourself, don't come crying to me."

"Me, either," says Fitch, coming through the door with Wayne's beer. "What we talking about?"

"We was just saying we don't think you got the brains God give a mailbox," says Wayne.

"Humph," says Fitch. He hands the beer to Wayne, and Wayne downs it in a quick series of chugs. He crushes the can and sits it on the porch railing. "Thanks, men," he says with a wave of his hand as he hops from the porch and climbs onto his Honda. "If it stops raining, I'll maybe give old John a talking to after all."

"Liar," says Benton.

"You're right," says Wayne, and he starts the engine with a belching of smoke and a grinding of gears. He heads over Route 536 and crosses the bridge, turning right onto the mud and gravel grooves that serve as the highway to the hills.

Most cabins along the route are hidden from view by the foliage. The homes are marked only by trampled, muddy footpaths leading from the roadway, with battered mailboxes stacked beside them. Several cabins are close enough to see from the path, their sagging stoops or screened porches weathered and unpainted, as much a part of the mountain terrain as the pines and vines and twisting, scabby crabapple trees. Wayne delivers mail to these homes, skidding his Honda to halts, cramming the mail into boxes without climbing off if he can reach. And as he rumbles up the trail again, pausing to do mail every few minutes, he lets his thoughts go where they will. And they always return to the same place.

They always return to Harry Callihan. Or Frank Furillo. Or Buford Pusser. Or Mike Torello. To all those lawmen, real and fictional, discovered through the wonder of his satellite dish. To all the lawmen that Wayne wants to be. To all those lawmen that he is.

Wayne is the sentinel of the mountain. He is the watcher of the path, the guardian of Beacon Cove. Twice a week he makes his run, listening for trouble, watching for need, dreaming that his rusty Honda is a trusty black-and-white, or an undercover convertible, or a sleek highway motorcycle. Wayne is the justice rider, like the circuit riders of long ago, bringing security to those he serves. Sometimes he imagines there is a forest fire, and he is needed to race the news to Ellison. Sometimes there is an illness without a phone near, and he must use his police medical training to ease the symptoms before getting the doctor. Sometimes he has been summoned by a distraught mother whose child has been abducted by Missy Campbell's crazy cult and Wayne must storm the hideout alone, wielding fist and gun, to free the child and swear the wrath of the American justice system for such crimes against innocents.

Of course, occasionally there is the daydream where the beautiful blond girl with amnesia and a torn dress wanders out of the woods, all confused and in need of first aid and comfort.

But now, with Patsy Campbell's mysterious disappearance, he spends much of his thought on a genuine crime, puzzling clues, watching the roadside, hoping now to have the chance to truly prove himself. To his parents, to Benton and to Fitch, and to Missy Campbell, who should be outraged and horrified at the loss of her daughter. But mainly, he wants to prove himself to himself. To the lawman inside himself.

As the Honda's odometer ticks over to 932 miles, almost three more than it had as Wayne crossed the West Path Bridge, the muddy path straightens again, nearing its end, and the home of the Barkers. Wayne slows the Honda and puts it in neutral, leaving the motor running as he always does, and climbs off to take the short path through the trees to the fence and the mail bucket beside the Barkers' front gate. Before he steps beneath the scraggly walnut branches that shade the path, he looks through the Barkers' mail. It is unusual that they get much more than the weekly flyers or notes about recent death from the members of the Cove Community. The notes, Wayne knows, are for the Barker family, not so much the father but the mother and the children. Wayne, as much a member of the mountain people as anyone else, knows that the sineater never needs to be told of a death. It is his duty to know, to come when it is time. But the ladies of Beacon Cove feel they should let the rest of the family know since the Barkers aren't exactly part of the gossiping chain. No Cove resident would ever talk with a Barker. It was much too chancy. There are no notes today, however. A healthy week, Wayne thinks, grinning grimly.

But there is a letter here again. The third one in a few months. Addressed to the youngest boy, Joel. Wayne knows it is from Andy Mason, whose father used to be the Baptist minister. Wayne knew of the friendship of the two boys, although he knew the relationship was a secret one off the school grounds. He would often see the boys down on the river bottom, or hiding out around the side of the Hardware. It used to make Wayne mad, the way the boys seemed unwilling to be bold and free as other children. Not so much mad at the boys, but mad that they lived where they could not even enjoy the pleasures of youth without the stigmas of traditions. Where was the justice to all of this? Even his own parents were part of the shunners.

Wayne holds Joel's letter up, wishing he knew what Andy was writing to his friend, but knowing he would never break confidence and try to see.

He goes up the path, through the shadows, to the Barkers' fence and galvanized mail bucket nailed to the wood. He looks at the cabin between the two huge spruce trees; he gazes at the dark and sagging screened porch. He does not feel comfortable here. He has lived in the Cove too long to shrug off all he has heard. But it is this very uneasiness that he spits in the face each time he delivers mail to the family of the sineater. It is his way of standing up for what he knows is just. Let his parents worry. Let the faithful of the Cove talk behind his back, and in many cases, to his face. Let Missy Campbell rave that the duty of sineater is now converted into a game of the devil, and the man of sin is now an insane demon, capable of any horrid thing, poisoned by the overload of evil that lays heavily in Ellison.

'Dangerous, yeah, bo,' thinks Wayne as he reaches for the hook latch. *'Avery Barker is about as harmful as a distant meteor, or a brown bat avoiding humans and smacking at the moon.'*

He pulls up the flat cover to the mailbucket.

The blast is blinding, hot, and Wayne's right hand is ripped from the arm in a searing, charred gout of blood, chunks of flesh, and screaming, naked nerves. The hand is shot back over Wayne's shoulder, mail trailing, and the mailman is thrown into the sharp weeds by the footpath. His eyes roll, fueled by panic and pain, but they see nothing except sparks of red and fiery white. He twists in the weeds, not comprehending what has happened, screaming "Oh God oh God OH GOD!" There is a blowtorch on his right arm, roaring full force, finding every single nerve ending and torturing it to the point of insanity. Wayne screams louder. Leaves and grit fall into his mouth as he rolls. "OH GOD OH GOD GOD GOD!"

And God must hear, because a blanket of unconsciousness pulls over Wayne's soul.

16

"You've got to touch him, Mama!" screams Joel. Beside him, Lelia stands with a dishrag over her arm, staring in dumb horror at the unconscious mailman in the weeds. Blood spouts from the burned, stubbed arm.

"He's gonna die! Wrap him up!"

Petrie stands behind the gate, watching, holding her cat, for once, like she needs it. Her eyes are wide and dark.

"Mama!"

"It ain't right," cries Lelia. "It's a danger for his soul for us to deal with him!"

"Mama, he'll die!"

"Go to town, Joel. Get someone to call the doctor."

"He'll be dead by then!"

Petrie begins to cry, and she flees into the cabin. Curry is in the shadows of the porch, unseen but watching.

Lelia's face twists in fear. "He won't die. God won't let him die. Go to town."

"Why is me going to town okay but touching him ain't?"

"Touching is too close! Go, Joel!"

Joel looks from his mother to the porch to Wayne. He turns to go, but then whips back around and grabs the dishrag from his mother's arm. He is remembering the cat Burke brought to the clearing last night. The cat Burke had killed. Joel did not see the cat's dying eyes. He is glad that Wayne's eyes are closed now, because he knows what horrid truth would be there. *'Killing is wrong,'* he thinks. *'Whether it is by your own hand or whether it is by keeping that hand from helping.'* "I'll do it, then!" he shouts.

"You can't, Joel."

Joel stoops beside Wayne. His gorge rises at the sight of the gushing stump, but he forces his fingers to work, to lift the stump and tie the rag about the forearm in a tight tourniquet. He snatches up a stick from the weeds and knots it into into the rag's loose ends, then twists it several times. He looks up at Lelia. "You gotta hold this while I'm gone," he says.

Lelia is almost in tears. "It's breaking the rules," she says.

"Mama, please. See, you won't even be touching him."

Lelia looks at the tourniquet. She licks her lips and then kneels slowly on the grass. She reaches for the stick.

Joel stands. "Don't worry, Mama. You ain't touching him." And then he races through the trees to the Path, passing Wayne's puttering Honda, thinking in a second that perhaps he should try taking the machine but knowing also in that same second that he did not know how to drive it and would probably wreck it and never make it to town on time; that his feet are more fleet than any bubble-tired scooter on these rough slopes and uncertain curves. And he knows his shortcuts.

"Keep holding it, Mama!" he cries as he races down the mountain. "Keep holding it!"

17

He makes it down the mountain in less than twenty minutes. His legs threaten retaliation from the abuse, rubbering out from under him in several steep spots. But he clambers up again, something odd and new driving him onward. Burke called it "power." Joel feels it as freedom. He has a duty to do and has grabbed the freedom with which to do it. There is a life in his hands, and he has the freedom to save it.

He runs to the Hardware, his mind screaming for help before he even sets foot on the bridge, but his lungs and tongue loosen the moment his shoes touch the pavement of Route 536.

"Someone help, please! Mailman's hurt! His hand is blown off!"

Fitch, who has been alone on the Hardware porch, has seen Joel approach, but when he hears the cry, he jumps from the bench, Woodmen of the World newsletter sliding to his feet. He stares at the boy as he comes across the road, sweating, shouting, the dust of the mountain caking his face and clothes.

"Hurry, please!" Joel gulps as he reaches the porch steps. "Wayne's dying! His hand's gone and he's bleeding to death!"

Joel doesn't have time to read anything in Fitch's face except for singleminded alarm as the man turns into the store to call for Benton. On his dash to town, Joel had known one of two things would happen. The townspeople would chase Joel away after getting the news and would then go help Wayne, or they would hail him a hero and then go help Wayne. Most likely, he knew, it would be the former. But his mind had enjoyed the brief thoughts of the latter.

But it is neither.

Benton and Fitch come back onto the porch, the door slamming behind.

"What's this?" demands Benton.

"Wayne Nelson's at our cabin. His hand's blown off and . . ."

But neither man is registering him anymore. They leave the porch, running, Benton circling left for his old VW Beetle, Fitch crossing the road to call for Rod Quarles at the Antique Store. "Phone Doctor Shuler!" he tells Ellen as her face appears at the door. "Up to the Barkers', Wayne's been hurt bad!" Ellen moves back as Rod comes past her, and out to join Fitch. The car pulls onto the road, and the two men jump in with Benton. Joel watches as the blue Beetle, with a whine of tires, turns onto the West Path. Rody Marshall is on the bridge as the car passes, and Benton pauses long enough for Rody to struggle into the backseat with Rod. And then they were gone.

It is then that Joel's body tells him off. It comes in waves of severe nausea, strong enough for him to bend over and heave into the leaf dust on the road. His legs cramp; his breath is forced out in heavy contractions, making him clamp his arms about his chest as well as his stomach.

"Ohhh," he moans. His vision swirls in and out of focus. He rocks himself back and forth, trying to work against the pain. Once he looks up, eyes full of tears, and sees Ellen Quarles watching him from the doorway of her shop. When she sees that he is looking, she closes the door.

It is only a matter of minutes before the doctor's Jeep is heard on the road. Joel holds himself gingerly and stands up. He thinks for a moment about waving the doctor down and asking for a ride because Dr. Shuler is not really of the community. Most of the doctoring is done by Melissa Benshoff and her daughter Jewel, both of whom are midwives and nurses. Dr. Shuler, Joel is certain, would not know a Barker if he came scratching at his window screen at night with a neon "I am a Barker" sign tied around his neck.

But Joel does not wave. The doctor does not stop.

It isn't until almost twenty minutes later, when Joel begins his trek back up the path, that he finds out that Wayne is, indeed, alive.

Joel is stepping off the path onto one of his shortcuts when the group passes him, heading down. Wayne is in the Jeep, his head leaning against the passenger window, his eyes shut. Behind the Jeep is the Beetle with Fitch and Benton, and behind that Rody, puttering along on the red four-wheeler, his face set with purpose, his eyebrows jumping with excitement.

When Joel arrives home, it is six o'clock and dark. He doesn't even pause to study the shards of steel that had been his mailbucket, but goes into the cabin and collapses on Petrie's sofa while his mother serves him supper. And as he bends wearily over his bowl of chicken and beets, his mother says, "It was Curry what saved the mailman's life." Joel looks up and squints. "He said that I could let go of him since it weren't right for a Barker to be so close to someone," she goes on. "I give Curry the tourniquet and Curry let it come off. Then he took a torch and cauterized the arm. Mailman was out the whole time. Then Curry and me, we come back into the cabin with Petrie, where we belong."

Joel sighs, the chicken flavor suddenly lost in his mouth.

He sighs, feeling betrayed.

PART TWO

JOEL AND PETRIE

1

They stand on the South Branch, not far from the bridge which is hidden behind them by a mass of tangled trees. At this moment, the trees bow in a November wind, and they rain their damp and brilliant leaves onto the pathway. The leaves swirl at the backs of the boys and about their feet in miniature sparkling whirlwinds, but only Joel watches them. Burke has his eyes glued to the front of the mailman's garage. On this low end of South Branch, only one other dwelling is visible, and that is the cabin of Frankie Ringgold. The cabin is not really a cabin, but an anchored camper trailer with a homemade deck to the front. Frankie is an old man who raises azaleas in his backyard. It has been said that Frankie hibernates in the fall and winter like his flowers, because nobody sees him then. A large television antenna and black wire satellite dish set near the deck give hint as to Frankie's cold-weather entertainment. Beyond the trailer, South Branch curves much like West Path, and disappears into the trees.

"Wayne know who you are?" asks Burke, and Joel jumps at the suddenness of the voice.

"I don't know. Why?" he answers, looking at the garage, then again at his leaf-covered shoes.

"Wondering." There is a pause. Then Burke says, "Go in with me."

Again Joel's head snaps around. "What are you talking about, you think I'm stupid?"

"No, but you're curious, like me."

"Curious about what? His old stumpy arm that got blown off? You want to see where I put the tourniquet? You want to see the old burned skin where Curry took a torch to it so Mama wouldn't have to touch the mailman no more?"

"Come on, Joel."

"Forget it!"

"Bullshit I will. We got to go, you and me. We got to go see Wayne."

"Just want to see somebody who got touched, got *saved* by a Barker and lived to tell about it?"

"Fuck you, Joel. I just want to talk to him."

"About what?"

"About helping him."

"Helping him what?"

"Come on."

"I can't. I ain't supposed to even be here with you."

"Why not?"

"It's breaking the rules!" Joel yells.

"Whose rules?"

"Damn you, Burke, the rules!"

"Your rules. Your mama's rules? Aunt Missy's rules? The *world's rules*?"

Joel rushes at Burke, stopping just short of hitting the older boy. "Rules!" he shouts again. "The right and wrong rules! God's rules!"

"Save me, Joel. *God's* rules? That's just what I'd expect from a Cove kid!"

"And you're a stupid asshole from West Virginia!"

Burke's face freezes, then a small, surprising smile crosses his face. "Now you're talking, Joel. Good for you. Come on. Let's go see Wayne."

Joel shakes his head.

"You already broke the damn rules, Joel. You already touched him, remember? I mean, *I* know you saved him even if nobody else in this place wants to admit it. So, if you touched him once, what's going to see him? What's one rule or two?"

Joel sniffs. His head hurts.

"The man don't even know you, Joel, I bet. You ain't the only kid in town. You don't wear no sign as far as I know."

"If you want to see, why don't you just sneak around back. There's got to be a window. You can peek in."

"His apartment's upstairs. Come on." Burke steps off the path and onto the brown gravel of Wayne's driveway. To the right of the drive is a simple sign: NELSON'S FIX-IT. PLOWING, TILLING, FARM SERVICE, REPAIRS. The garage itself is two-storied, dirty stucco over block. Two garage doors lead into the first door's interior, both of them pulled up, to Wayne's chagrin if he had known it. Inside are dismantled plows, a bushhog, broken riding mowers and push mowers, portable ramps, old tires, hoses, rags, cans, and buckets. A large standing toolbox sits against the right wall. Above it, extra wrenches and hammers are suspended on a bent aluminum wall rack.

Wayne's four-wheeler is parked just inside the doorway on the left. Joel knows it was parked there by Rody Marshall after the accident and it hasn't been moved in five days. Joel would never forget the scene as he hid on the side of the path, the parade of men and vehicles, with Rody behind them all, riding the Honda down from the mountain as proudly as Jesus riding a cloud down to earth on the Last Day.

"Get your butt over here before I start yelling the sineater's kid is running loose!"

Joel mutters, "This ain't right," and trots after Burke.

They enter the garage, Burke ahead of Joel. As they pass the toolbox, Burke glances up at the wrenches and hammers. He stops. Joel nearly runs up the back of Burke's shoes. Burke stares at the hammers, his eyes narrowing, his eyebrows twitching in a strange expression of confusion.

"What's your problem?" asks Joel.

Burke doesn't seem to hear him.

"Burke!"

Burke shudders, looks back down at Joel, and frowns. He says, "What?"

"I said, 'What's your problem?' "

"You," says Burke. "You're my problem." He turns and goes deeper into the garage.

The boys move to the back to the steps which run up the back wall and disappear into the ceiling. From the bottom of the stairs, the door at the top is visible, reminding Joel of the permanent stairs to the attic in Andy Mason's old house. There was a small storage area around the second-floor hole that the steps came up through, and Andy and Joel had spent a fun hour sitting on the ledge and bouncing rubber balls down the steps, then digging through the rotten bags that Mrs. Mason had filled with old magazines and put up behind the stephole.

Burke takes the steps two at a time, making tiny grunting sounds with each squeaking bounce. Joel stands at the bottom, looking up. Burke knocks on the door.

When the door at the top of the steps opens with a jerk, Burke steps back one step. Joel, still at the bottom, steps back three steps, knocking over a stack of Wolf Head oil cans.

It is Wayne's mother, Mrs. Stone, at the door, glaring down. Faint light shines past her; she holds a handmade cane before her like a weapon.

After a moment, Burke's shoulders straighten, and he moves back up a step.

"Afternoon, Mrs. Stone," he says. "I just wanted to check on Wayne. To see how he's doing and all. Could we come in?"

Mrs. Stone's face is dark in the shadowed landing above the doorhole, but her eyes are white and distrustful; her teeth work on the skin of her upper lip.

"Wayne's bad off," she says. "Lost a lot of blood. He's weak, and ain't up to seeing people."

"We just want to wish him well. We won't bother him none."

"We?" says Mrs. Stone. "I know you, don't I, boy?"

Burke nods and says, "Yes, ma'am." Joel can't believe he is hearing Burke talk like this. "Missy Campbell's nephew, Mrs. Stone. Burke Campbell."

Mrs. Stone lowers the cane. "Yes, that's right." Her voice is distracted, like she can't quite remember if Missy has a nephew or not. "And who is that with you down there?"

Joel is trying to set the oil cans right with his foot, but each falls again, rolling off in different directions. Two hit a stack of tires and stop.

"Just a friend from school," says Burke. "Can we see Wayne?"

Mrs. Stone breathes, sighs, and looks back over her shoulder into the room behind her. "I don't know," she says. "He's weak."

"Would you ask him, please, ma'am?"

"Well," says Mrs. Stone, and she shuts the door, cutting off the pale light and the radio music. Burke groans, then looks down at Joel. He chuckles. "Get up here, Joel. She's gonna let us in."

"You lied to her," says Joel. He stops kicking at the cans and moves back to the bottom of the stairs.

"What you worried about?"

"I ain't no friend from school. I'm a Barker."

"Just get up here."

"What if Wayne remembers me?"

"You ain't like the president. Not everybody knows you just by looking at you."

"Wayne might."

"Don't get like this, Joel."

The door opens and Mrs. Stone says, "Just for a minute. He's weak and needs his sleep."

"Okay," says Burke.

"You understand me?"

"Oh, yes, ma'am."

"And keep quiet."

"Yes, ma'am." Burke's voice is politely subdued, but Joel can see pleasure in Burke's grit-dancing feet.

Wayne's apartment is three rooms, a living room-kitchen off the front door, and a small bedroom and bath. In the living room is a monstrous sofa of splitting green Naugahyde, batting oozing and foam leaking from the cracks like coagulated toothpaste from many dead and gaping mouths. There is a black-and-white television on a cinder block and plank stand. The set is on, showing a program on inland trout fishing, but the sound is cut off. On the wall opposite the sofa is a round kitchen table with the hinged sides dropped down and two chairs shoved beneath the ends. Along the north wall are a grimy matched set of appliances—electric stove, refrigerator, water heater.

Burke takes Joel by the sleeves and pulls him through the doorway. Mrs. Stone closes the door behind them.

On the south wall is the only window in the living room. There is no curtain. Dust-softened venetian blinds are pulled all the way to the top of the frame. The glass is lined with cracks and water spots. Along the bottom panes of glass are a collection of super-hero sun-catchers. Wonder Woman, Batman, the Green Lantern, and Aquaman hang from little clear suction cups. Superman catches a particularly bright bit of sun, and he glows in a powerful concentration of red.

Mrs. Stone sits on a kitchen chair. Joel moves into the room behind Burke, scooting to the red-haired boy's right to keep out of the old lady's direct line of vision.

Wayne is on the sofa, facing away from the front door, gazing at the suncatchers and beyond. He is covered by an afghan of blue-and-green granny squares. His stump is hidden somewhere beneath. Burke makes a tsking sound, ready to launch into a speech, when Wayne's face shifts on the red throw pillow. His face is flushed, patterns of the pillow's crocheted design crossing his cheek like the veins of a drunk man's nose. "It would be all right for you to go on to the grocery store now, Mama," he says.

"Not now," Mrs. Stone says.

"You need some fresh air," says Wayne, "You've been holed up with me a long time."

"I'm fine, son," she says. She grips her knees and looks at the two boys. In her eyes is tolerant martyrdom and determined duty.

"Mother," says Wayne.

"I don't think I should leave now."

Wayne stares at his mother. His mother stares back. Burke says, "Hey, Wayne, you feeling better?" but his voice falls to the floor, unanswered.

"Christ," Wayne says finally.

"Is Lord, Wayne. Now watch your language," says Mrs. Stone.

"I really need those things on the list. If you don't want to get them for me, fine. I'm so glad you came along to help out."

Mrs. Stone frowns at her son. She then looks at Joel and Burke. "I don't see where as it needs to be done this moment, Wayne. I don't see where as you should be alone now what with these boys here."

"They ain't gonna steal me blind. I need those things from the grocery. My money's in my coat pocket. Take twenty."

Mrs. Stone stands from the chair, her anger causing the stiff chair legs to cry out on the aged linoleum of the floor. She snatches a paper from the small table and storms to the door. She grabs the cane from the corner.

"The money, Mama!" Wayne calls as she flings open the door and thuds down the wooden steps.

"Got my own money!" she calls back. "Don't you think your mama got no money?"

Burke looks at Joel, at Wayne, then closes the door.

Wayne turns from the boys and looks at the suncatchers on the window.

"What do you want?" he says then.

Burke glances at Joel, an urgent motion of flaring eyes that says "Get over here with me!" Joel glares back and does not move closer.

Wayne's head turns on the pillow, his hair on end like the fur of a static-ridden cat. His frown creases his face even further. Joel feels pain in the face, a drugged, sluggish pain, both physical and emotional. It makes Joel's hands go cold.

"So you came to stare at me?" says Wayne.

"Oh, heck, no," says Burke. "Wanna see if you're feeling better."

"Right. And I suppose Missy Campbell sent you."

"Well, to tell you the truth," says Burke, "she didn't exactly do that."

Wayne turns his eyes to Joel, rolling up to see beyond his shoulder. He says, "We got Campbell's nephew over there, but I can't imagine why you are here, Joel."

Joel swallows, and a stone drops to the base of his stomach. 'He knows me,' he thinks. 'Oh, God, I've done it now. He remembers who I am!

"Joel here's my main man," says Burke. He reaches over and wraps his fingers around Joel's upper arm. Joel is pulled into clear view of the mailman. "He came with me. And didn't nobody send us. We do what we want."

"Do you?" Wayne takes a slow breath. The afghan rises, then settles. Something moves beneath the thick cover. Joel imagines it is the charred stump. He thinks it is going to come out. But Wayne lies still, looking at the window. There is dust in the air, riding the sunlight from the window. Each speck is a suncatcher, a stupid piece of bright, worthless matter drifting without power on the whim of a current.

"You hang around a Barker, do you, Mr. Campbell?"

"Yeah," says Burke. "That's what I told you. Joel and me, we do what we want. Don't nobody tell us what to do."

"And you," says Wayne, looking at Joel. "You do what you want?"

Joel's breath enters his lungs in three shuddering spasms. He holds it until it forces itself back out again. "Yes," he says to the mailman.

"You go to school even though the Cove people feel it's wrong. You play with Missy Campbell's nephew. You come to visit a man who had his hand blown off at your cabin."

Joel's hands find each other and lock in a painful grasp. Bones crush bone. He wants to run down the steps, following Wayne's mother into the garage and on home.

"You used to play with that preacher's son, Andy. You don't make yourself scarce."

"No," whispers Joel. "Sir."

"You don't care about the way things are supposed to be, do you, Joel?"

Joel looks frantically at Burke. Burke will not look at Joel. "Yes, I care," Joel says softly.

"Maybe you do," says Wayne. "But you don't want to, do you?"

"I do," says Joel. He feels the strain of tears. He contorts his eyes, working the tears back into his head.

"Want to peek at the damage done, then have tales to tell, don't you?"

Joel's throat hitches; a tear falls. "No," he says. "I don't. I don't want to see. I just came because ..."

"Because what?"

"Because Burke ... Burke said ..." Joel stops. He can't talk anymore.

"Because nobody tells you what to do, isn't that right, Joel?"

Joel shrugs feebly.

Wayne sighs. He looks at Burke; he looks at Joel. He sits straight on the sofa, pulling his legs off the cushion and placing his feet on the floor. His right arm remains under the afghan, but the left hand comes out, and it rests in his lap. "Joel," he says.

Joel begins to cry.

"Joel," says Wayne. "Look at me."

Joel shakes his head.

"Joel."

Joel looks up at Wayne.

"It's good."

Joel's body trembles. He is confused. "What?" he manages.

"It's a good thing that you do what you want. A very, very good thing."

Burke watches between the two, his mouth slack.

"If you didn't do what you wanted to do, I would be dead now."

Joel looks at Burke, at the floor, the suncatchers, and again at Wayne. He shudders with the force of his sobs, his body as uncommanded as it was after his run down the mountain to tell of the mailman's accident. It is the confusion again. If only it was wrong to be here, he could make sense of it and leave. He wants to be wrong. He could then have punishment, could spend time in the toolshed alone, and have it over with. But he is not certain that he is wrong. It's not just Burke egging him on. He is hearing the seed of uncertainty being planted now by an adult.

And adults are to be respected.

Adults are to be believed.

'Aren't they?'

"Joel," says Wayne. He is extending his left hand. Joel stares through the tears, wiping his forearm up and down the length of his face. It is too much that the mailman offers. Joel cannot touch the man. It is not a matter of life and death anymore. There are rules . . .

"Can't I even shake your hand?"

'You are an adult, don't you know the rules?'

"He's kind of weird," says Burke. "But he's still my main man. Don't worry about him none."

Wayne sighs. "All right, then," he says. He drops his hand. "I'll just thank you from here. Thank you, Joel Barker, for my life."

Joel wipes his face.

Burke says, "Guess we should've brought you a get well present or something. Something to make you feel better."

Wayne shakes his head. "If you'd brought an elixir from your Aunt Missy, you could've just forgotten it. I wouldn't drink something from her any more than I'd drink horse piss."

Joel stops in mid-sob.

Burke gapes at Wayne.

Wayne's face is stone-cold serious.

And then Burke breaks into great gasps of laughter. He bends over, eyes closed, suffering with the hooting laughter that erupts from his gut like a good, long fart. Joel stares in amazement. Wayne begins to grin.

"That's great, man!" cries Burke. "That really is! Horse piss!"

Wayne chuckles a little.

"Man, I'm glad to hear you talk like that!"

Joel wipes his tears and blinks, watching between the two.

Wayne says, "I'm talking against your flesh and blood. You're not mad?"

"Oh, God, no way! I ain't never heard no grown-up talk like that about that old lady. It makes me think there's hope for old people after all!"

"Do you know what anyone else would think if they heard you talking like that?"

Burke stands straight. "Yeah," he says finally. "I think I do. And they'd have me up on Missy's table, trying to work out the demons."

"I've seen you around," says Wayne. "I figured you didn't want much to do with your aunt, but I didn't think you'd speak outright against her."

"So you learn something new everyday."

Wayne nods. His face becomes sober again. He looks at Joel. "And you, young Barker, I never thought I'd see you do anything except hang around corners, talking with that Mason boy, walking to school and back. It makes me think there's hope for young people after all."

Burke grins broadly at Joel.

"What do you boys really want, now? Did you really come to wish me well or to take a look at this arm?"

"To wish you well," says Burke. "And to look at the arm."

"I figured." Wayne looks at his lap, seeming reluctant. Joel wonders what it would be like to have a hand blown off. He wonders where Wayne's anger is, and what he think about when he is alone with the suncatchers. Wayne pulls his right arm out from the blanket. "Here you go," he says. Joel watches. The stump is wrapped in a clean white outer bandage. Wayne unwraps the white material. The cloth beneath is stained with yellow and brown blotches. This, too, comes off.

"Shit, look at that," says Burke. But Joel is no longer looking. He is staring at Superman, who has lost his bright red glow and is now a mere piece of colored glass. After a moment, Joel sees wrapping motions from the corner of his eyes, and he turns his gaze back.

Wayne works the bandages slowly and with ungainly awkwardness. It is something in his favor that he is left-handed. Again, Joel is aware of the medicated weariness in the man's eyes. He wonders what Wayne will do now, now that he cannot ride the four-wheeler. He wonders if he will try to commit suicide like Joannie Phipps' brother Taulsa did years ago when he lost his leg in a tractor mishap.

And then Burke says what Joel imagined he would, although the sound is as harsh and foreign as the mailbox blast had been.

"Who you think did it, Wayne?"

Wayne's head shakes ever so slightly as he finishes the wrap. He moves the stump beneath the blanket and tucks the afghan around it, a motion, Joel realizes now, not to hide the arm, but to keep it stationary. He wonders why Wayne doesn't have a sling. Wayne looks at Burke.

"What do you know about this?"

"Hey, I don't know nothing," says Burke, instantly agitated.

Wayne looks at Joel. "And you?"

Joel shakes his head. "Me, neither."

Wayne pinches the bridge of his nose. His eyes close briefly. Joel is afraid for Wayne's eyes to open again; this is why Burke brought him here.

They are down to what Lelia calls brass tacks.

And brass tacks can cut you deeply. They can make you bleed.

"Sit down, boys," says Wayne.

Burke looks at Joel and then sits in a kitchen chair. The splotches on Burke's face are a deep red; there is sweat along the hairline. In Burke's face, Joel sees the mad eyes of a horse with the bit in its mouth, running headlong into the woods, not knowing the destination or the dangers but high on the race.

Joel sits in the other chair.

Wayne's eyes open. "What do you know?" he asks. This time, the question is different. The tone is not suspicious, not demanding. It is slow, controlled, and without emotion.

"Your mama come to my aunt's meetings," says Burke. "Don't she tell you about them?"

"Just talk, Burke."

Joel can feel the sting of tacks, the burning chill on his back and arms.

"There was a big meeting last night. All the Brothers and Sisters were there. And some who don't come all the time. They talked about what happened to you."

"I'm sure they did."

"Missy said the time of insanity is here. She said we is the beginning of the last days."

Wayne nods. He looks at Superman on the window.

"Missy sacrificed some chickens. Everybody covered themselves with the blood. They said it was protection for the evil at hand. Said it was a sign of the human suffering that would happen before the devil was overthrown."

Joel wraps his arms about himself. He knows what Burke will say next.

"The sineater done it," says Burke.

Wayne's eyes turn, and stare at Joel. Joel knows now, in this instant, what it is like to be the devil's son. Shame and guilt and horror flood his heart and squeeze his chest with an unrelenting hand. Certainly Wayne will order Joel out of his home now, or worse, and it would be the right thing to do. Even if Joel did save his life. Maybe now Wayne will realize that it would have been better to die than to have been saved by Satan's child. Joel shuts his eyes, waiting.

There is no word spoken in the minute that follows. In the darkness behind his eyelids, Joel tries to see the accident again. To see the mailman in the grass, to see Lelia's twisted face and the dishrag on her arm. He tries to look beyond the scene, into the trees nearby, to see if there is a movement undetected before. To see if there is a man-shape in the shadow. To see if the sineater had indeed been hiding, watching, savoring the carnage.

But Joel cannot see anything beyond the hazy periphery of memory. He is, unfortunately, saved by his ignorance.

"Yes," says Wayne. "I know what they're thinking. I don't know they're wrong, either."

Joel opens his eyes and looks at the floor. There is a dead fly near his foot.

"But they're full of religious rantings, mindless beliefs. They turn my stomach."

Burke nods and looks at Joel. Joel cannot look up.

"I will have justice," says Wayne. "I don't know if Avery Barker is the one who stole my hand from me, though he probably is. Who but an insane man could live as he has these past years? But it is nothing of the devil. It is only human weakness. It was Patsy I wanted to avenge. Now, it is me."

"You gonna get him?" asks Burke.

"You want me to, Burke?"

Burke says nothing.

"Joel," says Wayne. "I don't know if it is good for you to be here for this. But hear me out. Understand what I'm saying. You saved my life. But my life won't ever be the same. I had dreams. And they're gone." Wayne stops, and Joel looks at him. His face is taut; his eyes drawn. It hurts to look at him now. When his shoulder shifts, there is a wincing, the first evidence of strong pain Joel has seen. "Joel, I believe your father is not in his right mind. No matter how terrible it might seem to you, you best accept it. You saw what he did to me. He stole my hand and my dreams. I don't think he wants anyone dealing with your family. And he will do what he can to stop them. I must do what I can to stop him."

"Yeah," whispers Joel.

"Can you understand? You should know the truth. I'm sorry, but I can't lie to you. You should understand what I'm saying."

"Joel's okay," says Burke. "My main man."

"I can see that," says Wayne.

"We'll even help you, Wayne," says Burke.

"Help me what?"

"Help you get justice."

"That's not necessary."

"So one's better than three?"

"No," says Wayne. "But this is a man's job. It is my job. It has nothing to do with you. You shouldn't be involved."

"Why not?"

"Don't play dumb with me."

"Don't want to hang around a Barker? Don't want to be seen with him?" asks Burke. "Don't want to break the rules?"

"Those rules are nothing."

"Oh, yeah? If Mrs. Stone knew it was a Barker boy with me today, you think she'd let us come in to see you? Hell, no. She'd be gone and burned the whole garage to clean out the place. Your mama knows the rules. She believes them."

Wayne's pained eyes register anger. "The rules are nothing."

"We want justice, too," says Burke.

"For what?"

"For you."

"Oh, really?"

"Yeah," says Burke.

But Joel thinks, *'No, it's not justice, it's power he wants.'*

"We'll help you, Wayne," says Burke. "We'll be really careful. We'll be good help. What do you say?"

"No."

"We're small, Joel and me. We're good at sneaking around. Don't you think a sineater's kid would be good at sneaking around, just to stay out of people's way?"

'Power,' thinks Joel. He shudders, remembering the cat by the fire in the clearing, remembering Curry's reprimand.

"It's too dangerous."

"So what ain't dangerous? You think life ain't dangerous?"

"And what would you do if we caught him, Burke?" asks Wayne. "Beat him up? Call the police? Kill him?"

Burke hesitates. Then he says, "Whatever I'd have to do."

Joel stands up and goes to the door. "I have to go home."

Burke stands up, too, his hands clenching tightly but his voice even. "Wayne, we want to help."

"No, Burke. It's not your job."

Then there is movement in the garage. Mrs. Stone is back with the groceries.

Wayne looks back at the window.

"Nice decorations," Burke says tightly.

"Belonged to the man who used to live here," says Wayne.

And then they hear Mrs. Stone on the steps. Burke joins Joel at the door. He opens it to let Wayne's mother enter. "You boys get on out of here now," she says. "You should have said your piece and been gone long ago."

Out again on South Branch, Burke snatches up a small branch and breaks it into tiny pieces as he walks as far as West Path with Joel. Joel wishes Burke wouldn't follow.

But as Joel starts up West Path, he hears Burke's footsteps stop. Joel keeps walking.

"I don't care what Wayne says," Burke calls out. Joel does not stop. "I'm going to help him with or without his permission."

Joel does not look back.

"Hell, I don't need anybody's damn permission!"

Joel kicks a small stone and continues to climb the path.

"And you, Mr. Joel Barker, you better think about helping me, too! Wayne Nelson the mailman ain't the only one in danger of a crazy sineater! You hear me?"

Joel hears, and keeps walking.

"He ain't the only one in danger! Joel!"

Joel rounds the first curve in the path, leaving the red-haired boy far behind.

2

Petrie arches her back, bunching up the old greasy coat beneath her. "Wait a second," she says. But Morton, the boy on top of her, is on a roll. He humps as fast as his knees in the rooty ground will let him. "Wait a second!" Petrie says again, but the boy keeps on.

Behind the fence, squatting down next to the compost pile, Joel watches his sister and the fat boy. He does not want to watch, but he wants to watch. He knew about a boy, but he didn't know his sister did this thing. And to do it so close to the cabin. Petrie must be more afraid of the woods than she is of letting a boy put his thing inside of her.

The sky is darkening early now; November is a queer month that teases with occasional warm weather but snatches light away right after supper. It is only six o'clock, but there are already stars above the trees. Joel cannot look at the stars, though. He is transfixed with the act which he's only seen his goats perform.

"Oh, baby," moans Morton.

Does Petrie want a baby? Joel wonders. Family-life class has hinted at baby-making. Does she want to get pregnant?

"Baby!" says Morton, and he bucks Petrie harder. The motion drives her back several inches into the pine needles, off the jacket.

And then, in the trees nearby, Joel hears a crack and thump. He strains to see in the faint light; it is most likely a deer. Bear are slowing down this time of year, and they usually run off if they come close to people. There is nothing visible, however, except for trunks and branches and night space beyond.

Then there is another crack, loud, close. Joel flinches. Petrie flinches, her eyes wide. She tries to see around the fat shoulder above her. There is another sound, like a low growl.

"Morton?" she says.

And then a rattle. Crackling. Moving, seeming to circle around the bodies on the ground, just within the dense trees. Electric fear surges Joel's veins.

"Morton," Petrie whispers urgently. She begins to struggle. But Morton says, "Wait, baby. Hang on."

Another growl, sounding humored, sounding cruel. Branches snap, footsteps shuffle. Joel looks frantically back at the cabin. He should run. He crouches lower, watching his sister.

"Morton!" Petrie throws herself backward, her hands fighting the pine needles. Her heels kick into the slick humus to each side of Morton's thick thighs. Morton slips out and falls flat.

Petrie jumps up, hands in fists, her skirt dropping about her knees.

"There's something . . ." she begins.

"Goddamn it!" roars Morton, face down in his jacket. He spits, pushes himself up, his bare ass working.

"Listen!" screams Petrie.

Morton stands, stumbling, and Petrie grabs his arm. Joel grabs his own elbows in a worthless gesture of protection.

"Christ, Petrie!" wails Morton. He jerks his arm free. "What the hell's the matter with you?"

"Something's out there, didn't you hear?"

"No, just you whining. Christ, I didn't even get to finish!"

"I shouldn't be out here, Morton. I know better than this! I ain't supposed to be out at night!"

"Shut up."

"Didn't you hear it?"

"No!"

"Just listen!"

Morton crosses his arms defiantly. Petrie's knees continue to clack against each other. They listen.

Joel, jaws dancing wildly, listens.

There is wind now, deep in the bowels of the forest. There are the late-season crickets, and creaking wood in wind.

"Ain't nothing," says Morton.

"It was."

"Maybe. But ain't now. Probably was nothing."

"I heard it!"

"Don't hear nothing. Don't see a damn thing, either."

"I gotta go home."

"I didn't get to finish!"

Petrie begins looking about on the ground. "So finish yourself! Where are my shoes?"

"I don't know," Morton growls. "Tossed them off somewhere."

Petrie bends close to see in the fading light. "Where are my shoes?" she cries.

"Back there," points Morton. His fury is obvious.

Petrie takes a few steps down the slope and her foot strikes something. She stoops quickly and picks up her canvas shoes and slips them on, not taking time to tie them.

Morton scrounges around as well, searching for the cowboy boots he'd unceremoniously wrenched off before he climbed into Petrie. He slips on loose soil and cusses under his breath.

"Walk me to the fence?" asks Petrie.

Joel pulls down tighter, his face nearly to the ground now.

"I don't know."

"Morton, please? I'm scared!"

"I don't know! Why should I?" Morton finds his boots, both standing upright beside a dead crabapple tree.

"Fine, I'll go alone! Big deal to you I'm scared!" Petrie turns on her heel and hurries up the slope. Joel scuttles around the pile, out of his sister's sight.

And then Morton screams, "Jesus Christ!"

Joel freezes. He hears Petrie stop at the fence, her breathing hard. "Morton?"

"Oh, God, oh shit, it's glass!" Morton crashes about down the slope, wailing like a trapped rabbit.

"Morton!"

"It's glass! My foot's full of glass, there was glass in my boot!" Morton is crying.

And then there is a sound again. This time hushed, slow. As much human as animal.

"Haaaaaaaaaaa." Close.

Joel's blood screams through his body; his heart races.

"Haaaaaaaaaaa." So very close.

"Petrie, help me! It hurts!"

And now the sound is quicker, like a horrid laugh. "Haaaaaaa. Haaaaa. HAAA!"

In the second Joel thinks he should help his sister, in the flash of moment that pity overpowers fright, his body says to hell with his mind and he races, holding low, across the dark yard to the cabin. Inside, he slams the pantry door.

Less than a minute later, from his bedroom, he hears his sister slam the pantry door and catch her breath before going to the kitchen to act as though everything was as normal as rhubarb pie.

3

It is nearly eleven-thirty Sunday night when Missy's praying begins to wind down. Burke has been watching the old wind-up clock on the crate by his cot, unable to sleep. Missy is in her bedroom, the only one in the Campbell cabin, and Burke is in the kitchen. Missy's door is ajar; light from her lantern is a mere puddle through the crack, an orange flickering film on the kitchen floor. Missy has been communicating with her Lord in her usual way, with every fiber of her soul and vocal cords. Usually, Burke hears Missy's prayers with his head beneath the pillow. Tonight, however, he listens from out in the open. The sounds still chill him, but he thinks of it now as a test. He must strengthen himself. There is so much he must do. Challenging his fear seems right. It feels good to know he is working for something important.

For control he has never had.

For the chance to see, to catch, the sineater.

Because to bring down the most powerful will be to become the most powerful.

And he is not alone. Joel will do as Burke says. Burke will make sure of it.

There is creaking in Aunt Missy's room. The bedsprings give under her as she climbs into bed. After a moment, the lantern is blown out. Burke feels under the sleeve of his undershirt and touches the star wound. It is rough and ugly. He traces it with his fingertips.

With all the courage he is feeling now, he should take Missy's cheese grater and scrape the star into oblivion.

"Burke," he says, testing his name. It sounds worthless, it sounds weak. "Burke." It is an old taste in his mouth, traced with bitter experiences and old hatreds and resentments. A name linked with bridled anger, and drowned in useless rage.

Burke licks his lips. "David Burke Campbell," he says. "David Campbell. David. Dave."

'Dave,' he thinks. It is different. It is somebody else. Someone who can make changes. Someone with guts.

"Dave Campbell," he says to the night-kitchen. He nods to himself. He is no longer Burke.

Dave closes his eyes. He would like new skin to go along with his new name. A new body. Not ridiculous hair that looks like an old mat of dead and tangled red fern. Not freckles that girls swear are dirt spots.

But he is different now.

He will have control.

And it will be all right.

4

As Burke Campbell is being transformed into Dave Campbell, Wayne is awakening in a panic, his face drenched with sweat, his arms shaking, his stump hot, and beneath the stump, his phantom arm being sawed apart. He sits bolt upright, the old quilt falling from his check. He cries out in the pain, and rubs his stump frantically against the quilt, trying to rub the pain away.

His mother is in the room in a second, jumping from the sofa on which she has slept the past nights.

"Wayne! It's past time for your pills! I told you to take an extra one afore you went to sleep!"

"STOP IT! I CAN'T STAND IT!"

Mrs. Stone races into the living room and runs water and puts several of Wayne's codeine pills into her hand. She goes back into the bedroom.

"Take them! I can't stand to see you like this!"

She holds the glass out to her screaming son, but his left hand lashes out, sending pills scattering and the glass in a water-trailed arc.

"Yes, you can stand it! You did this to me!"

"Stop it, that ain't you talking, it's the pain, it's the . . ."

"It's me, Mama! Me without my hand! And why? Because of your religious shit that drives people crazy with superstition! I gave my hand as a sacrifice to your goddamn religion!"

146

Mrs. Stone stares. "No, it ain't you, Wayne. It's the pain. The devil's using the pain to speak evil."

"Shut up!"

"The evil is working in your mind!"

"You're so ignorant! Can't you see your religion has led right up to this? Damn it! There'll be more, just wait!"

"No, Wayne, it ain't the beliefs. It ain't us. We love you. The sineater done it, son. Don't let the demon twist your mind into blaming the pure at heart. See it this way. Your arm was sacrificed but that might just save your soul!"

Wayne grabs his hair with his left hand, pulling it out into wild strands. "You'll never see. You'll never see, will you? You think I'll come to God now? Damn you all to hell!"

Mrs. Stone says, "I can't stay to hear this. I'm leaving."

"Of course you are! Close your ears! Feed the fire, Mama!" And he folds himself up, squeezing the stump because new pain is at least a change from the burning torture of the old pain. And above his own wails, he hears his mother puttering in the living room, and then the creak of the sofa springs. It is her duty to stay, she believes, and she will.

"Justice," he whispers through cracking lips, the word an appeal as if to God. "I'll have it."

5

It has been hours since he and Burke visited Wayne, but Joel cannot get to sleep. It is past midnight now, Monday morning has arrived in its dreadful darkness and stillness, but Joel cannot go to sleep.

Next to him, Curry snores softly. It won't be long before Curry is too tall for his cot. The teenager's big feet reach the full length of the thin mattress; his bare toes stick up in the dark-washed room like wet roots at the bottom of the river.

Curry is dreaming. Joel knows because there are intermittent moans and twitches. But Joel cannot cause himself to think about what it is Curry is dreaming, although he wishes he could. He wishes he could think about something other than what he is now thinking. Anything to divert his mind and make it weary and ready for sleep.

Joel is thinking about his father.

He thinks that this is the time of night when Avery comes home for his supper. After dinner, after chore time, after bedtime, after midnight, late in the silent hours, Avery comes home to eat, sleep a bit, and then go off again. Ever since Joel can remember, he has never been awake when his father has come home. As sure as Lelia Barker has taught her children Scriptures and chores and cleanliness, she has taught them that it is necessary to be asleep soon after going to bed. As sure as Joel knows that God and Christ and the Holy Ghost reign in heaven, he knows that to sleep at night is to be obedient and to be safe.

148

But he cannot sleep. His thoughts are rampant and worthless; they work themselves in his mind like a drunken spider weaving its web. They are images of Wayne and Burke and the Beacon River, and Andy and Patsy Campbell and Curry and Petrie and the fat boyfriend. He shakes his head, trying to still the images, but they merely re-arrange themselves and resurface again. He tries counting aloud, but quietly, hoping the repetition will lull his mind. After one hundred forty-six he stops. He rolls from stomach to back to stomach, dread-ing his wakefulness.

If there had been a wake today, Avery would not come home. But Lelia left the food out. He will come.

Curry groans and Joel looks at him. Right now, he wishes he were Curry. Curry knows how to be obedient. He can will himself to sleep when it is time. Joel had always been confident at his own ability, as well. He wonders if his dealings with Burke have begun to make him weak. But no, he tells himself. *'I ain't a baby. I ain't a wimp.'*

There is thumping outside, down near the path. Joel freezes. He rolls to his side and draws himself up, clutching his knees. *'Got to sleep.'* he thinks frantically. *'Got to sleep!'* Petrie is on her sofa, certainly asleep. Petrie more than anyone else in the family is re-quired to be sleeping when Avery comes home. She is more at risk, sleeping in the kitchen. Avery eats in the kitchen and then sleeps in the room with Lelia. If Petrie is at risk, what then of Joel's mother? Joel has always known how his father spent his nights, but the boy has never given serious thought to what it entails. Avery sleeps in the same room with Lelia. He spends hours in the same room with her.

The gate creaks. Joel winces. He squeezes his eyes so tightly that he sees specks of light.

'Avery sleeps with Mama!' Joel's brain chides. *'Does he sleep on the floor? Oh my God he must sleep on the floor! There is only one bed!'*

Bootsteps on the porch. Heavy. Terrifying.

Joel pulls in more tightly. *'Go to sleep!'* the Lelia in his mind cries. *'There is only one bed in Lelia's room!'* cries the fat boyfriend. *'He has the power, more than anyone else!'* reminds Burke. *'Hang on, Joel, hang on!'* Joel's chest constricts, hitching in fear, forcing a small squeak from his throat.

Joel wishes suddenly that Curry would wake up. At least there would be someone to share the fear.

The kitchen door opens. Bootsteps fall heavily on the kitchen floor. A chair scrapes, a plate moves. All other images fly from Joel's mind. In its place is the fissure, the opening, bringing into focus the physical form of the sineater. He is tall, oh Dear God, yes. Almost as tall as the kitchen ceiling. And his arms are like tree trunks, knotted with muscle, with hands of leather and nails as sharp as fish hooks. Legs thick and hard; boots of glistening reptile skin and toes pointed with metal caps. His neck like a bear's and his face . . .

Joel claps both hands over his mouth and muffles a scream. He cannot think this! He cannot! *'God help me! Let me sleep! Forgive me! Let me sleep!'*

But instead of the voice of the Lord, Joel hears Wayne's soft, gentle condemnation. "Thank you, Joel Barker, for my life."

And so Joel hugs himself as he listens to the moving in the kitchen, and he buries his eyes as he feels the floor of the hall give under the boots, and he bites his inner cheek as Lelia's bedroom door opens and then closes, but his sanity holds to the thread offered by the mailman.

And soon there are birds in the front yard and the sound of Curry chopping firewood in the back, and Lelia humming "Break Bread Together" in the kitchen, and Joel knows that night has come and gone in a heartbeat. He did indeed fall asleep at some point after Avery came home, and it is time to rise and face whatever the day and the Lord and Burke and his own new resolve would demand of him.

6

Dave's shoes are off the heels. The skin on the bottom of his feet is in contact with the worn carpet through the holes in his socks. If Aunt Missy had seen the socks, she would have dutifully darned them as well as run them through the boiling water of her washtub. Missy may have her thoughts on the Lord but she also believes in cleanliness and godliness and spends a good four hours a day at laundry and housework. She doesn't cook, however, as the Brotherhood provides a day's worth of hot meals early each morning. Dave hates the food they bring. It doesn't stay hot long, and Missy won't reheat it. And it is the things they bring that they expect a soul to eat. All ripe woodsy stuff, like squirrel, opossum, an occasional deer or rabbit. Not tasty canned food like he used to eat back in Tickton, West Virginia, or the cafeteria food they serve here at school. If he had his choice, he'd eat Kroger chili and spaghetti with meat balls till the day he died.

The guidance counselor's desk is not cluttered like the principal's desk. It is orderly and clean, with a little glass paperweight with a butterfly in it. The principle's desk looks like the floor of Missy's storage shed, all covered with paper and odds and ends that don't appear to have much meaning. Usually when Dave gets in trouble he goes to the principal's office. Now, however, he has been relegated to the cubicle of Mrs. Piper. Dave knows this either means he has reached the maximum point of Mr. Fort's tolerance and he is being launched into a new disciplinary approach, or Mr. Fort is tied up at the moment, and the paddle will fall as soon as the time is right.

Dave doesn't care one way or the other. Mr. Fort has about as much power behind his paddle as Missy would have behind a kickball. And there is no game Mrs. Piper can play that Dave hasn't played already in his other school and won.

Dave twists his heels on the carpet. It feels good.

Outside the closed door to Mrs. Piper's small office, Dave can hear the business of the school office. Mrs. Fort's typewriter. The voices of several students. The rumbling of the heat vent.

And then Dave hears the office door slam shut, and he sits straight, listening. He can't imagine who would slam shut a door at school, unless it was by the wind. And no wind blows down the main hallway.

There is a loud, high voice. He can't understand what it is saying, but the sound makes his head jerk around and his feet stop digging into the rug. The typewriter ceases its clacking. The students do not say any more.

"Where is Mr. Fort? I need to see him right away!"

"Oh, Christ a-mighty," breathes Dave. His eyes widen. He clutches the arms of the chair in which he sits.

The voice is angry, determined, and Aunt Missy's. "You's Mrs. Fort? Then tell me where he's at. This can't wait. It's important for the whole of this school!"

Mrs. Fort speaks, although Dave can't make it out. After a pause, however, her voice comes over the intercom system. "Mr. Fort, please report to the office right away. Mr. Fort to the office."

Dave gets up from the chair and presses his ear to the door crack. If Mrs. Piper comes now, he'll be knocked on his ass, but he has to hear. His feet work back into his shoes on their own accord, and the strings stay untied.

In a moment, he can hear Mr. Fort come into the office. Mr. Fort has an unmistakable habit of clearing his throat and making a tsking sound before saying something important. Perhaps he thinks Aunt Missy is important. Dave balls one fist into the other. Could she be here because of him? Has the school called her because of his behavior?

Mr. Fort obviously knows her. This could be because Patsy used to go to school here. He says, "Mrs. Campbell, why don't we talk in my office? I'm sure we will be more comfortable."

"I ain't got the time," says Missy. "Only the message. I ain't got no phone and what I have to say can't wait. It's about the safety of the school here."

Mr. Fort must be uncomfortable with this, because he sends the students from the office.

The telephone rings, and Dave can hear Mrs. Fort say, "Ellison Elementary School."

"Mrs. Campbell, let's go into my office."

"It's the Barker boy, Mr. Fort. Let me say my peace and I'll be gone. But hear me out. You got to be rid of the boy. He can't bring nothing but harm."

Mr. Fort lets out a large, deep breath that sounds like a cross between a shocked laugh and a reaction of disgust. "Mrs. Campbell, we have no reason to do such a thing. I don't appreciate you coming in like this and making such a demand."

"I've been praying," says Missy. "I've seen things and am compelled to tell you what I seen. Things of danger. Bad things. All to people what have dealings with the family of the evil one."

"Mrs. Campbell, I insist that we go into . . ."

"Joel Barker should never have been let go to school. It's a wrong we can correct, and maybe in time if you do it now. Maybe you don't see the whole of things, Mr. Fort, but God has borne it onto my shoulders to know. We've been weak and careless. And now it's falling down on us all."

"Mrs. Campbell, I think perhaps you should leave. I can't waste my time . . ."

"You call the Lord's will a waste of time? Joel Barker isn't to be at school. He isn't to be out among the rest of the community. He shouldn't even have been born, but he is alive, as are his brother and sister. How long can we let the wrongs go unchanged? Too much evil! Too much wrong! And it's in him now, and it won't be rid of! All we can do is watch and pray and be careful!"

"Mrs. Campbell, either you leave or I'll be forced to call the authorities. What you suggest is illegal and immoral. Removing a child because you think he is less than anyone else is absurd. Do you remember in which country we live?"

"God's will is above that of any nation. The sins ain't visited upon the child in this case, Mr. Fort, the sins is visited upon the father. Joel's father is transformed. He is consumed by our own sins, the sins of the dead before us, and is mad. He is the evil one. Avery Barker is a danger to body and soul. We must do what we can to protect ourselves and to make our lives holy unto the Lord."

Mr. Fort says nothing, but Dave can hear the thumping of the office door. He must be escorting Aunt Missy into the hall. Missy's voice is fainter as she says, "Get the danger behind us! Or it will be on the heads of those who don't heed the word!"

Dave slips back into the chair and sits holding his elbows. His hands are cold, his knees trembling. The witch is trying to wrap her claws around everything within reach. Anger and a trace of fear knot like marbles in the flesh of his neck. It hurts to swallow. He can't wait to tell Joel about this. If he gets the chance, he will talk to him during lunch.

The star tattoo feels suddenly like a tarantula, taunting and tickling and clinging to him, reminding him of his night of weakness and worthless hope.

7

The sixth- and seventh-grade classes have to sit separately in the cafeteria today because someone threw a whole tray into the garbage can last week and Mr. Fort decided that treating the older students like the primary students might shame them into acting like they were supposed to. Of course, all the sixth and seventh-graders know that it was Rennie who tossed the tray, and Mary Skipp's new retainer as well, although Mary would never rat on Rennie and so the crime went undetected by the adults. But Mr. Fort would calm down in another few days, and the older kids would be back to saving seats and goofing around with kids in the other classes.

A note is dropped onto Joel's tray near the end of the period, and as he looks up to see who gave it to him, all he can see is the retreating back of the red-haired boy. Joel swallows his bite of seaburger and opens the folded notebook paper.

"Go to the bathroom during sixth period," it says. "At 1:30. I'll meet you." And then it says, "Tear this up after you read it. Your friend, Dave."

Joel glances around again but Burke is vanished, swallowed by the crowd of tray-laden students waiting to dump their garbage in one of the plastic cans and be rid of their trays on the counter.

The bell sounds. The rest of the students clamber from the long tables, smacking each other on the back or trying to knock books and trays from each other's hands. Joel gets at the end of the crowd, tray in hand. The note is folded in his fingers, but he can see some of the ink of the words when he looks down at it. The note is from Burke, but Joel cannot figure the "Dave" part. Maybe it's a joke of some sort.

Ed and Rennie move beside Joel, both flourishing sick smiles. They whisper something to each other and laugh. Ed then moves around Joel, working his knees and hips into the previously nonexistent space between Joel and the skinny girl in front of him. Joel grimaces and begins to move back a step, but then stops. If Andy were there, he would have said, "Hey, butt, I see your butt." But Andy isn't there. There is no one there to take up for him, or to make the ridicule easier to take.

Joel leans slightly, getting his shoulder beside Ed, and he pulls himself up with it. He does not touch Ed, but is a hairbreadth from it.

Ed, now even with Joel, gapes. "Hey, what do you think you're doing? Rennie, this fag is trying to butt in front of me."

Joel's heart pounds. He looks straight ahead, holding tightly to his tray in case revenge will be an upper cut to the bottom of it. The skinny girl moves up, now right in front of the trash can and the kitchen window. Joel moves up also. Rennie says, "Nobody butts in front of my buddy."

And then comes the fist, more suddenly than Joel expected, but his fingers ready. The tray bounces once, uneaten cake crumbs spraying the air and Joel's face.

Joel does not look at Ed, or speak, but calmly puts his tray on the shelf of the window and turns to leave the cafeteria. On his way to class, he thinks that next time, he might even look Ed or Rennie in the face. A real stare-down. The thought is frightening, but the fright is coated a bit by a sense of uneasy satisfaction.

He does not tear up the note. In fifth period, he pulls it out many times to read behind his English book. "Dave?" He plays with the letters, thinking perhaps they spell a code he is supposed to be quick to decipher. It spells nothing backward, as do the messages on the boulder. "Dump apples very early," he scribbles on his paper. No sense there. "Dumb awful Vivian Eastman." Joel looks over at Vivian Eastman at the far side of the room. Yes, she was dumb all right, but Joel doesn't think Burke even knows Vivian Eastman. Maybe the letters backward stand for some other words. "Eat vegetables after doughnuts." *'Crap.'*

He puts the note away until sixth period. And when Mrs. Grant assigns the story from the reading book, one which Joel has already read because one night he had no homework and Lelia said he had better well have homework, Joel raises his hand and asks to be excused. He is a few minutes early, but then again, he really does need to go. A little.

In the boys' bathroom across the hall from his class, Joel is alone. He relieves himself in one of the two urinals, then looks at himself in the grimy mirror. "Don't always vibrate eagles," he says to himself. He shakes his head, and then makes several faces. He frowns, making his dark brows into a single black line. It reminds him of his mother so he stops. He then stretches his lips wide, looking at his teeth. He does not have a mirror in his room at home. And so it is at school where he appraises his looks, which isn't often. There are two mirrors at his cabin. One is Petrie's, and she keeps it with her things in a box under her sofa. The other is Lelia's. It stands on the old dresser in Lelia's bedroom.

'Does she turn it over at night when Avery has no wake so she won't see him?' Joel thinks, and turns suddenly from the mirror to end these thoughts.

And the bathroom door opens, and it is Burke.

"Hey, amigo," says Burke.

"Don't ask Viking eggheads," says Joel.

"What the fuck are you talking about?"

"I don't know. You tell me."

Burke frowns amusedly, and moves to the mirror and leans in close. "Do I look different to you?"

"No. Should you?"

Burke turns his face side to side slowly. Then he says, "You know how to lock that door?"

Joel looks around. "What door?"

"How many doors in here? This ain't the girls' john."

"No. Munsen's got the key. Why?"

"Got to shut the door." Burke moves from the mirror and pulls a triangular piece of rubber from his flannel shirt pocket. "This'll have to do,'' he says. He taps the doorstop under the bottom of the door.

"Why'd you do that?"

"We got to talk. I don't want no first grader coming around."

"Where'd you get that stopper?"

"Hardware."

"When?"

"Before school. What's it to you, anyway?"

"How much did it cost?"

"So I borrowed it. Big deal. We got important things to deal with and can't let dumb stuff get in the way. Happy?"

Joel shrugs. Then he remembers the note and says, "Hey, Burke, I didn't understand the last part of . . ."

"Name's Dave."

"What?"

"I'm Dave. Not Burke. I'm a different person."

"You're crazy."

"Maybe. But I'm not Burke anymore. I'm Dave."

Joel shakes his head. "You telling your aunt Missy this? You telling your teacher?"

"Gonna sign my papers Dave now. As to Missy, it don't make no difference. She's got other things on her mind now besides me."

"You think I'm supposed to change my name, too?"

"That's up to you."

"It's stupid."

"It's different."

Joel crosses his arms and watches the older boy. Then he says, "So why you want me in here?"

"We got to talk. About what we're gonna do to help Wayne."

"I never said I was gonna help."

"Listen to me. We're gonna be around a lot. We're gonna go out whenever we can, or whenever we can make a chance. We got to keep our ears and eyes open. We can find clues and shit. We can find out where he is."

"You mean . . ."

"Of course I do. We gonna catch us a mailman killer."

Joel turns from Dave. He frowns at the floor, sweat popping out on his face. Finally, he says, "He didn't kill Wayne."

Dave laughs, and it is an ugly sound. "No, he didn't kill him, but he tried his damndest, didn't he?"

Joel says nothing. He squints at the tiles on the floor.

"He sure did take the hand clean offa old Wayne, didn't he?"

Finally, Joel says softly, "Don't you understand?"

"Yeah," says Dave, his voice rising. "I understand about your stupid rules. I hear 'em enough from Aunt Missy! I know you ain't supposed to look at Avery Barker, I know you ain't supposed to speak in tongues without an interpreter, I know you ain't supposed to handle a rattler 'less you feel the spirit of God floating round your head! But I thought you was growing out of 'em, Joel!"

"It's more than that."

"More than what?" Dave's impatience is palpable. Joel looks at him. The irises of his eyes almost seem red now, reflecting the fire of his hair and the fire in his soul. It is awesome. "More than what?"

"I don't know," Joel mumbles. "It don't make sense."

"Goddamn it, tell me what you're talking about!"

"He's my father, Dave!" Joel spits out the words, alien beings with a strange taste. Once out, they hang like pathetic bits of nonsense.

Dave's face flinches. He hesitates, his tongue moving against the inside of his mouth, feeling it out. The red in the eyes concentrates between narrowed lids as Dave studies Joel. Then he says, "Hell, if it was my father I'd hunt him in a second flat. He's the asshole what sent me to this town in the first place."

There is a thumping on the door as someone tries to enter. It lasts a moment, then stops.

"Now, you got to help me, Joel," says Dave. He begins unbuttoning his shirt. He undoes buttons at his cuffs, and slips the shirt from his shoulders. It falls and hangs about his hips, still tucked in at the waist.

"See?" asks Dave, turning his left arm toward Joel.

Joel gasps softly. There is a rough, dark-lined star on Dave's upper arm. Dave's eyes are closed, like he is praying, or thinking, or even ashamed. Joel cannot imagine that it is anything but thinking.

"Where'd it come from?"

"Missy marked me to save me."

"What do you want me to do?" But Joel knows already, because

Dave has pulled a large square of coarse-grain sandpaper from the bookbag on the floor. "I won't."

Dave opens his eyes. "I want it off, Joel."

The door thumps from outside, and a small male voice says, "Oh, no, it won't open."

Another little boy says, "Mr. Munsen must be cleaning. Let's go to the one in the cafeteria."

Joel looks away from the door, back to the dreadful star.

"I can't," he says.

Dave thrusts the sandpaper at Joel. "We ain't got time to argue. I got to have it off."

Joel takes the paper. It makes his skin crawl. Imagining Dave's flesh rubbing off in a sheet of pulpy red makes his mind crawl.

"I can't."

"I hate it, Joel. I hate who gave it to me. You should hate her, too. She came to school today. She told Mr. Fort you should be kicked out of school."

Joel stares at Dave. "Why?"

"Because you're a Barker, asshole! You're a danger to us all, because you should have stayed where you belonged, back in the woods. Hell, back in your mama's womb!"

Joel's fists clench. He fights against the urge to lunge at Dave. "Don't say that!"

"I wasn't me! It was dear Aunt Missy! You hate her, Joel? Get rid of this star for me!"

"I . . . I can't!"

"You're a pussy, Joel! Is that all Barkers are, crazy psychos and wimps?"

"Damn you."

"Do it, quick! We got to get back to class before they come looking for us."

Joel drives his fists into each other, cracking knuckles. He works on his breathing, trying to slow it down. Then he straightens and looks at the older boy. "All right," he says. "I'll do it, if you do something for me."

"What's that?"

"Get rid of the coon dick."

Dave's jaw drops. "That old thing? I ain't got it no more!"

"I'm not so sure. Let me see."

Dave picks his pockets inside out, revealing nothing but lint. "See? It was just a joke. Shit."

Joel nods. "Okay," he says. "Okay, then." He looks at the star again. "But it's gonna . . ."

"I got a rag." Dave produces a frayed-edged strip of cloth from the inside of his sock. He tosses it over Joel's shoulder, then turns to the sink and grips it until his muscles stand out in tight cords. "Don't stop, Joel, no matter what." His voice is raspy, urgent. "Don't stop till it's done."

Joel grits his teeth, feeling sandpaper in his bite, and drawing back his lips in distaste. He takes Dave's arm in one hand and presses the sandpaper onto the star. Again, the feel of another human's warm skin is a shock, and the flinching of anticipation of Dave's arm is horrid.

"Do it, Joel."

Joel scrubs the paper hard against the star. Dave bolts once, then bends into the sink, drawing air through his teeth. White skin papers off, then beads of blood well up. Joel scrubs harder, clutching the edge of the paper in his fingers to fight the resistance of the once-freckled skin. Dermis is churned up and spit out like tilled soil. Dave moans, driving his chin down into his chest. The palm of Joel's hand is hot. Blood currents from under the sandpaper and runs down Dave's arm. It drops onto the floor.

"Is it finished?" The words are through clamped jaws.

Joel peels the paper back and looks. The patch of arm is too raw, too red to tell. He wipes at the blood with the side of his hand. Only a few disjointed traces of star outline can be seen.

"Just about. I think it's enough."

"No," says Dave. "Get it all."

Joel scrubs again. His chest hurts. He bites the side of his mouth, but it does not take the pain away. Blood makes him sick. Blood is ugly; it is foul. How can the blood of Jesus wash sinners clean? Blood is dark and thick, and it stinks of anger and hate.

Joel stops and looks under the paper, wiping the blood away. "It's gone," he says.

Dave stays frozen at the sink. Joel ties the rag around the arm and knots the short ends. The red-haired boy turns then and wraps his fingers about the bandage. "Just squeeze it a little and it'll be good as new." His eyes are glazed with uncried tears, but they blaze in a defiance and a craziness that keeps Joel silent.

"Now I can get on with business," Dave says.

Joel nods.

The bathroom door rattles. A woman's voice says, "What is going on in there?"

Joel moves to get the stopper, but Dave says, "Wait." He shrugs his shirt up and buttons it quickly with barely disguised pain, then tears an uneven piece of paper towel from the dispenser and swabs the blood from the floor. "Okay," he whispers.

Joel pulls out the stopper and kicks it into a corner. The door flies open, and Mrs. Grant comes in. Hands on hips, she seems to have no problem in disciplining wherever she finds trouble.

"And just what is going on here, Joel? You've been gone quite long enough to do what you had to do."

"And we're glad you came, Mrs. Grant," says Dave. "Door was stuck. We didn't think we'd ever get out of here. Rusty hinges or something. Maybe wet weather's got the wood all swolled up. Mr. Munsen better check it out."

"I know you," says Mrs. Grant to Dave. "You're the new boy, the one who is always in the office for something."

"I got to get to class," says Dave, and he brushes by Mrs. Grant. Mrs. Grant seems for a moment that she will grab Dave to turn him back around, but instead she watches him go with an adult's indignant rage. Then to Joel she says, "What was going on?"

Joel taps his teeth. "Nothing," he says.

"Joel," says Mrs. Grant. Her body droops, and some of the intensity leaves her face. When she speaks again, it is softer. "Joel, I don't want you hanging around that boy. He's trouble, I'm sure you know. He bothers other kids, always picking on them, pushing them around. You always seemed to be a nice boy."

Joel feels instantly ill at ease with his teacher. Never has a teacher spoken directly to him about anything, except to ask him to read or to empty the pencil sharpener. It was comfortable that way. Now he is alone in the boys' room with his teacher, and she is, in her own way, trying to help him. His toes squirm in his shoes.

"Joel, if that boy tries anything with you, I mean, bothers you or tries to get you to do something you know is wrong, please let me know.'' She nods her head as if Joel has agreed. ''Let me know, all right?''

Joel nods his head barely. ''All right,'' he says.

''Good,'' says Mrs. Grant. Her stern teacher look pulls back onto her face like a living mask. ''Now, out to the room with you. We've got work to do.''

Mrs. Grant goes out of the bathroom.

Joel takes deep breaths, grabbing for composure. He then moves to the sink and flushes the blood from beneath his fingernails. So what if Avery is his father, he wonders. It doesn't matter. It shouldn't matter. If Avery is a psycho as Dave says, then let Dave or Wayne find him and have their justice. If Avery is the devil, let Missy find her answer in prayer and stop the evil before it can harm more people.

As the water runs through Joel's fingers, he thinks about the story of Pilate in the Bible, and how he washed his hands of Jesus. Joel washes his hands of the sineater.

Moving back into the hallway, Joel's mind sends a twinge to his heart. He knows it must be his conscience, taunting him for erasing a Brother from the family of the Light. But he shakes his head, reminding his conscience that the Brother he removed did not want to be part of it. The Brother he erased would have been nothing but a hindrance. ''It was right,'' he says to himself. ''I done what was right.''

And he strolls into reading class, where Mrs. Grant is back on her stool with a doughnut stick and the kids are yawning over the story of Alfred Nobel.

8

Dave has not gone back to his classroom yet. He stands just inside the janitor's closet near the gym. He holds his burning arm still and breathes heavily, working down the pain so he can return to class as though nothing has happened. The closet door is closed, the light is off. He hits his thigh heavily, rhythmically, with the head of his hammer. It helps take his mind from the angry raw nerves of his arm. He had tried to hit the pain in his arm away, hoping it would make it numb, but striking the bloody mass only made it worse.

In the pain, though, he takes heart. The star is gone.

He is no longer a Brother.

At least Joel hadn't pussied out.

Dave sighs, and hits his thigh with the hammer.

The closet door bangs open. The light is switched on. Joshua Munsen blinks, then stares at Dave.

"You taking a smoke, boy?"

Dave lowers the hammer. He wonders if he could smash the man's face and make it look normal again. "No," he says.

Joshua shakes his head, scowling, then grabs his jacket from a nail on the wall. "I don't care if you is, anyway. I'm quitting. Today."

Dave says, "Yeah?"

"It's too dangerous to stay here."

Dave watches as Mr. Munsen jams his arms into his jacket. The man's arms tremble. Then he looks back at Dave. "They get that

Barker boy outta school and I'll stay. But Mr. Fort says we can't do that. Says it's unconstitutional to even think it. But I say we can't argue with the Lord.''

Dave's heart hops. Mr. Munsen is quitting because Joel goes to school.

"We sure can't," says Dave.

Mr. Munsen, his hand on the doorknob, his damaged face shaking, says, "Missy Campbell came to the office today. She told Mr. Fort what to do, but he ignored her. I heard her, though, and know she's right. I always knew she was for the Lord, my wife goes to Missy's meetings. But now I heard the woman for myself, and I see that God speaks through her.''

Dave can hardly keep from grinning with excitement. But he says, ''You're right.''

Mr. Munsen's eyes light up for a second, and look at Dave with appreciation. "Praise God," he says. And then he is gone.

Dave puts his hammer away and goes back to his classroom with much on his mind.

9

Joel plods down Route 536 after school, heading for the West Path Bridge. He feels strangely brave this afternoon. A small yet exhilarating sense of control stirs his veins. Today he almost stood up to Ed and Rennie at lunch. Today he dared to touch Dave and sand Missy Campbell's sign from his arm. And Joel is still alive, and nothing terrible has fallen on his head.

Joel stops in front of the Hardware. He looks at the empty porch. There won't be any mail anymore, he realizes. Wayne is not mailman now. People of the Cove will have to come down for their own letters now.

So how will Joel get mail? And if Missy Campbell has her way and changes tradition, nobody will be sending any death notices, either. How will the dead now be saved from their sin? What else can there be to do? But he shakes that thought to concentrate on the mail issue. Perhaps Benton could leave the mail out on nights when Curry is scheduled to deliver baskets.

But Joel knows that Curry wouldn't want to be involved with mail. And what if Andy writes again? Joel will have to do this himself. As Dave would say, "Go for it."

'Go for it. You've broken one rule, another won't hurt,' Lelia would put him in the toolshed if she knew.

'And how would she know?'

The store porch is still and empty. Benton playing solitaire, probably, or dozing behind his register. If ever there was a time to try, it is now. Joel jogs back to the store and steps onto the porch.

There is no sound from inside, but then the windows are all shut tightly against November. Joel stretches his finger out, and taps lightly on the wood frame of the screen door. He balls his fist, and hits again, harder.

He hears muffled movement, and steps back reflexively. A voice, heavy and grumbling, grows louder. But then, another voice, that of a woman, and a spear drives into Joel's heart. In a panic, he crouches and scuttles off the porch and around the corner.

The wooden door scrapes open, then the screen door. Joel hears footsteps on the floor of the porch. Benton says, "Wind, I guess. People don't knock on store doors."

And then the woman's voice, Missy Campbell's voice, causes Joel to press his fists up beneath his neck and draw his back as tightly into the rough wall of the store as he can without going through.

"Be rid of 'em, Benton," she says.

"Don't let them cans fall out of the bottom of that bag, now," says Benton. "I could still double-bag that if you want me to."

"A little bit of commission ain't worth it, Benton. Be rid of 'em all."

Benton says nothing more, but Joel can hear the screen door clap, and the heavy door thump shut. He slides down onto the ground, daring to let his eyes strain to the left, watching the edge of the porch. Missy coughs, and whispers something to herself, then he hears her footsteps down on the gravel to the side of the road. Joel slowly slides his fists down onto his chest and presses them into his ribs, feeling the hammering heart. And then he can see Missy's back, just beyond the porch side, on the street, turning off toward the path.

Joel closes his eyes, taps his teeth, and listens to his heart.

In a moment, control returns. He struggles upward, pushing his hands onto the store wall and moving his neck outward to gulp a good strong taste of air, then he goes back onto the porch. He looks over his shoulder, and sees that Missy is over the bridge now, and gone.

'Thank God.'

Joel knocks on the screen door, and waits.

Nothing.

He knocks again. And again, he hears the grumbling voice of a perturbed Benton coming to the front.

Joel pulls his fingers back and tucks them safely inside his jacket pockets. The fingers of his right hand find a long, loose thread, and they begin an intricate braiding.

The heavy door pulls open. Benton's face is at the screen.

"Well, God bless America," says Benton.

Joel cannot look Benton in the face. The unfamiliarity of such a familiar character in his life is unnerving. "I just wanted to ask you a question," he says finally.

"It's cold. Come on in. Then ask."

"I just wanted to ask about the mail. Is there any? I mean, did we get any?"

Benton tips his head down, coming into eye level with Joel's lowered gaze. "Well, I don't exactly know. I'd have to look. And I'm letting all my heat out with us talking through this screen."

"I can wait. I ain't cold."

Benton pushes against the screen door, knocking Joel out of the way. "Get in here, Joel. You can look for yourself. I'm nobody's slave."

Again, Joel is dumbfounded. It is not that Benton knows his name, but that the same is being spoken. Spoken like a normal name, of a normal person. Joel lets himself look at Benton, and he sees something of what he saw in Wayne's face. Tolerance, perhaps. Patience. And no distrust.

He goes into the store. Benton shuts the door.

The interior of the store itself is a marvel. Andy had described the rows and rows of items and the smells of the goods and the gleam of new tools and the glint of new paint and varnish cans. But seeing it all is something altogether different. Joel's eyes widen, and he stares. Benton moves beside the boy and says, "Never been in here, have you?"

"No," says Joel.

"Guess you're the first one, huh?"

Joel knows he means the first Barker, and he nods his head.

"Mail's in my bag over here." Benton goes to the counter with the cash register, and draws out a canvas sack. "Come on and look. I was busy reading."

Joel follows to the counter. He picks up the sack and peers inside. There is not much. Cove people are already looking out for themselves.

"Dump it out if you'd like," says Benton, pulling out a Wheel Horse brochure from beneath the register.

Joel upends the sack; envelopes of all sizes scatter about the countertop. He wonders if some of them contain money. It would be something to receive a letter with money in it. He looks up at Benton. The store owner is leaning against the closed window behind the register, frowning over the brochure.

"You trust me?" Joel asks suddenly.

Benton does not look up. "Shouldn't I?"

"I guess." Joel fingers through the letters and manila envelopes, magazines, and newspapery advertisements for Moore's Building Supply in Penloe. Many envelopes were on their faces; he turns them over to read the addresses.

"I trust people," Benton continues. "Only way you can run a business in a small place like Ellison. I can't stand to shop in those larger cities. All those beepers and security men and hidden cameras and funny round mirrors above your head. I know it's a sign of the times, but I like my times a little slower."

Joel reads the envelopes. Rody Marshall. Preston Vicks. Mr. and Mrs. Richard Benshoff. Mr. Andrew R. Cook. Mrs. Candace Stone. And for Mr. Ringgold, a slick new seed catalog.

"Find anything?"

Joel shakes his head. "No." He spreads the envelopes out and looks more carefully. There is nothing from Arlington.

"Hmmmm," says Benton. He folds the brochure and looks at Joel. "Maybe another day."

"Maybe," says Joel. He licks his lips and looks back around the store. "You said you trust people. Ain't you never had nothing stolen? There's some really good stuff in here."

"Stolen?" Benton laughs. Although at least fifteen years older, Benton reminds Joel again of Wayne. Not that Wayne had been smiling when Joel had gone visiting, but there is a strange adult compassion that seems to move just below the features, an understanding, or at least a desire to understand. Joel cannot believe that Lelia is completely unaware of people on the outside who do not see the Barkers as a plague. Maybe she *is* aware but has followed the rules not only with her actions but with her mind, and has forgotten about them. It is a very sad thing to think about.

"Oh, yes," Benton says. "I get stuff stolen all the time. Some of it is kids, just playing around and picking up a piece of candy or a screwdriver. Sometimes it's some grown-up who takes wire or little fixtures or tubes of glue. And I've even had a couple break-ins at night. Through the window, I reckon. It never got broken, just had the screen latches popped out. Missed some chain, tools, odds and ends."

Joel is amazed at Benton's calm. "You call the police?"

Benton shakes his head. "We ain't got real criminals here, Joel. Not the stealing kind, that is. Kids take stuff. When they come in the next time, I ask them how they liked that candy, or if the marbles they snuck out rolled good. If they get uncomfortable, they learned something. Maybe they'll think about it before they do it again. The adults now, that's a little different. Why do adults take stuff? Because they don't like themselves. Because they never got taught right. Because they really are poor and need these things. Nothing's been messed up too bad. So I just let what will happen, happen."

Joel ponders this. Then he says, "What if somebody stole Creeper?"

"Then that would be real criminal," says Benton, his eyes narrowing with cold seriousness. "That ain't just messing around, in my book. Any one mess with my dogs, and I'd have the police here before you could count your big toes."

The phone rings. Benton picks the receiver up from the chunky black phone beside the cash register. Joel begins to put the mail back into the sack.

"Howdy, Sam," Benton says. "Busy?" Benton looks about the store, a comical expression on his face. "Hell, yeah, Sam, I'm busy. But let me tell my customers who I'm talking to and they won't mind waiting." Benton puts his hand over the receiver and says to Joel, "I'm talking to Sam Fort. Can you wait before I help you with your order?"

Joel smiles uncertainly. "Yeah."

"No problem, Sam," Benton says back into the phone. "They all said they'd be glad to wait. I mean, they know that nothing tops education, or the man in charge of education. Now, what can I do for you?''

Joel folds the top of the sack over, then moves from the counter toward the closet shelf. On it are fishing tackle; plastic boxes with snap-shut lids, plastic bags of purple and orange rubber worms, assorted hooks in a cardboard display box. Joel touches a hook, turns it over, and considers its vicious purpose.

'Do fish have souls?'

"She still works there, yes," says Benton. "Philicia goes to the church after the youngest two get home from school. They do their homework there and all. I told her it's best they not do it around the store 'cause it gets right noisy at times." Pause. "Yes, can you believe my oldest two are in the high school already? None of them do part-time here, though. Not that I don't want them in the old man's footsteps or anything, but they do lots of sports and all." Pause. "Well, I don't rightly know. I could ask her. I could have her call you in the morning. Mind me asking why you are asking?"

Joel wiggles a bag of rubber beetles. They almost look real. Andy and he could have had a grand time playing with them.

"Quit, hmm? What in the Sam-hill did he do that for? He's always been there. He sick or what?" Pause.

Joel moves from the fishing gear and looks at the assortment of seed packs and Jobe's Plant Spikes. Benton's pause becomes longer. Joel marvels at the variety of colorful blooms on the package covers. He wonders if Benton would notice, or mind, if he slipped some into his pocket and tried to get them to grow at home.

'Such neat things at a hardware store!' Joel thinks. He moves to boxes of matches, pocket knives, lighter fluids in little squeeze cans, rolls of bare and insulated wires, batteries, hooks and latches, all shiny in their factory-wrapped packages.

Benton says, "Oh, dear."

Joel glances around. Benton, who had obviously been looking at the boy, looks away quickly.

There is another pause. Joel spots a jar of striped candy sticks on a small shelf by the register counter, and wishes he had at least a quarter.

"I see your problem," says Benton. "Ain't gonna get no better, either, the way things are looking. Not until some people grow a good strong set of balls.'' Benton glances at Joel. ''I mean guts.''

The door bangs open, and Fitch comes in. He sees Joel, and his face darkens a little. Instead of going to the register counter, he shakes off his coat and drops it onto a rack beside the door, then moves over to the magazine display and picks up an issue that has a large picture of a wood duck on the front.

''I'll ask her, Sam. I can't really say. She's obligated to the church, you know, but the mornings might be something she could handle. I don't dare to speak for that woman, you know.''

Joel moves close to the candy-stick jar. He can see his reflection, filmy and curved around and making him look a little like Petrie's fat boyfriend.

''Mmmm hmmm,'' says Benton. ''Like I said, I can't speak for her, but I'll have her give you a ring tonight when she gets home. It'll be late.''

Joel looks from the jar to Fitch. He doesn't like being in here with anyone but Benton, although he knows the next best person would be Fitch. Benton and Fitch have been bookends on the Hardware porch ever since Joel can remember, ever since Joel started first grade and he had to make the long journey from his cabin to the Ellison Elementary School alone. Benton and Fitch have always seemed like men of contentment, maybe not with the world in general, but at least with their place in it. Fitch looks up from his wood duck magazine. Joel tries a small smile.

''Howdy,'' says Fitch. He doesn't smile, though. Joel realizes that seeing a Barker in the hardware store is as much a shock as waking up to find your house on the moon.

''Surely, Sam,'' says Benton. ''Will do. You take care, now. Kids get right wild what with Thanksgiving and Christmas coming up. Lord knows *I* know. Bye-bye.'' The receiver is returned to the cradle. Benton comes around the counter to Joel. ''Sorry weren't no mail in there for you,'' he says.

Joel shrugs. ''It's okay. Would it be all right if I came by after school on other days? I know we don't get a lot of stuff but sometimes we do, you know, and I don't want to miss nothing. Maybe win a sweepstakes or something, you never know.''

Benton smiles. ''No, you never know.'' He gestures toward the front door, and Joel knows the visit is over. He walks to the door and Benton follows. "You see who actually come in here to chew the fat for a while?" he says to Fitch.

Fitch says, "Ain't that something?" A magazine page flips over. "Joel Barker, ain't it?"

Benton laughs. "Only the same scrawny little guy we seen walking to and from school for the last umpteen years. Got a bit taller, you think?"

"A bit," says Fitch.

Benton opens the two doors and goes out onto the porch with Joel.

"You just come on over whenever you want to check on the mail," says Benton. "I should've asked you to come on in a lot sooner, back when your little friend Andy Mason was around, but sometimes it takes a good eye-opener to make somebody see what's for what. So you come on anytime, Joel. You hear?"

"Yes," says Joel. *'Ah, Mama, can't you see this? If only you could know!'*

"And here," Benton says, pulling out three sticks of blue-and-red striped candy. "It ain't much, but it's to say you done a fine, brave thing coming to tell us about Wayne Nelson. You should be mighty proud of yourself. This whole town should be."

Joel takes the candy shyly, and nods his thanks. There is a most amazing sensation swelling in his chest. He wishes Benton would offer his hand like Wayne had. This time, Joel would accept it. He would like to know if hands are warm like the voices they go with. But thinking about it is almost as good.

"But," says Benton as Joel starts for the road. "Even though you should keep your head up proud, keep your eyes wide, too. Be careful, Joel."

The man moves back into his store, the screen door still banging softly after the heavy door has been heaved shut.

10

Dave slaps two pieces of bread around a slice of cold turkey and goes out to the front stoop. He sits on the hard stone and works his fingers around the bread crusts, pinching it down like a Ziploc bag. It is a habit he has had since he was very little in West Virginia. A nervous habit, his mother used to swear, and she would take the sandwich away because it was the wrong way to eat. Sometimes he'd go without supper for days on end because he would forget himself and begin pinching down the bread crusts, and away would go the sandwich into the trash. Sometimes along with the peaches or the raisins or the chips, just for good measure, to show him he couldn't do whatever he wanted to do and get away with it. When he got older, he would do it for spite when he was angry with her, and the battle of wills would ensue, with Dave winning even though he would wind up in his room, without supper. He'd made her good and fire-engine mad, and that was sweet victory.

Missy doesn't care how he eats his sandwiches. He could pull the crust off in a string and eat that, then eat the turkey and then tear the bread up into confetti, and it would not bother her in the least. When Dave had first arrived in the summer, Missy had paid him plenty of attention. Cut his arm and made him a real honest-to-God Brother of the Light. But then he became part of her unnoticed environment, no more than a spider on the ceiling or a cat under her rotting, empty storage barn. She still thinks of Patsy, however. Still has her school photograph under a piece of glass on the wall of the kitchen, and Dave has caught her, many times, staring at the picture as if it were of the Lord Himself. In the photo Patsy is a chubby, pleasant-faced girl with curly hair and the barest of smiles. Sometimes Dave wonders what Patsy had been like; if she had been a miniature Missy, or if there had been some normal things about the girl, like a sense of humor, or mischief, or of reality.

Dave begins to chew the pinched-edge sandwich. The bread is very dry, and there is a tang to the turkey, like it's been stored a few days too many. But he eats it anyway, staring into the gathering darkness of the trees that rim the clearing of Missy's cabin. In the house behind him, Missy is talking with Ricky Benshoff. Ricky and his wife and daughter have set up a tent in the backyard. They have decided that in order to survive the growing evil they should band together not only in spirit but in body as well. They have no heat except for a steady fire going in a large aluminum basin. They have been in the backyard since the meeting Sunday night, but they don't come into the cabin unless they are specifically asked by Missy. They don't talk to Dave and Dave doesn't talk to them. Dave thinks it will be a matter of little time before others follow the Benshoffs' lead and the Campbells wind up with a regular Valley Forge in the backyard.

It begins to rain. Not a heavy rain, but a steady misting that softens the sandwich bread and coats the red hairs on his arms like tiny, perfect pearls. He eats most of the sandwich and tosses the rest out into the grass. The rain begins to soak his shirt, and he feels the flannel stick to the bandaged wound on his upper arm. He would like to unwrap it and look at it, but he knows it would not be possible until he is certain to be alone. But there is a true thrill in knowing that the star is gone, and in knowing that the Brothers and Sister don't know.

Dave touches the shirt-sleeve, and traces the outline of the bandage. It stings like the granddaddy of all rug burns, but it is a proud, haughty sting. He wishes his parents could see him now. He wishes they could know that he has already begun to turn their great idea sour. They had been sick and tired of him. He knew because they told him often enough. Sick and tired of his demands and his selfishness and his misbehavior and his temper. They wished he had never been born, they wished he'd go on and do something really terrible so the police could lock him up in the detention home and give them some rest. But Dave was smart. He knew how to keep his head above water. He knew how to punish his parents and yet dance just this side of delinquency. He never was arrested, never even suspended from school. But he was a burr under their hateful saddles, yes sir. He knew enough to know he needed food and shelter, and not from juvenile hall, yet he would make his parents pay for all the love they withheld from their only son.

But then Cousin Patsy, whom Dave had never met, disappeared, leaving Missy Campbell alone in the mountains of Virginia. Dave never knew what correspondence transpired, as he never found letters or overheard any phone calls, but less than a month later, he was bus bound for Staunton, and was picked up by a lady he later found out was Mrs. Phipps, one of Missy's Sisters. En route to Virginia, Dave considered butting out heading north, but he had been given no money, and his parents had threatened that if he didn't make it to Ellison, they would have the FBI after him as quick as a hungry dog after a Japanese beetle. Dave wasn't sure they'd really do it, or if the FBI would take on such a case, but the thought and the lack of money carried enough rationality to bring him safely into the care of his God-loving aunt.

A plan, now that's what he and Joel need. They must be careful and strong, and they must keep ears and eyes open and listen to all that goes on around them. The skin on Dave's arms prickle in excitement. They will do what no one in the Cove has ever dared to do. They will show them all what it is to be your own man. They will catch the sineater.

"Burke." Dave jumps slightly, then looks back over his shoulder. Missy is at the door. "It's raining. Come help the Benshoffs get their wood onto the back porch."

"Just a second," says Dave. Missy pulls back into the house.

Wayne wants to catch the sineater for his own justice. Dave understands that, but it cannot be. Joel needs to catch the sineater to come face-to-face with his own dark heredity. And Dave needs to catch the sineater so he can see, so he can understand, so he can clasp the very essence of human power. If Wayne will not let them help him with his purpose, then Dave and Joel must do it on their own, and do it first. Wayne will not screw it for them.

"Burke," says Missy from in the kitchen.

'Human power,' thinks Dave. *'And maybe even supernatural power at that.'*

"Burke!"

Dave stands and brushes wet crumbs from his lap. He goes into the kitchen, around the table and past his cot, to the back porch. Missy and Ricky are hoisting damp logs through the opened screen doorway and laying them on the rickety slats of the porch floor. Ricky is an old man, nearing seventy, Dave thinks. He has no hair on his head, but the gray brush that cuts a solid line over his eyes is dense enough to be shaved and used as a wig. He is one of the oldest Brothers, with Manny Vicks vying for the honor. Ricky's wife is holding the torn screen door. She is half Ricky's age, not quite forty, and she never speaks unless Ricky or Missy speaks first. Melissa Benshoff's hair is short and straight, and except for some prominent lines across her forehead, she is a dead ringer for her daughter, Jewel. Jewel is twenty-seven, born when Melissa was thirteen, nine months to the day after Melissa and Ricky were married. There is a younger brother Jay, and two younger twin sisters, Molly and Bernadette, but none of them are part of the Brotherhood. They live in homes about the Cove and still attend the Baptist Church, much to Melissa's dismay. Missy has comforted her, saying that soon they will come home to the Lord. Special prayers have been offered at night meetings on the behalf of the Benshoffs' fallen younger children.

Jewel stares at Dave, then looks back at the logs, wrapping her arms about the slick, black wood and slinging it to her mother who slings it to Ricky on the porch. Melissa is distraught over Jewel's spinsterhood. But Missy has promised that if Jewel reaches the age of twenty-eight without a suitable man claiming her as his own, the older woman will make arrangements. Dave thinks the arrangements will include himself, even though he is barely a teenager. A Sister must wed a Brother, and at the moment, he can't think of any other single Brothers.

Dave puts himself into the assembly line, replacing Missy. Jewel passes logs to her mother who gives them to Ricky who gives them to Dave who stacks them on the porch. The rain begins to fall harder, and Jewel whines but continues to pass the wood. Soon it is done, and the three retire to their tent. Dave tries to imagine, for the hundredth time, what it would be like married to a skinny old midwife, and it makes his stomach cramp. But he needn't worry. The star is gone. He has passed from Light into darkness, and it feels good.

"Burke," calls Missy.

Dave goes into the kitchen and closes the solid door behind him.

"There will be more coming like the Benshoffs," his aunt says. She stares at Patsy's portrait and does not look at her nephew. "In the morning I want you to cut an extra load of wood and put it in the old barn. I can't say how many and for how long, but God told me they were coming."

"Get me up early, then," says Dave. "I can't be late for school."

Missy's head leans in, studying the photo. "You aren't going to school anymore."

Dave steps closer. "What do you mean?"

"It's unholy, Burke. They have the sineater's son there. They allow him to go to school, and it is wrong."

"But . . ." Dave grabs for words. He cannot believe what she is telling him. "You let Patsy go to school. Joel Barker was in school when Patsy was there." And he braces himself for the backlash that will follow.

But Missy's voice does not rise. She still does not look at Dave. "I know that. I was weak. I was unseeing. But things have changed. I know what is right and I will make sure that we are returned to the state of obedience where we should be."

"But, Aunt Missy. I got to go to school. It's a law."

Missy looks around from the picture, and her mind is long past school. "Joshua Munsen is joining us at our meeting tomorrow night," she says. Her face is glowing. Frightening. "He has asked for the star. God bless him." She goes into her bedroom and closes the door.

Dave imagines what her face would look like if he smashed her fucking door down with the hammer and said he was going to school anyway.

He can hear her repeat, "God bless him."

11

After supper it begins to rain. Joel, his homework done, goes out the back way to the barn. Before he gets to the barn door, he hears Petrie inside, crying. He peeks in.

Petrie is sitting on the floor near the goats' pens, rubbing her stomach. Beside her, a floor plank is wedged up, there are little containers of makeup by her feet. Joel steps back, he calls out.

"Petrie, you in there?"

He counts to three, then goes into the barn.

Petrie is sweeping makeup back into the hole. She frowns. "What are you doing in here? You got homework."

"Finished. What are you doing here?"

"Got chores. Curry and me, we got chores, brat."

"I don't want to fuss with you, Petrie," says Joel.

"Why? I ain't got no money you can borrow. I ain't got nothing you want. I ain't got nothing nobody wants."

"I don't want nothing. Just to talk to you."

"Really," sneers Petrie. "Like about what?"

"About stuff. Family stuff." Joel shrugs.

"What do you mean, family stuff?"

Joel takes his place on the barrel. There are no chickens clucking about his feet. They are in their coop, heads under wings.

"I bet Mama tells you stuff about our family, you being a girl."

"What do you mean?" asks Petrie.

"I want to talk about Mama. And about Avery."

Petrie blinks. Her hands move like unsteady beetles, scuttling over the wood slat and pushing it down over the sinful makeup. "Oh, no you don't, Joel."

"Yes, I do. I think you know about him. Don't mamas talk more to their girls? Like when they do chores together?"

"Sometimes," says Petrie. It is almost a whisper.

Joel watches Petrie. He wants to talk with her but doesn't want to scare her off. "Have you ever seen Avery?"

"Of course not."

"Has Curry?"

"Of course not."

"Has Mama?"

Petrie swallows. "I . . . of course. Before they got married."

"But he was sineater before they got married."

"I mean before they got married and before he was sineater."

"You see? You know more than me. What else do you know?"

Petrie shivers. "Why do you want to know this stuff?"

Joel shifts on the barrel. "Today I went into the Hardware. I knocked, and Benton Hodge let me come in. It was something, Petrie. Like I was somebody who wouldn't be a harm to be around. Like it was okay that I was in town. After I left, I started thinking about our family. I don't know hardly nothing about it. I felt dumb. I want you to tell me anything you know."

"I know that when Mama was young, when she lived here with Grandma and Grandpa, she fell in love with Avery. He was nineteen and the sineater was an old man named Curtis Terrell. Joel . . ." she pauses. Then she says, "I don't think it's right to talk about this."

"Mama told you. Was that right?"

"But she only told me one time, when I was ten or so. She was real sad then. We was doing the garden. She said I ought to know how we all got started as a family. But after that, she never said no more. Like she was sorry she told me."

"But she did."

Petrie sighs. "Curtis Terrell was the sineater, like I said. He lived alone in the woods, like he was supposed to. No family or nothing. Anyway, he died. He crawled down to the edge of the river and somebody found him, realized who he was. I don't know who found him, but the man covered him up real quick with a coat. Missy's papa Glory Campbell needed to find someone to take Curtis's place. Someone who would eat Curtis's sin so Curtis could finally go into heaven.''

Joel's fingers interlink, almost prayer-like, and he leans over his knees, listening to his sister.

''Avery was an orphan, you know that. Living with that old lady, Sister Sally. Mama said Glory saw Avery to be the best choice. He didn't have no family 'cause his mama died when he was born and his daddy burned himself up for the love of the Lord a long time before. Mama said there was a big group come up to Sister Sally's house, all calling for Avery to come out because God had pointed His finger in his direction. Sister Sally was all excited; Mama said maybe because Avery had been called for God's service, but probably 'cause she was tired of looking after him.''

''Did Avery come out?''

''Mama said he did, but it was out the back way. He run down to Ellison and hid in the church. Glory and his wife and Missy chased after him, and dragged him out even though the Baptist preacher was telling them to leave Avery alone.''

A goat in the pen bleats, and Joel jumps. The fall insects are chirring a soft, discordant chant outside. It is getting late.

''But they took him back, anyway. Said he couldn't run from the eye of the Lord. Said it was ordained, and he must accept what was given him.''

''What did Mama do?''

''I guess she couldn't do nothing. She didn't say she did anything. How could she, what with everybody else saying what was right?''

''I don't know.''

''And maybe she knew it was right, too, even though she loved him.''

''Maybe.''

''So they made him eat Curtis's sin. Spread out bread and apples on the sineater's chest and made Avery eat it while they watched. Then when he was finished, they all turned toward the wall, 'cause nobody could ever look at him again.''

''How did Mama know about what food he ate?''

"She had to go watch, Joel. She had to watch him eat the food, then turn away when it was over, like everybody else."

Petrie hesitates, touches her stomach. It seems as if she's going to cry again.

"They got married, anyway," prods Joel.

Petrie nods. "Mama said Avery left her notes in the barn, asking her to marry him. He said it didn't matter if she couldn't look at him, 'cause he could at least look at her. And even if he had to spend most of his time alone in the woods, at least he would know he had a wife and then it wouldn't be so lonely."

"That was before he got so much sin and went insane."

"What?"

Lelia calls suddenly from the back of the cabin. Both Joel and Petrie start, and stare at each other with eyes wide.

"What is it, Mama?" Petrie shouts.

"It's late, that's what! Come on in! And where's Joel?"

Petrie looks at her brother. "I'll find him, Mama."

"Got to hang laundry in the pantry so it'll dry. Hurry up!"

Joel and Petrie wait, and then Petrie stands up. "Got to hang laundry."

"But I want to ask you . . ."

"Not now, Joel. Maybe later. Maybe never. This was stupid. We ain't supposed to talk about it."

"How about later, then? When I'm in my room. You could come in when Mama's gone to sewing in her room, and we could talk for just a minute or two. Please?"

"I don't know. What about Curry?"

"He's taking baskets down tonight."

"I don't know. It don't matter none, anyway. All that stuff is a long time ago. It's all different now. We're born. Mama's old. And Avery, well, he's been sineater for a long time. You know what that means. Knowing any more won't change nothing."

"Just a little more, Petrie, please?"

"I just don't know! So shut up and let me do my chores, you little moron!" And she flees the barn, through the spattering rain.

As Joel jumps from the barrel and steps outside, he feels eyes from the woods on his back, and the hair on his neck stands straight in the wind which carries the laugh of the damned.

"Haaaaaaaa. Haaaaaaaaaaaaaaaaaaa."

12

Joel checks Benton's hardware store for any mail the next few days, and always get the same message from Benton. "I don't think so. But you can look."

Dave is his usual obnoxious self at school, insisting that Joel meet him in the bathroom at various times so the two of them can check on the progress of his healing scab. It remains a scab, however, much to Dave's frustration.

Friday after school, Dave catches Joel in the front school parking lot and makes his heavy demand.

"Hey, dude," the red-haired boy says, slapping Joel vigorously on the shoulder. "So you're going into the Hardware now, looking for mail. You're getting pretty brave in your old age, ain't you?"

Joel shrugs. "I guess."

"Then try this one on for size. Come to my cabin tonight. There's another meeting. A big deal, this time."

"That ain't brave. That's stupid. Besides, according to you, all them meetings is big deals."

"This is different, really. Important. Missy's gonna rewrite a God rule."

"What do you mean?"

"I ain't telling. Unless you promise to come."

"No," says Joel. "I ain't got no reason to come. You're all both-

183

ered about Avery, Wayne's all bothered about Avery. I ain't got nothing to do with it.''

"Listen, stupid!'' shouts Dave. "You know I ain't even supposed to be coming to school no more since you go? Missy told me I couldn't. But I sneak out, anyway. She don't know. I do it so I can see you and keep you informed. You got to know what's happening, Joel!''

Joel turns and walks toward the road.

Dave chases after Joel, a looseleaf page, stuck carelessly in the front of his math book, flapping crazily.

"What do you mean, you ain't got nothing to do with it, Joel? You and me, we's a team! We's in this together!''

"I ain't got nothing to do with it,'' repeats Joel, still walking.

"Fuck you, man! And you're the kid with no friends! No wonder!''

"Stop it, Dave,'' says Joel, turning around. Dave's statement stings, and Joel wants to know exactly what Dave is driving at.

"You hear me, asshole. You don't come tonight, you can forget about being friends. You'll be back on your own.'' Dave glowers, the sunlight sparkling on his brows and eyelashes.

But before Joel can say any more, there is an adult voice piercing the air, and a flurry of movement behind Dave. Joel looks over the older boy's shoulder. Mrs. Grant is coming after them, arms pumping.

"Boys!''

Dave pivots about. "What the hell ... ?''

"Boys!'' Mrs. Grant reaches them and skids to a stop, her hands finding her hips and clutching them like they were two old ski poles. "School is out. What are you doing?''

Joel looks at Dave, then back at Mrs. Grant. "We're talking,'' he says.

"We're talking,'' repeats Dave. "What's the big problem?''

"There seem to be a lot of problems where you are concerned, Mr. Campbell. And I don't want to hear you speak disrespectfully to a teacher again.''

Dave draws up. Joel can feel the anger radiating from him in thick waves. "Why you on my case? I ain't never done nothing.''

Mrs. Grant licks her lips and her cheek muscles flinch. She leans in to Dave, one hand rising from her hip and forming a claw of accusation. "You are constantly at the base of problems. And I won't have you corrupting one of my students. Joel Barker is not your type of person, Mr. Campbell. You will have nothing to do with him, you hear me? You will leave him alone."

"You can't tell me who to talk to. We ain't even on school property no more!"

"Joel is my student whether he is on the school property or not. And you will leave him alone, you understand?"

Dave's mouth works in silent rage. His eyes glare. Joel thinks he will cuss Mrs. Grant out, but he does not. He doesn't seem able to get beyond a stare-down.

And then Mrs. Grant turns to Joel. "Let me know if he bothers you, Joel. He's a bad influence. You want nothing to do with him." She looks back at Dave then, and crosses her arms, waiting for Dave to leave.

Dave stares. He does not blink. Joel feels his own eyelids refusing to close in fear he will miss something. His stomach makes little flip-flops, bringing the taste of the chicken lunch back into his mouth.

Mrs. Grant stares. Dave stares. And then, Dave's eyelids give, and he blinks. He glances at Joel, then spins on his heel and heads off down the road. Joel can see a small smile of relief cross Mrs. Grant's face. She stands with Joel as if she is his bodyguard.

But when he is yards away, Dave makes his point, over his shoulder, striding down the road. "Fonda Clark died, Joel! She's been dead two days! Missy's gonna get rid of her sin tonight!"

"Get on with you, Burke Campbell!" shouts Mrs. Grant.

"You can bet Avery will try to come to the wake, to do his duty! You gotta be there with me!"

"Get on!" Mrs. Grant cries.

"You got to stick with me, Joel! You got to come tonight!" And then Dave is turned around again, his legs taking him down Route 536 in long steps, heading for West Path and home.

Mrs. Grant sighs. Joel does not want to look at her. Her concern is unsettling. He does not want to go to Dave's cabin, but he feels sickened at the thought of losing his only friend. Again. He does not know how Mrs. Grant's interest fits into all of this.

"Now, then," says Mrs. Grant, pleased with herself. "You go on home, Joel. That boy won't be doing anything he wants while I have any say about it. Go on.''

Joel looks at her, then back down the road at Dave's vanishing figure.

''Go on,'' says Mrs. Grant.

Joel goes.

13

There is the beginning of fog on the road, and rolling across the Hardware's porch, coming up from the lowland behind the eastern rows of stores on Route 536. Joel glances around the porch at the dog pen, and sees the hounds looking out at the approaching white. The parking lot of the grocery next door is swirled with wet mist, and beyond that, the work lot of the Exxon is vanished from view. Joel hopes it is a pocket that will move on. Perhaps Dave will beat the fog home. But if it is not a small cloud, Joel will have to go up the Path in it. Fog can double travel time, and even though it is still daylight, it makes the day seem like night, and makes him think about the things that travel in the night.

He knocks on the Hardware door. Benton opens it after a moment, and waves Joel inside.

"You're in luck this time, Joel," says Benton, leading the way to the counter. "There's a letter for you. Maybe it's from a secret admirer."

Joel anxiously picks up the envelope, immediately recognizing the pencil script. He knows Benton is curious, and he's been nice enough to have his curiosity answered. "It's from Andy Mason," says Joel. "Remember him?"

"Of course I do. Reverend Mason's boy. You two used to feed my dogs."

"You knew about that?"

Benton chuckles. "My dogs mean a lot to me. And anybody messing with them drives me crazy. But I watched you boys out there a number of times. You were always gentle, always easy with Creeper. I don't know why those dogs like that old candy, I don't believe they even have the taste buds for it, but it never was no harm done." Benton leans against the counter. "You got a dog, Joel?"

"What, at home? No, but I got goats. They're kinda like dogs. They follow me around when they ain't penned up."

"Goats," repeats Benton. "You best be getting home to read your letter."

"Yeah. Thanks." The letter goes into the spelling book, beneath the cover flap.

Joel goes to the front door, pausing to glance out of the small dirty window at the rolling fog. He zips his jacket up to his neck, wishing he had worn a flannel shirt instead of the old cotton one he has on. He wishes, too, that Benton would invite him to stay long enough to see if the fog will move on. But he cannot ask something like that. So he says, "See you later," and pushes out the door to the porch. Coming up to the store from the road is Mr. Ringgold, making a rare appearance, and the man does not take notice of Joel at all. Joel steps to the side to let the man enter, and then moves off the side of the porch.

He shivers in the dampness, and tucks his fingers deep into the pockets of his coat.

"Creeper?" he calls in the direction of the pen. The frame of the fenced area is visible, but everything else around it and inside it are softened into gray oblivion. Joel then remembers the quarter he found at school, the one deep inside his jeans pockets. He wonders if Benton would mind him sharing some chocolate with the dogs after all this time.

Joel hops back onto the porch and goes inside. Benton is to the rear of the store, talking with Mr. Ringgold. Joel takes a Hershey bar from the rack near the jar of candy sticks.

"How much are the Hershey bars?" he calls.

"I thought you were gone. They're thirty cents."

"Oh," says Joel. He puts the candy back, and picks up a bite-size Tootsie Roll. "How about the Tootsie Rolls?"

"Two for seven cents."

"Can I take . . ." Joel pauses, working the math in his head. "Can I take six and just leave the quarter beside the cash register?"

"What? Yes, sure, Joel, go ahead."

"Great," Joel says to himself. He unwraps one piece of chocolate and sticks it into his mouth. His tongue swirls it around, tracing the smooth texture, before his teeth crush down. The taste is glorious; a flavor of summer and goofy times and Andy. The rest of the pieces go into his pocket, and he goes back to the door.

As he touches the knob, his attention is drawn to the left. On the floor between the wall and the first row of shelves stands the display of Curry's baskets and hampers. It is strange seeing them like this, all in a row with little orange tags dangling from the handles. There are dried flowers in some of the smaller ones. In one larger hamper is a folded gingham cloth, making it look like it is ready for a picnic. Joel is impressed, and suddenly proud of his brother's talent. The younger Barker has always thought the work was good, and has always wondered what it would be like to make useful creations from useless little trees in the woods, but now he feels a true pride. He wonders what the tourists say when they come into the store and see Curry's baskets. He wonders if they marvel and ogle; if the wives beg the husbands to go ahead and spend the extra it costs so they can have something so lovely in their home.

Joel smiles. He goes outside.

There are patches of sunlight in the fog now, streaking the wet white with orange and pink. The cloudy mass continues to roll across the road and up into the mountain, a large yet insubstantial monster lumbering after itself. It makes Joel think of the old song, "The bear went over the mountain, the bear went over the mountain." He grins at the thought. Such a stupid song, and he had loved it in kindergarten.

Joel jumps from the side of the porch and walks to the dog pen. Wide strands of fog still move through the fencing, and it is hard to see much except the frame and the wide doghouse in the center of the pen. He stops at the gate and touches the Yale lock that dangles on the latch. "Creeper? Hey, you, I got something for you!" There is no movement; no sound.

Joel frowns. The fog continues to pour through the chain links of the pen, the cloudy strands thinner with each passing moment. *'He's taken them home,'* Joel thinks. *'Benton has taken the dogs home for the weekend for some reason. Maybe to the vet. Maybe they had to get shots.'*

Joel drops his spelling book onto the ground, and pulls another Tootsie Roll from his pocket, unwraps it, and sticks it into his mouth.

'But weren't they here just before I went into the store the first time?'

Joel's teeth crunch down; the dark, sweet flavor coats his tongue. He looks up at the closed window over the pen. He shivers in the fog. For some reason, he remembers Benton's comment not long ago. "Be careful, Joel."

"Creeper?" Joel tries again.

And again, nothing. Joel swallows the candy. He moves around the side of the pen, trying to see inside the dark maw of the doghouse. It is too dark.

"Hey, Creeper, you asleep?"

The last of the thick fog strands clears out of the pen. Nothing but tiny puffs of mist follow after. The air is clear now, and the sun finds the pen, the doghouse, and Joel. The sun even finds two sluggish flies, crazy with the lateness of the year, bumping into the front of the doghouse, looping downward and bumping into the ground, flying to the left and bumping into the large plastic container in which Benton stores his dog food, flying over the top to the space between the container and the wall of the store.

Joel walks around the fence to the back and looks into the small space behind the container.

The dizzy, late-year flies thump into Creeper and the two other hounds.

The chocolate candy rockets upward in Joel's throat, driven by an eruption of burning bile. Joel's mouth croaks open, and he clutches the fencing with one hand, and his mouth in the other. There is a scream behind the hand, silenced by horror.

There is a scream behind Creeper's lolling tongue, silenced by the chain that has strangled him, and by the fleshy, wet-slick coils of ropy intestines that have fallen from his slit belly and join the chain in a tangle about the dog's matted neck. The flies find the entrails, and land delicately, then proceed to take opposite pathways along the guts, one feeling its way toward the neck, the other moving to the blood-crusted opening of the belly. Another fly, buzzing through a link beside Joel, moves to the open eyes of the dog, and trots happily over the drying cornea.

Joel spits chocolate into the leaves at his feet. He grasps for his mouth again, and looks back into the pen. Behind Creeper are the other two hounds, each dead from a slit throat. The blood in which they lie is black on the ground, and is sprinkled with wind-churned dirt flakes. Taped to the side of the plastic dog food bin is a piece of notebook paper. The words are legible through the fence.

"HE WHO COMMUNES WITH THE FORBIDDEN WILL REAP THE HARVEST OF THE UNFORGIVEN. SEE CLEARLY AND BE SAVED!"

A fly thwacks the note, making a heavy sound like a spitball on a chalkboard, then returns to the pathetic opening of Creeper's abdomen. It crawls inside and disappears.

And Joel runs away from that place, his hands shaking around his schoolbook, his eyes blurred with tears, and he does not go tell Benton, because Joel is the sineater's son.

Joel is the forbidden.

14

At 5:10 P.M., Wayne decides that he will go to Missy's meeting later tonight. Wayne's mother has been after him all week, telling him about the gathering in Missy's backyard, and how it is a sign of the coming conflict. She left Wayne's apartment fifteen minutes earlier, and Wayne has spent the previous moments alone, chewing aspirin and musing angrily over the letter sent by the state police.

It is actually a short note. A response to the bit of wire sent to Richmond in hopes there was something, anything, to help Wayne know who set the bomb. The wire was a small remnant that had lodged in his torn shirt during the explosion, one the doctor insisted on discarding but which Candace Stone had wanted as some sort of morbid souvenir.

The note read, ''Dear Mr. Nelson,

I'm not supposed to respond to requests from private citizens with personal grievances, but it has been a slow day and as long as the supervisor doesn't know, I figure what the hell. I'm not using my real name for reasons I'm sure you now understand.

As to your wire, there's little I can tell. This could have come from a handmade grenade, for which parts are easily obtainable. Of course, we can't find prints on something which has been blasted, so I can't help you there, either. You should go to your local sheriff's department. Was there personal injury involved here? Of course, me asking this is rhetorical, because I don't expect you to write back and get me into trouble. But if you were hurt, please follow through on your local channels. I'd hate to think you guys out in the mountains are letting the criminal have his day. I grew up in Hot Springs.

Sorry to be of little help.

Richard Shaft Roundtree.''

Wayne slides the letter back under a copy of POPULAR ME-CHANICS and sits straight on the kitchen chair. It isn't that he really expected to find out great details about the explosion, but at least there could have been something.

Something.

Richard Shaft Roundtree suggested that he follow through. There is no doubt he will do just that.

He stands from the chair, wrapping his fingers about the stub of his left arm. The throbbing is less intense than it has been, although the phantom pain of the missing hand and wrist and the itching come without warning. He hates to admit, even to himself, that at the moment he has seven aspirins in his system. They make his head ring and buzz like an electric wire without insulation. When he shakes his head, he can play a rhythm with the buzzing.

Wayne pours a drink of vodka from the cabinet over the small refrigerator. He mixes nothing with it this time, it is too much trouble. He wonders if aspirin and vodka will make a toxic combination. How could he know? He shakes his head at his ignorance and the buzzing jingles a monotonic tune. How could he know anything, living in this backwater community for so long? He is suddenly ashamed and angry about his lack of knowledge. He hurls the nearly empty glass across the room and it hits the window. Superman falls to the floor and a large crack flowers on the window glass. How could he have been so stupid to have stayed here this long? If he had gone to Richmond a couple of years earlier, how much more worldly would he have been? At least he'd be a state policeman by now. At least he'd have his goddamned hand.

He goes to the window and scoops the broken glass from the floor. He needs to find Avery Barker, to confront him. The thought actually scares him, even though his conscious mind doesn't want to admit it. But if he doesn't get on with it, if he doesn't see justice through to its end, then the Missys and the Candaces will turn it to their twisted advantage.

Candace had said that tonight there was a soul to send to heaven; there was sin to be rid of. And without the aid of the sineater. It was not without a certain pious glee that she told Wayne that the sineater would be angry, and might feel betrayed. It was as though his mother was hoping Avery would come to the meeting so the Brotherhood could confront him in all his evil. *'Without looking at him, of course,'* Wayne thinks with a dark laugh. *'Perhaps it will be like the old mythology. They will slay the creature by gazing in the shining surface of a shield.'*

"You'll turn to stone if you ain't careful, Mama," Wayne says to the empty room.

The meeting begins at seven-thirty, according to Candace Stone. She wanted him to know. Hoping he'd join the ranks, he is certain. Supposedly the Benshoff daughter is without a husband, and Missy has her eyes open for possible candidates. Wayne shakes his head. It rings. He puts the broken glass on the kitchen table and goes into the bedroom to find his shoes. They are, naturally, under the bed, just far enough away to prevent Wayne from reaching them without dragging his head and shoulders up beneath the springs. He scoots carefully, but when his left shoulder hits the bed frame, a shock of hot pain goes down to his stump. He curses, but grabs the shoes and comes out panting.

His case is a single situation, a lone violation. It will require lone retribution. He will not allow anyone to become involved. He will see it through. He sits on the bed. The buzzing of the aspirin is still in his head, but the pain in the missing hand is beginning to grow again. This would be a hell of a time to live in Richmond, where you could get some real drugs. Wayne bets that Mr. Richard Shaft Roundtree can get his hands on drugs whenever he needs them. Fuck the fact that he used to be a good old country boy.

He doesn't want to go out. He doesn't want to walk past his Honda, silent and still in the garage. He doesn't want to sneak up to Missy's cabin and eavesdrop on the howling of her group. But most of all, he doesn't want to chase down Avery Barker and see the man who ruined his life. He wants to stay in the garage apartment and die.

The pain is greater now. He pulls the stump close to his body; he draws it up under his right arm pit. It warms it, but doesn't stop the pain. "God," he says. He knows it is going to be bad. It always becomes bad. "God, don't let it happen, let it stop just this once. Just this once." But it does not. Wayne lays on his back, his stump tucked under his arm, and tries to ride it out. How could he have thought he could go out? It is time to die now. "Now, God, let me die!" He writhes about on the unmade covers, groaning and sweating. Chills sting every inch of flesh on his body. There is nothing but pain now. Pain like a chain saw on his wrist, torturous and relentless and profound.

He hears the heater click on in the living room. He pulls his legs up and tries holding his breath. Then he screams, not caring how loud he is, and he screams again, then again. To hell with bravery. He does not have to be brave here. The bed springs squeak with his rolling, but he can only feel them beneath his cries.

And it begins to slow. Wayne bites his lip, thinking it is a trick. But the agony is less severe now, the itching not as hot. He stops struggling, and holds still on the bed. He can hear the buzzing of his brain again. He sighs, carefully. And he sits up on the mattress.

"Of course I'm going out," he says. "A man did this to me. I can't let it go." He stands shakily, and moves into the living room. He fixes a small meal of canned creamed corn and chili, and watches the clock, giving himself the pep talk he'll need when he dons his coat and heads for the steps outside the apartment door.

15

Lelia cannot understand why Joel won't eat more than two tiny carrot slices, but he tells her he isn't feeling well and wants to stay in his room and go to bed. She agrees reluctantly, touching his head for possible temperature, then waving him on. Curry is out in search of vines in the last hour of light, and Petrie sits on her sofa, mending one of her mother's plain blouses.

In his room, Joel presses the door shut and falls onto his cot. He cannot get the image of Creeper out of his mind. The glassy eyes, the ultimate degredation of his slit bowels and his tangled intestines. *'Why?'* he thinks, and he almost cries out. He has no answers. But he knows it has to do with him. He vows he will never set foot in the hardware store again. Not only did he bring this horror on Benton, but maybe Benton will think Joel actually did it himself. Maybe more will happen, maybe something worse.

Avery is insane. Joel thought he could wash his hands of his father. But he cannot. These bad things Avery has done are part of Joel as well.

He takes the letter from his pocket and looks at it. Nothing Andy can say could cheer him now. Nothing will be funny. But he opens it anyway.

"Dear Joel,

Sorry it has been so long since I wrote you last. How do you like this letter? I'm doing it on the computer. It gets printed out on a machine. We have computers at school and everybody gets to take six weeks of it. School's kinda neat now that I'm used to it.

Anyway, I'm doing the letter hear instead of at home because daddy won't even want me writing you any more. He's gotten weird. I mean bad wierd not good wierd like a funny person.

I'm getting a envelop from my teacher Miss Petersen. Then I can mail this from here and Daddy won't know about it. I brought a stamp to school today.

Daddy stopped preaching. Mama got a job at social services giving out food stamps to poor people. I don't mean poor like you. You know what I mean. Daddy is going to see a doctor every week, well two times a week because mama says he is having a lot of stress. She says he needs time off. He won't talk to me much. He walks around a lot. Sometimes he talks about something that he says he knew about but didn't stop. Sometimes he just says, "It's my fault." And sometimes he uses cuss words. Like fuck and stuff. I hope Miss Petersen doesn't want to look this letter over before I mail it.

If you want to write to me anymore, send it to school, not to my house. Daddy would hit the roof. Send it to the address at the bottom of this letter.

School is okay. I'm okay. I miss you and the rock. I bet it is cold there now. Bet the river is really high, too.

Write to me, okay?

Your frend,

Andy.''

Joel rereads the letter and then puts it under his cot. Andy's father cussing? He cannot imagine it. It is true that Reverend Mason did not like Andy and Joel playing together; it is true that Reverend Mason and Missy Campbell get along, and that he thought mountain customs were fine because of their traditional value. But why does Andy keep saying his father refused to talk about Ellison and Beacon Cove? Why did he stop preaching? Andy used to say his father said there was no calling finer than that of a reverend, and that his love was his family, his God, and his calling.

There is a tapping on the bedroom door. Petrie's muffled voice says, "Joel?"

"What?"

"Can I come in?"

"Why?"

There is a pause. When Petrie speaks, Joel can hear the beginning of aggravation. "I thought you wanted to talk. Do you want to talk or not?"

Joel almost says, "Yeah, but that was Monday, this is Friday," because he really doesn't want to talk, he wants to go to sleep and try to forget the horrid image of Creeper and the other dogs and the memory of Wayne bleeding on the path in front of the mail bucket. But he says, "Yeah, I guess."

Petrie pushes the door open, glances over her shoulder toward the kitchen, and comes softly inside.

Joel rolls back against the wall at the head of the cot. "What you got to tell me?"

Petrie scowls slightly, but she sits on Curry's bed and says, "Why did you bring up all this stuff in the first place? What difference does it make?"

"You mean about Avery?"

"Of course I do. Why do you want to know?"

"Because I want to know."

"Because you think it was him what tried to kill Wayne Nelson."

"Yeah."

"You aren't the only one, you know. Curry says he heard that a lot of Missy Campbell's people say he did it, too."

Joel shrugs.

"I think he did it."

Joel looks at her, hard.

"But that's not the only thing he's done, Joel. I know about something else, too."

Joel's throat clenches. *'I know about something else, I know about something else, too, Petrie!'*

Petrie hesitates. She looks around the room, her eyes pinched and full of an obvious agony. She shakes her foot, and then it stops. "You tell me why you think so, Joel. You tell me first."

"What about Mama? What if she comes in and finds us talking?"

"She's not in the house. She wanted to finish killing them chickens before her hands started hurting in the cold. She wants them down so we can pluck them in the morning."

"And Curry?"

"He's still out, getting wood."

"I was at Benton's today," says Joel. "The hardware store, I mean. Do you know I've even gone inside the store? Petrie, you wouldn't believe what it's like in there."

Petrie's hands move to each other and clasp together. "You've gone inside a store? Joel, don't you know how wrong that is?"

"It's like good magic. Candy and food and tools like you never seen before. Like a real magic place."

"Don't talk about magic. It's a sin."

"You want to talk about this? It's a sin, too, don't you think?"

Petrie massages her fingers. She sighs. "I want to talk."

"I seen something terrible today. I seen what can happen when somebody has something to do with a Barker."

"Not counting Wayne."

"Not counting Wayne."

"Tell me."

"Lots of blood," says Joel. He twists his back for a more comfortable position and cannot find it. "I seen Benton's dogs all cut up and bleeding and . . ." Joel feels tears inside his head. "And dead," he finishes. "I think Avery killed them. He put a note on the pen. It was a warning. I knew he was the sineater, Petrie. I heard he was crazy with too much sin. But I didn't know what that meant. Until now."

Petrie says, "I didn't, either."

"He wants people to be afraid of us. He wants everyone to stay away."

"I know."

Joel leans forward. He wraps himself tightly with his arms. "What do you know about?"

"I have . . . a friend. He came to visit me. And he took off his boots for a few minutes. Later on, when he put them on again, they were full of glass."

"Who?"

"Doesn't matter, Joel. I'm just telling. That's all." Petrie's voice rises, and it is trembling.

"No," says Joel. "It don't matter." He knows it is the fat boyfriend. The fat boyfriend has been hurt by Avery, too.

"He hasn't come back to see me no more. I don't know if he's hurt bad or not. But it was awful, Joel. It was so awful.'' She looks at her brother, and he feels that she is pleading with him, as if he can do something to make the scary things stop happening. Joel wants to say he can make them stop, wants to tell her about Dave's plans and about Wayne's, but he cannot. He isn't sure that even if he tried, the words would form in his mouth. And so he says, ''I know.''

There is silence for a moment. Joel looks at his sister while she looks at the floor. Then Petrie says, ''I know where there is a picture of Avery.''

Joel's mouth flies open. There is a hot, fiery explosion in his chest that shakes his whole body. ''No, Petrie.''

She nods. ''I put clothes away in Mama's room, in her dresser. In the bottom of the drawers is where the towels go. Way in the back is a stack of photographs. I seen some of them. There ain't many, mostly Mama when she was little and Grandpa all around the cabin. But at the bottom of the stack is a picture turned upside down. You know I can't read, but I know my letters. I know how most of them sound, since Mama taught me. And there's writing on the back of this picture. It says, ''Avery Barker. Sept. 4, 1964.'' The ink looks real old.''

''When were Avery and Mama married?''

''October 5, 1966. Avery was twenty-two. Mama was seventeen.''

''And when,'' Joel takes a breath. ''When did Avery become the sineater?''

''I don't know exactly. I don't know how long it was after he was sineater that he and Mama got married.''

''So that picture could be of Avery before he was sineater.''

''Or it could be from after he became sineater,'' says Petrie.

Sister and brother stare at each other.

Then Joel asks what he has to ask. ''Have you looked at the picture, Petrie?''

''No.''

''So why did you tell me? What good will it do to know there is a picture of Avery?''

''I don't know,'' she says.

Joel digs his fingernails into his knees.

"I just thought you might want to know. You might want to look."

Joel glances up at his sister. "Why? If it is a picture of Avery after he became sineater, I'd lose my mind. I'd die. You know what would happen."

"I wonder if the person who took the picture died?"

Joel does not answer. Knowing there is a picture of Avery in the house makes him feel sick to his stomach. It makes him feel unsafe in his house, even though his father is not actually there. Yet, there is an intrigue, an appeal of morbid terror that has Joel already imagining himself in his mother's room, digging in the bottom drawer, lifting the old photograph and beginning to turn it over.

"Do you want to get it?"

Joel flinches from his thoughts. "Why?"

"I don't know. We could burn it. Something."

Joel considers this. It is probably the best thing to do. But could he really touch it? What if it accidentally turned over, and he came face-to-face with the sineater?

"What do you think?" asks Petrie.

"No," says Joel aloud.

"No what?" asks Petrie. "You don't want to burn it?"

"No," says Joel. He will get the picture and somehow give it to Wayne. Joel wants nothing to do with it, and maybe Wayne can use it. Wayne will have to decide himself if he will look at it or not. It won't be Joel's problem then, it will be the mailman's.

"Joel?"

It will be out of the house. It will be gone.

Petrie stands from Curry's cot. She touches the doorknob and then looks back at Joel. "I knew it would be dumb to talk to you. I thought maybe you could do something. I thought since you'd spent a lot of time in Ellison, out where real people are, you might know something, or you might know what to do. Boy, was I dumb."

Joel grits his teeth behind a placid face. He can't tell Petrie any of what he has been thinking. It might be dangerous if she knew what was going on. Because knowing would involve her, and he does not want that.

"Sorry," he manages.

"Bastard," she hisses, and slams through the door, leaving him alone. He wonders where she heard that word. Probably from the fat boyfriend. Joel bets the fat boyfriend said more than that when he stepped onto the mess of glass inside his fat boots.

Joel stands and listens through the closed door. Curry is still out, and if the older brother took a lantern, he will be out for perhaps another hour. Lelia is still outside, but might be in at any time. Petrie has gone out to the front porch, because the kitchen door has slammed, and he can hear her talking to herself.

He has to get the picture, and like it or not, he has to take it to Wayne tonight.

Joel opens his door and looks to the right and left. The cabin is quiet; the door to his mother's bedroom on the right is closed. It is always closed. The nausea in his stomach returns, but he tries to picture Wayne's face in his mind. He forces himself to remember the warmth of Benton's welcome, the confident concern in the two men's faces. The vision of the dogs comes, but he squeezes it out again. He will not look at that now. He slips through his door and stops in front of his mother's room.

"God," he whispers, surprised at his own need to pray, because it has been his mother who prays for the family. Joel cannot think of a time when he himself has ever talked to the Lord. "Let me get the picture. Don't let nobody catch me. And don't let me see what's on the other side of it." Joel opens his mother's door and wiggles inside.

The room is dark, with outlines of simple furniture about the log walls. Joel was told that he was born in this room, and he has not set foot inside it since. It is an alien place, smelling differently than the rest of the cabin. The atmosphere is heavy with the private things women are all about, and heavy with a sense of caution, of whispers, of thoughts unspoken and of tiptoes and closed eyes.

"God," Joel says again. But he cannot speak more, because his eyes are adjusting, and he can see clearly the large dresser with the five drawers. His gaze locks on the bottom drawer. His throat is tight and hard, dry and beyond speech. He listens for noises outside the bedroom, but cannot hear any.

'Get the picture,' he tells himself. *'No big deal.'* He presses the door shut behind him and takes several steps into the room. Suddenly his legs feel vulnerable and he pulls them together. It is as if there

is something lurking beneath his mother's bed, something that would shoot out and grab his ankles and pull him to his death. Something like a monster or a troll, as in those fairy-tale books in the school library. Or something like a deranged man with long fingers and claw nails.

'Jesus, guard me,' he thinks. He steps toward the dresser. It looks as though it is miles away. *'Jesus loves the little children, all the children of the world.'* He moves closer. There are strange things on the dresser top. Funny things that would seem more at home on Benton's Hardware shelf. Bottles, jars, little boxes.

Three feet from the dresser, Joel hears a creaking in the hall behind him. He stops short, not turning, but pulling his head down as far as it will go onto his chest and squeezing his eyes shut. *'Red and yellow, black and white, they are precious in his sight . . .'* He hears the pantry door open and footsteps move in. *'Let it be Petrie,'* Joel prays, sweat prickling the space between his chin and his chest. *'Let it be Petrie!'*

He listens. Jars rattle, a wooden box scrapes the bare floor. Then the footsteps go back into the hall and away, heading for the kitchen. Just at the edge of audibility, Joel hears the person's throat clear with a soft grumble. It is indeed Petrie.

Joel moves to the dresser and bends down. He slides his fingers into the carved indentions and pulls out the drawer. His hands move among the towels, carefully pushing them aside, and he sees the white stack of photos in the back. The top ones are slid over, revealing a single large photograph, face-down in the drawer. In the dark, Joel cannot read the writing on the back, but he know what it says.

Blackness suddenly swims over Joel's field of vision, and he flattens his palms against the wood floor to keep from toppling over. He sees nothing, but feels his own body threatening to give way beneath him. His arms tense with the threat. And then the crack of light in his mind pulls open, and the fissure of his imagination widens, more rapidly now than ever before. "Is he tall?" Dave asks from somewhere in Joel's mind. "Yes," Joel whispers. "Oh, yes!" The crack opens more, and Joel sees the sineater's boots, the large, threatening curve of taut and angry legs, the large torso, the shoulders, broad and thick and hardened, with arms and hands spread outward, clawed and ready to swipe the face off an intrusive boy. Joel tries to close his mind's eye but it will not shut. He sees a neck, large and dark, sweaty and pulsing with rage. A chin, hair on it dense and spiked like the vicious thorns of a swordbrush tree. A mouth snarled with crazed anger. Deformed cheeks of leather, flat flaring nose, and eyes . . .

Joel throws his body back and he cracks his head on the floor. The vision shatters and vanishes. Stars take the place of the vision, and they spin about the dim sight of the bedroom ceiling.

Joel regains his balance and reaches into the drawer. His fingers touch the old photo and cringe at the feeling. It is slick and cool, and then sensation makes every nerve in his body crawl. His nails work beneath the side and the picture comes free.

Holding the photo at arm's length, he pulls it out. He stands and turns toward the door, then on a thought, slips it beneath his shirt. His skin recoils but he moves forward, keeping it close. He grasps the doorknob and gives it a tug. The door opens.

Lelia is standing in the hall, looking at him.

"What are you doing in there, Joel?"

Joel holds his arms close around him, pressing the foul picture to his flesh.

"I heard a mouse, Mama," he says. "It ran through the hall and into your room."

Lelia frowns. "Ain't no mice in this house. Not since Curry brung that set of traps and put them up under the corners."

"Cat musta brought it in, then. Stupid cat always dragging in things."

"Cat kills things."

"Not this one, Mama. Cat was playing with it, I bet."

Lelia moves past Joel and into her room. She looks about as if she thinks something might be moved around or missing. The feeling that his mother does not trust him is surprising and uncomfortable. "You catch that mouse, Joel?"

"No, Mama."

"Hmmmm," says Lelia. She turns around a few more times, then looks at her son. "Best get Curry to put up another trap in here, then. Don't want nothing in here what don't belong."

Joel nods, knowing it's not mice his mother wants to keep out.

16

Inside his room, Joel pulls the photo from beneath his shirt. He puts it facedown on the cot and rubs his stomach to make the sting of horror go away.

Beneath the cot is a stack of old school papers, good ones, ones with A's and B's that Joel didn't want to throw away. He pulls out some of them and looks them over. One is a social studies test on Virginia history, from two years ago, back in the fourth grade. Another is a math homework assignment on decimals. Joel wishes his family had some clear tape like they use at school, but if it is not a necessity and Curry's money can't buy it through the roundabout grapevine of the ladies of the Cove, the Barkers don't have it. Joel gets on his knees beside the cot and digs deeper. He digs quickly through the dust and webs, thinking that the power of the crazed sineater will make the picture hop off his bed and onto his neck and bite him to death.

Coughing, Joel emerges from beneath the cot with three old shoestrings. He ties them end to end, making one long string. He gathers up the school papers, and then looks back at the picture. For the first time, he lets himself see it clearly. It reads, ''Avery Warren Barker. Sept. 4, 1966.'' Joel knows the handwriting is his mother's. Hurrying, Joel wraps the school papers about the picture and secures them with the string. Then he puts the picture under Curry's cot and slides his shoes in front of it so he won't have to see it.

Then pencil and fresh paper in hand, he writes a note to Andy.

"Dear Andy,

Got your letter. I'm going to send this to your school so there won't be no trouble. There's lots of trouble here, though. I feel wierd writing about it. Like it might makes things worse. You remember the mailman Wayne Nelson? He got his hand blown off not long ago. At our house, putting mail in the bucket. And Benton's dogs is dead, all cut up. Even Creeper. And Petrie's boyfriend got glass in his boots when he wasn't looking. It's Avery, Andy. Evil's swelling up like Missy Campbell said it would, and it's coming out in Avery. Wayne wants to stop him. Wants to take him to the police or kill him, I don't know which. Dave, this kind of friend of mine, wants to catch Avery. Can you believe it? He wants to catch the sineater.

I don't know what to do.

Dave wants me to come to his cabin tonight and watch Missy, 'cause there's been a death and they is gonna get rid of the sin without the sineater. Dave thinks this will make Avery mad enough to come around. Dave doesn't want to catch the sineater alone. That's why he wants me there.

What would Missy do if the sineater came tonight?

I don't want to go."

Joel pauses, and listens. Lelia is in her room. Petrie is in the kitchen. Suddenly, a panic fills Joel's chest. What if his mother looks in the bottom drawer? She'll know that Joel took the picture. His breathing quickens.

"I gotta go now," he writes. "Hope your dad is better. Having a crazy dad is scary.

Write to me soon.

Your friend,

Joel."

Joel folds the letter over, then realizes he has no envelopes. He scrounges about and finds an old envelope from Andy, and he scratches out the address and pencils in the address of Andy's school beneath it. He marks out the canceled stamp and hopes he can find a new one to put beside the old one. The letter is folded and inserted, and Joel finds enough unlicked glue to adhere the flap.

He will take the picture to Wayne. Wayne will know how to

handle everything. Wayne can be trusted. And Wayne might have a stamp for Andy's letter.

Joel gathers up his jacket, the letter, and the wrapped picture. The letter and the picture go beneath Joel's shirt; the jacket is slipped over Joel's shoulders. He goes into the kitchen, where Petrie is letting the hem down in a skirt.

"Gonna check on the goats," he lies, knowing Petrie knows it is a lie but knowing she probably doesn't care now.

Outside, he goes to the barn and sees that Curry does indeed have the good lantern. But the old rusty one still hangs in a curtain of straw in the back corner. Joel dusts it off and fills it with kerosene. The goats, lying in the hay in their pens, pay no attention to the boy. Joel wonders what it would feel like to have your belly slit and your intestines pulled out. He wonders if he would cry if someone did it to his goats.

With a few sputters, the old lantern blinks into life. The goats turn their heads and blink. Joel finds a burlap bag behind the barrel, still a third full with chicken feed. He takes the top off the barrel, hoping to pour the feed into it. But the barrel is full. The chickens, hearing movement in the barrel, hop from their roosts outside the barn fence and come into the barn. They begin clucking and picking around Joel's feet.

Knowing he can't travel alone to Wayne's apartment with the sineater's picture in his shirt, Joel upends the bag of grain, dumping it on the floor in a large mound. The chickens go into a feeding frenzy. Joel shakes the dust from the empty bag, then drops the letter and the wrapped picture inside.

Pulling his jacket tightly, and holding the lantern and sack, Joel crosses the front yard to the gate and moves out to the path.

17

It reminds Dave of a carnival he saw once. The smells of fatty meats cooking over the backyard fire. Tents litter the ground behind the Campbell cabin. The number of people beside the fire in the shadows cannot be counted, as they continually shift and wander about and among each other. They talk little except in soft undertones. Several children sit the closest to the fire, putting sticks in and pulling them out to watch them glow. It reminds Dave of his visit to the clearing with Joel, and makes Dave wonder what is keeping the sineater's son.

Certainly Joel will come tonight.

Missy's cabin is mysteriously bright, a united force of many lanterns shining through the opened back door and through the small unshuttered windows. More faithful are in the cabin, awaiting Missy's return from praying in the woods nearby. In the cabin, also, is the body of Fonda Clark, laid out on the long table in the kitchen, hands folded across her chest, dressed in a cream-colored dress and surrounded with wildflowers Dave had been made to collect when he got home a few hours ago.

Some people here tonight are merely honoring the wake of Fonda, but those who pitched tents this week are looking for more. Many, Dave knows, have already received the star.

He watches as a cat moves toward one of the children by the fire and is scared off by a red-hot stick. Jewel Benshoff climbs from her tent, smoothes her black skirt, then throws a strange, restrained smile in Dave's direction. He pretends he doesn't see. He squats in the dirt beside a small tulip poplar. Joel should already be in the tool shed, watching. Maybe he isn't coming. Maybe he really meant no when he said no. The thought races uneasily in his mind. He doesn't want to be alone for this.

"Brother Burke," says Jewel. She is by the fire, her face turned over her shoulder. "You should be inside. As man of the house you should be in your aunt's place until she returns."

"I don't think nobody's gonna steal nothing," says Burke. He looks away. He can feel Jewel's gaze linger on him, then move off as she gets up and goes into the cabin. Damn witch, he thinks nervously. I wouldn't marry her before I'd cut off my dick and swing it on a piece of yarn.

And then he flinches, because there is rustling movement in the side yard, coming through the thick shrubbery. If it is Joel, then the boy is dead meat. Can Joel truly be this stupid? But it is Missy, moving into focus as firelight chases shadows from her body. Her head is held high.

Those who have gathered in the back yard see Missy. In reverence they stand, discarding their meals and moving toward her.

Missy waits until all are close and all are silent. Dave stands but stays beside the tree, straining beyond Missy to watch for movement near the shed that would indicate Joel had come.

"Tonight is a holy night," begins Missy. "We see the signs and we move ahead knowing the Lord done give us the right to do as we must do. We pull away from the danger of the devil. We make a new way for our brethren to get into the grace of heaven without sin. A new way." No one in the crowd looks at each other. They stare steadfastly at Missy Campbell. "Before we go to our sister Fonda, we must purify our souls and humble ourselves. Ziah?"

A man about forty leaves the group and goes onto the back porch. He brings out a stack of old washpans. Behind him, those in the cabin who realize that Missy has returned follow out to the yard. Immediately, the men and women form themselves into separate groups. Everyone removes their shoes as Ziah and several other men help fill the pans with water from the rain barrel. It is time for footwashing. Dave bears down on his teeth but removes his shoes and leaves them under the tree. He joins the men.

"As Jesus washed the feet of the disciples," wails Ziah, "let us do unto each other, praying for the spirit to uphold us and clean us and make us worthy."

"Amen," answers the Brotherhood and the mourners.

"Fear not the dark nor the day," says Ziah. "Give no thought to the evil nor the haughty, knowing we are sustained in righteousness and upheld in the Way."

"Amen."

As Dave stands between the tight circle of men, and as someone kneels before him, lifting one of Dave's bare feet and putting it into the pan, as the smiling men to Dave's left and right catch his arms and smile at him, and the cold water is worked about Dave's toes and arch and heel, with soft praying drifting upward from the man who does the washing, Dave thinks he indeed will have to face this night alone.

Several harsh tears of anger spill down Dave's face, but he does not wipe them away, because the others are crying, too, but out of holiness, and they will think nothing of it.

18

Wayne stands in the middle of South Branch, his apartment directly behind him. He takes breaths, counting them, grabbing hold of his resolve and his nerve. His head had spun when he came down the steps into the garage. His heart had lurched when he walked by the four-wheeler. Motion of an imaginary engine rumbled his muscles, and he could feel the handlebars, both of them, and the clutch at his foot and the mountain wind on his face.

His teeth had crushed down, anger cracking beneath anguish.

But he pulls it back. He stands on the pathway and holds himself, directing his thoughts beyond the heat of his stump and to the issue at hand.

Avery Barker will go to the wake tonight, and Wayne will be there.

And then, as he turns and takes the first steps up the South Branch, he hears something whining in the distance, moving up the main road through Ellison. He stops, turns and faces north, and listens.

It is a siren. Coming from the north, heading south. It is not fire, or police. Wayne leans his head, concentrating. It is an ambulance. The whine grows louder. Wayne can see faint flickers of red flashing lights on the tree branches just beyond the end of the West Path Bridge.

There is an emergency somewhere nearby. And for some reason, it does not sit right. There is something profoundly compelling about the siren's wail.

Wayne licks his lips. He thinks of the wake, just beginning at the Campbell cabin. He thinks about the ambulance, and about what it could mean. The piercing sound pricks his skull. It demands his attention.

He turns and looks at the four-wheeler. The only way he could check out the emergency would be to drive. And he could never drive with only one hand.

The four-wheeler sits in the opening of the garage door. Rody Marshall had left the keys beneath the mud mat at the base of the steps, Wayne's mother had told him.

The siren begins to fade at the south end of town, and then cuts off with a slow drawl. The emergency is not far. Down near the school, it sounds like.

"Fuck it," Wayne says. He goes into the garage, finds the keys where his mother had said, and climbs onto the seat of the Honda. "This'll work," he tells himself. "I know this machine."

The key goes into the ignition. And with a twist, the engine growls and lurches into life. Wayne's stump reaches for the handlebar, and he curses himself. He grasps the other bar with his only hand, and sets his feet up. He will not be able to do the clutch, but at least will have control of the brake. He can ride in first gear, and just hold for all his life to keep the steering straight.

"Do it," he says to himself. "Come on, man." He turns the handle grip, and the Honda bolts forward. He leans into the motion, and with a violent twist, maneuvers the machine right. He drives to the bridge and turns again, sweating and single-minded, not letting his surprise at what he is doing override the situation he is investigating. Precious few ambulances have cause to come into Ellison, and his own emergency is not so far removed as to keep the dread of what he might find from swimming his gut like a sick fish.

He turns right again, onto Route 536. The Honda whines like the ambulance, pushed to the edge of first gear and beyond. Wayne feels the stump awake to the harsh vibrations of the engine. Soon, it will be hell again.

He drives on.

And then he sees the reflecting red flashes again, to his left, and he knows the house. It is the only stone house in Ellison, a neat and trim home kept by two respected individuals of the town. He slows and pulls off beside the mailbox. The ambulance is in the short driveway; lights are on all over the house. Wayne climbs from the four-wheeler and cradles his throbbing stump. He goes up to a lone paramedic by the rear of the ambulance.

"Who is it?" Wayne asks. "What happened?"

"You a friend?"

Wayne nods.

"Sam Fort," says the paramedic. "Maybe you best go in and see for yourself."

Wayne nods again, fear growing like a thistled vine in his throat, and goes to the front door.

Benton Hodge answers the knock, and only then does Wayne realize that Benton's Volkswagen bug is in the drive beside the ambulance.

"Wayne," Benton begins, surprised.

Wayne holds his stump more tightly, but the throbbing grows. "Benton, what happened here?"

Benton shakes his head, hesitates, then steps aside. "It's bad," he says softly. "I don't think I never seen a worse tragedy in my life. The waste. The waste." Benton stops, unable to speak for a moment. Wayne looks past the man to the scene in the Forts' front sitting room. Christine Fort is on a small sofa, her face hidden by her hands. Her hair is matted and wild, as if she had tried to pull it out. Philicia Hodge sits beside her, one arm around Christine, the hand patting. The other hand is in Philicia's lap, picking a crease in her skirt. She looks at Benton with an expression that is at once horrified and stoic.

"We're waiting on the police," says Benton. "Ambulance got here first, but now we got to wait on the police."

"What do you mean?"

"Go 'round the house,"says Benton. "Look over the wall."

Wayne's throat clamps. "Tell me," he says.

Benton's face does not change. But his voice drops to a hardened, enraged snarl. It makes Wayne's veins turn cold; it makes his mind picture what he has yet to see.

"Go 'round," Benton repeats. "Look over the wall."

'Goddam,' thinks Wayne.

"Go on," says Benton. Behind him, on the sofa, Christine lets go of her hair and looks up at Wayne. Her face is horrible.

'Goddam it.'

Wayne turns and goes around the garage. He can hear men below the retaining wall, talking softly to each other, and he can hear the liquid rush of the stream.

The slope is slick. There are leaves on the grass, patches here and there as if someone had tried to rake them away but had not finished. Wayne works his way down to the wall, and stops on top of the bright green moss.

Below are three men in white coats and pants, standing on the side of the stream. One has his hands in his coat pockets and looks out past the stream into the woods beyond. Another squats beside a stretcher, hands braced on the edge, chin down. The third pats his foot in the wet ground beside the water's edge and looks at his watch.

'Oh, goddam it.'

There is a blanket over the stretcher; a form beneath the blanket. Wayne's foot jumps, pushing a crumble of rock from the top of the wall. The three men look up at him.

"You police?" one asks.

Wayne shakes his head.

"They fucked if they think they can come whenever they want to," says the man with the watch.

Wayne licks his lower lip. His arm sings out, but he does not pay attention to it.

Sam is dead.

From behind, sirens come. The law.

"How . . ." begins Wayne, but he stops.

The man who squats says, "Don't know. You a friend?"

Wayne nods.

The man sniffs. He crooks his head, indicating the space of grassy soil near the far end of the wall. "Note over there," he says. "We can't pick it up, but we read it. Damndest thing."

"Damn thing," says another.

The sirens grow louder.

"What does it say?" asks Wayne.

"Something like 'You can't invite evil to stay without asking for the consequences as well.' Yeah, it was like that, only more biblical sounding."

"Don't know if it was the skull blows or the loss of blood," says the man who had looked at the woods. "We ain't doctors. But it makes me sick to my stomach, I'll tell you that."

"Goddam it," says Wayne.

"Yeah."

Lights come before the police cars, blue lights cold in the translucent blackness of the night.

Wayne cannot face the police. They are worthless; they are incompetent. He wants to tear their eyes out for their uselessness, but instead he says to the paramedics, "Tell the police to go to visit the Barkers. I may leave a scrap for them to paste in their souvenir book."

The three men blink, not understanding.

But they cannot ask the mailman what he means, because Wayne is moving along the Forts' side yard, near the dead hollyhock patch. The police climb from their car to interrogate the paramedic with the ambulance.

Wayne spits the grit from Route 536 out of his teeth and leans into the jerking movement of the Honda.

There is a pistol in his apartment, and Wayne knows where Charlie stored the rounds.

19

The footwashing is over. Men had washed men, women had washed women. It culminated with crying and speaking in tongues and dancing in the yard. Missy has ordered a time of silent vigil now, and the mourners are clustered in little groups. Some of the younger children have fallen asleep.

Dave has moved back to the small tree. He holds the stance of prayer, but his jaws grind violently, his eyes burn in frustration. He begins to count. Joel will come when he is finished counting. Joel will come before the sineater does.

20

Wayne's stump has taken the crest of pain and is riding the downslide. It swings evenly with his good arm, clutching forward to help move the man up the rugged slope of South Branch. His Honda is left behind in the garage; what he has to do now is an act of solitude. A revenge for two, but acted on by the one who can still walk and breathe and pull a trigger.

'Sam is dead. Goddam it!'

Wayne carries a large, boxy flashlight in one hand. Beneath his other arm, pressed to his side, is the loaded pistol. It burns through his shirt like molten iron, and Wayne coaxes it on.

"Two lives ruined. Burn, you bastard. This one's for Sam.'

He squeezes his arm to his side; the pistol crushes into the muscle and Wayne walks on.

He will hide. He will find a place to hide and watch the crazed gathering of the Brotherhood and whatever bizarre rituals they have planned. And he will wait for the sineater to appear. And when he does, Wayne will watch and then follow. He will not kill the man before the gathering. He does not want an audience for this. Avery Barker's blood is due the mailman. And blood is best collected one on one.

It takes only seconds for Wayne to identify soft sounds behind him. He stops and looks around. The sounds are back about two hundred feet, around a curve, moving up the path.

They are footsteps. And they are human.

And they are cautious, attempting to be silent.

Wayne squints into the dark, knowing he will see nothing. The footsteps continue, closing the gap.

An unsummoned chill races Wayne's shoulder, and he almost calls out to protect himself from sudden discovery. He holds the flashlight out, fanning it back and forth, but he cannot see past the ragged curve. And so he turns the flashlight off, throwing himself into total darkness. He steps carefully to the side of the path, and listens to the movement coming up the road.

It is most likely one of the Brotherhood, Wayne tells himself. Someone late to the meeting, hurrying to Missy's cabin.

The footsteps are closer, with a pale beacon of light preceding them, coming around the curve before the one who holds the lighted lantern.

It could be any one of the Cove inhabitants, coming back from town a little later than usual.

Wayne steps back another three steps, his heels riding up on the ungiving root of an unseen tree. People don't go out late at night, he thinks. They don't go out in the dark, especially not alone. Brotherhood or not, they are afraid to solo the mountain.

Someone is out alone, someone who is not afraid of the dark things of Beacon Cove.

"Avery," Wayne breathes, not certain if the words are audible or merely his thoughts screaming at him. "That's Avery Barker."

Wayne lets the pistol slide down to his waist. He grapples his coat open with fingers freed from the flashlight. He finds the barrel; his fingers move down into place. His neck trembles and his sweat goes cold beneath his arms.

The lantern light swells, and a form appears around the curve, obscured in the branches that canopy the lower edges of the South Branch. Wayne steps back again, and a stick snaps beneath his foot. He curses silently.

'The sineater,' his mind pronounces boldly.

Wayne pulls the pistol from inside the coat. There is a twinge in his stump, his left arm crying for vengence. Justice. Earlier it might have been an arm for an arm. But not now. Death is justice now.

The form is closer, still a dark, fluid blot in the center of the lantern light. Wayne cannot breathe. To see the sineater is to look upon death, to see the face of evil. And more so now than anytime before. The sineater, in his determined duty, has collapsed beneath the evil he has consumed.

To see the face of the sineater is to die.

'Your mother is talking!' A gust of brittle wind raps Wayne's face. *'Don't believe that rubbish, he's a man and nothing more!'*

Wayne's beard itches, but he cannot reach out of his pocket to scratch it. If he had a left hand he could.

If he had a left hand.

The figure is close now; arms are visible, legs working against the uphill slope, a chest, a jacket. Wayne levels the pistol and points it.

'Justice!' he thinks. The pistol steadies. *'Fairness! For you, Sam, and for me!'*

And then the figure with the lantern clears his throat, and it is a sound much softer and higher than Wayne would have expected. The lantern swings slightly, bringing the lower portion of the face into view. It is a young face, the mouth a tight line across the upper ridge of the jaw.

Wayne lowers the gun. "Joel," he says.

The boy jumps violently, the lantern clattering and smacking into his legs. He cries out and whirls toward the sound.

Wayne pockets the pistol and clicks the flashlight. Joel stares at the mailman as if he were Satan himself. "Joel," says Wayne, stepping out onto the path. "It's all right. It's me, Wayne Nelson."

"Jesus Christ!" says Joel, his eyes wide in horror. "What are you trying to do, give me a heart attack?"

"No, Joel. I didn't know it was you. I . . ." Wayne isn't sure how to explain, then decides to try a variation of the truth. "I didn't know who might be out at night, maybe somebody I wouldn't want to deal with in the dark. And so I stood to the side and waited to be sure."

Joel understands instantly. "Avery don't use the paths. I thought you knew that. And he don't use a lantern, either. He can see into the dark like a tiger."

Wayne moves to Joel's side, and tries to smile. It is a feeble attempt. "Listen, I'm sorry I scared you."

"It's okay," says Joel, and it is obvious he has already forgotten about being scared by Wayne. His face works with something heavy.

"Why are you out here, Joel? I didn't think you'd come out at night like this. What business you got?"

"I was looking for you," says the boy. "Stopped by your apartment just a short time ago. The engine of the Honda was hot, like you'd been somewhere. And your light ain't on or nothing. I figured you was going to go to the meeting at the Campbells'."

"How'd you figure that?"

The boy sighs, but the sound isn't one of relaxation. "Dave told me about the wake. How he hopes Avery comes, even though he won't be welcome this time. I figure you'd want to go, too. To be there when he comes. To do . . . whatever you is going to do about getting even."

Wayne wants to tell Joel about Sam Fort, but the boy seems frightened enough already. He doesn't see any good it could accomplish. "So why you need to see me?"

Joel touches a burlap bag which is slung over his shoulder. "Got something here for you. Something you can use. If you ain't scared, that is. If you don't believe seeing . . ." The boy's eyes looks very small in the shadows. Fear radiates from him like heat in the autumn night. "If you don't believe in our beliefs."

"What is it, Joel?"

"A picture of Avery."

'Oh, my God.'

"Petrie told me it was in our house. I had to get it, to get it out. But I couldn't burn it, or tear it up. I thought you could use it. If you don't believe that seeing Avery will kill you, then maybe you will be safe. I don't know for sure, but I thought you would know. You can use it, can't you Wayne?"

"Oh, dear God. A picture of the sineater.'

"How, Joel?" asks Wayne. His lips hurt, like they are going to crack apart. He knows he has been breathing through his mouth these past minutes, but he cannot stop it now. "How can I use the picture?"

"So you'll know him. So you can stop him before he does any more bad things. It ain't just you no more, Wayne."

"What do you mean?"

"He killed Benton's dogs. He ripped them up. He hurt Petrie's boyfriend."

"And he killed Sam Fort," says Wayne, not realizing he is going to tell the boy until the words have hit air.

"What?"

"Sam Fort is killed," says Wayne. "Beat to death. There was a note beside the body. About breaking the rules of God."

Joel looks away from Wayne, and Wayne thinks the boy is crying. He waits. Then Joel looks back. "Take the picture. Please."

Wayne nods. Joel pulls a photograph from the bag and gives it to the man. Wayne slips the bottom of it beneath his belt. "Go on home, Joel. Thanks."

Joel looks down the path, into the lightlessness and beyond. Then he says, "I gotta come with you, now."

"Why?"

Joel's eyes are wet; straining.

"Why do you have to come? It's best you go home."

Joel says, "I'm scared, Wayne. I didn't know he'd kill nobody. I don't want to go home alone! Let me come with you. I'll hide at the Campbells' until daylight. I won't look at nothing, I won't do nothing wrong! I won't break the rules! Please, let me come along."

Wayne hesitates. He wants to put his arm around the boy's shoulder, but knows that, too, is breaking the rules, and the boy needs the rules tonight.

"All right," Wayne says. "Stay close. I may have to leave the Campbells', but not until I know you got a safe place to hide."

Joel nods slowly. Whatever relief there is, is minimal.

They begin the last leg of the South Branch toward Missy's meeting.

21

Two-tenths of a mile east of the Campbell cabin, the flashlight and lantern are turned off. Wayne and Joel pick their footing carefully, keeping their eyes focused on the glowing of the cabin in the clearing. They can hear singing, and faint chanting, and the sound chills Joel's blood. He is afraid, and wonders if he will actually be able to sneak around and into the empty shed once they get to the edge of the front yard. His conscience screams, ''Sinner!'' and he sees his mother's face, torn with anguish at the broad path of destruction her son has chosen to follow. The only thing that keeps his feet moving ahead is the man beside him. In this dark, he cannot really see Wayne, but the physical presence is very close, keeping pace, breathing heavily. Joel fights a childish need to reach out and grab the man's hand. Wayne would surely jerk away, would surely be offended. And it would be a rule broken. Yet another one. Joel's gut shudders. He remembers in the bathroom at school, washing his hands of the sineater. Surely his own weakness, his own stupid need of friends and want of power has led him to this terrible situation. His hands are not clean. They hold blood as surely as they did when he scoured Dave's star from his arm.

''You been here before?'' asks Wayne in a whisper.

''No,'' says Joel. ''I always knew Missy didn't like me and my family. I always stayed off the South Branch 'cause of that.''

Wayne clucks softly in response. The two slow, stopping at the head of Missy's footpath. The cabin is close now; Joel can pick out individual voices. He can see silhouettes through the cabin windows and the open door of the front stoop. There are several people seated on the stoop, several standing with backs against the log wall.

"Dave said there was a shed round back" says Joel.

Wayne nods, and the man and boy step from the path into the trees to the left. In spite of the singing and moaning of the Brotherhood, Joel finds a bit of consolation in the fact that their noise drowns out any sound of footsteps in the woods. It is not hard to see the larger stumps and logs, but briars make their presence known by catching his face and snagging on the burlap bag which is wrapped and folded and held tightly beside the dark lantern.

They move around the side of the cabin. Joel leads now, Wayne follows. A campfire comes into view behind the cabin, with a few people standing beside it and a number of tents holding a ghostlike sentry in the drained light behind the fire. And behind the tents, the squat and silent shed. Joel stops and Wayne draws up beside him. *'Silent and deadly,'* thinks Joel, remembering that as a term Andy Mason had used to describe Joel's classroom farts. But Joel cannot think of it as funny, because the words describe the shed too accurately. Silent and deadly. With the emphasis on deadly.

"In there," Joel says to Wayne.

They move behind the shed, wait until none of the gathering are facing that direction, and slip between the brush and climb into the shed through a splintered window.

22

The silent vigil is done. Singing has begun again. Jewel is particularly overcome, rolling in the leaves and dust, covering her head with grass and dirt, saying "I am nothing before you, Lord!" Dave figures she is in rapture because her twenty-eighth birthday is in December, less than three weeks away, and Missy has promised her a husband. Dave touches the inner skin of his arm, and feels the crumbling scab. In less than three weeks Dave will be a legend to these people. And not one Missy would dream of matching up with that ugly old midwife.

He has stopped counting. Joel is still not there. Dave walks to the campfire and kicks a pebble into it. The children who slept during the vigil have been awakened and are in the cabin now. They can be heard screaming as the parents force them to kiss the cold, white cheek of the dead woman.

'Joel isn't here yet.' Dave plucks a small rock from the ground and balances it in his hand. Not ten minutes ago, Dave checked the shed to find nothing inside but three cats and a half-dead rat they were playing with. Dave had cursed and come out again, to find Jewel grinning at him from the ground. The skin on the nape of his neck had prickled. He thought she would be one who would respect his new status if he caught the sineater.

Dave glances again at the shed. It appears empty and still. The boy rakes his finger through his red hair and crosses his arms.

Damn Joel, anyway. Dave looks at the porch as several Sisters come out from paying their final respects. They wipe their eyes and hold each other's hands. Dave has paid his respects, all right. He had stared at the dead woman and chanted in his mind, *'You got your sins now go to hell with them, you got your sins now go to hell with them.'*

The whole thing was such a monstrous farce. The smoky, smelly, bright carnival of lies. Fonda would not lose her sin anymore than she would had the sineater done his duty. But, of course, in the farce was the power.

Missy appears on the back porch step, and gathers the group around with a wave of her arm. Dave steps back away from the center of people, slipping out to stand at the back, near one of the tents. "Time is here," she says, and the group becomes quiet. "We shall send the spirit of Sister Fonda to the Lord in a cloak of purity. White was snow and clean as wool."

Four men come from the cabin, bearing the body of Fonda Clark. The crowd parts, letting them through. They lower the body gently on the ground near the fire. The group draws in again, watching.

"We spit in Satan's face," says Missy.

"Amen," mutter some of the men.

"We do not spit at holy traditions, for that would be to scoff at the Lord. And we know the straight and the narrow. We know that the narrow path leads to life eternal."

More men now, and women say, "Amen."

"We make a change so as to pull away from the evil one. The evil one, who has corrupted the lowly servant. The evil one, who has taken the man of sin and made him the man of Satan."

"Amen."

Missy's thin arms rise, her fingers toward the sky. Her eyes flutter and close. Her body is still, although it seems as though a secret breeze, undetected by the others near her, strokes her loose clothes in a mysterious rhythm, billowing, slacking, billowing, slacking. It is hypnotic. Dave's eyes are drawn to her and are held fast.

Missy looks around at the following. Her clothes ripple like slow waves on a deep and dangerous lake.

"And it is in this way that we will rid our Sister of her sin."
She takes her knife from her skirt and kneels beside the corpse
of Fonda.

Dave glances frantically over his shoulder toward the shed. He
must go back and look one more time. And if Joel is not there, then
the sineater's son be damned, and may he look upon the face of his
father and receive his foul reward.

23

The phone rings in the Hardware, and Fitch catches it before it sounds a second time. Benton glances over from the front door, where he has been standing the last half hour, gazing through the window to his right and thinking about Sam.

"It's the police from the hospital," says Fitch. "They want to ask you a question."

Benton takes a long swig from the can of Milwaukee and sniffs.

"They got a question, Benton," repeats Fitch. "You want to talk or you want me to tell them you can't now."

"Tell them I'm in the john. What's the question?"

Fitch speaks into the receiver. "He can't get to the phone now. What do you want?"

Benton looks back out of the window. The only thing he can see is the road a few feet beyond his own store, and the lamp beside the door of the antique shop. A quiet town, used to be, he muses. But what used to be used to be. He wonders if he shouldn't up and move and start over again. Somewhere else. He doesn't think Philicia would miss him all that much.

Fitch says, "They want to know if you sell baseball bats. I said you did. Then they want to know who bought a baseball bat recently. I said how the hell would we know."

"Jesus," says Benton. He turns and strides to the phone. "And I think I just tossed my latest baseball purchaser list out with the garbage.'' He takes up the receiver. Even before he speaks, he can hear the hospital commotion in the background. ''Baseball bats?'' he says.

It is the dumb young cop on the other end, the one who smudged the note when he took it from the stream side. ''Mr. Hodge, this is Floyd. We've got a preliminary report here. Looks like Fort was struck by heavy wood, possibly a baseball bat. Can you remember anyone buying a baseball bat recently?''

Benton bites back a sarcastic retort. ''Floyd,'' he says. ''There is a lot of wood in this part of the state, if you hadn't noticed. Called trees. What hits like a baseball bat could be a two-by-four, or a branch.''

''Got the smooth form of a bat. Forensics man says so.''

''All right, then. I haven't sold a baseball bat since July. Not many boys batting balls around in the fall. They like to follow the pro schedule. Do you know that baseball bats, old or new, probably make the same kind of mark.''

Floyd says nothing for a moment. Benton feels no pleasure in the stupid man's growing frustration. ''Yeah, I know that, Mr. Hodge. It ain't helping me none, though.''

Benton thinks of holding back a scrap of information, but then figures it won't make much difference. He gives the policemen the bite. ''I did have a bat stolen from my store not two weeks ago.''

Floyd catches his breath. Benton can picture the goofy eyes bugging out in the pleasure of discovery. ''Really? Stolen?''

''No big deal,'' says Benton. ''I lose things now and then.''

Fitch frowns at Benton. Fitch had not known about the thefts. Benton shrugs at the other man.

''Did you report the theft, Mr. Hodge?''

''Of course not. I got better things to do with my time.''

''Could we discuss this matter further? In person?''

''I don't think that's necessary. I'm going to bed in a few minutes. It's been a hell of an afternoon, and I think a little sleep is preferable to meeting with you. Why don't you go to bed? Maybe you can come up with the answer to your puzzle in your dreams.''

''We're coming back out that way, Mr. Hodge. We could just stop in for a minute.''

''Don't come here,'' says Benton. ''Try the Barker cabin.''

"Who's that?"

Fitch looks back at the window. Benton feels a new surge of anger grip his body, and his hand crushes around the receiver. He had seen the note, smudged though it was. He had seen Wayne's bloody stump, and had heard the rumors of Avery's possible insanity. If it was Avery Barker, then the police should by all means get the bastard. If not, they can determine what else to try. He feels bad for the Barker boy, for Joel, but if the boy's father is a murderer, then let the chips fall.

"Go up West Path. Gets kind of rough, but you tough law men can make it I'm sure. It's the last cabin at the top of the mountain, the last one on the trail. Ask for the father. They won't know where he is, but they might be able to tell when he last was home."

"The man's name?"

"Avery Barker."

"Why do you think he'd know something?"

"You're the detectives," says Benton. "You figure it out." And the receiver goes back into the cradle.

Fitch looks back sternly at Benton. "You never told me about no stealings."

Benton throws up his hands. "Hey, don't worry about it. I have a few things taken now and then. If it don't bother me, don't let it bother you. Stolen things ain't the end of the world."

Fitch sniffs.

"Stolen things ain't murder," says Benton.

Fitch shakes his head.

"Now go on and go home. I really am going to go home and go to bed."

"One more for the road, Benton," says Fitch.

"Help yourself, you old bloodsucker."

Fitch goes to the rear of the store and digs in the cooler. Benton pulls on his red hunting jacket and goes out to the porch. He looks up and down the road, seeing little but darkness lying on the road. He scratches his neck, feeling the wiry texture of black hair gone gray. For a brief moment, he feels a frightened love for what is around him. He thinks of the early years of the Hardware, of how he and Philicia had worked together to get it going. How each of his four children had been baptized in the Methodist Church a few miles down Route 536. How, as a family, the Hodges had actually been regular in attendance for a while. How pretty Philicia had looked as a bride, and as a new mother. How the two of them had marveled as each child had learned to walk, to talk. How proud Philicia had been when she first took the job at the Baptist Church, on the one hand shy because she thought it was a duty looked down on, and yet bursting with fierce pride because she was producing pay checks for the family's account.

There is a quick stirring in Benton's chest. Something like love for his wife, for what they had, together, brought into being and into existence.

But as he holds the feeling, it slips away from him, leaving him sad and bewildered. *'What used to be used to be,'* he thinks, then reaches behind him to switch on the floodlight which illuminates the area of the dog pen.

Fitch comes out on the porch. The door slams behind him. "Running low on brew," he says, then steps from the porch and moves out of view beyond the reach of the porch light.

"So go to the grocery store next time," calls Benton after. Fitch, down the road, says, "Humph."

Benton hops off the side of the porch and goes to the pen. "Hey, buddies, you asleep on me or what?"

And then he goes around the back, and sees his dogs, and his knees buckle and he falls, clasping the wire of the fence, a wail of anguish ripping from his throat and cutting the air like the sound of a man crucified.

24

Dave is halfway to the shed when Missy calls out, "Burke, come here!"

The whole crowd turns to him, and he is trapped by their eyes. He licks his lips and stops.

"Burke, I need your help."

Dave looks at Missy, crouched on the ground beside the dead woman. She holds the knife. Dave has no idea of what it is she wants of him, but he does not want to be part of it, he is certain. "Come here, Burke."

Dave swallows hard against the stone in his throat. He goes to his aunt, and squats beside her. "We will be first, Burke. And this will become a holy act. The others will follow." She takes his hand. He cringes at the cool, bony grasp. Her other hand lifts, and what is in it glints and sparkles, throwing off the white brightness of the campfire and the cold callousness of the distant stars.

Dave can feel the Brotherhood and the other mourners pulling in, can feel their eyes still locked on him, their hot breath on his face. His arm rebels against Missy's hold, but her fingers tighten and pull back.

The knife winks, held aloft.

And then there is movement in the cedars beside the house. A crackling, rattling of branches pushed apart and snapping together. Footsteps coming through the trees.

231

Dave turns his eyes toward the cedars. Missy's head jerks about on her neck, her face full of instant terror and hardened rapture.

No one speaks, but Dave feels that everyone else in the yard has turned their faces away. Dave's stomach contracts. It is the sineater coming.

Dave's own gaze falls to the dirt. His heart beats his chest with death blows.

But then he hears Missy say, "Mannie Vicks. Welcome to our ceremony."

Dave licks his lips and looks up. The others do the same. Mannie stands just beyond the circle of believers, his hat from his head.

"Missy," says Mannie by way of greeting. His voice is deep and quiet.

"We is glad you seen fit to join us, Mannie," says Missy. "The Lord seen that you was to be saved. That you was to accept His changes."

Mannie nods at a funny, slanted angle that makes his neck appear broken. He says, "Murder has come on us now. Been to town earlier. Sam Fort's a dead man. You . . ." His voice cracks, giving in to a shuddering, grating sob. Then Mannie says, "You was right and I didn't see it now. We can't let it go on. I never thought this could happen. Murder, maiming . . ."

"Join us now, Mannie."

"Was Carter saved, Missy?" Mannie looks at the woman with the knife. "When he came to her at the wake, was he so fouled then that her sin was not taken? Has Carter been sent to the Lord, or is she burning with the demons for her sin?"

"Trust in the Lord" is all Missy will say. "Trust in the Lord with His good ways."

Mannie stares at the woman, then at the fire, then at the crowd. He moves into the circle and puts his hat slowly back onto his head.

Above the group, in the ebony air, an owl cries.

"This is her blood!" Missy says. "Full of pride and deceit. Take, drink, in order to see her to the Lord of hosts!"

The knife swings down and cuts into the skin of the old woman's throat. Blood does not come out, but Missy puts her lips to the wound and draws in. When she sits straight, there is a dull, pale-orange fluid on her mouth. She grins at Dave.

"And this," says Missy, moving the knife to the edge of the cut and slicing a small chunk of skin away, "is of her body. Take, eat, in remembrance that we are but dust in the eyes of God. Take her evil and consume it to make her free." Missy lifts the skin, and in a motion that resembles a kiss, puts it to her lips. She licks it between her teeth then, and swallows it down.

Dave reels back, pulling, knees struggling in the dirt and leaves, but Missy holds him more tightly, and it is as though her strength indeed comes from somewhere beyond her. Dave cannot get free.

"Burke," says Missy, her eyes rolling in ecstasy, handing the knife to the boy. "Take up this blade and follow me."

Dave cannot hold the knife for the shaking of his hand. Missy guides the hand to a lower place on Fonda's neck and presses the blade until a small slit is made. She puts her hand on the back of Dave's neck and pushes his mouth to the cut.

"Drink," she whispers.

Dave sucks. He comes up, gagging.

"And of her body," says Missy. She uses the knife in Dave's hand to saw a tiny bit of flesh free. She holds it before Dave. He licks it into the mouth and begins to cry. He chokes, and swallows.

'Weakling!' his mind screams. *'Worthless, fucking coward!'* And the words roar at him in not only his own voice, but in that of his parents in West Virginia, and in the voices of Wayne and Joel. Dave cries aloud, but is ignored, because Sisters and Brothers and those who will soon become Sisters and Brothers are moving around him now to take their turns at the feast of redemption. Missy lets go of his arm.

Dave stands, stumbling away from the nightmare. He drops into the grass by the shrubs and heaves the foul, death-ripe taste of the dead woman's flesh. He spits into the grass, and spits again and again and again. Behind him is chanting and singing. Children are dancing. Dave glances over his shoulder, his eyes blurred with tears. The crowd swarms over the corpse, making cuts and hunching down to suckle the body like a frantic gathering of obscene hairless kittens over a wrinkled, decaying mother.

'Fucking coward!'

Dave's face buries into the sharp cedar needles on the ground. His body spasms, and without knowing or caring, he wets himself.

25

"How long can this insanity go on?" whispers Wayne.

Joel does not look at the man, because the words aren't for him, and because he cannot take his eyes from the horrific play which is being danced before him in firelight. Through the crack beneath a shuttered shed window, Joel can see much of the backyard. There are people all over the dead woman, and Joel knows they are cutting her and sucking her body. It looks like they are kissing her, like they would kiss the feet of Jesus. Joel's breath is painful in his throat. He feels he stands on the cliff side of hell, and it is only a matter of minutes before the whole gathering turns and stares at him, a boy peeking through a shed window crack, and with accusing screams, direct Missy to find him and kill him.

He swallows and it feels like fire, but he cannot look away.

"Damn it, this can't take all night," says Wayne.

Then Joel sees Dave move beside some small evergreen trees, and fall on the ground and throw up. Behind the red-haired boy, the people cut and drink and eat, then dance about on bedeviled feet.

"Damn," whispers Wayne.

The people dance and sing. Many chant loudly. Joel feels his stomach clamp, and part of his undigested lunch fills his mouth. He wipes it away. He wants to hide in the shed corner, but he is afraid not to see. He is afraid that whatever will come unknown will be worse than that which will come as he watches.

Missy's face rises with the fire's smoke, and it is like a witch's face, a smile that is horrid and all-knowing and white as death. It seems to spin above the others on the ground. Spinning like a crazy star, fueled by God's own wrath and truth.

The motion is sickening. Joel holds his stomach.

The crowd dances. Missy spins. Faster. Faster.

And then the spinning stops.

The people who dance freeze in place, faces turning in unison to the back porch of Missy's cabin. Those on the ground by Fonda sit bolt upright. Dave whips about to stare in the same direction as the others.

"What . . ." begins Wayne, questioning the silence.

"It's a goat," says Joel.

On the sagging porch beside the stack of firewood is a lone goat, standing stock-still, staring out at the gathering with wide eyes. A piece of twine is tied about its neck, with what had been a lead cut short and hanging loose. It is a large animal, of dark, wooly coat and knobby, familiar knees.

"It's one of my goats," says Joel.

A child in the yard hops up, squealing, "Ha! Look! A goat done come through Sister Missy's house!"

The child is hushed immediately by her mother.

Joel's fingernails scratch the scabby wood of the window frame as he tries to press more closely to the crack. A spiderweb goes up his nose and he fights back a sneeze. He squints. Dangling from the twine around the goat's neck, Joel can see a piece of paper. A note. "Why . . . ?" he whispers.

The goat's pointed jaw falls open, emitting a harsh bleat. The eyes blink, sparkling with the fire's light.

Mannie Vicks moves, turning to Missy. He says softly, "You want me to?"

Missy, her face turned away toward the porch, nods very slowly.

Mannie moves toward the porch. His hands catch each other in a nervous struggle for composure. He clears his throat. The goat watches carefully, then stamps its hooves as if it is playing King of the Mountain. Its head lowers as the man approaches.

"Hold," says Mannie. "Hold now." He reaches out and snatches the note, then hops back as the goat takes a step forward. The child who had laughed says, "Ha!" again. No one else says anything.

Mannie rubs the bristly back of his neck, then coughs uncertainly. He says, "The note is from him."

"Dear God!" screams a woman suddenly.

"Him?" whispers Joel to Wayne.

Mannie's gaze flicks about the yard. There is a glowing terror in his eyes. "Do you want me to read it?" he says.

"No!" screams the woman, and someone says, "Hush."

Missy hands slowly fold themselves in an attitude of prayer. Then she says, "Yes."

Mannie's tongue flicks across his lower hip. He reads the note. " 'This is a wake. Fonda is dead. Where is my food?' "

"God, no!" screams the woman, and several other women begin wailing and clutching each other. "God save us!"

Men begin to talk excitedly among themselves. Several people hurry to Missy's side, and cling to her arms.

"What are we to do?" one asks her.

Joel's chin scrapes the blistered wood. "Him," he says. "He used my goat for a message. He was in my barn. He touched my animals!" Joel's heart flips painfully.

Missy turns about to face the crowd. Her face is hard and small now. She says, "Fear not, my Sisters and Brothers. He will not come into our Brotherhood!"

"His animal came through your house!" calls someone. "His goat! His animal of Satan!"

"Yes!" shouts another man. "He chose the animal of the devil! He chose a goat to bring us a note!"

An uproar swells; Missy calms them with her hands. Then she says, "Let us be rid of this animal, then. We will show him what we do with the unholy!"

"Yes, Sister!" cry some of the women. "Be rid of it!"

"Mannie," Missy says, "bring me the goat."

Mannie frowns, hesitating, then nods. He goes to the porch where the goat still stands, watching them all. He slips his fingers beneath the twine and gives the goat a tug. The animal balks, kicking back on its heels, then hops off the porch and follows Mannie to the center of the group where Missy waits.

Missy moves a small way into the crowd which surrounds her, then returns to the center with a gasoline can. She holds it up for the people to see. "Purify and destroy," she says. She uncaps the can and douses the goat, who struggles and tries to pull from Mannie's grip.

"God help us!" says Missy.

"God help us!" the people echo.

"Oh, no!" says Joel. "Please, no!"

Wayne presses in, trying to see through the crack beside Joel. "What is it, Joel?"

Joel is nearly sobbing. "My goat!" he says.

Missy reaches down to the campfire beside her. She knocks a large, burning stick from the fire and holds it up by the uncharred end.

"Purify!" cries Mannie, and he leans into the goat, holding it with both arms wrapped about its chest and belly. Missy lowers the torch and touches the dark, damp wool on the back of the goat's neck.

"NO!" says Joel.

The goat explodes into a white fireball. Missy jumps back and the crowd cheers. The faces of the Brotherhood are crossed with red and orange and yellow as the dying goat bolts among them, trying to run away from its death. Shadows are cast long and sharp and flickering between the dancing, shouting people. "Purify!" they cry. The children laugh shrilly and catch each other's hands to spin in celebration.

The goat jumps and twitches. Its cries of horror and supreme torment cheer the onlookers further. It crashes to the ground on its side, then rolls up to run again. The people give it room, with several men swiping with their boots as the creature passes. The living bonfire stumbles, then suddenly shoots out of the crowd toward the woods to the west of the backyard.

Joel's eyes burn as if it were his own body on fire. "No," he wails.

Tall, trembling shadows follow the dying goat into the forest. They stretch out beside it as it runs, black as hell, with halos of an unearthly orange glow. There are no more bleats. Only the huge shadows.

An image of rock and log is cast three times their size on the trunks of barren trees.

The shadow of a frightened bat is cast in monster dimensions as it flies among the oaks.

Shadows of thorns and thistles, themselves a black and horrific forest as tall as a house, wave their deadly spines in the wake of the passing goat.

"Goat'll start a forest fire!" shouts one child.

"Woods is too wet," begins one of the mothers. And then she stops.

The others stop and gape.

Joel grabs a scream that wants to rocket from his throat. His eyes pull open so far, it feels as if his lids will rip.

There is the shadow of a man, forty feet tall, his arms outstretched in anger and his hands clutching the air like giant claws, thrown against an enormous spruce tree. The black head throws back. The arms raise higher, coming together into monstrous, deadly fists.

And he shouts, "Missy Campbell!"

The voice is from the very pit of hell.

"Missy Campbell, where is my food?!"

The goat vanishes. The shadow falls from the tree and is swallowed up in the midnight darkness of the forest.

Joel puts his hands over his ears. He does not shut his eyes because to do so would be to invite the picture into his mind again. He stares at the people in the yard and watches as they cower and cover their faces. Even Missy flinches, but then turns her face to the woods.

"You have no right to be here!" she shouts. "Be gone!"

Joel can hear her, and he pushes his hands harder against his head. He thinks of the code he and Andy invented, and he recites the alphabet in his mind. '*ZXYWVUT . . .*' By the cedar, Dave gets up onto his knees, watching his aunt. '*. . . SRQPONMLK . . .*'

But the voice is strong over Joel's palms. The sound thunders against the dam of fingers and pours through.

"You dare to change God's tradition!"

Joel cries out. But still the voices come.

"You are not of God! We know what you are now. You can't trick the righteous! Leave our holy ground!"

'*. . . JIHGFED . . .!*' Joel glances away from the window, and sees on the floor of the shed the image of the sineater. The claws, the thick and brutal arms, the spiked beard and cruel, twisted, inhuman mouth.

"You say I am the devil!" comes the answer. "Do children of God have no faith to look evil in the eye, then? If I am Satan, come to me and see me now. Face me, then ask me to leave!"

"She's going to do it!" says Wayne.

Joel looks at Wayne. Wayne puts his arm around Joel's shoulder. "Watch, Joel."

'No!' Joel wants to scream. *'I don't want to see!'* But his words have no voice.

Joel looks out at the yard again.

Missy stands by the fire. She is a photograph, a statue, and the world at her feet is stopped in time. Even Joel's eyes won't blink, having become part of the scene beyond the shed. Only the fire sways.

There is no sound at all, not even popping of cinders. Joel wonders wildly if he had heard a voice at all, or if he were truly here with this man's arm about his shoulder.

But then Missy's foot moves very slightly. It lifts and moves, her body gliding with the small movement. Her other foot moves also, and she follows.

One of the Sisters hears her steps and says, "Missy, no!"

Missy says nothing. Her hands held outward, her eyes stare into the woods where the goat is gone. Where the sineater waits.

A Brother says, "Missy, don't look."

"Come!" It is the sineater. "Meet me. Look at me."

Joel jams his fingers into his ears.

'No No No No No No! . . . CBA, CBA, CBA!'

A chorus erupts from the crowd. But Missy moves through the grass toward the edge of the yard. And Joel can see a dark figure moving through the thinned trees of the forest edge toward Missy.

The Brotherhood cower, faces away. "Missy, no!" they shout.

The figure is closer now, at the very edge of the brush. Missy stares, entranced.

"See me now!" shouts the sineater, and he leaps from the darkness into the firelight. At the same moment, Missy turns her face away, and Joel falls from the window.

"Oh God oh God!" Joel screams. Wayne reaches out for the boy but Joel scoots into a corner. Joel would claw his eyes out if he could and save himself from what he might see.

''Be gone, Satan!'' says Missy. And the Brotherhood repeat the chant. ''You shall not tempt the Lord your God. Be gone from here, we will not let the devil sway us!''

''Be gone!'' shout the Brothers and Sisters.

There is nothing then.

There is silence.

Joel thinks he hears a whispered, ''Praise Jesus.''

And then there is the soft sound of movement in the woods. Footsteps crunching branches and scattering leaves. They grow more loudly, as though they are coming around toward the shed. Fire and glass bear into Joel's heart. He drops from the window and wraps himself with his arms. The sineater knows where he is! His father is coming to get him, to punish him for listening, for being there, for knowing!

Beside him, Wayne shifts from the side of the shed and moves toward the rear window through which they entered.

The sineater comes closer. Joel can hear his breathing now, and a low rumbling which can only be the devil's snarl.

'. . . *CBA!*' Joel's brain screams. *'Leave me alone! God forgive me!'*

Footsteps closer. Near the shed.

Joel curls more tightly. *'NOOOOO!'*

And then the footsteps are moving away, are becoming faint. Joel shudders, and dares to look up above the safety of his forearms.

The sineater is going away, into the depths of the mountains.

And Wayne is gone, too.

26

Fonda is taken by the four men who carried her from the cabin, taken back inside and placed into her pine coffin where she will wait until daybreak to be buried in a plot just east of the Campbell home. The campfire is a glow now in the darkness, a red eye staring at anyone who will stare back. Missy has retired to her room; the people who have tents are moving slowly, collecting blankets and children and climbing quietly away for a night's rest.

Dave sits on the ground as he has ever since he drank Fonda's sin and eaten her unholiness.

'He came. Fucking coward, he came and you did nothing!'

Dave's legs are wet. He knows that it is more than mud or frost; he can smell himself, and his anger is fanned higher.

'He came, he called out to us. Missy did what you thought she'd do, but you only pissed yourself!' Dave spits on the ground, his tongue still cringing against the obscene taste of Fonda Clark.

He looks at the silent shed. If he had a torch, he would set the thing on fire and watch the rats run with their fur ablaze. If he saw Joel Barker at this minute, he would hammer his head in for leaving Dave to face this alone. Something, someone, should pay for this. Hate and fury shake Dave's lungs until he has to bend over for breath.

Then he stands, and brushes dirt from his jeans. He looks at the Benshoffs' tent. It is quiet. That is good, Dave thinks, because if he'd seen Jewel at that moment he would have gone and kicked her teeth into her face.

Dave looks about the yard. The clutter and slow motion of the scattering crowd cross him with a wave a nausea. He rocks with it. When it is gone, he goes to the shed.

The door to the side is bolted simply with a slat of wood. Dave can see that it is still cocked up in the half-bolted angle he'd left it in this afternoon, so Joel had never come after all.

Dave knocks the slat up with his fist and shoves his shoulder against the door.

'I may be a coward, but you're worse than me, you little sineater's son!'

There is someone in the corner. The someone looks up. The wide eyes belong to Joel.

"You fucking bastard shit!" Dave rushes at Joel with his hands clenched. He falls on the younger boy and begins hitting him in the face and stomach. Joel ducks his head and lets the blows fall. He doesn't try to shield himself.

"Why didn't you come on time, you shit! Goddam you and your stupid fucked-up family to hell!"

Joel ducks further. "I did come," he says through his arms.

Dave continues to strike out. He does not feel better, so he hits harder.

"I did come!" says Joel.

Dave stops, and look at the dark-haired boy. "You did not," he pants. "I checked."

"I did," sputters Joel. "I been here a long time. You didn't check for a long time."

Dave wipes his mouth. The dead taste of Fonda makes him want to heave again, but he doesn't. "What did you see?"

Joel rubs his arms. "I seen what you did to the dead person. I seen everybody cutting and sucking on her. I heard Avery come to the meeting."

Dave narrows his eyes. "You seen it all?" Joel saw him suck Fonda. Joel saw him at his weakest moment. He knows Joel heard the sineater, and also saw Dave motionless with fear. "Goddam you!" Dave pulls the hammer from his pocket and slams it into Joel's shoulder. Joel cries out and rolls away. Dave strikes with the hammer again, but Joel catches his wrist and jerks the hammer free. It falls to the floor.

"Wayne was here!" Joel manages.

"Here? With you? How long?"

Joel turns his neck and draws further against the wall. He looks tiny and scared and weary. "A long time. He came with me. Then he left."

"When did he leave?"

"He left after Avery."

Dave slumps onto the floor. He frowns and looks about. His head reels, his gorge threatens to rise once again. "I hate them all," he says. He does not care anymore if he thinks it or if Joel hears it. "I hate them and I won't let myself be weak anymore. I don't care if I die. I won't be weak anymore."

Joel watches silently.

Dave thinks suddenly of his arm, and he rips open his jacket and strips his shirt. Surely the scabs will be gone. And with them, the star.

But the scabs hold tightly. He picks at one and it begins to bleed.

"Fuck it," he says. He looks at Joel. The dark-haired boy's eyes are fluttering, closing.

Dave thinks a short rest might not be bad after all.

Just a short rest to get his balance again and to get rid of the sickness that clings to his tonsils.

'A five-minute rest,' Dave thinks, but his mind won't allow more because sleep has already decided to consume the boy with its relentless power.

27

Wayne steps and leans on a tree, holding the large flashlight in his hand and pressing his burning stump to his body. He no longer can hear the footsteps of the sineater, and he is no longer certain where he is. West somewhere, he knows, but there is nothing on which he can base his directions. The flashlight is not on; when following he did not want Avery Baker to know he was behind. But now, with moonlight banished behind clouds, he no longer can see even the largest of branches in his way.

There are loose aspirin in his pocket. He drops his flashlight to pick some out. He gulps them down dry.

He feels foolish now. His anger has not died, but some is now reflected back from the black trees and onto himself. The pistol is not hot anymore. It is cold steel, impotent and worthless.

The sineater is probably a quarter mile ahead of Wayne now, and the case beyond hope.

Pain comes hard. Wayne rides it and fights it, then the aspirin kicks in and takes the edge off. He looks at the clouds and thinks he will try another time.

He moves from the tree and turns the flashlight on. This is not the end. But seeking out the hermit in the dead of night was a stupid idea. The man is not a vampire; he will not be asleep in a coffin or hiding in a root cellar by day.

Wayne will find the man when the odds are in the mailman's favor. He will find the man in the daylight.

He steps over a broken limb, then turns to a rustling behind him.

A mind-shattering crack sends him into unconsciousness and he falls to the forest floor.

28

It is not the cold of the ground, not the dirty glow of sunlight seeping into the shed that awakens Joel, but the pain on his neck and shoulders. He groans and tries to pull away from the hurt, but it isn't a dream, and is there to stay. His eyes open, close again. In that fraction of a second, he saw Dave beside him, sleeping.

He is awake, and he is in Missy Campbell's old shed behind her house.

His mouth is dry and tastes like mud.

'But what does Dave's mouth taste like?'

The thought makes Joel feel grossly sick himself; he sees the moment when Dave's mouth went to the corpse's waxy neck and sucked the cut Missy had made.

Uneasily, he stands, gripping the rough walls. He hobbles over to the window and looks out. It is indeed daytime, but still early. Most of the people are still in the tents except for a single man who has started a new fire.

'Soon they will wake up and take the dead woman to bury her.'

Joel glances at the broken window through which he and Wayne had entered last night. *'Got to get out. Get out now!'*

He goes to the window, stepping over Dave. As his knee goes up to scale the hole, he thinks of Avery.

His stomach clamps like a piece of meat in a steel press. He groans and tucks his head. Avery had come last night and had seen the change Missy had created. He had seen all the people, had seen the dead woman, and had not been invited to eat food from her to save her from her sin.

And he had spoken.

Joel had heard the voice of the sineater.

Joel groans again. He is dizzy; the window seems to crawl beneath his fingers.

The sineater is not only insane now, he is also angry.

Joel raises his head and forces himself out through the window. He struggles through the trees that border the Campbell clearing, holding low and out of sight of the man at the campfire. When his feet touch the South Branch, they break into a run.

As if the devil were breathing fire at his heels, he runs.

Near the bottom of the path, by Wayne's garage, he passes several uniformed policemen, starting up the Branch. They do not notice him, and he feels like a ghost, a transparent wisp that runs by the men on the foul wind of morning.

He goes to the boulder and climbs up. Exhaustion takes him then, and lying out on the coded graffiti, he sleeps.

29

"Joel."

'No.'

"Joel!"

'NO!'

Then there is thumping on his back, and though he tries to wish it away, to dream it into the water of the Beacon River, the thumping continues.

Joel opens his eyes. The sun is bright, hanging over the trees and reflected in the brisk river current. A starling crosses over, followed by a rain of leaves from an unseen oak tree. They whirl, cluster and break away. Joel shuts his eyes and feels the cold rock beneath him.

The thumping starts again.

"Joel."

Joel looks up. Curry's face is in the center of the sky.

Joel shuts his eyes.

"Joel!"

Joel looks at Curry. In the morning November air, Curry's young beard sparkles. His blue eyes are like the sky itself, clear and pure. The face, although etched with concern, is like that of a savior. A face of comfort, of safety.

"Curry," says Joel.

Curry helps Joel sit up, brushing debris from the younger boy's clothes.

"You've given Mama a scare, Joel. A big scare. She's been crying all morning."

"What time is it, Curry? Is it late?"

"Late, yes," says Curry. "Where have you been all night? Here on this rock?"

Joel tries to remember what he had done the night before, but can only feel the air and smell the earth around him.

"How did you know I was here?"

"Finding my brother is important. It didn't take long."

Joel licks his lips. One foot is asleep, and he has to look to see if he still has a shoe on that foot. He does.

"Police came to our cabin last night. They wanted to come in. Do you know a man named Fort?"

Joel touches his head. Thoughts are like glass shards in his brain. "Mr. Fort is our principal at school."

"He's dead. Beat to death. The police wanted to talk with us. I sent them away. They didn't know the danger to their souls, just coming to our house."

"Mr. Fort?" It is a whisper, a whimper.

"Mama's so upset she won't stop crying."

Joel feels bile rise, but when his stomach cramps, it is a dry heave. The glass of his headache spreads to his neck.

"Mama found your cot empty," says Curry. "She went crazy, crying you had disappeared like Patsy Campbell. And then she saw Petrie was gone, too."

"Petrie is gone?"

"Mama thought she was doing early chores. But she wasn't in the yard or barn. Mama looked all around. Petrie has disappeared, Joel."

Joel slams his first into the side of his head. Panic catches him; he begins to remember the night before. "This is Saturday," he manages.

"Yes," says Curry.

Yesterday was Friday. Yesterday he saw Benton's dogs dead, and Sam Fort was beat to death. Yesterday he took Avery's picture from his mother's room and gave it to Wayne Nelson. Last night he went to the Campbell cabin and saw people cut a dead woman and drink from her.

And last night he heard the voice of Satan. He heard the voice of the sineater.

"Come home with me," says Curry. "Mama needs us."

"Yesterday," whispers Joel.

"Joel, come home."

Joel looks at the face of his brother. And in the presence of comfort and safety, he falls into waiting arms and cries.

Curry carries him home.

PART THREE

JOEL AND CURRY

1

"It is Friday."

"No, Joel. It is today. It is Saturday."

'There is fire in the yard and it burns my face. I have to get away from it!'

Joel feels sweat on his chest and thighs. He is naked beside the fire in Missy Campbell's yard, and he cannot move away.

"Joel, you are ill. It is Saturday."

'No, it's not. Can't you see? Can't you see where we are?'

There are tents to Joel's back. There is a shed behind him also, and Wayne calls to Joel but Joel cannot answer. He can only stare at the fire. Where is Benton? He should be here. He could help.

Missy comes out of her cabin. She wears a torn dress, and carries a vicious, shredded mail bucket. She does not look at Joel, but moves to the fire's side and lies down on the ground.

"This is my body," she says, and drags the ragged shards of the bucket over her arms. Blood pours out. Then her eyes roll over, and take Joel's in a horrid stare. "Come drink, boy. It is the only way."

Joel says, "No!"

"Lie still, Joel." It is Lelia, her voice from somewhere in the sky.

'Mama, help me!'

"Come, Joel. Blood of the Lamb, waiting for you. Sineater'll get you if you don't watch out." Missy grins.

"Watch out!" screams Wayne from the shed.

"Watch out," says Missy.

And then Dave is beside Joel. The red-haired boy swings a burned and ragged hand from a piece of blue yarn. "Hot enough?" he asks.

Joel looks down. His legs are on fire. Red flames lick upward, wrapping his skin like a living cocoon, turning his flesh to black. The fire creeps upward, crisping his body, reaching for his eyes.

"Will save you, Joel," says Missy. "Burn your eyes and you won't have to worry 'bout seeing the sineater."

"It's a blessing, Joel, accept it," says Dave.

Joel raises his blackened and peeling arms above his head. "Mama, help me!"

"Joel, it's all right. It's Sunday," Lelia speaks from beyond Joel's vision.

And then the fire is gone. He is standing in water. He looks down and sees the Beacon River swirling about his feet. He knows the boulder is beside him, although he cannot turn to see it. He can only look down the river at the West Path Bridge.

A raft comes from beneath the bridge. It bears Missy and Dave Campbell. And between them, standing as tall as a giant blue spruce tree, with eyes of red embers and teeth of sharp, whittled pine branches, is Avery.

Joel covers his face. "Mama!" he cries.

"Look at us!" calls Missy. Joel looks.

The eyes of the sineater burn into Joel. They spark in bloodlust. The wooden teeth open and shut, chattering in anticipation of the taste of Joel's flesh.

"Mama, help me!"

"I'm here, Joel."

Avery towers now, close enough for the heat of his eyes to singe Joel's face. The terrifying face leers, looms close. The teeth clack rapidly.

"Eat!" screams Missy. "It's the only way!" She laughs. Dave laughs. The mouth of the sineater closes in.

"Mama!"

Joel shudders. He jerks his head, and the river is gone. Avery is gone. There are walls, and the feel of a familiar mattress beneath his back.

"Mama!"

Lelia leans over her son. She holds a rag, and her brows are drawn. "Fever's broke, Joel. You'll be all right now."

Joel swallows. The fire in his head has burned all his spit away. "Mama," he says. "It ain't safe no more. I heard his voice. It ain't even safe for us no more."

"Hush, Joel." Lelia twists the rag about her fingers and dabs his face. The rag is warm.

"Do you hear me, Mama? Petrie's gone. Where do you think she is?"

"Shhh." The sound is tense. The dabbing quickens.

"Mama, he's killing people. He's gonna kill more! And he don't care if it's them or us now. We's just people to him, people who can bleed and die!"

"Stop, Joel!" Lelia pulls the rag from Joel's face. "I won't hear of it! You be quiet!"

"He coulda killed Petrie! We got to get away. We can go stay with Andy. He won't care. His daddy's a preacher, he's got to understand!"

Lelia stands, so abruptly that she knocks the cot and it skips a step on the floor. "You's sick, Joel. It's the sickness talking. Get a good night's sleep and all this nonsense will be gone from your head in the morning."

"Mama, please!"

"It's Sunday night, Joel. Say an extra prayer tonight."

"Mama . . ."

Lelia leaves the room and closes the door.

"God," Joel whispers in obedience to his mother, but can go no further. He wraps himself in his arms. "Wayne," he says. "Benton." He wants to be with them. He wants to be where strength does not die in fear.

He wants to fly away. To go away from sickness and evil and sin and sadness.

If God can do anything, he can take boys away and put them where there is sun and laughter and no hate.

'Curry is safe, Joel. He will take care of you.'

But Curry is a Barker, too. No matter how much he cares, he will always be a Barker, and will always be feared by the other people of the world. And one day, he will become sineater. And then even Joel won't be able to look at him.

And then who will be there?

Lelia.

Only Lelia.

For his whole life, Joel will have only his family to be with him. Only his family to attend him. And together, they will cower in the dark and be shunned by day and will cry and shiver and pray.

God can do anything, but He doesn't want to.

Joel turns on his side and sleeps.

He does not dream this time.

The emptiness and the nothingness lasts forever.

And then he jerks awake to find that late night is on him, and Curry is sleeping on the bed beside Joel.

Joel rubs his eyes, and tries to sit up, but dizziness puts him back down. He coughs and spits into his hand a trickle of phlegm. The fever is returning; his pillow is soaked.

He shifts his face on the wet cotton of the pillowcase. His lids flutter. If he can get through the night, it will be better. Lelia always said pain was worse at night.

'Go to sleep.'

Thump.

Joel's eyes fly open.

Thump.

Another dream, he thinks. Sounds working in his sickened mind.

Bootsteps thump on the porch, and the kitchen door opens.

'Not again!'

Steps in the kitchen, scraping on the floor.

'Christ, Jesus, God, No! I can't be awake for this. Not again!'

Joel's body begins to shake violently. The fever, the sickness, tossing his body about, out of control. *'Stop it! Stop it!'*

Thump, thump, thump. In the hall now. Outside of Joel's closed bedroom door.

'He knows I was at the Campbells'! God, help me! Put me to sleep now, or let me die! Don't let me shake here for him to see!'

Joel rolls onto his arms, but they tremble beneath him like fevered snakes.

The doorknob is turned.

'Go away! I'm asleep! Please, God, I'm asleep!'

The door opens.

Joel's body shakes. Sweat pours from his skin.

The bootsteps move into the room. There is breathing with the bootsteps.

Tears cut down Joel's face. His eyes are shut so tightly they tremble with the rest of him.

There is no sound then, except the breathing. The sineater is staring at Joel. Avery is staring at his son. Joel listens for the clicking of the wooden spiked teeth.

But all he hears is the breathing. The harsh rasp of the sineater's breath. Hot. Close.

And on his neck.

'GOD!'

And then it moves away.

The steps go into the hall.

The door is closed.

Joel tastes blood from the cut his teeth have made deep in his lip.

2

Just inside the front door of the school, Joel stops and puts his bookbag on the floor. Other kids push around him, blowing in on the cold outside wind and ripping scarves and hats off as they hit the heat of the main hall. Across from where he stands, Joel can see the large window of the office. Christine Fort is not there, of course. Some strange lady mans the phone. The assistant principal Mr. Hamilton paces in the office, talking to the strange lady while several students sit on the bench there and wait.

Joel leans on the wall for a moment, trying to find a second wind. His head is light, his stomach empty and uneasy. Lelia had not wanted him to go to school today, but had protested very little. Joel told her that he should get out for fresh air and exercise, and promised that if he felt worse during school he would go to the sick room. Joel couldn't believe she had gone for that excuse; he had been very ill all weekend, and the fever had broken a second time only five hours ago during Monday's wee hours. But Mama was too tired and confused to put up much of an argument. She bore an expression of dazed astonishment at all that had come upon her. Petrie had not returned all weekend. And as Joel was leaving the cabin this morning, two policemen arrived, calling for Mama and saying that this time they had a warrant.

Joel would have stayed for that. But he had something else he had to do.

He stopped by Wayne's apartment before he crossed the bridge, but the mailman was not there. Joel's heart tightened. He wanted to tell Wayne about Petrie. He wanted to ask the mailman to take his family away for a while, to find somewhere safe the Barkers could hide.

Joel knocked on the door at the top of the stairs for a long time, until his fist ached and he had to sit on a step. He wondered where the mailman would be this early in the day, and thought at first that he would wait for the man's return.

But Wayne had a mother who was part of Missy's group, and she would come and find the Barker boy on the steps.

After a spell of blackness passed, Joel climbed down the stairs and went to school.

A second hope was there at school.

The bell rings. Joel moves from the main hall to his classroom. His bookbag drags behind him on its strap. There are three minutes until the next bell sounds for homeroom to begin. Three minutes to plead his case.

Mrs. Grant had sounded truthful when she offered concern to Joel earlier. She had sounded like she really wanted to know if she could help if there was trouble. The thought of talking to his old-lady teacher about what had been happening was terrifying. He couldn't even imagine standing before her and forming the words on his lips. But as he had walked to school he had found his courage. She was an adult. She was a teacher. She had power in her own right. She would help him if he asked her.

Sixth graders flood into the classroom. Joel stops at the door, peeking inside. Mrs. Grant is not yet inside, thank God. It will make it easier. He looks up and down the hall. His hands run cold; his barren stomach squeezes uncomfortably, questioning what Joel plans to do.

Rennie plows past Joel, swinging a backpack which catches Joel in the side of the ribs. Ed and Mary Skipp follow through, holding hands, which come apart as soon as they are in the room.

Mr. Hamilton is in the hall now, ushering children to their proper rooms. He acts as though it is the first day of school, not the middle of November. Joel wonders what they will say over the intercom this morning about Mr. Fort.

Joel's fingers strum the strap of his bookbag.

He stares down the hall, watching for Mrs. Grant. He hopes Mr. Hamilton will not shoo him inside before he comes.

And then he sees her head above the morning students, a stern balloon with a top of gray hair.

Joel licks his lips and strums his bookbag strap.

Mrs. Grant works through the crowd and stops at the classroom door. She looks at Joel.

"Is something the matter?"

Joel licks his lips again. His fingers hold still on the strap.

"Yes." *'No! This isn't right. Too many people all around. Not now! Can't we talk somewhere else?'*

"What is it, Joel? I've got a class waiting."

"I want to talk to you."

"All right," says Mrs. Grant as she looks into her classroom.

"It's about stuff . . . this weekend. I want . . ." He stops. Ed is making faces from his desk at the teacher, but the teacher doesn't see.

Mrs. Grant thinks she understands. "We all feel terrible about Mr. Fort, Joel. Such a crime is incomprehensible."

"Well, it's sort of about that," says Joel. "And more."

Mrs. Grant looks into her classroom and shakes a finger at Rennie.

"It's about my family."

Mrs. Grant looks at Joel. She is obviously surprised.

"This is serious, Joel?"

'Yes!' "Yes, ma'am."

She frowns, glances inside her classroom and then looks at Joel again.

"Now isn't the best time, Joel. Things are very hectic this morning," she says. "Lunch, maybe, Joel? Let's talk at lunch time."

Joel picks up his bookbag strap again, then looks to see Mr. Hamilton distracted by one of the young janitors. Several other students slip along the hallway in a race to class.

Dave strolls at the back of the jumble.

"Will that be all right with you, Joel?"

Dave sees Joel, and his expression is dark and terrifying. It dares Joel to talk to his teacher.

"I don't . . ."

"Rennie, get in your seat this minute, I won't say it again!"

Dave gets closer. Joel has never seen such fury on a face before.

"It ain't really nothing," Joel whispers.

"Rennie, I said sit! Joel, what did you say?"

"It ain't nothing, Mrs. Grant. I just don't feel too well. I'll be okay."

Mrs. Grant shakes her head. "If you're sick you should be at home."

"I'll be okay."

"Well, come on inside, then."

"Can I go to the bathroom?"

"Can you go?"

"May I go?"

"Hurry up about it."

The teacher enters the classroom. Joel slides across the hall and into the boys' bathroom. Dave follows.

"What the fuck was all that about?" Dave says as Joel goes to the sink.

"What the fuck was what?"

"Goddam you!" Dave shoves Joel's shoulder. "What was you saying to that teacher?"

"Nothing! I just told her I was sick!"

"You told her about Friday night. You's spilling your guts, you little coward!"

Joel spits into the sink. "I didn't. I didn't say nothing."

"Your eyes looked all sneaky. This stuff is between us, Joel. Nobody else, especially not no goddamn teacher!"

"I didn't say nothing."

Dave stops and looks away. Joel watches him in the mirror. Then the red-haired boy says, "They came to our house, did they come to yours?"

"Who?"

"The police. They think they're gonna find out who killed Sam Fort by checking a couple of cabins. What a joke."

Joel says nothing. He wipes his mouth with a paper towel.

"They don't know what they're dealing with. I should just tell them to go home and wait for me to take care of it."

Joel says nothing.

Dave pats his arm, and for a second Joel thinks the coon dick will be pulled out from some tucked-away place in the older boy's sleeve.

"Ain't nothing I can't do," says Dave. "I ain't supposed to be at school and I come. I ain't supposed to talk to you and I do."

Then Joel knows it is the scab that Dave is caressing. The scab Joel put there with the sandpaper. The scab that replaces the star of light.

"They don't know nothing, do they, Joel? Soon they will. Soon they will." And Dave's smile looks like Avery's dream smile, all sharp and hateful and deadly.

3

Joel is relieved that Dave is in trouble for fighting during the beginning of lunch, and will spend the rest of the day in Mr. Hamilton's office. Joel eats alone and in silence, hoping that Mrs. Grant will remember his appeal this morning and approach him. But she sits at a far table with the fifth-grade teachers. Their voices are low and their faces are drawn. Talking, most likely, about the tragedy Friday afternoon. It seems she took his final denial, his excuse of sickness, seriously. Perhaps he'll be able to talk to her at the end of the day. He takes a small bite of the tasteless potatoes.

But the day ends early. Classes are dismissed at two o'clock, and those with arrangements leave in carpools to Mr. Fort's funeral in Christine's hometown of Penloe.

Joel gets out to the parking lot in time to see the rear of Mrs. Grant's Toyota join the long line of automobiles heading north.

He stands with his bookbag on the blacktop, his hands in his jacket pockets. Above him, unsanctioned but allowed, the Virginia flag flies at half-mast beneath the Stars and Stripes.

'Tomorrow', he thinks. He hopes to God that tomorrow will not be too late.

Joel shudders. The state flag pops and cracks in the wind, high above Joel's head.

'Benton.'

No, Benton will not want to see him. Benton's dogs are dead, and it is Joel's fault. His fault for coming around the Hardware in the first place. His fault for being a Barker.

Joel starts down Route 536. He hopes that perhaps Benton will be on the porch as he passes, and that the man might call Joel up to look for mail, and then Joel can tell the man all that has happened.

'Yes, Benton will be on the porch. It ain't raining, and it ain't all that cold. He will be on the porch. I can talk to Benton.'

As Joel approaches the store, he can see someone on the porch. His heart jumps. *'Oh, thank God!'* His feet pick up speed, and his bookbag seems suddenly lighter. A small smile forms on his lips, and one free hand raises slightly, ready to wave if the reception seems kind enough.

A car on the road honks at Joel as the boy veers a bit onto the pavement. Joel begins to run.

The man on the Hardware porch stops watching cars and looks at Joel.

It is not Benton.

It is Fitch Spencer.

Joel's feet slow. His bookbag thumps his thigh. Fitch Spencer. And the man looks very unhappy.

Joel slows for a moment. He gathers himself, then goes to the bottom of the porch steps.

"Mr. Spencer," he begins.

Fitch looks around, his interest momentarily taken from the flow of cars going north.

Joel does not want to talk to the man. It was bad coming here now. Fitch does not like him.

"Well, what is it, boy?" Fitch crosses his arms. He has no gloves on and his fingers are red and rough.

"I came to see if there is any mail today," says Joel.

Fitch look back at the road. He creaks back slightly on the bench, bracing the heels of his rubber boots on the floor. "Well, I don't know. I ain't Benton. And Benton ain't here. Gone to the funeral."

'Of course.'

Fitch pulls a can of Coors he had on the bench to his lips and poises it there, drinking silently. Joel steps back, nodding stupidly, muttering "Okay, sorry."

"Gone to the funeral," Fitch repeats. Joel turns and trots across the road in front of another car blaring its horn.

"Gone to the damn funeral!"

4

Tuesday morning, Earlie arrives at school before seven-thirty. It is unusually cold this morning, not even out of the teens, and in spite of the layers she wore, her body still shakes. She drops her books onto her desk and unwraps her scarf; peels off her mittens. She is still depressed about Sam Fort, and the depression is edged with a touch of miff she holds for herself. Last night, she and several other teachers had visited with Christine, a Christian enough duty, but when Earlie had gone home she had fallen into bed without grading a single paper. Without reading a single book report. It only goes to show that socializing can become a force that takes one away from one's truer purposes. A force like television, like alcohol, like too many magazines or too much free time.

Before she takes off her coat, she opens her plan book and spreads the science quizzes out like a fan over the desktop. With a little luck and no interruptions, she can at least get these taken care of. The book reports will have to wait until music class.

One of the hippie janitors strolls by with a pair of headphones on his hippie head. Earlie scowls. The school was never clean enough to suit her, and now with Joshua Munsen gone, sometimes her room is left untouched by a broom for two days in a row. She has no beef with Philicia Hodge; the woman is only a part-time temporary, and the hippies don't respect her enough to do as she says. She wonders if Mr. Hamilton will be appointed as a principal by the school board

266

or if they'll cart someone in from elsewhere. She doubts that Christine will come back. The whole school has been tossed upside down like a bowl of lettuce and mushrooms.

Earlie goes to the back of the room and opens the door to the walk-in coat closet. She shrugs from her coat and lifts the scarf from her shoulders, then goes inside and pulls the chain to the light. The room is small, with rods about three sides for the students' wraps. Shelves above the rods store many of Earlie's materials. In about a week she will take the Christmas box from its resting place, and decorate the room with the old ropes of golden garland and cardboard cutouts of huge holly leaves and candy canes. She has a manger scene that she likes to display, but one of the new teachers last year told her she shouldn't put it out. Of course, Earlie still plans on setting it in its place of honor by the window, but now the act will hold a tinge of anger. Anger at the uppity teacher and the school board which would support the uppity teacher if they saw the manger by the window.

She takes a hanger from the rod on the far wall and slips her coat onto it. She bends to unbuckle her boots, when there is a thumping behind her, in the doorway.

"Who's that . . ." she begins as she turns around.

All she can see at that moment is a huge packing box being flung into the closet with her, striking her on the hip and falling to the floor at her feet. Her eyes cut up instantly to see who tossed the box, but only hands are there then, fingers wrapped around the edge of the closet door as it is being slammed shut. The fingers pull away right before the door clicks.

And there is scratching.

Earlie hops to the door and rattles the knob.

Scratching. Skittering.

The knob turns, but the door won't budge as she pushes into it.

"Who's that? What is going on?"

Something heavy is behind the door now, on the classroom side, wedged so Earlie cannot get the door open.

Skittering, scratching. Squeaking.

Something crosses the top of Earlie's boot. She looks down.

A scream rockets to the top of her throat, then locks, and she gags on it.

She falls against the door, and it holds as tightly as if it were nailed.

From the box, digging through a loose flap in the top, are rats. Gray rats, black rats, frantic and squeaking and twitching noses and horrid, naked pink tails.

They spill onto the floor, running as their claws touch the wood, circling and racing around the walls and across Earlie's feet.

Earlie catches her neck with both hands. Her eyes pop.

More fall from the box. They bare their teeth in fear.

A rat jumps and catches to the bottom of Earlie's skirt. She shakes, tossing it free. She dances, her feet moving between some of the rats and coming down on others.

She screams.

The box itself moves now. An enormous wet nose rams through the loose flap. One huge paw comes in contact with the floor. The last rat, too large to come through, scoots the box about the closet.

Earlie screams. She lunges up, catching the bottom of a shelf and trying to pull herself up onto it. The shelf gives from its nails and drops her onto the floor.

A rat tangles its feet in her hair.

She jumps up, screaming again, and shakes her hair until the rat falls.

She hurls herself up to the next shelf. One hand catches, then the other. Her booted feet kick the air, trying to walk up to the shelf. One knee finds the steel rod and braces her for a moment. Hangers clatter. One heel goes over the rod. Her palms, splintered and crying in pain, hold on to the shelf. Below, the rats run circles in the closet.

"Help me!" she shouts.

The largest rat gets its second foot through the flap. The claws glint in the light of the single bulb.

"Help me!"

She swings her other boot, trying to get her foot up to the clothes rod. And then the shelf cracks and gives. She is tossed outward and down. Her clutching fingers grab at air and find the string to the light.

The light snaps off. The string pulls from the bulb as she drops to the floor.

And only the rats can see in that darkness.

5

Joel stands beside a bare walnut tree across the road from the hardware store. Next to him, the antique store is silent and empty. The Quarles, according to the note on the door, are on vacation for a week. Joel wonders where they went. He wonders if Rod and Ellen will really come back.

There is no one on the porch of Benton's store. Joel has stood here since school let out a half hour ago, and he has seen no one enter or leave. Perhaps there is a note on Benton's door as well, telling of an early vacation, although Joel can't see any paper.

Joel feels the shreds of a note in his pocket. The note he had written to give to Mrs. Grant today. The note that told everything, from Dave to Missy to Avery and Petrie. Last night in bed he had convinced himself that it was the only way to do it. She would read the note today and this afternoon she would think of something to do to help.

But she wasn't in school today. Or, as the rumor went in the halls this morning, she had come, but had had a stroke in the closet. Or a heart attack. Something serious. Something that brought an ambulance from Penloe.

Mr. Hamilton had fumed in the front of the class, acting as though he had forgotten how to be a teacher, until a substitute arrived, a Miss Conlon with fat arms and yellow teeth. With each change of subject during the day, with math and spelling and social studies and

269

science, Joel tore a little more of the note up and crammed it into his pocket.

"She won't be back, not for a long time," Ed had said with a grin.

"She had a seizure and fell in the closet," said Mary Skipp to the girls at lunch. "They said she had scratches all over. She was bleeding and everything."

"She was *crying*, I heard!" laughed Ed during reading. "Can you see that?"

By dismissal time, the note, all three pages of it, was like a rabbit's nest, soft strips of crumpled paper in a ball.

And now Joel stands watching the hardware store. A few cars rumble by. It begins to sleet.

It does not matter about the mail anymore. Whatever Andy might have to say would mean nothing. Joel has to talk to Benton. Even if Fitch is there, he has to beg for help.

Joel lets the sleet collect in his hair without taking the knit hat from his coat and putting it on.

No one comes to the store. No one comes out. Joel wonders why he is waiting.

There is crunching on the side of the road, and Joel looks around to see Dave kicking his way toward the West Path. Joel dives down and scoots, hiding himself behind a lump of slick, icy earth. Dave passes. Joel waits. When he looks up, the older boy is gone.

He cannot wait longer. He hurries across the road and goes up onto the Hardware porch. His hand shakes, but he knocks. Closing his eyes, he listens. There is no sound of dogs around the store, and his mind serves up the picture again of the hounds in the dirt, bodies slashed and degraded. Joel shakes his head, knocking out the image, and he looks again at the door.

"It'll be all right. Benton will help.'

The doorknob twists.

'Benton will help.'

Benton stands in the doorway. Joel can barely see the man's face through the screen.

Joel shivers in relief. "Benton . . ." he says.

"What do you want?"

Joel blinks. The man's voice was hard. "I want to talk to you. Is that okay?"

Benton does not open the screen door. Joel still cannot see his face.

"No," says Benton finally. "I don't think so."

Joel swallows, and his bowels suddenly hurt. His lips open. Sleet, melting on his head, slides down his cheek. "Why?"

"Dogs are dead, Joel. Got a note. And now Wayne is missing. This ain't mentioning Sam Fort."

'Wayne, missing? God, no.'

Benton shifts behind the door. "Dog's are *dead*, Joel!" The fury in Benton's voice drives a knife into the boy's heart.

"I know."

"You know, do you? And you know that I can't take chances no more? Do you know that I have a family and I can't take chances?"

Joel feels his head nod.

"Jesus!" swears Benton. The man looks around into his store, then back out the screen door. "My dogs, damn it! What did they ever do to anyone? Damn it! I'm sorry, Joel. I just can't take no more chances, not now."

Joel wants to scream, "What does this have to do with me? Why can't you like me anymore?", but he knows. Everyone who has had something to do with the Bankers is now the hated target. The rule breakers are receiving the insane revenge.

"Here," says Benton, pushing the door open a slit and dropping something through. "A letter. But don't come here again. I'm sorry, Joel. But they were my dogs!"

The heavy door shuts. Joel stares at the envelope on the porch.

Sleet, cold and melting, falls in large drops and smudges the ink letters of Andy's return address.

6

With a slam, the kitchen stool is flung across the room, crashes against the steel sink and falls. A chair follows, and a basket of kindling, then pans and spoons and forks fly after, clanging and pinging on the sink and the front of the stove and then falling to the floor. Missy says nothing because Missy is not home, of course. She and the tent dwellers from the backyard are about their daily duties. Some have gone to their respective cabins to retrieve stored food and to tend animals left behind. Others are in town with a communal fund, gathering other supplies from the grocery and hardware stores. Some are with Missy, visiting the fresh grave of Fonda Clark.

Jewel has not gone with the others. Dave thinks she is the only one remaining in the backyard. She keeps the campfire burning so it will be hot for dinner in an hour or so. Dave thinks Missy left her behind so when Dave got home, the two of them would have time together. Dave does not know what Missy thinks he does with his time during the day. As long as he is not going to school, then she doesn't give a flying fuck what he does all those hours. She does not even ask him. But when he is there, and when she happens to think of him, she is constantly making references to Jewel and her meekness and her virtue. It makes Dave want to puke.

When Dave got home from school not twenty minutes ago, Jewel was on the back porch, getting larger logs to add to the fire. She heard him come in, and she stuck her ugly face in through the door

272

and said hello. Dave did not speak, but immediately went out to the front stoop until she was in the backyard again.

The bucket of old magazines and fliers, used for fire starters, crashes into the stove. Paper scatters. Dave's work boots take the air, thumping into the wall above the sink, barely missing the small window.

The rats had worked. Waiting in the boys' bathroom in the dark and cold with a cardboard box of frightened rats from Missy's shed had been worth it. Joel won't be able to talk to that teacher anymore. The old lady is out of commission, spending time in the hospital and hopefully retiring for the rest of her damned life. She had tried to keep Joel from Dave. She had hated Dave, had thought she could ''help'' Joel be safe from all the dangers Dave presented. But screw her now. Let her have nightmares of rats. Let her sit in a wheelchair in her house and look out at the trees and realize that Dave had stopped her.

But Joel is hiding from Dave. All day long at school, Dave watched for the younger boy, but only caught glimpses of him. When Joel saw Dave he would hurry around a corner or into a crowd to be lost.

Hiding like a wimp.

Dave throws a pillow from his cot and a box of screws from a shelf.

Hiding like a goddam wimp!

Leaving Dave alone to do what he had vowed to do.

So screw Joel! So forget him. How could Dave had expected more? Why would Dave have wanted a friend in the first place?

Dave drops onto the cot and hammers his heels on the floor. He looks at the mess about the room.

Missy won't notice. She and her followers are so into the spirit these days, she'll think they were tossed around by a Sister in a trance, or a Brother filled with the holy ghost. And there are more Brothers and Sisters now than you can shake a stack of Bibles at. Missy's Last Day sermons have recruited at least another twenty-five. Lots of stars have been carved these past days. Mutilations and deaths are still to come, she said. Only safety is in the gathering of God's own.

Dave's shoulders tremble with impotent fury. He must regain the power he was seeking. He must forget Joel and Wayne and get on with catching the sineater.

He shivers.

He hears Jewel on the porch, getting more logs.

A paralysis holds his muscles and his mind. He knows what he must do, but something will not let him. Something holds power over him even now, letting him dream his dreams but stopping him from acting.

On impulse, Dave finds the coon dick in a box beneath his cot. He slides it into his jeans pocket beside the hammer.

Is it fear that stops him? Cowardice? Is Dave a wimp like Joel, all talk and dreams and nothing but shit for guts?

Suddenly, the scabs beneath Dave's upper arm begin to itch. His fingers creep beneath the shirt material and scratch. Bits of scab flake free. He traces the flesh; it is smooth now. No scab is left.

"Christ," he whispers. "The star is gone."

His mouth goes dry. He ducks his head through the neck of his shirt and comes out, peeling the sleeves free. He feels the smooth underside of his arm. At last, the terrible reminder of Aunt Missy's power is gone.

Dave turns his arm over and looks.

"Christ."

He stares, his hand falling from the smooth skin.

"Fucking Christ," he hisses.

The star is still there. It is faint, the corners softened in scar tissue, but it is still there. Plain and garishly simple. Horrid. Mocking.

'She still holds it over you, Dave. She can make you eat dead people, and can keep you in line.'

"Fuck it!"

'You aren't any more than you were back in West Virginia, where they even told you how to eat a goddam sandwich!"

"Fuck it!" Dave stands and grabs the platters from the mantel. They crash across the room. He takes Patsy's picture, and without looking at the girl's timid face, hurls it to the floor. He snatches the hammer from his pocket and smashes the picture glass into bright, vicious shards.

He hits again, again, again. Each strike feels like a death blow.

The face of Patsy is the face of every Sister, every Brother, of the sineater, and of Missy Campbell.

And he is killing them. The hammer is for killing.

Yes.

The hammer blazes in his hands and he smashes the glass, pulverizing it.

The hammer is for killing.

Burke stops abruptly and the hammer falls from his grasp.

'The hammer is for killing.' Why does he know that?

His heart is a hammer, too. It thunders, trying to kill him itself. He picks the hammer back up. He can almost touch a dark memory; it laughs horribly at him from under his ribs.

Then he goes into his aunt's room, and takes the shotgun from the case. He grabs a handful of shells and crams them into his pocket. A backup for the hammer.

He slams through out front door and into the sleet.

He will find the sineater. He will smash the demon himself, then send the head back to Missy on a silver platter.

Joel sits on the barrel in the barn, letter in hand, watching the address smear under the dampness of his thumb. No Wayne now. He is gone. Perhaps he found the same fate as Petrie. Joel shudders. He cannot imagine what that fate is, and the thought is unbearable.

Mrs. Grant cannot help now. Benton will not help.

Lelia does not want to leave. She does not believe in the danger, only that Petrie is gone. Curry does not want to leave, either. He believes he is where he should be.

'Run away, Joel!'

Joel balls up, tucking his head into his elbows and crushing the envelope. Sleet taps the ground outside.

'Run away, Joel!'

"I want to run away," he whispers.

A gust of wind blows through the open door, bringing the sleet, which stings his face and hands. He wonders if anyone ever stole gloves from Benton.

"I'm scared."

The wind subsides. He looks at the soggy letter, then rips it open. The pencil print inside is not smeared. It says,

"Dear Joel,

I didn't want to write but I got to. You got to know. It's real bad."

Joel shifts on the barrel. He reads on.

"It's bad. Daddy's not at home no more. He's at a place called

Brandon House, for sick people sick in the head. He's been gone a couple days now. What he told us before he went to Brandon House is really bad."

'It's really bad here, too, Andy. You wouldn't believe it."

"You and me wondered what happened to Patsy Campbell. She saw the sineater, Joel. In June she was in the woods near her cabin and she saw Avery Barker."

Joel pulls the paper taut. Patsy saw the sineater.

"Daddy said what happened was his fault because he never told Missy Campbell what she did and believed was wrong. He said he didn't think they were wrong, just different. Missy liked him for that. That's why she came to church when we was in Ellison."

Joel's heart hammers. Patsy Campbell saw the sineater!

"Daddy said he didn't care if Missy and those people handled snakes and stuff like that. He said it was their business. Now he says he was wrong. He says he should have told them to stop doing things like that. The other Baptist preachers were right all along."

Joel turns the letter over.

"Daddy said Missy trusted him. She believed Daddy came from God. And then Patsy saw Avery in the woods.

"She came home screaming. Missy could tell Patsy had already lost her mind for seeing him. Missy put Patsy in the shed and came to see my daddy. She told Daddy what happened. Said Patsy seen the sineater. Daddy asked Missy what she wanted to do about it. All Missy said was 'Guide me in God's way.'

"Daddy told her to go home and pray. She'd know what to do.

"Daddy told me and Mommy that God will damn him, but he will never tell nobody to pray about nothing again. Never."

Joel's hands shake. It is hard to hold the paper still.

"Daddy said he thought things would be okay. He thought God would help Missy, and Patsy would get over what happened.

"Daddy didn't believe seeing the sineater would make you die.

"But it did."

Joel's breathing matches his heartbeat; irregular, painful.

"Missy went home and prayed about it, like Daddy said. Then she did what she thought she was supposed to do. She's crazy, please be careful! Missy did what she said she had to do when somebody seen the sineater . . .''

"Joel!"

Joel jumps, startled, dropping the letter. He looks up.

Lelia stands in the barn doorway. Her hair is full of sleet; her eyes are red with anguish.

"What?" Every nerve of Joel's body challenges her. Every fiber is piqued with fear and urgency. Missy did what she had to do when somebody sees the sineater. What, dear God, was that? She did something terrible to Patsy!

"I thought you had disappeared!"

"I'm here, Mama."

His mother's eyes spin. They find the letter on the floor. "What's that?"

"Letter."

"From Andy?" Lelia steps in and grabs up the letter and shakes it in Joel's face. "No more letters! You hear me? No more, we don't need this!" She tears the letter into strips and takes it with her out into the sleet.

Joel doesn't know now.

But he knows enough.

It is Missy. He holds his head and rocks back and forth. It is Missy. The mail bucket and the dogs and Sam's death and Petrie missing and Wayne missing isn't Avery. It is Missy. Andy says she is crazy. He says Joel must be careful.

Dave said it was all about power, and Joel knows without a doubt now that Dave was right. Missy is fighting for her power, and doing anything for it.

Anything.

'Dave.'

Dave has had something to do with the Barkers. Dave has been Joel's friend.

Dave is in the dead-center of the danger. What would Missy do to him if she found out?

Joel slides off the barrel, catching a large splinter in his calf. His feet hit the ground and drive him forward.

He has to tell Dave. He has to warn his friend. Without Wayne, or Mrs. Grant, or Benton to help him.

He has to do it on his own.

8

There is pain, hot and driving, in the back of Wayne's neck, and at his wrist, his elbows, his legs. He tries to open his eyes but there is the blackness of a cloth blindfold over his eyeballs. The cloth scrapes them through the slit and it hurts, so he squeezes them shut again. A strand of lint from the cloth catches under his lid and makes the eye water fiercely.

He is aware of a thirst which is almost as bad as the pain and the lint. His tongue finds his lips and the sticky bit of saliva only burns. The muscles of his shoulders suddenly buckle, and Wayne drops an inch against the hard surface to which he is held.

Cords cut his flesh.

'God, yes.' He remembers. He has been here a long time, bound to something that has his arms outstretched and his forehead strapped with a tight piece of rope. Unconsciously, his shoulders have worked at holding him upright, relieving the strain on his arms and neck. But they cannot hold indefinitely, and with his knees drooped now, he feels the cords will tear right through.

He tries to get some weight on his feet, but they, too, are bound backward, braced awkwardly on the flat surface behind.

He remembers. Anger and realization surge with his headache. He had been hit on the head some time ago. He had been at the Campbells' cabin, and had gone after Avery Barker. And then in the darkness, he had been struck.

And now he is here. Wherever the hell that is.

His stomach clamps, empty and angry, and Wayne swallows nothing in answer. The circles of pain across his body cause him to shove himself upward again with the use of his shoulders, and give the job back to them.

He has never been so afraid in his life.

There is the sound of bugs and birds beyond his darkness, but they are hard to hear over the headache and fear.

And then the sound becomes feet, and he feels the closeness of someone directly in front of him.

'God, no.'

A hand is on his elbow, and Wayne knows now for the first time that his shirt is gone. Cold fingers touch bare flesh. Wayne grinds his teeth so he will no cry out.

The whisper that comes is horrifying.

"You have damned yourself."

Wayne begins to tremble, and his shoulders threaten to let go.

"You have ignored God. You've had dealings with the unholy."

Wayne's dry lips open. Through his terror, he mumbles, "Fuck you."

There is a sound of rattling, and then something sharp is pressed to the skin of his arms. Wayne's throbbing brain reels, trying to imagine what it is, what is coming.

The sharp thing is wriggled, finding muscle immediately beneath the bone of his upper arm. And then there is a second of silence, and then a grunt and a motion quick to the side of Wayne's face.

With a smack, the nail is driven through the arm muscle and into the surface behind. Wayne opens his mouth and shrieks. Fire races his blood, taking the pain to every corner of his body and soul.

"You must suffer the punishment," says the whisper.

Wayne feels the hand on his other arm, and another sharp point nestles the skin, seeking muscle.

"Noooo!"

"Yes," says the whisper. There is the pause, and the quick motion. Even before the nail drives into his body, Wayne is screaming and screaming and screaming.

9

The sleet stopped before Joel had even reached the Campbell cabin, but the boy is still soaked, his jeans wrapped about his legs like wet paper to a tree trunk, and his shoes sloshing. He walks down South Branch toward the bridge and the beginning of West Path.

Dave had not been home.

Joel had waited behind a tall shrub, watching the front door to the Campbell cabin, listening, hoping the red-haired boy would come outside or at least look out the door so Joel could get his attention. For a minute, Joel even thought of calling out, but he had no idea if anyone else might be there.

He waited for many minutes. And then, a young woman had come calling through the cabin.

"Burke?" she said. "Burke, where are you? I need some help with these larger logs."

Joel pulled low, watching.

"Burke?"

The woman's face appeared at the front door, and then she came out onto the stoop. She wore a bulky sweater and long gray skirt. A plaid flannel shirt showed from under the sweater, and her hair was wound into a massive bun.

"Burke?"

She went back inside. Joel slid down and sat on the wet ground.

281

His heart hurt. His body only then registered the discomfort of the wet clothes he wore.

And he got up then and headed home.

He would tell Dave at school. It was the only other choice. There was no way Joel could find Dave in the mountains if the boy wanted to be hidden.

Joel passes Wayne's garage, but nothing seems disturbed since he last looked. Joel does not want to think about where Petrie is now, or what has kept Wayne away for these past four days.

And then he is at the bridge. He stops and looks down its length, over Route 536 and at the front of the Hardware.

Benton had been Joel's friend, at least for a while. Joel feels his ribs draw in, making his chest hurt. Damn Missy Campbell! Damn her!

Angrily, Joel rips off his soaking jacket and lets it drag in the mud at his feet.

He stares at the hardware store.

10

Benton rubs his eyes and starts the money count all over. He cannot keep his mind on it. All he can see before him are his dead dogs and Philicia crying and Wayne's bloody stump in the weeds in front of the Barker cabin. And Joel Barker's face when Benton threw the letter at him and told him not to come back.

Joel Barker.

Avery Barker.

Damn them for being who they were and damn Ellison and Beacon Cove for making them who they were.

Fitch went home a few minutes ago, announcing through the door before he left that the sleet was ended.

Alone, Benton slams the cash register closed and sweeps his arm across the counter, sending papers and a jar of candy to the floor.

Benton is ashamed for taking it out on the boy. It isn't the boy's fault, and yet Benton knows what happened wouldn't have if Benton had kept the boy at arms distance as the tradition had commanded.

He goes to the front door and opens it, wondering if Joel might still be on the porch after all this time. He knows that is not possible; it has been nearly an hour and a half since Benton slammed the door on the boy. Maybe even longer.

Looking out, his eyes see the porch empty, and the road still. The door of the antique shop has the "Closed" sign hanging on the window, and the shade is drawn. But then Benton sees some-thing on the other side of the Bridge, a small figure staring at him. It is Joel Barker.

Benton shudders and sighs, almost in relief. He will call the boy back, and talk to him again. He will not let him in the store, but maybe Benton can fix some of the damage he himself has done.

He raises his hand to wave.

11

Joel cannot believe what he is seeing. Benton is waving at him from the door of the store. Joel hesitates, then lifts his own hand. The communication lasts nearly three seconds.

And then Philicia Hodge's car rumbles up to the store and pauses. Joel can see Benton's wife roll the window of the passenger's seat down and speak briefly to her husband. Joel lets his hand drop to the edge of the bridge's handrail. He watches the short conversation, and then Philicia's car pulls away, driving the short distance and pulling off into the parking lot of the Baptist Church. Joel watches through the bushes and hedges, trying to watch the woman until she is in the church. He is afraid to look back at the hardware store. He is afraid Benton will have gone back inside, or that Joel made a mistake and that the wave was actually for Philicia, who was coming down the road. Philicia works at the doorknob to the church's side door, and then pushes inside.

Joel looks at his jacket in the mud, then at his hand on the railing and then at Philicia's car on the church parking lot. He looks down into the water of the Beacon River and stares until a large stick vanishes beneath the bridge, carried along by the fast-moving flow.

Then he looks back up at Benton Hodge.

The man is still there, still standing in the doorway. The man's hand raises again, seeming to beckon Joel to come over.

Joel feels a surge of anger and hurt at Benton's treatment of him.

But just as quickly comes the memory of Creeper and the flies. He stares at Benton, suddenly wanting to go to him, but his feet uncertain.

"Joel," calls Benton.

Joel flinches.

"Joel, please come here for a minute."

And Joel's feet loosen. He swoops down and picks up the jacket and drapes it over his arm. He starts over the bridge.

He can't tell for sure, but it looks like Benton might be smiling just a tiny bit. A small smile, of relief, or of sadness.

And then there is a deafening roar, and a flash of intense heat and light, and Joel is knocked to his knees. A shower of grit and small pieces of rock fall about him and on him. He shields himself with his arms.

From over the road, he can hear Benton shouting.

And then Joel wipes his face and feels for the bridge railing. Finding it, he grabs hold and pulls himself upright. He opens his eyes. Benton is no longer on the store porch, he is running across the road to the church.

Joel looks to his left.

The church is destroyed, the side section a burning, ravaged pile of stone and wood.

12

Dave does not know where he is heading, except that he is going northwest. Fury, kept at a head like a stinging pimple, drives him on, forcing his feet along among the trees and brambles and brush, and keeps the gun tight in his sweaty grip. The hammer rides his hip in his pocket.

The tattoo remains. Aunt Missy might never touch his soul, but her repulsive mark taints his skin even now.

Goddam the bitch.

The evening descends in the forest, soaking up sunlight, but Dave has a lantern he snatched up from the porch on his way out. He does not want to turn it on until he has to, though. He will sneak like a fox in the forest, his eyes keening in and keeping him on track.

He will find the sineater. He will look at him, then kill him. Then Missy and her followers will know their star is nothing. They will know Dave is fearless. They will know his power. Some might even leave to follow him.

And Joel will see Dave as he truly is, not a whimpering fag drinking blood and washing old men's feet.

Needle leaves of a fir tree scratch his face. He pushes on.

Goddam Missy! Goddam his mother and father. Goddam Wayne Nelson and Jewel Benshoff. Goddam God.

Maybe when he comes back with the sineater's head, he will rape Jewel Benshoff. She won't care, she'll love him to. Then he will make Jewel's mama lick mud from his filthy shoes, and say she will do anything for him.

The trees break. Dave emerges into a grassy area. It is a clearing, the same one where he and Joel had had their late-night campfire. Dave is slightly to the south of where he had come out the last time. In the late autumn, the weeds have not grown taller, and the campfire site is visible, although barely a black chalk smudge across the field.

West, Dave tells himself. West feels right. The sineater might follow the setting sun, slinking after the bright, burning ball until it is gone, then fall into the onrushing shadows. The crazed man would then hide behind trees, starving if the crop of dead has been lean, slavering and slobbering and watching for careless wanderers.

A chilling thrill fires through Dave from toe to skull. He shivers, and pulls the shotgun close. He imagines the sineater jumping out from behind any of the trees lining the clearing. He imagines having to pull the trigger. He thinks of the unsettling excitement of the dying cat, and wonders how much more thrill there will be in the face of a dying devil.

Tears swell; Dave blinks them away with a toss of his head. He strides out across the clearing, not swerving to avoid patches of dense thistle but plowing right through. The butt of the shotgun snags and jerks in his hands. He passes the blackened campfire remains, thinking for a second about the taste of marshmallows. But then he cannot think of more. Everything to him now exists in the future. Briars biting his jeans and into the skin of his legs do not register. Gnats and moths and invisible flying things batting his face are without meaning. Everything is future, near future, what he will see and what he will do.

The clearing is a long meadow, dipping down on the western edge. Dave stamps ahead, fingers clamped to the gun barrel. He descends with the sloping ground. And at the edge, where trees again swallow the land, he sees a small wooden structure.

He stops.

He squints across the glare of the shiny, dead grass.

It seems to have once been a building. A cabin, perhaps. He moves closer. He sees, in his future, Avery jumping from behind the structure, and he sees the slow motion path of the shot as it flies from the gun, he feels the heavy kick of the butt and hears the loud crack.

Closer now, the grass thinning to what may have once been a yard, he recognizes it as, indeed, a cabin. Or the burned remains of one. A long-abandoned, burned husk of a cabin, left to weather and be grown over with ages of honeysuckle.

Dave tilts his head. The future pauses; it gives room for remembering. This is the remains of Joe McDonald's cabin, set afire many years ago by the community of Beacon Cove. This is where, according to the stories he had been told, three young men burned themselves to death in the name of the Lord. Missy had said that one of the dead men had been Avery Barker's father.

Avery Barker's father. Peculiar to think that the sineater had been a child once. Evil is hard to picture as a baby.

Moving slowly, Dave goes to the cabin, to the open hole which was once a front door. The smell is strong of decaying wood and dampness and mildew. It is strange to be inside such a burned place and not smell the carbony stink. But years have wiped that smell away. Dave steps through the doorway and into the weed-infested hull. There is no ceiling. Early-evening sky hangs above. The right wall of the cabin is gone. The other three are of various splintered heights.

Holding the gun before him, he moves into the center of the hull. Beneath his feet, he can feel mice and meadow moles squirming.

"Come on," he says. "Come on, you bastard. Have you been here? Are you here now?"

A swallow flutters from the vines on the south wall and takes to the sky through the opening of the roof. Dave jumps, jabbing his chin with the shotgun.

"Jesus," he says. Then points the gun away from himself.

There must be something here. This place reeks of mystery and old, terrible traditions. This place is on the downside of a slope, sitting where the shadows would fall quickly, and someone could easily hide. This place means something.

Dave scratches his forehead. This place means *something*.

He kicks around, overturning sticks and rocks and clusters of leaves. There is nothing. He begins swinging the gun angrily, swiping the grass like a scythe. Then he sits in the grass.

The sky darkens. He flicks on the lantern. He watches a spider jump from weed stem to weed stem. Like molasses from a cracked jar, he feels his resolve begin to drain with encroaching weariness.

A moth flies against the lantern. Others join it.

Stupid things, like Missy's followers. Kill themselves for the light. Obedient fools. Crying and praying and cutting their arms for an obscene tattoo.

'TATTOO!'

Dave jumps to his feet. He cannot believe he has been sitting in the weeds of an old cabin while he has a crucial job to do! This cabin is nothing, perhaps, but Avery Barker is real, and Dave will find him.

He goes back toward the doorway, but a pile of planks to his left catches his attention. He stops, and looks. They seem out of place, too neatly stacked to have fallen with the ancient fire.

Dave swings the lantern around and moves to the stack of wood. He kicks one aside with his foot. There is something beneath it. He stoops down.

It is paper of some sort, plastic it looks like, and Dave hoists the plank up and off. It is a plastic bag full of magazines.

For a second, Dave imagines that some sort of secret boys' club meets here, a group of young teenagers who drink and fart around and read their newest issues of *Hustler*. But the magazines are a strange assortment, he sees as he dumps them out. Farm magazines, *Newsweek, Reader's Digest.* And of course, as daring as young teenage boys are around Beacon Cove, they still would not come this far from their homes at night with a sineater in their midst.

Dave shoves aside other planks. Beneath them he finds other plastic bags, with some coins, an old pocket knife, and several old greeting cards. More planks move. There is a small hole in the ground, and in the hole are photographs. Dave settles himself again on the cold ground, his mind buzzing with his find. Gingerly, he opens the bag with the cards. Their age has turned them rough and yellow. One is a birthday card with pink roses. Outside it says, "On your tenth birthday." Inside it is signed "With love from Sister Sally." Another card is faded, actually a postcard that says, "We missed you in Sunday School." It is from the Beacon Baptist Church. Had the owner of this card gone to Sunday school once and then never returned? Had the church once launched a program to bring in all the Cove children to prove the teachings of the church were true and right? The last card is homemade, of folded school paper and written with a scratchy handwriting. Outside it says, "I Love You." Inside there is a crudely drawn cabin and flowers. The "I Love You" is repeated, and a signature is at the bottom. "Lelia."

Dave drops the cards onto the ground.

He knows now what he has found.

Joel's mama's name is Lelia.

He nearly knocks the lantern over as he digs the photographs from the hole in the ground. There are only two of them, both in black and white. Dave does not look directly at them at first, fearing what he will see. Then, slowly, he looks at the first one. It is only a picture of the river, taken from the middle of the Bridge. The date on the back says 1960. Then Dave lets his gaze slide onto the glossy image of the second. It is a photo of the Barkers' cabin. The two pines are noticeably shorter than they are now. There is a girl on the porch, her hands in the pockets of her apron. She has long black hair in two braids. There is a dog under one of the pine trees. On the back again, is only a date. 1959. June.

Lelia Barker. Joel's mama. And this is the secret place of Joel's daddy. Avery Barker. The sineater.

Suddenly, there is a muffled groan from somewhere outside the burned cabin. Dave's heart leaps at the sound. He throws the photos back into the hole and whips about. There is silence.

Silence.

And then the moan again. Goosebumps race Dave's arms. He holds the gun and the lantern with equal fierceness. Outside, the moan stops again, and the faint sound of new sleet takes its place.

"Who is that?" he says.

Trickles of the icy rain fall through the opening of the roof and pat the grass around him; it thumbs his hair. Then he stands. His eyes cut rapidly to all sides of him. He backs out through the front doorway.

"Who is that?" There comes no answer, and he does not expect one. If this be the final confrontation, then let him be ready.

The moan rises again on the air like thin, eerie smoke. It comes from behind the building. The sound is human, and Dave's blood becomes like the sleet. He creeps through the weeds, rounding the burned shell. The gun points outward, the lantern does not swing.

"Who is that?" he begins again. And then there is a rush behind him and a shriek of rabid anger, and a plank smacks him on the back of the neck and the ground rushes up to catch him.

13

Joel sits on the barrel in the barn, his school books scattered at his feet like so much chicken feed. The hens jump around the books, squawking and complaining. All but one of the goats are out in the yard, grazing and trying to get into the dead garden. The other, pregnant, lies in her pen.

Lelia thinks he has gone to school this morning. She won't know any better because she is too sad to come outside to do any chores. She has not been outside the house since Monday. Curry thinks Joel has gone to school, too, but he won't find out because he is off gathering more wood.

He cannot go to school. He cannot stop thinking about the church explosion. When he came home last night, he told his mother and his brother. They seemed temporarily concerned, but then the thick, sullen cloud settled again and wiped out the subject completely. And again, last night, Lelia set a place for Petrie at the supper table.

"It's only been four days," she said. "She will be home."

Curry had nodded along with his mother.

And Joel went into his room and cried. He just at that moment had seen that not only was the shunning against the Barkers, but it came from the Barkers as well.

He, alone, longs for his world to be bigger.

'Philicia Hodge is dead,' he thinks. *'Sam Fort is dead. Petrie is probably dead, and Wayne is probably dead, too.'*

He kicks at a hen and catches her in the wing. She grunts and runs away. Joel picks at his fingers. He wonders what it feels like to be dead. He wonders if it truly hurts, or if the soul leaving is a painless thing. He wonders if he died, if Avery would try to eat his son's sin.

There is a piece of twine on the floor in the grain dust. Joel picks it up and loops it around his neck. He crosses the ends and begins to pull.

It hurts immediately, but he continues to pull.

At first there is nothing but the pain of the twine digging into the skin. And then, as Joel tries to take a breath, he cannot. He continues to pull. His tongue works out of his mouth, almost an evacuation attempt. Joel continues to pull. The pain grows, hot and exquisite. He suddenly feels a dizziness as well. Suddenly, he thinks that this is a stupid idea. But his hands are into the flow of it and do not want to stop pulling. His eyes bulge. He squirms on the barrel.

And then his mind shouts, *Stop it, you idiot Barker! You don't want this yet!'*

And his hands obey. They drop to his sides. The twine falls away. Joel gulps air. The chickens peck his shoes.

After a few minutes, he climbs down and goes out into the yard. The goats stop and look at him, then busy themselves again with the wire around the garden. Joel goes to the back and climbs the fence. He does not want to die like Missy's cat.

But if the terrible thoughts would go away forever, he would be happy. If he would see Avery Barker face-to-face and go insane, he would not have to think about the horrors anymore.

14

His head spins. There is a blindfold across his eyes, but there is a gap at the bottom caused by his nose, and he can see the ground and a pair of feet. But he cannot tip his head back far enough to see whoever it is who holds him up and ties his arms and legs. With the churning of his head, the small bit of vision he has is blurred, and he cannot recognize the feet. Dave feels ropes wrap his arms, his head, his legs. His bruised brain will not give him control enough to lash out, to fight his captor.

Someone else is nearby. Dave can hear the coughing, the shallow breathing. Someone else, maybe, in Dave's situation. Dave wants to shout, "Let me go, you motherfucker!", but his voice is dead. It is like the night he received his star.

He feels drugged.

"Brought your own hammer, I see," the figure hisses. "Think it can drive home my point?"

Dave feels the taunting cold of the hammer's head against his cheek, being rubbed along his face as if it were a silk scarf.

And he remembers. *'The hammer is for killing.'*

The hammer, the drugs. The night he received his star; the night his mind swam with pain and the effects of Missy's potion.

"I think so," the figure answers itself. "Let's give it a try."

A nail is placed against Dave's arm. His muscles are beyond command. He cannot struggle. And he remembers.

The hammer, the nails, the shed in the backyard of Missy's house. Patsy was there. She had seen the sineater. And Missy said there was only one thing to do.

Nail her eyes closed.

So she would never again see the sineater.

'The hammer is a killer.'

Missy drove nails into Patsy's eyes while Dave watched. And she had died.

Dave remembers, and his voice finds itself.

"I'll kill you, you motherfucker!"

The nails made mockery of his threat.

15

The path Joel follows is one of Curry's. He calls out for Avery. He wanders a long time, moving south. After a while, he loses the path and stops and sits on a rock. He wishes he hadn't given the photo of Avery to Wayne. If he had it, he would look at it now. He wishes Benton's dogs weren't dead, because one now would be a comfort. He tries to pray, but cannot. He wishes he had gloves because his hands are cold.

Squirrels dig nearby, unearthing hidden acorns. How many of these creatures have seen the sineater? How many of them have witnessed Missy Campbell in her insane rages? A centipede flutters across Joel's foot.

He stands then, thinking he should go home. There are no answers in the woods any more than in his room in his cabin. He touches the tender circle around his neck and wonders if there will be a scar.

And he begins down the small slope to flatter ground, he hears a voice in the forest, just above him, just beyond the ridge. He stops and listens, but cannot recognize the voice. He climbs back up the slope and struggles between a dense patch of cedars. Beyond him a good sixty yards, there are two figures moving among the trees. The trees strobe their motion, and Joel's vision of them is only brief glimpses, but there are two of them, he is certain. One leading, the other following, and it appears the second one is having a difficult time.

Joel bends down and continues to follow. It is most probably some hunters, out this November day, but for some reason, Joel's mind will not believe that. He knows he best not be seen.

The voice sounds again, and it is not a pleasant sound. Joel stops and waits and listens.

The people are going west, toward Pine Clearing.

And then, still holding low, he follows again. Up the steep ridges that lead to the clearing he moves, his heart racing of his feet. He moves as he learned the Indians moved, silently, steadily.

The trees thin then, and he reaches the edge of the clearing. He looks all around, watching for the two figures. He does not see them. His shoulders fall; his neck is caught in a fresh stab of pain. Surely they came here. Where are they?

And then he sees movement, far west, on the other side of the field. The two are moving down the knoll that leads to the trees. Joel knows that that is where Joe McDonald's old cabin is, although he has never ventured there. Nobody goes there. Missy claims that holy spirits live there, and want to remain undisturbed. Most people in Beacon Cove believe that to be true. Joel just never ventured that much alone, and the thought of standing where his grandfather was burned to death was frightening.

He watches and waits. His eyes hurt for trying to see so far.

And then he sees one of the people come from the trees, and cut across the side of the clearing and back into the forest to the north. Joel tries to identify the figure, but the bright sun and the distance allow the boy to see merely a shape in motion, hurrying, gliding the grass and disappearing into the woods.

He waits. He watches.

He wonders, and his curiosity grows unbearable.

Keeping to the edge of the trees, Joel moves around the side of the clearing and down to the west side. The burned cabin comes into view. He stops, listens, then continues around. When he is very near the cabin, he stops and watches again.

No one moves about it. He can hear nothing. Perhaps the second person left through the woods behind the cabin.

He stares at the cabin longer. He doesn't want to, but he imagines the fire those many years back, and sees the three men walking calmly to their fiery deaths. The vivid story, told him with as much reverence and awe as any tale from the Bible, comes playing in his memory. He can see the flames, can hear the cracking of the wood of the cabin; he can see Joe McDonald cowering in fear, with the ruins of the still behind him. Orville Campbell raises his hand, blessing the all-consuming heat, and Floyd Ramsey, Bobby Stone, and Donald Barker move forward, not praying, but entranced.

Donald Barker, as Joel sees him, is blond like Curry. He is thin and tall and pale like a birch tree. The fire seems to take him last, because he is the color of fire.

Joel closes his eyes and looks away. The image is too strong for him, and if he continues to watch it, he will become rightfully afraid and will leave. Now, he does not want to leave. He looks back at the cabin. Still, he sees no one. He creeps to it carefully.

The north side of the cabin has little left of a wall. Most of the front is gone, with blackened wood barely holding its place. Joel moves around the front of the cabin, stepping through the thorny thickets which hold the remains tightly like a green rush of water against an old dam. He peeks into the doorway, and sees a tall garden of nature; tall, brown grasses blow in a breeze from the many openings of the building. There are small cedars and hunks of fallen wood in process of becoming mud. Planks are scattered about to the right near the door.

Joel steps away from the front door and inches along the wall to the south side. He rounds the corner.

He stops.

His heart stops, too.

There is something behind the cabin, he can hear it. He hopes it is an animal, a small furry thing with more guts than brains, something brave enough to stay even with the scent of a human on the air. He flattens himself against the side wall, or what is left of it, and holds his breath. If the second person is still here, working behind the cabin, then Joel cannot imagine getting away undetected.

Who is it?

Joel listens unwillingly. There is scraping, and thumping, and what seems to be a low humming. He turns his head slightly. He listens.

The sounds stop, then begin again. He tries to imagine what it is, and cannot. He knows the sound of chopping, of stripping wood, of nailing and digging and stacking. He knows outdoor work sounds. He cannot figure these.

His feet slide sideways, taking them toward the end of the south wall. He does not want to go with them, but he does. His hands, flattened outward, jump across the huge holes of the wall and catch large splinters on the burned planks. His hands pull away but then go back. For some reason, it feels safer that way, as if his hands will push him away quickly if need be, and give him a running start. The splinters hurt but he cannot care.

The thumping becomes louder, then stops. The humming stops as well, and then starts up again. Joel prays it is a dog, caught in a hunter's trap. He reaches the end of the wall. His left hand moves slowly over to join his right. His left foot moves away from the wall. He braves himself to look around.

And as he swings about, he suddenly does not want to see Avery anymore. He does not want to go crazy. He does not want to lose his mind.

'I don't want to see Avery!'

But his body goes around. He stands at the corner of Joe McDonald's backyard.

The horrifying sight drives him to his knees in the middle of the thistles.

Against the back wall, which has large sections of unfallen boards, are Wayne and Dave. They stand straight, as if at absurd attention, their backs nearly arched and their heads held high.

Joel stands slowly, his eyes not moving from the two on the wall. He steps out into the yard, staring. He takes in each terrible detail one at a time. Foreheads bound by white cord to the wood. Dirty blindfolds over the eyes. Rags tied tightly across the mouths.

The humming is Dave, crying through his gag.

"Oh, God," says Joel.

Neither has on a shirt, and the skin is white with cold. There are chains around their waists, tight enough to bear into the flesh, secured with padlocks. Their knees are bent slightly, with the bottoms of their feet up against the wall and held with the same kind of cord that binds their foreheads. Cords also hold the arms outward at the elbows, and smaller chains support them around their upper arms.

"Oh, God, no."

Both Wayne and Dave have nails driven through the lower flesh of each arm.

Joel convulses and spits curdled breakfast milk into the weeds. He wipes his mouth and looks again. The blood around and under the nails in Wayne is brown and crusted. The blood around and under Dave's nails is still red.

"Wayne?" Joel says.

The man does not move.

Then Joel says, "Dave? It's me, Joel."

Dave's feet begin struggling on the wood; his head strains against the cord around his forehead. His humming is louder.

Joel moves across the yard to Dave. He must take off the boy's blindfold, but he does not want to see Dave's eyes.

He works his fingers under the gag, clawing it down to Dave's chin. Dave begins to cough violently.

"Dave, it's me."

Dave is caught in a spasm. Joel knows it is the pain. He reaches up and lifts the blindfold.

Dave's eyes fly open. They are red and dreadful.

"Dave," says Joel. "You got to listen. I know who done this to you. I know who it is."

Dave's breath hitches, and his lips curl back into a snarl. Joel thinks he may be crazy from the torture. Through his teeth he hisses, "The hammer killed her!"

Joel steps back a step.

The crucified red-haired boy stares at Joel with his crazy eyes. Then he twists his gaze down to the hammer in the grass. Sweat-fear drenches his shirt.

He says, "I got a letter from Andy, Dave. He wanted me to be careful. He wanted me to know what was going on . . ."

Dave screams "The hammer killed her! The hammer drove nails in Patsy's eyes!"

Oh God oh God oh God. Andy tried to tell him. "Missy?"

"Yes."

Joel feels his legs try to give way, but he fights back. "Then she was the one. Andy's letter said so. She's lost her mind, Dave. She's so crazy she's trying to kill everyone who has anything to do with our family. It isn't Avery, Dave. It's Missy who did this to you!"

Dave's tongue, fat and dry, lolls across his lips. He croaks, "You're wrong."

"No," says Joel. "I'm right. She's the danger, Dave!"

Dave's eyes close. He moans. "You're wrong, Joel"

"I'm going to town," says Joel. "I'll get help right away." He feels anguish in his gut like a poisoned piece of meat. "Do you know, is Wayne dead?"

"You're wrong," says Dave again. "Look around, Joel." The eyes close.

Joel steps back, confused. He turns around, looking, not knowing what he is looking for. He turns left and right, seeing only the edge of the yard and the curving forest that surrounds it. He looks behind him, and sees only trees.

But something else.

"I was brought here last night," says Dave. "Not today."

There is something behind a nearby oak, something indistinguishable in the shadow. Joel goes toward it.

"Look," says Dave.

Joel comes close to the tree. He can see now a chain about the trunk, and several cords tied above it. He can see the very edge of shoulders, and the very tips of elbows.

"Jesus," he says. "Oh, Jesus, not more."

He goes around the tree.

Tied as are the other two, with her hair loose and falling in ratty strings to her waist, her old wrinkled neck covered with the drool that has leaked through her gag, is Missy Campbell.

There is a note above her head, nailed to the tree, in the same print as the note in Creeper's pen. "Beware the sineater! Respect him and this won't be your fate!" Below the note, Missy bleeds fresh blood from facial scratches.

"It's Avery Barker!" screams Dave, and Joel jumps. He looks back at the boy nailed to the wall. "It's your fucking daddy! Get help. Get me off of here! I'm going to find the bastard and look him in the fucking face before I kill him!"

16

'Metal cutters. Wire cutters. Let Benton be there. Bandages. Pliers. Oh God let Benton be there!'

His legs are almost worthless, and they give with every fourth step he takes. He crosses the West Path Bridge, holding his stomach. There is a large scratch across his cheek and it bleeds. There are countless bruises forming, and cuts on his jeans and legs. He took the straightest path to town; he came due east, finding only pieces of pathways, and working the rest of the way down the rough and wild growth of nature undisturbed.

'A jeep would work. Metal cutters, and pliers. Benton, please be there! Just this once don't send me away!'

Wayne might be dead. He might have bled to death, or starved to death. He might have frozen to death; the man had no shirt, and only a small bandage had been left on the stump.

'Wayne is not dead!'

In the corner of his vision, he can see the destroyed church. 'Philicia is dead, too, blown up by the sineater.'

When Dave is free, Joel will do what he can to help kill his father.

Joel goes across the road. His knees buckle in the center, and he drops down with his palms to the gravel. He pushes back up. Benton will help. Wayne is Benton's friend.

'You were Benton's friend, too, remember?'

Benton will help Wayne. He will help Dave, too, and Missy.

'Remember, Joel? Friendship is a myth. Ain't no such true thing.'

Joel grasps the porch post and hauls himself up to the porch. He pants. His cheek burns furiously.

'Friendship is nothing.'

"I'll help kill him," Joel says aloud. "I don't care. I'll do it, I swear on Jesus' name."

He knocks on the store door.

No one comes. He knocks again. No one comes.

"Damn it," says Joel. He opens the screen door. He grabs the knob to the wooden door and gives it a turn and a push. He steps inside.

Fitch is at the counter, beside the cash register, writing.

He looks up at Joel.

"You got to get Benton. You got to come, too. Wayne and Dave and Missy Campbell is hurt bad up at the clearing. You got to hurry."

Fitch blinks slowly, then looks back at his work. He says, "Benton ain't here. He's at the funeral home. Wife got blowed up yesterday, or didn't you know?"

Joel comes closer.

"I know. You got to call the police. You got to come. Quickly."

Fitch continues to write. He does not look up at Joel.

Joel goes up to the counter. He watches in amazement as Fitch calmly writes out an order for paint. "What are you *doing?*"

"You don't belong here. Go away," says Fitch.

"Goddam it! You got to call the police! Wayne might be dying! He might already be dead! You got to help me!"

Fitch writes, "One can primer, Dutch. Two paintbrushes, one roller."

"Please!"

"You are lying."

"No! I don't care if you hate me, help me!"

"I don't believe no Barkers. Go away."

Furious tears spring to Joel's eyes. "I'll get the Quarles to help if you won't!"

"They ain't opened their store in three days 'cause of the problems round here. They ain't there."

"The grocery store, then! I'll find somebody!"

"Grocery's closed. Got damaged in the explosion."

"If everyone is closed, why are you here, then? Huh? Why aren't you home safe and sound?"

Fitch does not look up. He continues to write his order.

Joel runs from the store.

17

'*Thank God*' is his first thought. Then, '*Please let me find the key!*'

He hurries to the open door of Wayne's garage and places his hands on the seat of the four-wheeler. Surely he could drive it. It has a key, the key starts the engine. Joel has seen the boys at Ozzy's Exxon play with their motorcycles; he knows that you flip your foot sometimes and turn the handle grips to make it move.

Where did Rody leave the key? Has Wayne moved it since that day?

The key is not in the ignition.

Joel goes to the steps inside the garage and looks under a bristly floor mat. There are no keys there, either. He goes up the steps. Another, small mat is on the top step. He look beneath. No keys.

He throws his shoulder into the door, and it does not give. He goes downstairs into the garage, and finds a sledgehammer. He takes it upstairs. With four swings, he makes a crack. And then with each swing the crack grows. He stops a moment, catching his breath, then swings again. The wooden door chips, and then a chunk falls away, into the apartment. He swings again. The hole widens. Again. It opens more.

Joel throws the hammer to the bottom of the steps. He reaches in through the hole and opens the door.

Inside, he finds the Honda keys on the tiny kitchen table by the bedroom door. '*Faster than walking,*' he thinks.

Outside, he puts the keys into the ignition and gives it a turn. The switch clicks, nothing more. Joel panics. There is a button, and in desperation he pushes it. The engine hums.

Awkwardly, he walks the Honda around and faces it toward the path. He sits, presses his foot, and twists the handle. It bolts forward, nearly tossing him off backward. The engine screams, and he knows he is not doing it right, but it is moving, thank God, it is moving. He steers it to West Path, and begins the climb home.

If anything, Joel knows his family will believe him. He twists harder on the grip. The engine screams, but he picks up speed. His family will believe him. His family will help. They may not want to touch, but they will help.

Working around the curves is much harder than Joel would have imagined, but he leans forward and talks to the machine. It seems to work. He does not flip over.

'Lelia will help,' Joel thinks. *'She will know it is the right thing to do. She helped save Wayne once, she will do it again.'*

Joel leans further forward. The Honda skids on rock but continues to climb.

'And what about Curry?'

"I don't know," says Joel. The four-wheeler rounds the last curve before his cabin. "I really don't know."

At the bottom of the Barkers' footpath, Joel turns the key and climbs off. His legs ache horribly. He has to stand for a moment and let the ache reach its peak and then subside.

"Mama!"

He walks up to the gate; through the gate and up the crumbling walkway to the screened porch.

"Mama!"

He collapses on the bottom step, his arms on his knees, breathing down onto the pebbles at his feet.

"Mama!"

The kitchen door opens and closes. The screen door opens, and Curry says, "What do you want? Mama ain't feeling good."

Joel looks around at his brother. He is certain Curry will say no before Joel has finished asking him, but he plunges on.

"You got to help me. Wayne is probably dead. Dave is hurt and Missy Campbell is, too. You got to come help get them down."

Curry steps slowly down onto the first stair. He is frowning. "What are you talking about? You don't have dealings with those people."

"That don't matter now. They's hurt, bad. Please, Curry. You are strong. You can help me. I can't do it alone!"

"It ain't right, Joel. We ain't supposed to have nothing to do with them. Don't you believe all that Mama's taught us?"

Joel stands and turns. His vocal cords feel hard like rocks, and his eyes burn like there is ash in them. "Stop it, Curry! You got to help me, there ain't no choice! They're nailed up, Curry! They're all bloody! They're gonna *die*! Do unto others, even if we are Barkers! Please Curry!" Joel's voice breaks. "Please, Curry. I don't want them to die."

The blue eyes flicker, then look away from Joel. Curry seems to ponder heavily, then he says, "Where they at, then?"

"Pine clearing. Behind the burned cabin."

"It ain't right, Joel. We ain't supposed to deal with other people. It's bad for their souls."

"God can forgive their souls! But their souls'll be gone if we don't help them, gone on to heaven or hell!"

Curry sighs. He says, "All right. Don't tell Mama where we're going."

"I won't."

"We can take some of my trails. It won't take long."

"Okay. And Curry, they got chains on them, with locks. We got to get them cut or unlocked somehow."

Curry nods. He goes around the side of the house to the toolshed. He brings out some shiny tools Joel never knew they had.

"Bandages?" says Curry, and Joel runs into the house to find some old cloth. Mama's door is shut, and she is most likely inside taking a nap. Joel cannot take towels from her bottom drawer and tear them into strips. And so he settles with the washed and folded dust rags on the shelf in the pantry. He hurries back outside. Curry already seems impatient.

Joel trots over to his big brother. "Thanks," he says.

But Curry turns without speaking, and they leave the yard for the forest.

18

It does not take long, as Curry promised. The trails Curry uses are small but amazingly smooth and concise, angling along steep slopes, yet making the most of stretches of flat land. Curry is truly a mountain man; Joel feels his hopes rise with his brother beside him. Curry will know what to do.

They reach the clearing, and Joel is barely winded. His legs still hurt, but it is a second concern below his thoughts of Dave and Wayne.

'Be alive,' he pleads of Wayne and Dave. He knows God will think it wrong, but he cannot think of Missy.

Curry leads across the clearing, Joel follows. Curry still does not speak, and Joel wonders what it is he is thinking. He wonders if Curry knows the sineater has lost his mind and has become a killer. Joel trips over a stump; he grunts and Curry does not look back. Joel shivers and moves on. They reach the top of the slope and the cabin is there, a long-dead, blackened monster of old.

Joel's heart skips. His feet slow, though Curry's continue with the same place. He is afraid to look behind the cabin. It must be early afternoon by now. The sun is straight up over their heads, a mocking eye of fire in the cold midday.

"Curry, wait," Joel says suddenly. Curry stops and looks over his shoulder.

"What?"

"I don't know. Just wait a second. What if someone else is back there? What if . . . ?" The question trails. Joel looks at his brother, hoping Curry will understand.

"Who, Joel? We've come all this way and you are worried about who is there? If this is truly what God wants us to do, as you seem to believe, then He will protect us. Do you believe in His protection?"

"Curry, it ain't that simple."

"God protects the pure, Joel." Curry turns on his heel and walks down to the cabin. Joel follows.

Curry rounds the south side of the cabin. The tools click in his hands as he grips tightens and loosens. Joel picks up his feet, trying to catch up. He does not want the gap between the two to be any larger than it is. He reaches the cabin and goes around it. Curry is already in the backyard. Joel moves around the corner and catches up with him. Slowly, he lets his eyes glance up to see the two on the wall.

Dave's gag and blindfold are still off, but the boy's eyes are closed. Joel hopes he is dozing. Then he looks at Wayne. The man is still, but the nails beneath his arms are ringed with fresh blots of red blood.

Wayne is still alive. Sometime since Joel left, he had awakened and had struggled.

"Wayne," whispers Joel.

"Let's do this quickly," says Curry matter-of-factly. He drops tools into the weeds, then picks up the metal cutter.

"Wayne," says Joel. He approaches the man, one hand out slightly. He wants to touch the man, to feel warmth in the body, to feel the shallow breathing. He gets two feet from Wayne. His hand moves out further.

"Joel!"

Joel whips about. Curry points the cutters at Joel; they shake in stern reprimand. "Stay away, Joel. We will do this quickly, but the less touch there is, the better."

"I want to know . . ."

"Let's do it." Curry goes to Dave. The red-haired boy's eyes twitch as Curry works the steel clamps about the links. "Joel," he says. "Get them pliers."

Joel backs away from Wayne. Then he stoops and picks up the vise-grips, leaving the hammer and the chisel.

Curry twists and presses on the cutters. He does not look Dave in the face, but stares intently at his work. *'If he has to touch, he won't look,'* Joel thinks. *'Curry don't want to see what's in Dave's face. He wants it done quick and let it be over.'*

Joel goes to Curry. He looks at Dave's face. Dave's eyes are open slightly now, red slits full of pain and fear. His mouth is clamped as tightly as Curry's cutters. The boy's shoulders jerk in a tethered spasm, and Dave's neck follows. He twists his head and looks directly at Joel.

"You get the bastard yet?" he hisses.

Joel shakes his head.

"I want you to help me," says Joel.

With a sharp twist, the link breaks; the chain drops. "Help you what?" Curry stands straight. Joel looks away into the woods.

"Oh, nothing," Joel answers. "Dave ain't feeling good. Just talking is all."

Curry snorts silently. "Pliers," he says. Joel hands the pliers to his brother. Curry grips the first nail. Dave cries out as the flesh is pinched and pulled against the steel. "Don't move," says Curry. Blood flows. Joel cannot look at the nail or at Dave's face. He looks at the fallen chain instead.

A bloodied nail drops onto the ground. Dave cries again as Curry pulls on the other one. It falls beside the first.

"Bandages?"

Joel pulls the rags from his pockets. As Curry cuts the cords with his small knife, Joel's shaking fingers form folded strips. Gently he wraps one about Dave's bleeding arm and ties the ends.

"Too tight?" he asks softly.

Dave shakes his head.

And then Dave is free, his feet unbound, his body stumbling forward. Curry steps back to let Dave catch himself. Joel reaches out, then sees Curry's face and stops. Dave drops onto his hands and knees; he coughs for a long minute. His body shakes like Petrie's cat when it has been left out in a rainstorm.

"Next one," says Curry. He goes to Wayne. Joel looks between Dave and Wayne, then goes with Curry.

The cutters work beneath the chain. Joel lets himself look Wayne in the face. The blindfolded face is horrifying. A man facing execution. A man already executed. Joel inches up to the mailman. His hand lifts; moves to the gag. It is tighter than Dave's, and Joel cannot get a good grip. Without saying anything, Curry indicates the knife in his pocket. Joel takes it out and carefully slices the gag. It loosens and he pulls it away.

Wayne's mouth falls slack. The lips are split and deathly white.

Curry grunts and jerks the cutters back and forth.

Joel moves the knife to Wayne's hair and slips the blade beneath the blindfold above Wayne's ear. He saws. The blindfold peels off. The eyes remain closed.

Joel looks over at Dave. The boy is now on his knees, rubbing his face.

"You okay, Dave?"

Dave says nothing, but looks at Joel. "We'll find him," the look says.

"Joel." Curry is finished with the chain. It swings and drops down around the mailman's feet. "Get them bandages ready."

Joel folds another set of rags. Wayne does not protest the removal of the nails. Very little blood shows from the raw wounds. As Joel ties the bandage he lets his hands wrap about Wayne's arm. The skin itself is cold, but as Joel squeezes, he can feel warmth deep inside. Wayne is alive.

'Thank God.'

"Wayne's alive, Dave!"

"Where's my goddam shirt?" mumbles Dave. He works himself into a sitting position on the ground.

"Joel! The other bandage!" Curry is already slicing off the cords on Wayne's forehead, arms, and feet. Joel obeys.

Gingerly, Curry lays the freed man into the grass.

Joel stares, wanting to comfort the man, and to try to wake him up. But Curry is already going to Missy at the tree.

"I'll be back," he whispers to Wayne. "Hang in there. I'll be right back."

He goes to Missy.

Curry does not take notice of the note over the woman's head, but Joel rips it down first. He look at it once more before stuffing it into his pants pocket.

"Beware of the sineater."

'Damn the sineater!'

There are no nails in the old woman; her clothes are intact as though the torturer had had respect for the fact that she was a woman.

Joel reaches up and pulls the blindfold off Missy. Touching her is creepy, like reaching into a deep pit without looking. Her eyes fly open. Joel steps back a step. Curry struggles with the chain.

Avoiding the staring, accusing eyes, Joel hooks his fingers and pulls on the mouth gag. It is wet with the old woman's spit, and his stomach hitches.

The chain drops. The gag comes off. Missy screams.

Curry calmly cuts the cords. Joel puts his hands over his ears and turns away. Missy's scream is like a ghost, high and loud and long. He cannot look at her. She is screaming at him, and at Curry. She is screaming at the crime done against her, and at the fate she had expected. She screams in rage and terror. Her rules have been broken, and she is being saved by the sons of the devil.

Joel turns and looks at the ground. Missy screams, and he feels her hot breath on his neck.

And then she cries, "Don't touch me!"

Joel looks around. Missy is freed. She flails her arms at Curry to keep him away.

Curry collects his tools and goes back to the center of the yard.

"Don't touch me, you demons!" Her words come in sobs, but they are strong and powerful. "Get away, and be home with you! What do you mean to come here?"

Dave, his arms wrapped about his naked chest to keep out the cold, says, "We was gonna die, Aunt Missy. They saved us."

Missy will not hear this. She backs around the tree, as if in any moment she will flee into the woods. "They are the Barkers! Don't you know who they are?"

"Yes."

"They are Barkers! They can't touch us, they can't let us see them! It's against all what's holy!"

"They saved us, Missy. Avery Barker meant to have us dead. He nailed me and Wayne."

Joel looks at Wayne. The man has not stirred. He still lies on the ground, shirtless and white, with the side of his face deep in thistles. If only Joel's coat were bigger, he would give it to the mailman. Joel thinks Wayne will freeze to death if they don't go soon.

Missy raises an accusing finger, and points at them all. "God will have His day!"

"Shut up, Aunt Missy."

"God will right what is evil!"

"I said shut up!"

Missy stares, shocked. Then she whispers, "God will damn you for that, Burke."

"Good," says Dave. "And it ain't Burke, it's Dave." He looks at Joel and shivers. "Give me your coat."

"We can't move this one," says Curry, standing over Wayne. "Still out. We'll send help to get him."

"No," says Joel. "We can't leave him. He'll die."

"It's decided," says Curry. "Help the boy. The woman can walk herself, she ain't hurt bad. We'll take a shortcut to town."

"We can't leave him!" Tears suddenly burn his eyes. Joel does not blink them away. "He's my friend! He'll die!"

Curry turns sharply, and grabs Joel by the upper arm. "Don't never say that, Joel. He ain't your friend. You's a Barker! You know your place!"

"He is my friend. And he ain't got no shirt, no coat!"

Curry's blue eyes are ice. Slowly, he repeats, "He ain't your friend, Joel. Let's go." Curry lets go of Joel's arm and strides out of the yard and up to the slope which leads to the clearing. Joel watches him, dumbfounded. Wayne will surely die. He takes his coat off and lays it across Wayne's white back. "We'll be back," he says. "You hear me? Wayne?"

Wayne does not move.

"I'm coming!" he calls out to Curry, who stops at the top of the knoll. "Wait one second." Then he strips from his flannel shirt and hands it over to Dave.

"But," says Dave. "But then you ain't got one."

"If it was bigger I'd give it to Wayne," says Joel. "But it ain't. You take it."

"You hate me," says Dave.

Joel says nothing. Dave takes the shirt and puts it on. Curry calls down, "Now!"

Dave takes a few steps and then folds over in a violent fit of coughing. Joel goes over to the boy. "Go on," manages Dave. "I can make it." He steps out again, then immediately vomits bile onto his feet. Joel moves beside him. He puts his arm around the red-haired boy's shoulder and waits until the sickness has passed.

"No," Joel says then.

Dave wipes his mouth. He does not look up at Joel, but says softly, "No, what?"

"No, I don't hate you."

Missy roars forward from beside the tree, her hair flying. "Get your hands off Burke! Don't touch him!"

Joel backs away.

"Come now!" shouts Curry from the knolltop.

"He needs help," Joel says to Missy.

"Not help from you! I'll help him! I'm his family. You're the sineater's son!"

"I can help."

"You just go. Lead the short way to Ellison. We'll follow, but don't you look back at us. You hear me?"

Joel sighs, and look at Dave. Dave still looks at the ground. "All right," Joel says.

He turns and walks off to join Curry. Halfway up the slope he thinks he hears something behind him, calling his name in a soft, reedy voice. He stops, peers back, only to see Missy with her arm about Dave's waist, helping him along.

"Don't turn around!" screams Missy.

Joel continues up to the clearing.

They walk through the high grasses and infant trees, a straggling line, Curry ahead, Joel not far behind, Missy and Dave a good distance to the rear. Joel cannot feel the cold on his bare skin; but the other things around him crash into his senses with unbearable clarity. The ash-gray of the sky, threatening early snow. The patch of starlings to his right, pecking for food, their greasy black feathers like oil, their chattering brash and steady. The scent of mud and pine, the taste of salt in his mouth.

"Joel."

He stops, and turns back again. He ignores Missy's instant complaints and stares back toward the slope. No, there was no voice. It was his mind. His stupid, hopeful mind.

"We will have the boy call from the Hardware," Curry calls over his shoulder.

Joel follows. "Fitch was the only one there when I went. He didn't believe me. He wouldn't call."

"Fitch," says Curry. "How do you know Fitch?"

Curry seems to slow, but Joel does not really want to catch up with him. He knows what Curry thinks of Joel talking with outsiders.

"I go to school," begins Joel. He slows, but Curry slows as well. Curry stops then, and waits for Joel. "I go to school," he repeats. "You know that. I know people, that's all. I can't help it."

Joel reaches Curry's side. He crosses his arms over his chest, suddenly cold.

Curry looks up at the sky. He wipes his chin. "Gonna get an early snow." Then he walks ahead.

Joel and Curry reach the edge of the clearing, and they pause to let Missy and Dave close the gap. Curry leans on a tree and finds a small twig to pick his fingernails.

Joel stands with his hands in his pockets, looking out to where a campfire once held a party for two boys late at night.

"Joel!"

Joel's eyes widen. He had heard it. From somewhere. From . . .

"Where are you going?" shouts Curry, but Joel is running as fast as he can back across the clearing. His feet strike the ground with fury, his face flushed and strained. He passes Missy and Dave. He runs, runs, runs. To the other side of the clearing, to the slope, down to the burned hull of the Joe McDonald's cabin.

He runs around the back. He stops beside Wayne.

"Wayne!" he says.

The man is facedown in the thistles. The coat has blown askew on the bare back.

Joel drops to his knees. "Wayne? Did you call me?"

Wayne does not move. Joel moves his hand slowly, and touches the white of the skin. It is cold. He presses down. There is still cold.

"Did you call?"

Wayne does not move. He does not speak. Joel's throat spasms. His mouth jerks.

"We'll be back, then," Joel says. He lifts his hand from the man.

And then there is something shiny, only a corner, jutting from Wayne's pants pocket. Joel hesitates, then reaches for it and pulls it out. He immediately thanks God it was upside down. The back of the white square says, "Avery Barker, Sept. 4, 1966." His father's picture.

He almost lets it go to the wind, but he will not do that now. He puts it into his own pants pocket. He had promised to help Dave. When Wayne is all right, that is what he is going to do, so help him.

Joel returns to Curry, who still waits in the trees at the far side of the clearing. Missy and Dave stand back twenty feet.

"Don't look!" Missy says as Joel goes by them.

"I don't want to look at you," Joel answers.

19

The path seems longer than it should, but Joel believes his weariness is making time slow to a crawl. He fumes behind Curry, trying to hurry his big brother up. His body hurts, his soul hurts, his brain hurts. Jumbled thoughts stir furiously. Sweat pops from his arms and then freezes in the air.

He shoves his hands in and out of his pockets as they move along. He fumbles with the note and the edge of the photo, then jerks his hand away as if they were lighted matches.

'Why wouldn't Fitch help? It wasn't for me, it was for Wayne, and Dave, and Missy.'

Curry turns left, and they go up a small rise. Joel is confused, but then he thinks again.

'Fitch don't have nothing to do with me. Just calling isn't dealing with me. Why was he scared?'

In and out of the pockets go the hands. From behind there is the crunching of four cautious feet.

Joel takes the note out and looks at it again. This was a warning. This was part of the horror, part of the pain Wayne and Dave suffered. Joel's anger swells, threatening to take off the top of his head.

And then he nearly drops the note. He stops dead on the path and his heart quickens. He stares at the paper.

"Oh Jesus."

318

The crunching of feet behind grows louder as Missy and Dave start up the rise.

Joel swallows. He can hear blood racing in his temples.

"Oh sweet Jesus."

Curry stops and looks back. Missy and Dave halt nearby.

"What's wrong, Joel?" Curry's voice does not hide his aggravation.

There is something familiar about the print on the note. Joel puts one hand to his forehead and pushes. It is certainly the same print as the note at the dog pen. He closes his eyes. A myriad of scenes of memory want to replay themselves, but he scans them all. And he picks the scene at the Hardware. He sees himself go to phone for help, he sees Fitch at the counter, ignoring Joel's pleas, writing that goddam paint order.

The paint order. Primer, Dutch. And some brushes and roller. All written down on the order slip with the neatest of print. Almost childlike in its slow attempt at perfection.

Joel's fingers open. The note drifts like a dirty feather.

"Fitch," he says.

"Let's go, Joel," says Curry.

"Fitch." Joel looks at his brother. "It was *Fitch*! The notes were written by Fitch! Curry, Fitch has done this all! Fitch killed Mr. Fort, Fitch nailed Dave and Wayne ..."

Curry stares, then laughs once, a terrible, astounded sound.

"Fitch!" Curry says.

Joel nods. His head rings.

"That's ridiculous."

"It's true."

Curry turns and starts to walk on. Joel runs and grabs him. "Listen to me, Curry. It's true! We got to stop Fitch."

Curry frowns. He holds up the new metal cutter. "And what do you want me to do, hit him with this?"

"I don't know ..." Joel begins. "Curry, where did you get those tools? I been in the toolshed lots and never seen them."

"They're mine."

"But how did you get them? Where did they come from?"

Curry chuckles. It is an odd sound in the winter air.

"Ain't no place got new stuff like that except the Hardware," says Joel. "You can't go into the Hardware, you're a Barker."

"I take my chairs at night."

"But nobody is there." Joel feels a cramp in his throat. "You break in, Curry, and take them tools?"

"No."

Joel takes a breath. Fitch. Curry. Dear Savior Jesus. "Fitch gave them to you."

Curry grins as if his brother just passed a science test. His eyes take the color of the sky, draining the calm blue and becoming something wild and dangerous. "Yes," he says.

"When?" whispers Joel.

"It don't matter. Many nights he has done work for me." Curry stretches his shoulders. He laughs again. Then he laughs and laughs. Joel looks at Missy and Dave. They stand on the path, terrified of Curry's strange reactions.

Curry stops laughing abruptly. His face metamorphoses. He sneers. "Fitch wants heaven, Joel. Do you see?"

"Fitch wrote them notes. But they were from you. You done all this. You done it all, didn't you, Curry?"

"Yes. Don't give any credit to that weasel. I can make Fitch do what I want. He wants heaven, Joel."

"It don't make sense."

"Of course it does!" Curry roars. He thrusts his face at Joel's. Joel cries out. "Who am I, Joel?"

Joel rakes his teeth on his lip. "Curry Barker," he says.

"Yes. And do you know what our father's position has become?"

"No."

"It's nothing. It's soft and worthless. There ain't respect for it. But I'm changing that."

"What do you mean?"

"I'm changing it! They'll fear the sineater now, like they never have before. Do you see?"

Barely a murmur. "No, Curry."

Curry strikes himself in the chest with his fist. "I'm his firstborn son. I will become what he is now when he is dead. And I will have the fear that is due me! I will have it, Joel!"

Joel says, "Curry, don't."

Curry puts his hand on Joel's arm. Joe's flesh cringes. "If I can't have what my spoiled little brother has, then I want what I can have. If I can't go into town, if I can't go to school and learn to read and write or walk in the daylight where other people walk, then I will be feared like nobody was ever feared in Beacon Cove. And they fear me now, don't they!"

"Yes."

"Fitch did what I told him. He knows I'll be sineater, and I told him if he didn't obey me, I would not eat his sin when he died. He wrote my notes for me." The horrible laugh again. "I can't write, so Fitch wrote my notes! He stole what I needed from the store. Rope, cutters, nails, a ball bat. I promised I'd send him to heaven someday."

Joel says, "Where were you taking us, Curry?"

"Us?" Curry slides his hand from Joel's shoulder and ruffles the younger boy's hair. "Joel, you sound scared. You're my little brother! You're a Barker. You ain't supposed to be scared! Now, them . . ." he nods toward the Campbells. "They should be scared outa their skins."

Dave backs away, down the path, watching bug-eyed as Curry grins at him. Missy stands squarely in the center of the trail, chanting, "Jesus'll shelter us, Jesus'll watch over us."

"The man and boy'd been gone by now if it wasn't for you, Joel. I told you it was wrong to go in the woods. I told you your place was at home. But you didn't listen to me, did you?" Curry looks from Dave to Joel. The grin vanishes; cold anger takes it place. He is crazy, Joel thinks. *Jesus shelter me.*

"No," Joel answers.

"You didn't listen to me! They would've had their punishment. They would've set their example! But you go where you want and do what you want."

From the corner of his eye, Joel sees Dave continue his cautious retreat. And then Joel screams, "Run, Dave! Get away!"

Dave spins on his heels and kicks dirt, taking off in a run. In the same second, Curry is after him, passing the woman and striding the ground as if he were racing on air. He catches Dave before the boy can get to the flat; Dave wails as Curry's long fingers dig his arms. Dave struggles, turning about, and he slashes at Curry's face. Curry drops his fingers to the bandaged places on Dave's arms and twists harshly. Dave screams in pain and his legs give way. Curry twists again. Spots of blood appear on the sleeves of Joel's shirt. Dave groans, his face contorted.

Curry leads him back. When he gets to Missy, he stops.

Missy closes her eyes and continues to chant.

"And you give this atheist your shirt, huh? He's a heathen, Joel." Curry snorts. "You look pathetic."

"Where were you taking us, Curry?"

"I hoped you would get tired and go home," says Curry. "Then I could do what I had to do without you being here. But I guess it don't matter now, does it?"

"Curry, please!"

"Don't worry, Joel. You're my brother. See His righteousness. See His place regained!" Curry pulls his whittling knife from his coat and, smiling, plunges it into Missy Campbell's neck. Her eyes fly wide like a surprised fish on a hook. Joel lunges forward, grappling for Curry's arm. Curry sidesteps his brother and Missy falls free from the knife. She bucks on the ground, her hands at her throat, blood spouting.

"Do you see?" Curry shouts in triumph.

Dave jumps on Curry's back. "I'll kill you!" he roars. "Fuck you fuck you fuck you!" He bites Curry's face, his knees wrap Curry's waist. Joel, seeing a chance, drives into Curry's chest. Curry back pedals but does not fall. Joel drives into him again. Again he steps back but does not go down. And then Curry's whittling knife flashes in the air, and slashes viciously across Dave's leg. Dave cries out and the leg pulls away. Curry slashes the other leg. Dave crashes into the leaves by the path. Curry whirls on him, knife raised.

"Beware . . . the . . . sineater!"

Joel reaches out to stop his brother. Dave lifts his hands in a final attempt at protection. And a small pocket knife catches Curry between his shoulders, and he bellows and spins around.

Joel watches as Curry claws at his back, trying to dislodge the knife. It will not come out. Curry shakes his body, but the knife will not come free. He cries in fury then, and dashes across the path and into the trees.

"Who . . ." begins Dave, between silent sobs.

Joel swallows. "I don't know."

"Go get him, Joel. He's hurt. You got to stop him."

"Somebody already . . ."

"Goddamn you, Joel, go stop your brother! He's hurt, you can do it!"

Joel looks at Dave.

"Screw the fucking rules, kill the bastard!"

Joel dashes after Curry.

He runs among the trees, dodging, dipping, twisting. He smells blood, like a dog, like a wild animal, and he follows. He jumps and runs. His mind fades to blank. He does not think of what he will do. He only feels it.

Until he dashes around a fallen tree. Until his foot strikes a soft, solid something and makes him stumble. He falls onto his hands. Cones and sticks gore his bare chest.

Panting, he looks back.

Curry is lying on the ground. The pocket knife is out of his back and is now up to the handle in Curry's chest.

There is a bizarre, bloody smile on his dead face.

PART FOUR

JOEL AND AVERY

1

Joel stares at his brother. He almost expects Curry to roll over, pull out the knife and laugh. Then he would collect up a bunch of sticks and begin shaving the bark for hamper twigs.

Curry does not move.

A quick, fierce shudder tosses Joel's body, then passes.

He stares at his brother.

Certainly there is a prayer Joel should be saying, but he cannot think of what it would be. Certainly he should be full of anguish, but he cannot find those feelings. Instead, he is numb. His muscles, and his skin, and his emotions, are surrounded by a dull, soft coating of unrealness.

Then he hears something moving not far from where he kneels. The sound is steady, not moving nearer nor farther away. Joel lets his eyes move from Curry. He looks ahead, toward the sound, trying to see through a thicket of brambled crabapple trees.

The numbness draws away from Joel's heart. It quickens. His lips part. He knows who is beyond the trees. The one who killed Curry is just past the dense thicket.

Joel's father.

"Avery," whispers Joel.

Rocking with the painful hammering of his heart, Joel stands. He walks to the crabapple trees.

The rustling sounds again, less definitive now, slower. As Joel's foot snaps a twig, the rustling stops.

'He hears you.'

A breeze tosses Joel's dark hair. He lets his gaze travel to the top branches of the tangled trees and to the snow-heavy sky beyond. God is up there, watching this. God has seen the deaths, the cruelties. Let God see this last act.

Joel crouches and squirms between the tight branches. His foot slips on a loose patch of moss, and he catches himself on the trunk of one of the trees. He emerges on the other side. He is ready to see what he will be damned to see.

Just several yards beyond, a man lies on the ground. He is on his side, facing away from Joel, one knee drawn up. One arm is stretched out above his head, and it clutches open and shut, rattling the leaves beneath it.

Holding his chest, Joel takes one step forward.

The clutching hand stops. Joel sees blood on the man's back and legs, soaking his faded trousers and spreading across the pale green of his jacket.

'Sineater,' Joel thinks.

The man moans.

Joel steps closer.

Then the man coughs and drags his clutching hand back up under his head. He seems tall, as Curry, and his hair is pale with strands of gray. *'And his face?'* Joel thinks. *'What of his face?'*

Joel pulls himself straight. His arms draw down to his sides. And then he says, "Avery."

The man rolls over.

Joel looks his father in the face.

2

Before Avery raises his arms over his face to shield his son, Joel sees the truth. In the flesh, he sees the dream he has feared, the nightmare he has dreaded. His father's face is bearded, the whiskers crudely cut with some sort of dull knife. His hair is unkempt, uneven locks framing his forehead. There are lines on the face, although the lines do not so much speak of age as care. And his eyes are blue. Curry's blue. Petrie's blue. And yet not. There is a vulnerability there, and fear, and sorrow.

The arms go up and Avery rolls away on his side.

"Don't look."

"Avery."

"Go away. You are not to look at me."

Joel's chest constricts. He moves closer. "I looked," he says. "It's all right."

The sineater's body convulses. The jacket grows a darker red.

"I'm sorry, Joel," the man says softly.

Joel's heart tightens at the sound of his name. He remembered hearing it spoken by Benton so long ago, and the thrill it had caused. And now, his father is speaking it.

Joel stoops beside his father. The wounds on his body are brutal.

"I knew what Curry was doing. I'm so sorry," says Avery.

"It's all right. It wasn't your fault."

The man coughs. Then for a moment, it sounds as if he will not catch his breath. In a few seconds, he does.

329

"I'm glad," begins Avery. "I'm glad I've seen you now, Joel. God forgive me, but I am. Even though it was never meant for you to see me, I'm glad I've seen you once in the daylight. There have only been two other times. The first, when you were born. The other, just days ago. You were very sick. I looked in on you. You'd never been so sick. I was afraid you might die."

Joel cannot answer. He can only stare at the blood and the back of his father's pale hair.

"Let it die with me," says Avery.

Joel reaches out.

"Curry is dead. Let it die with me. I have the sin. I will not get into heaven. But no one should bear this godforsaken fate."

Joel's hand hovers over his father's head.

"Do you hear me, Joel? Let it die with me."

Joel's tears fall onto Avery's butchered body. "It will be all right," he says. "Don't worry. It will be . . ." and the last words die on his tongue. Crying, he gently strokes his father's hair.

3

After a long while, Joel stands. He cannot tell how long he has been there, and he is not certain how long Avery has been dead. The sky, long promising an early snow, begins to rain.

Joel goes to the crabapple trees. The leaves of the tree are dead, with a few stragglers dangling like strips of old paper from the knotty branches. He looks beneath the tree, clawing the moss and humus and mud with his nails until he finds what he is looking for. Then he goes back to the sineater.

Where is Avery's soul now? Is it waiting for release, or is it in hell bearing the sins of all of Beacon Cove? Is it nowhere at all, but dead like the body on the ground?

Joel shakes his head and kneels down. He carefully turns his father over onto his back, then places the cluster of rotting crabapples onto his chest.

He eats the crabapples off.

And he takes the picture from his jeans pocket and turns it face up. The photo is fuzzy and out-of-date, but the openness and happiness on the young Avery Barker's face is clear.

Joel leaves the picture with his father.

PART FIVE

JOEL

The Beacon River is slow now, with a sheen of ice pieces riding the flow. It is late January. It has been a frigid month, and yet there has still been no snow.

Joel sits on the boulder. He wears Curry's long coat. It reaches Joel's ankles, but that is good, because he sits on the rock more now than ever before. He does not go to school anymore, and as of yet, there has been no one from the school looking for him. Lelia doesn't know or care.

There is new graffiti on the rock beside him, scratched with a firm hand into the boulder's surface with the blade of a small pocket knife.

In his hand is a letter, the postmark from Monterey. Petrie works there as a maid in a local motel. "Mountain View, Hospitality in the Hollow." Someone with nice penmanship has written the note for her. She says in the note that she couldn't stay in the Cove anymore, and had to run away. She says she is happy, and the woman who owns the motel is very nice and lets her have her own room on the second floor. Earlier this morning, Joel gave the letter to Lelia, but she wouldn't believe it was true. She wouldn't even read it. There was a canceled stamp and a "Mountain View" logo, complete with a tiny picture of a pine tree, on the envelope. But Lelia threw it back at Joel. She accused him of making it up to ease her suffering. She was mad enough to assign him to the toolshed for the day, but then too wearied to follow it up. She went back to bed, and Joel made himself an early lunch and brought the letter down to the river.

Dave has gone back to West Virginia. With Missy dead, there is no one else to care for him. Joel had thought of asking Lelia to let Dave have Curry's cot, but no sooner had the thought crossed his mind did he dismiss the request as ridiculous.

Dave survived the final ordeal fairly well. After Joel had chased Curry into the woods, Dave tore Joel's shirt into strips and bandaged his legs, then limped east, eventually finding the cabin of Preston and Candace Stone. The Stones tended him, and Dave did not mention Wayne. Melissa Benshoff was called in to stitch his wounds. Six days later, a collection was taken up among the members of the community to send Dave home to his parents. Dave did not tell Joel good-bye. Joel likes to think he would have, had there been the chance.

Missy was not found until two days after Dave left for West Virginia. She was in too bad a shape for an open-casket wake. Her body lay in state in a closed wooden coffin in the kitchen of her cabin for a day and a night. Mourners came in and ate from the dishes of potatoes, beef, and beans. They stared at the coffin and patted the lid carefully. They did not know how to send Missy Campbell to heaven.

Joel attended the wake. He had stood in the corner of the kitchen unnoticed for a long time. He thought the loss of Missy had clouded their minds, and they did not know who he was. Later, when the night-darkness began to creep along the wooden floor, and when women began to put matches to lantern wicks, Joel took a cloth napkin full of cubed potatoes and rested it on the coffin lid.

Several mourners frowned at him with numbed confusion, but said nothing. Joel then ate the potatoes. When done, he scanned the faces in the lantern light, making eye contact with as many as possible.

Then he went home.

Wayne was found the day after Missy. There was no wake. Joel does not know what Wayne's parents did with the body. And so Joel went down to the garage on South Branch a week ago, broke into the building and sat on the Honda seat. After a silent prayer, he ate the radish from Lelia's pantry he'd hid in his pocket.

Joel stretches his neck and puts his palms down on the cold of the boulder. He remembers, again, the burned cabin, the nails through the flesh, the blood, and the blindfolds. Again, he tells himself that it was the voice of God calling him from across the clearing as they had left the cabin behind. It was not Wayne.

It could not have been Wayne.

"It was You, wasn't it?" Joel screams to the river. "It was You, not Wayne! He was already dead! He had to have been dead!"

There is a strange half-echo off the bank over the river, then the sound is swallowed with the water.

"He was already dead," Joel says.

A raccoon stares at the icy water from the muddy bank.

A starling cries above the oak trees.

There is discomfort deep in Joel's gut. He wonders if it is the sin, or just loneliness.

He has not told anyone that he is now the sineater.

He puts one fist to the pain in his stomach and pushes, but it does not go away. It only goes deeper.

He is the sineater. And slowly, one soul at a time, they will come to know it. He will eat their sin, he will offer cleansing to the spirits weighed to the earth by wrongdoings. But the ritual will not be the same. The sineater will eat in full view. The people may never welcome him, but their caution will be respect, not fear. Curry wanted it changed but Curry is dead, and now Joel will change it his way. It will take a long time, but Missy is gone and time is all there is. Joel will look at the mourners and they will look at him. They will see the good there, not the evil. They will see the salvation, not the damnation.

This Joel will do for the sineater who was hated.

This he will do for the memory of the sineater who was reviled unjustly.

This he will do for Avery.

Joel touches the graffiti on the boulder. It says, "ZEVIB R OLEV BLF."

Joel shreds Petrie's letter into tiny fragments and lets them fly. Then he wraps his arms about himself and watches the Beacon River wash the mountain debris down to the bridge and far away.